Knight and Day
Widow Evelyn Gerhard Stanford ke... ten-year-old son a secret from her prospective groom. When she arrives in Sagebrush, she's shocked to realize her groom forgot to mention *his* ten-year-old daughter. While Evelyn tries to teach Gareth's daughter some manners, Gareth tries to teach Evelyn's son what it means to be a man. And all the while, they are learning to be a family.

Lady-in-Waiting
Jane Gerhard, the invisible sister, longs to be special to someone. But the man she weds is a workaholic who spends all his time on the range. Harrison Garvey's father made him a wager: double his ranch's production within three years or move back East. Jane tries to win Harrison's attention, but it isn't until she works herself to exhaustion that Harrison learns what winning her love is really worth.

Shining Armor
Gwendolyn Gerhard is shocked to find out the man she intended to marry has died while she journeyed to meet him. His grandson, Matthew Parker determined to send the woman home, convinced that she is a gold digger. When he learns she has no family to return to, he has no choice but to marry her. . .but that doesn't mean he'll fall in love.

On a White Charger
Emmeline Gerhard has long dreamed of living on a ranch, so she's thrilled to be heading to Sagebrush. Imagine her surprise when her cowboy turns out to have a ranch all right. . .a sheep ranch. With gentle persistence, Joseph Barrett shows Emme-line the reality of life in the West. And when area cattlemen threaten the flock, Emmeline and Joseph must band together to save their ranch.

SAGEBRUSH KNIGHTS

SAGEBRUSH KNIGHTS

FOUR-IN-ONE COLLECTION

ERICA VETSCH

BARBOUR
PUBLISHING

© 2012 by Erica Vetsch

Print ISBN 978-1-61626-642-4

eBook Editions:
Adobe Digital Edition (.epub) 978-1-62029-630-1
Kindle and MobiPocket Edition (.prc) 978-1-62029-629-5

All scripture quotations are taken from the King James Version of the Bible.

This book is a work of fiction. Names, characters, places, and incidents are either products of the author's imagination or used fictitiously. Any similarity to actual people, organizations, and/or events is purely coincidental.

Cover image: Kirk DouPonce, DogEared Design

Published by Barbour Publishing, Inc., P.O. Box 719, Uhrichsville, Ohio 44683, www.barbourbooks.com

Our mission is to publish and distribute inspirational products offering exceptional value and biblical encouragement to the masses.

ecpa Member of the
Evangelical Christian
Publishers Association

Printed in the United States of America.

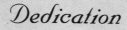

Dedication

For Peter, Heather, and James,
as always

Prologue

Four sisters, Christian, 18–28, seek matrimony with four God-fearing men as soon as possible. Must live in close proximity. Apply: Matrimonial News, #278.

The final eviction notice and the marriage proposals arrived in the same post. Though she couldn't help but wince at the comedown in their circumstances to be driven to posting an advertisement for husbands, Evelyn Gerhard Stanford couldn't cavil at the timing of the response.

She presented these missives to her sisters as matter-of-factly as possible, but inside, insecurities and doubts roiled. The advertisement had been her idea, after all, arrived at after many a sleepless, prayer-filled night.

With each of her three younger sisters looking to her for guidance and assurance that they were making the correct—the only—decision they could, she kept her fears to herself and put on a brave front. All through the packing, the leave-taking, and the jolting journey via hissing, sooty train and bone-jarring stagecoach, she maintained her calm, controlled demeanor.

She could do this. She could get her family across more than half this continent and see them safely ensconced in new homes with new husbands. She would meet every crisis and obstacle with determination, intelligence, and fortitude. And try to pretend she wasn't scared out of her mind at the unknown racing toward them all.

Evelyn clutched her reticule, crackling the papers inside. Two letters, the only communication she'd had with her prospective groom, one Gareth Kittrick. Not much to build a marriage on, two single-sheet missives. The first was from the *Matrimonial News*, passing along the marriage proposals of four men from the town of Sagebrush in Wyoming Territory to advertisement #278. The second was from Mr. Kittrick himself and contained tickets for the journey and a few lines about himself and his ranch. A widower—that thought gave her some solace, being a widow herself—looking for a kind woman to grace his home.

With the eviction notice hanging over her head like the Sword of Damocles, Evelyn had expedited their departure from Seabury. They'd barely had time to think. But now, as mile after mile rolled under the train and stagecoach wheels, her doubts and fears ran rampant.

Glancing down, she touched the thin gold circle on her left ring finger. A lump formed in her throat as she slipped it off and moved it to her right hand. For more than ten years, she'd worn Jamison's ring, though she'd been widowed nearly all that time. Still, it would be bad form to show up in Sagebrush to meet her new husband while still wearing her first wedding band.

Not that Mr. Kittrick would need that reminder of her previous marriage. No, the permanent reminder lay on the seat beside her with his head pillowed on her lap. She stroked his sable curls. Guilt chased anxiety and fear through a twisting maze in her head.

In her brief and hurried communication with her intended husband, she'd neglected to mention she had a son.

KNIGHT AND DAY

Chapter 1

Wyoming Territory, April 1874

They aren't even here?" Evelyn dropped her valise onto the boardwalk in front of the general store. "We were supposed to meet them in Sagebrush." What kind of a beginning was this?

The lean, gray-haired man in a ratty black suit shrugged and ran his hand through his hair, making it stand on end. "Things have changed." His cantankerous scowl belied his claim to be a preacher.

Her hands went to her hips. "Just how have things changed?" Surely the men weren't backing out now. Not after all the travel and travail the girls had encountered just getting to this desolate outpost. Dread spiked its way up her windpipe, shortening her breath and sharpening her temper. "We've had a long trip, and if I never see the inside of a stagecoach again, it will be far too soon. The stage was supposed to arrive here yesterday afternoon, and instead we've spent an entire night in that dreadful conveyance making up lost time. We're tired, hungry, and in no mood to be trifled with. Kindly point us in the direction of the nearest hotel so we may refresh ourselves and await our intended husbands."

He inserted one of his long, bony fingers between his collar and his turkey-red neck and swallowed, making his scraggly beard lurch. "You want a hotel, get back on board and head fifty miles back to Cheyenne. If you want to get married, get yourself and your gear into the wagon. I have to be over to Dellsville tonight. I'm doing this as a favor to Kittrick and the rest, and you being late has set me back. I'll haul you out to the ranches and do the marryin', but only if we can leave right now." His eyes bulged a bit, with more than a hint of wildness to them.

"But I thought the men all lived close together, in Sagebrush." First their husbands failed to meet their stage, and now they didn't even live in the town?

"Naw, they don't live in town." He looked at her as if she had gravel for brains. "They're ranchers. They do live close together. . .well, close as far as Wyoming distances go. It'll be late afternoon before I get the last one of you dropped off." His scowl could've curdled fresh milk. "That is, *if* we ever get going in the first place."

Evelyn sized him up, wary that this John Brown look-alike might be trying to pull the wool over their eyes. "Are you really a preacher? I've never encountered such a cranky, caustic man of God before." She tugged her cloak tighter around her shoulders to ward off the fresh breeze.

"Yeah, I'm a preacher. If you don't believe me, head into the store and ask Jake. But don't take all day." He turned away, muttering. "Cranky, am I?"

Jane, Gwendolyn, and Emmeline all looked to her for a decision, just as they always had. Little Jamie held Emmeline's hand, his face—so like his father's—pale with exhaustion. He yawned, and Evelyn fought the need to yawn as well.

Exhaustion after their night of travel tugged at her limbs and eyelids. She couldn't remember her last decent night's sleep, and every muscle ached from that butter churn of a stagecoach.

She bit her lip, her thoughts chasing one another until they all merged into one. They had no choice but to accept the situation. Just as they'd had to accept Papa's death, the notice to vacate the teachers' quarters at the academy, and the marriage proposals of four strangers two thousand miles from all that was dear and familiar. She wanted to press her fists to her temples and scream, but she confined herself to a silent prayer.

God, why do You keep doing this to us? Why do You take, take, take from us without giving us even a choice in the matter?

"Very well, Reverend. . . ?"

"Cummings. Most folks just call me Preacher."

"Reverend Cummings. If you will be so kind as to load our luggage, we'll just step into the store for a few minutes." Not giving him time to protest, she herded the girls and Jamie inside, casting a look back over her shoulder as she entered the mercantile. "We won't be long." She just needed a few minutes to adjust her thinking to the new situation and plan out what to do.

A rounded man with a jolly face and healthy side-whiskers wiped down a counter. "You must be the brides." His face split in a grin. "Preacher's been cooling his heels for half a week waiting for you. Worked himself into a froth, he has."

A shaft of weak relief shot through Evelyn. The man outside really was the preacher, and he really would take them to their new homes. At least that hurdle had been taken without her having to ask.

"Is there anything I can get for you before you head out?" The shopkeeper—Jake, wasn't it?—tossed his cloth aside and rubbed his hands together as if anticipating a big sale.

She shook her head. "No, there's nothing we need." Nor could afford to buy. The store appeared crammed with lots of items they might find useful, but their budget didn't stretch to anything beyond the barest of necessities. Her reticule held exactly four silver dollars; the sum total of the family's estate after all the bills had been discharged. If it hadn't been for their prospective grooms' generosity in arranging travel and lodging, they wouldn't even have made it this far— especially as the money had needed to stretch for an extra ticket for Jamie.

"Emmeline, keep hold of Jamie's hand. Gwendolyn, be careful with that china." Her youngest sister trailed her fingers across a white teapot painted with a spray of roses and violets. Jane stood before a wall of shelving loaded with bolts of fabric. Sturdy calicos, twills, flannels, and muslins in a rainbow of hues. Her lace gloves just brushed a bolt of pale green cloth, a wistful expression in her hazel eyes.

Evelyn gathered her courage. "Let's go." She squared her shoulders and marched them all outside. Their trunks—one for each sister and a small one for Jamie—sat in a tidy row in the wagon bed along with their valises and satchels, and Reverend Cummings sat on the wagon seat with the reins in his hands.

Rattling away from the settlement, Evelyn couldn't help but look back at the huddle of brown buildings. Sagebrush. Aptly named, for sagebrush seemed to be the only thing the area had in abundance. Unless you counted empty. There was a fair bit of empty, too.

Jamie stood up behind the wagon seat and stuck his head between Evelyn's and the reverend's. "Are we going to live in the mountains?" He pointed to the purple-blue hills rising in the far distance.

Evelyn gently lowered his hand. "It's impolite to point, Jamie." She straightened his straw hat. "Please sit down and be quiet." She turned to the preacher, who sat, hunch-shouldered with his elbows on his knees. "How far are we going?"

He flicked a glance at the sky. "Two hours to Kittrick's. Which of you is Gareth marrying, or is it first choice after he gets a gander at all of you?"

Evelyn tried to ignore how her heart hitched at hearing his name aloud. "I am." *And may he be as kind and chivalrous as his name implies.* As the daughter of a medieval scholar, she knew intimately the legend of Sir Gareth of the Round Table.

"Good. I'm supposed to marry you and Gareth, then I'll tote the rest of these gals to their husbands one at a time. If I push it, I can still make my appointment in Dellsville by nightfall."

"Won't all the gentlemen be at Gareth's for the weddings?"

"Naw, can't take the time off in the spring."

Her racing heart sank. She would miss her sisters' weddings.

Jane tapped the reverend on the shoulder. "Excuse me, but you know each of these men we're to marry, right? Can you tell us what they're like?"

Evelyn shot her sister a grateful look. Why hadn't she thought of that? A little information ahead of time would help her control the situation better.

"Bit late to be wondering now, ain't it?" He slapped the reins against the horses' rumps. "Guess you'll meet them soon enough."

"But you must know something of the men we are to marry." Emmeline shifted on the board laid across the wagon box.

"They're ranchers." He shrugged. "I haven't heard anything against them."

Hmm, not much to go on. "All their properties adjoin?" If they were going to have to leave Seabury and marry strangers, Evelyn at least wanted her sisters where she could keep an eye on them.

Again the shrug. "Not really. They each own the property their houses sit on, but most of the land out here is open range. The ranches are miles apart with lots of free range between. Take all day to get to all of them."

Miles apart? All day? The bottom dropped out of Evelyn's chest, and from the gasps and frowns of her sisters, she assumed they felt the same. They had counted on being able to support one another, to see one another frequently. They'd never been separated, not even by Evelyn's marriage to Jamison. Because of the war and Jamison needing to return to his post, Evelyn had never left home. Delighted to find she was carrying his child, she had been devastated when her husband had been killed. Her family had held her together through that terrible time. She'd practically raised her sisters. What would she do without them in her everyday life?

Gwendolyn said, "I thought we'd live closer together, that we'd be neighbors." Her blue eyes widened as if she'd just thought of the enormity of what they were doing. The youngest of the Gerhard sisters at just under nineteen, Gwendolyn had been accepting and easygoing about the entire enterprise. Evelyn had particularly hoped to live closest to Gwendolyn to help her all she could.

Her glance went to Emmeline, who could barely suppress her joy at finally getting to see the American West and to meet a real-live cowboy in person. Evelyn worried about Emmeline, who was so enamored of learning to ride a horse and perhaps encountering danger and desperadoes. Evelyn blamed those ridiculous dime novels and serialized stories Emmeline was addicted to for filling her head with such nonsense.

And Jane, dear, dependable Jane, who was a born home-maker and worked harder than all of them, who could sew and cook and bake and clean. The sister Evelyn leaned on the most to help her take care of everyone.

God, You've done it again. You've taken my expectations and ripped them away. How am I supposed to watch over my sisters if they're a day's ride away? How am I supposed to make sure their husbands are good men if I don't get to even meet them before the weddings? Why did You take Jamison and Papa from me? If they were alive, we wouldn't be in this mess.

Reverend Cummings broke into her prayer—if it could be called a prayer. "That boy yours?"

"Yes, Jamie is my son."

"He legitimate?"

The preacher's bluntness took her breath away.

"My husband was killed in the war a few months before Jamie was born." She infused her voice with all the ice she could muster. Which was considerable every time she thought of the way God had taken Jamison from her. In a cruel twist, Jamison had been killed two weeks after Lee's surrender. Ambushed by bandits on his way home from the war, he'd been murdered and robbed only a few miles from Seabury. But it was easier to say he'd died in the war than try to explain. Not that she could explain the way God seemed to delight in foiling her plans.

Chapter 2

Gareth looked up from the forge and wiped the sweat from his forehead. Chilly as this spring had been, bending over hot coals, wrestling with balky cow ponies, and molding metal to his will sure chased away any cold.

A light brown smudge of road dust followed a dark brown dot out on the prairie. He sucked in a deep breath, bellows-like. That had to be her.

Rimfire Dawson, his friend and right-hand man, led another horse into the shop. "Did ya see it?"

"Yeah." He removed his gloves and shoved them into his pocket then yanked them out and tugged them onto his hands again.

"Was you this jumpy the first time you got married?"

His first wedding day, a subject he'd been trying not to think about. All his friends and family packed into the church. The flowers, the meal, and dancing afterward. But most of all, Justine. Big green eyes, dark shiny hair, and a smile that said he was the only man on earth.

This time he didn't even know what his bride looked like. He should've asked for a photograph at least, but there hadn't been time. Was she tall? Short? Dark? Fair? Did she like kids? Did she snore?

What he did know about her made a pretty short list. Twenty-eight, a widow, and from Massachusetts. A Christian woman. Evelyn. Pretty name. And she wrote with a very nice hand, though her letter wasn't overly long. His heart shied and skittered around his chest like a green-broke horse.

Gareth ripped his hat off and whacked his thigh. Dust flew from his pants. He smelled of smoke and horse and hot iron. Delightful.

"No."

Rimfire scratched his ear. "No, what?"

"No, I wasn't this nervous the first time I got married."

"Why you gettin' married now?"

Gareth shrugged. "It's time."

"You don't look exactly settled to the idea. You've been skitin' around here, nervous as a mouse in a rattlesnake nest. I suppose it's too late to back out now, but the donnybrook that blew up over breakfast this morning. . .whew."

"My mind's set. And I'm not going to be swayed by a tantrum. It's those kinds of things that make me more certain than ever that I'm doing the right thing."

"Tell that to Mad Dog."

"I tried. It wasn't pretty."

The dot grew larger. Now that the situation was at hand, his stomach started acting like he'd swallowed a chestnut hull. He reminded himself of all the reasons why his getting married was the best course of action, and that though it might take them all a little while to adjust, eventually the dust would settle.

"Four unmarried sisters." Rimfire tied off the horse to a ring high on the wall and shoved his hands into his pockets.

"How old did you say they were?"

"According to the advertisement, the youngest is eighteen and the oldest is twenty-eight."

"And you're getting the oldest one?"

"Yes, a widow woman. Lost her husband in the war."

A grunt. "And she didn't get married again after ten years? Is she ugly? Or devoted to her dead husband?"

Questions Gareth hadn't thought to ask himself. New worries cropped up like weeds after a rain. Was something wrong with her that she hadn't married again before now?

The dot had grown so he could make out Preacher Cummings and several passengers. Though he strained his eyes, he couldn't discern anything beyond bonnets. The woman beside the preacher was smallish, and she wore a dark cloak. Was that Evelyn or one of her sisters?

Rimfire joined him in the wide doorway of the smithy. "Maybe I better scout around and see if I can find Mad Dog."

"Good idea. Go ahead and leave the horse here. I'll come back and finish the job in a while. I'll meet you up at the house."

His foreman gave him a strange look and headed for the barn—the most likely spot to find his quarry. Gareth made for the house and arrived at the same time as the wagon.

"Morning, Preacher." Though he spoke to Cummings, he looked from one female face to the next. Then his eyes lit on a small straw hat.

"I brung 'em." Preacher wrapped the reins around the brake handle and jumped down.

The woman on the front seat stared at him so hard he wondered if she were trying to read his thoughts. Beautiful blue eyes, fair skin, and from what he could see under the rim of her somber bonnet, pale yellow hair.

"Evelyn?"

She nodded, and a tight place in his chest loosened. She looked nothing like his dead wife. Justine, with her brown hair and green eyes. He hadn't even been aware of his desire that his mail-order bride not resemble his dead wife, but surely that would make things easier for everyone.

Instead of waiting for her hand to help her alight, he reached up and spanned her waist, lifting her over the edge of the wagon and setting her down before him. He found himself staring down into her eyes. She was small. The top of her head barely came to his chin. And she was light as a tumbleweed. Her hands gripped his forearms.

Preacher pulled the pins from the tailgate and let it fall with a clank. "Burnin' daylight, Kittrick. I have a lot of miles to go yet." He dragged a trunk toward him, scraping along the wagon bed. "Which ones belong to her?"

One of the girls in the back of the wagon directed him to the correct luggage.

Gareth couldn't take his eyes off Evelyn. When she tried to move, he realized he still held her waist, and stepped back, letting his hands fall to his sides. Though travel-stained and weary, she had a look about her that drew him. Attraction wasn't something he'd counted on or even expected, at least not at this stage of the game. He flattened his lips, rolling the idea around.

"I'm Gareth Kittrick."

"Yes." She turned back to the wagon. "These are my sisters and. . ." She trailed off.

His attention was drawn to a little face, the owner of the straw hat, peeking over the side of the wagon. Coal-dark eyes and curly hair to match.

"And who might you be, young man?"

The boy scrambled over the side of the wagon and stuck out his hand. "Jamison Trent Stanford Jr., sir. I'm pleased to meet you. Are you going to be my father now?"

A gut punch couldn't have been more effective at knocking the wind right out of him. Evelyn chewed her bottom lip and bunched her eyebrows. Not just a widow, but a mother. She placed her hand on his arm and sparks flew up his veins. "I know I should have told you, but things happened so quickly, and I was hoping. . ."

He knew. "It's not a problem." Bending, he took the boy's hand. "Nice to know you. And to answer your question, it would seem that, yes, I am going to be your pa."

The child gave a quick shake of Gareth's hand and moved to his mother's side. A regular little gentleman, though the wide collar and short pants would have to go. What Mad Dog would make of him, Gareth could hardly guess.

He reached up to assist each of the girls to the ground, and though each was pretty enough, none set his heart to racing like Evelyn did.

Preacher hoisted a trunk and *thunked* it onto the porch. Two satchels followed while Evelyn made introductions. Her voice had a clipped, eastern quality, and she spoke rather quickly, but it was a nice voice for all that and sounded like her letter.

"Let's get to the marryin'." Preacher reached into his coat pocket and withdrew a tattered Bible. "I've got to make tracks."

Gareth winced at this abruptness, though he expected no less from Cummings. "Just a minute. There's something I need to talk to Evelyn about before we have the ceremony." He motioned for her to step away from everyone and kept his voice low. "I don't mind about the boy. In fact, I'm relieved you have a son, because—"

A scream erupted from the barn. Rimfire appeared in the doorway, a writhing bundle under his arm. He marched up to the house and dropped the squirming mass onto the porch. Legs and arms and braids sorted themselves out into a furious child.

"Don't do it, Pa. It ain't too late if you ain't said the words yet. Send her back." A little boot stomped the packed dirt, and fists jammed onto nonexistent hips. "We don't need her around here. Look at her, dressed like an undertaker and thin as a fence post. She won't last one winter."

Gareth stepped forward, hauled the child up against his side, and wrapped his hand over her mouth. "You'll keep a civil tongue in your head, Mad Dog. We've been through this. We need her, and she stays. And look, she brought her son with her. You're going to have a brother."

Evelyn's eyebrows rose. "Did you just call this child 'Mad Dog'?"

Keeping the furious kid pinned to his side, Gareth nodded. "This is my daughter, Madelyn. The boys took to calling her Mad Dog because she gets so worked up about things, and the name stuck." He prepared himself, awaiting his prospective bride's response.

After her initial shock, a rueful humor flickered in her blue eyes, and something in his middle eased a fraction.

"It seems we are each hoist with our own petards, Mr. Kittrick."

"If that means strung up with our own nooses, then you're

right." He braced against the bucking and kicking Maddie put up. "I need some help with this one. She's wild as a Texas steer and can be more trouble than a wagonload of wildcats. That's one of the reasons I sent for you."

"I see."

The boy stood halfway behind his mother, dark eyes round as he watched the struggle. Rimfire stepped onto the porch and swept his hat off his head. "Ma'am. I'm Rimfire. I work for Gareth. Welcome to the Lazy K. Glad you're here." He cast a look askance at Gareth and the wriggling Maddie.

Enough. Gareth hauled his daughter up against his chest and took her around the corner of the house. "Stop it, Maddie. I'm ashamed of you."

The child went limp, and as he eased her to the ground, her lower lip quivered. She scrubbed at her eyes but didn't cry. Maddie never cried. Shout, stomp, rage, yes, but tears, never.

"Why'd you do it, Pa? We don't need anyone else." Anger radiated from her skinny, overalls-clad body. "We're doing fine."

He squatted in front of her and pushed his hat back on his head. "We're not, or you wouldn't have thrown a tantrum like that. You're growing up wild as a mustang out here without anyone to teach you any manners and show you how to be a lady."

"I don't want to be a lady. I want to be your pard."

"You are my pard, kiddo, but you need to learn all that girl stuff I can't teach you. You need a woman for that, a mother."

She shook her head so hard her ginger braids flopped on her shoulders. "You didn't tell me she had a kid."

"I didn't know she did."

"I don't want a brother."

"I'm sorry, Maddie, but you'll just have to accept it. We both will. And you're not giving him a chance. He seems like a nice kid."

She sniffed and scowled. "He looks like a greenhorn. What kind of a hat is he wearing, anyway? One good breeze and it'll sail right into Sagebrush Creek. And his clothes are all wrong."

"Stop it now. I know you're not in favor of the idea, but I'm getting married, and you're going to treat your new mama with respect *and* be civil to your new brother. You're going to start acting like a girl and learning to be a lady."

Maddie's arms crossed on her chest, and her jaw set. "She won't be my mama, and he's not my brother. You can have them."

Tired of the fight, Gareth straightened. "I've had about all I'm going to take today, Maddie. If you can't be nice, then at least be quiet. You want to be my pard, you'd better show some manners, and that's that. Now, come on. Preacher's in a hurry."

They returned to the group, and Gareth put his hands on Maddie's shoulders, bringing her around to stand in front of him. "I apologize for my daughter's behavior. She's having a bit of a hard time adjusting to the idea of me marrying again." A quiver went through Maddie's shoulders, but she remained rooted to the spot and tight-lipped.

Cummings scowled and smoothed his beard. "Let's get to it then. You ain't the last stop I have to make today, you know."

In an almost indecent amount of time, Gareth found himself promising to love, honor, and cherish Evelyn Stanford for the rest of their lives. Before they could hardly blink, Preacher was chivying the sisters into the wagon.

The good-byes were hard to take. Clinging to each other, whispering encouragements, and wiping a few tears. Not even Preacher seemed to have the heart to pull them apart too quickly. Finally, the three youngest girls were loaded and headed west, and Evelyn and her son stood on the porch watching them go, as forlorn a pair as Gareth had ever seen. In small measure, he began to understand the complete upheaval of Evelyn's life by coming across the country to marry him.

When the wagon finally disappeared, Evelyn blinked and brushed at her cheeks before turning to her son. "Jamie, if you will gather the satchels, perhaps we'd best go inside."

"Where you gonna put him, Pa? He ain't takin' my room." Maddie crossed her eyes and stuck out her tongue at the boy, who regarded her as if she were an animal in a menagerie. His assessment seemed not far wrong as she swung from the porch post like an organ-grinder's monkey.

"Jamie can sleep in the loft. Plenty of room up there." Gareth hoisted the trunk and shouldered it into the cabin. He was proud of his house. Made of square-cut logs and chinked against the winter winds, it boasted two bedrooms and a large front room, with a loft besides—a spacious abode for the frontier. He'd built it with his own two hands right after the war, when he and Justine had first settled along Sagebrush Creek, hauling the logs from near Laramie Peak and sawing them himself.

Letting the trunk come to rest just inside his bedroom door, he ignored the nervousness hopping under his skin and returned to the front room. He was married. The deal was done, and soon his daughter would become the young lady God and her mother intended her to be. And he'd gained a son in the bargain. A tenderfoot to be sure, but the boy would soon toughen up. He'd have to if he wanted to survive around Maddie.

Evelyn removed her bonnet and smoothed her yellow hair. Though *yellow* didn't seem the right word. More the color of pale, creamy butter, it caught the light and drew the eyes.

Gareth rubbed his hands down the outsides of his thighs, wondering if her hair was as soft as it looked. "I have a horse tied up in the smithy that still needs shoeing. We're all running flat out getting ready for the spring roundup. Maddie"—he turned to his daughter—"you stay in here and help them get settled. Show them where everything is. And, Evelyn, don't worry about cooking tonight. There's some ham and bread and some beans we made yesterday. Those will do for lunch and supper both." Maddie's eyes blazed green fire at him, and Evelyn's eyebrows—a couple shades darker than her hair—rose.

"You're leaving?"

"Well, yes, I told you, I have a horse tied up in the smithy."

"But we just got here. There are a hundred things we need to discuss, not the least of which is your expectations regarding—"

Heat shot through him. "Ma'am, we don't need to discuss that right now. Especially not in front of the children."

She blinked, and rosy color tinted her cheeks. Without meeting his stare, she cleared her throat. "I was referring to your expectations regarding your daughter."

Embarrassment of another kind trickled through him

and tightened his collar. "We'll talk about all that later." He clapped his hat back onto his head and made his escape.

Down at the smithy, Rimfire pumped the bellows and fitted a horseshoe into a pair of tongs. "How'd it go in there? Everybody playing nice?"

Gareth rolled his shoulders to loosen the tension knotted there. "It will take some time, but she'll settle in."

"You talking about your new bride or Mad Dog?"

"Either, come to that, and you need to stop calling her Mad Dog. Her name is Madelyn or Maddie. The Mad Dog days are over."

The front door slammed, and his daughter took off for the barn like a streak of redheaded lightning.

"Maybe not quite over." Rimfire chuckled. "Your marriage set off a stick of dynamite in the henhouse. I have a feeling it's going to rain feathers for a long time."

Chapter 3

Evelyn descended the steep stairs from the loft after tucking Jamie in for the night and hearing his bedtime prayers. Maddie's bedroom door remained firmly shut, as it had been all evening.

Gareth tipped his chair back and hooked one boot heel over a rung. He angled a small book toward the lamplight over his shoulder. The heavy knot Evelyn had been carrying around in her middle squirmed, and her mouth went dry. Alone with this stranger who was also her husband. He was so different from Jamison, so. . .manly and rugged.

She pounced on that thought and chastised herself. Jamison had been manly, just in a different way. He'd been intellectual, a man of ideas and thoughts. A man who fought ignorance by education and enlightenment. Everything about Gareth shouted action and physicality. A man who fought nature and the elements to hew a living from the prairie through sheer labor.

"Get him settled?"

She jumped as Gareth's words broke through her thoughts. "Yes."

"We'll have to see about getting a real bed made for him. Though sleeping on a pallet won't hurt him. We're right on the edge of spring branding, the busiest time of the year. Over the next couple of weeks we'll be gearing up, hiring summer hands, fixing equipment. I won't have time to make any furniture."

Evelyn perched on the edge of a chair and made sure her feet were side by side and her hem straight. The house—cabin, actually—couldn't be more different from their home in Seabury. The house at the boys' school had been a graceful redbrick with lots of windows and spacious rooms. This dark abode, with its rough-hewn walls and uneven flooring, made her want to hunch her shoulders. A wave of homesickness swept over her, leaving her hollowed out and echoing inside.

What was happening to her sisters right now? Had they gotten to their new homes safely? Were they all married women by now? None of this was working out the way she'd thought it would. They were scattered from pillar to post and might as well be in different states. She felt alone without the support and closeness of her sisters, and she could hardly bear to think about what this decision meant for their futures.

Wind rattled the door, and Gareth rose to stir the fire. A chill draft scuttled over the floor and across her ankles. Back in Seabury, lilacs budded, daffodils and crocuses bloomed, and tulips and irises thrust jade spears up through the dirt. Would the new tenant care for her garden? How had she come to be here, so far from all that was dear and familiar?

"Evelyn?"

Again she jumped. He stood right beside her.

"Yes?" Her heart thrashed in her chest like a buoy on stormy seas.

He squatted, bringing his eyes to the same level as hers.

Kind, brown eyes that held an inkling of humor somewhere in their depths. "I think it might be a good idea if we had a talk. Just to clear the air, so to speak."

A good idea. If only her tongue didn't lie in her head like a useless block of wood. She searched his face. Warmth lit his eyes, and he tilted his head, inviting her to relax. But with him so close, relaxing was out of the question. He rose and resumed his chair, propping his forearms on the table and lacing his fingers together. Large, work-rough hands, tanned and scarred. She swallowed. Where did one start?

He made the decision for her. "I'll go first. As you might have guessed, I answered your advertisement primarily because of Maddie. She's growing up wild as a well-watered weed, and she needs a woman to take her in hand. I chose you because you are the oldest of four sisters, and I figured you'd have some maturity and experience in dealing with girls." He smiled and tugged on his earlobe. "I never figured you'd be such a fine-looking lady or that you'd have a child of your own. Not that I mind either of those things."

He thought she was fine looking? The frivolous thought blazed across her mind.

"What I can't figure is why a pretty woman like you would place an advertisement in the first place? Every one of your sisters is fine looking, too. How come you all didn't marry back east? Why place an ad at all?"

She eased back in the chair and studied her hands in her lap. "We had no other options, really. My father was a master at a boys' school. Medieval studies. He passed away just after the first of the year. The school owned the house we lived in, and they needed it for the next instructor. Though my sisters and I are well educated in medieval history and literature and can speak and read Anglo-Saxon and Middle English, we aren't trained in anything that would support us. Jobs are scarce for women, and because of the war, single men are even scarcer. The Seabury area was particularly hard hit. So many of our young men were killed at Gettysburg. Placing an advertisement for husbands seemed the logical choice."

"Didn't your father make any provisions for you? What about your mother?"

"My mother passed away when my youngest sister was born. I was ten. And my father lived in another world most of the time. His thoughts were occupied with Chaucer and Alfred the Great, not saving money or planning for the future. Especially after my mother passed away. It fell to me and Jane, my next oldest sister, to see to the household. Papa's salary just stretched to meet our needs. There wasn't anything left over."

"You married though."

"Jamison. He was a teacher at the school and one of my father's former students. He was a general's aide during the war. We married when he was on leave, just before the war ended, and he was killed three months later."

"So you've raised your sisters and your son alone." Admiration shone in his eyes, making her flush and shift in her chair.

"What about you?"

"I was a Union soldier, too, but stationed over at Fort Laramie to protect the Oregon Trail. When I was discharged, I married Justine. She passed away when Maddie was three. Blood poisoning from a cut on her leg that wouldn't heal." He blew out a breath. "Maddie's grown up here on the ranch surrounded by men. She can ride and rope and clean the barn, but she hasn't had a lot of schooling. As for her cooking and sewing? Her last attempt to sew a button on one of my shirts ended in me having to throw it in the ragbag, and she's never made anything edible yet. She sure could use a woman's touch."

Evelyn eyed the parts of the stark cabin she could see in the lamplight. More than just Maddie could use a woman's touch.

"While you see to training up Maddie, I'll take the boy in hand. He'll toughen up after he's spent awhile with the hands. He's green now, but in a few months you won't even know him."

"What? There's nothing wrong with Jamie."

"Nothing that a few chores and time out in the sun won't cure. He'll be riding like a Comanche and herding cattle like a *vaquero* in no time."

Evelyn blinked. "I don't think so."

"Sure he will. I know he's kinda puny now, but he'll grow. Best thing in the world for him, you moving out here. He needs a man in his life to toughen him up. Here, he'll have a dozen men to learn from."

Ice flowed through her veins. Nobody had ever interfered with her parenting before. "The same men who have influenced and molded your daughter?"

"Sure. Me, Rimfire, and the boys."

"No, thank you. My son is destined for greater things than to be a common cowhand. You act as if riding like a Comanche is a thing to aspire to. I will help you with your daughter as much as I can, but you will leave my son to me. He will continue his studies. He has his father's intelligence, and such a gift shouldn't be wasted on cows."

Gareth leaned back and scratched his cheek. "Well, there's smart and there's smart. Out here, it isn't so much what a man knows, as what he does that is important. All the book learning in the world isn't going to get the barn clean or the cattle branded."

"You don't think boys need schooling?"

"That's not what I said. The boy can continue with his book learning, but he'll be expected to do chores and learn the ways of the ranch. He's not in Massachusetts anymore."

"I insist you leave my son's future in my hands. Location notwithstanding, he'll be raised the way his father would have wanted him to be." She clenched her hands.

"Evelyn, we're a family now, for better or for worse. You, me, and the kids. We're going to need to pull in the traces together if we're ever going to get where we want to go."

Had he just likened her to a cart horse?

Gareth stood and went to the mantel to wind the clock. "I think it would be better for everyone if we didn't talk in terms of your son or my daughter. I'll treat Jamie as I would my very own flesh and blood, and I'll expect you to treat Maddie the same way. That's not to say we'll forget our first marriages, but if we're going to make this work, we'll have to be a team. We have to present a united front to the children."

"A united front." This was so much more complicated than it had seemed back in Seabury. There, needing a way out, a way to survive, marriage had seemed so simple. Here, face-to-face with the realities of marrying a stranger, the situation grew more complex by the minute. And she was at a loss to control any of it.

Gareth nodded and yawned, stretching and rolling his

shoulders. "It's getting late, and we have a big day tomorrow. I'll step outside if you want to get ready for bed."

Her heart started hurling itself against her ribs as he addressed the issue her mind had been avoiding from the moment she accepted his proposal. Biting her lower lip, she stared at her hands and nodded.

He cleared his throat, crossed the room, and lifted her to her feet, keeping hold of her hands. The warmth of his touch told her how cold her hands had become. Surely that was the only reason she found his handclasp both comforting and disturbing.

"Evelyn, our correspondence was so brief, we didn't have time to discuss the boundaries of this marriage." He squeezed her hands and released one to place his finger under her chin, raising it until she had to look at him. The warmth in his brown eyes heated her skin. "I want this to be a real marriage in every way. I'd like to have more children eventually." His voice deepened. "But I'm not going to rush you. We'll share a room and sleep in the same bed, but nothing else will happen until we're both ready."

The lump in her throat shrank, and her pulse slowed. He'd just handed her back a measure of control. Perhaps they could pull together as a team. Perhaps everything would work out fine. Perhaps she hadn't made such a terrible mistake after all.

Chapter 4

Moving to Wyoming was the worst decision she'd ever made. In the three weeks since her arrival, Evelyn had made no progress with Maddie, and Jamie had become so enamored of Gareth, she hardly ever saw the boy.

Maddie disobeyed, ignored, sabotaged, and defied Evelyn at every opportunity. Though never overtly in her father's presence. She was too canny for that. When Gareth was in the house, Maddie toed the line, but with all the preparations for the roundup going on, Gareth wasn't often in the house. And Maddie wasn't either, escaping outside the minute Evelyn's back was turned.

Evelyn didn't want to admit that the little horror had bested her. But no more. Today, instead of cajoling or suggesting the child behave only to find herself routed horse, foot, and artillery, Evelyn was going to take the battle to Maddie.

While she finished pinning up her hair for the day, Gareth wiped residual lather from his face, leaning around her to replace the towel on the wall hook. She tried not to notice the breadth of his shoulders or the way his torso tapered to a lean waist. The smell of soap pricked her nose. She turned to pull back the quilts to air the bed. "Will you be working near the house today?"

"Most likely. Jamie and I are going to clean out the barn, and he's going to help me repair the pigsty fence. That sow keeps trying to root her way out."

Evelyn set her jaw and took a deep, calming breath through her nose. Smoothing the quilts one last time, she tried to brush past him in the doorway, but he caught her gently by the elbows.

"I need to get breakfast started." Her skin prickled at his touch. He'd kept his word and given her space, never pushing, but several times she'd caught him looking at her in a way that made her throat close up and her blood warm. But she wasn't ready for that. Not yet.

"In a minute. I know you're still not happy about Jamie being in the barn and around the men, but he's having the time of his life. I think he was born to be a rancher. He can't seem to learn fast enough."

"I haven't complained." And only she knew what it cost her to bite her tongue and refrain from begging him to be careful with her son.

"I know, but your mouth gets all tight around the corners every time I talk about Jamie learning to cowboy." His eyes twinkled, and he smiled, making her heart trip. "I best go roust the kids."

Tearing her mind away from his handsome features and charming manner, she shook her head. "Just Jamie. Let Maddie sleep. I'll wake her in a bit."

After a quick breakfast with the boys, Evelyn hugged Jamie and brushed a kiss atop his curly hair. "Have a good morning. Obey Gareth. And be careful. Come home safe."

"I will, Mama." He squirmed, broke free, and scampered toward the door. "I'm going to go find Rimfire."

"That's a nice custom you have." Gareth drained his coffee cup.

"What?"

"The hug and kiss you always give Jamie before we head out in the morning."

He leaned around her to place his cup in the dishpan, brushing her arm. She turned and found herself face-to-face with him. . .or rather face-to-chest, as he was so tall. Looking up, she caught the playful warmth in his eyes. Involuntarily, she moistened her lips, and his gaze focused on her mouth.

Gentle as a whisper, he brushed the hair at her temple. He leaned closer. "Yep, a very nice custom. Lucky Jamie."

He strode away, leaving her sagging against the workbench.

Stop it, Evelyn Stan—Kittrick. You vowed never to care for anyone like you once cared for Jamison. You can like Gareth, you can even be fond of him, but you cannot, you will not *be so foolish as to fall in love with him.*

Loving meant caring too much. Loving meant loss of control. Loving meant ruin when God took that person away from you. And she never intended to go through that kind of devastation again.

⌁

An hour later, Evelyn knocked on Maddie's door. "Time to get up. We have lots to do today."

A groan seeped under the door. Evelyn waited a moment and knocked again.

"Hey, where'd my pants go?" The door wrenched open, and Maddie stuck her tousled head out. "I can't find any of my clothes."

Evelyn pushed the door wider. "All your clothing is in the wash. And that's where you'll be soon. Today you're going to take a proper bath and put on clean clothes. The bathwater is heated, and the tub is ready."

Mutiny gleamed in Maddie's eyes and hardened her jaw. She scanned the room, and when she saw her father wasn't in the house, her thin arms crossed in a gesture Evelyn had grown to loathe. "No. I washed in the creek already this week."

"Dogs and cows bathe in creeks. Little girls use the bathtub. And soap."

The child didn't even have a proper nightgown. Faded red-flannel underwear only emphasized her skinny frame and clashed with her flaming-orange hair.

"I ain't going to take a bath."

"You are if I have to drag you to the tub and hold you there."

Maddie's eyes narrowed to angry slits. "You better bring your lunch, because it's going to be a long day. Wait until my pa hears about this."

"Your father has given me the staggering task of turning you into a lady. I've tried to be nice, to guide and assist you in learning some manners and the basics of hygiene, but you've chosen to ignore everything I've said. Obviously, a change in tactics is necessary." She planted her foot firmly along the base of the door when Maddie went to slam it and grabbed her by the upper arm. "As to your bath taking all day, that's up to you, but I assure you, I'm equal to the task. If you want to be so undignified as to hiss and spit like a frightened barn cat, go ahead, but it won't do you a speck of good."

In the end, Maddie got clean, but Evelyn was hard pressed to decide who had gotten wetter. Halfway through the struggle, the child gave up trying to escape and became a block of stone. Though relieved not to be wrestling the slippery eellike body any longer, Evelyn didn't labor under the notion that Maddie had given up. She could almost hear the gears churning in the child's mind, and she tensed for the next onslaught.

This came when Evelyn finished rubbing Maddie dry and handed her the new garments she'd spent every night for the last three weeks sewing.

"What are those?" Maddie scowled.

"Drawers, chemise, petticoat, dress, pinafore."

"I ain't wearing those. Those are for girls."

"I have news for you, Madelyn Kittrick. You *are* a girl, and you're going to act like it from now on. Now get dressed. You have a cooking lesson awaiting you."

"I'm not wearing that sissy stuff. I can't ride or work in a getup like that."

"You won't be riding anytime soon, and when you do, it will be sidesaddle like a proper lady. If you won't dress yourself, I'll have to do it." Evelyn's muscles chided her, worn out from bath time, but she ignored them. "As to work, you surely can work wearing a dress. I do it every day. You're going to learn to cook, clean, sew, garden, and you're going to study."

"Study?" Maddie's jaw dropped. "Study what? I can read some, and I can add some. That's enough."

"You've barely scratched the surface. You're going to study grammar and history and spelling and much more. I refuse to raise an ignorant child."

"Ignorant? You're the one who's ignorant! You don't know anything that's worth a hill of wormy beans."

After a protracted battle, Maddie donned the new clothing, but Evelyn suspected it was because the only other option was to walk around in a bath towel until her other clothes were clean.

When Evelyn had asked about appropriate clothing for Maddie or a shopping trip to procure material, Gareth had shrugged. "I can't sew worth a lick, and it was easier to buy ready-made boy's clothing at the mercantile. But Justine's stuff is upstairs in a trunk. Maybe you can cut down a dress or two for Maddie, though you can expect some pretty heavy ordnance to go off when you try to make her wear it."

Heavy ordnance indeed. However, except for the black scowl on Maddie's face, she would've looked quite sweet in the light blue calico dress and snowy pinafore.

"Roll up your sleeves, please. You're going to learn to make biscuits."

The girl's green eyes blazed, but she unbuttoned her cuffs, shoving them up before crossing her arms.

Training this child was like dragging an elephant through a knothole backward, but Evelyn wasn't about to give up.

⁖

Gareth listened at the barn door, but the caterwauling from the house had quit. Though his first instinct had been to race over to see what was happening, he refrained. The showdown had come at last. Three weeks. About time.

Even knowing how stubborn his daughter could be, his money was on Evelyn. She had some steel to her. Her stubborn insistence on coddling Jamie showed how, once she latched on to an idea, she wouldn't let go.

Jamie wielded the hay rake awkwardly but with his mother's same determination. "What else are we going to do today?" The handle bounced off a partition and jumped from his hands, but he grabbed it and attacked the soiled hay in the stall again. "Besides clean the barn, I mean."

"Grease the axles on the wagon and go over the equipment. Bridles, saddles, branding irons, knives, the lot. That way we'll be ready when it's time to roll out."

"And I can really go with you? On the roundup?" He searched Gareth's face. His shoulders bunched, and he quivered like a happy pup as if he couldn't quite contain his joy at the prospect.

"That's right. You'll never learn any younger." Though what Evelyn would say, Gareth hated to think. She had a hard enough time letting the boy out of her sight long enough to do a few simple chores. Roundup could last a month and took in a fair amount of range. "You've done a good job on the barn here. How about we take care of the wagon?"

Jamie dropped the rake and headed for the tack room then stopped and scampered back to get the tool and hang it up properly. Gareth tousled the boy's hair and winked at him. "That's right. Always take care of your equipment and put it back where it goes. That way, if you need something in a hurry, you'll never have to waste time looking for it."

The boy nodded. "That's what Mama says, too. 'A place for everything, and everything in its place.'"

"You've got a smart mama." *And pretty, too.* Sharing a house and a bedroom with Evelyn, seeing her go about her duties, having her so near, was taking a toll on Gareth. He'd had to stop himself from reaching for her several times. And in her sleep, she forgot to keep her distance. She crossed the no-man's-land center of the mattress and cuddled up against his side as if they'd been married for years. He always made sure he left their bed first, and the minute he slid out from under the covers, she rolled back over to her own pillows as if he'd dreamed the whole thing.

"Gareth?" Jamie's voice broke through his thoughts, and from the impatient edge, the boy must've called his name more than once. "Aren't we going to grease the wagon?"

With Jamie's help, he worked his way down his chore list. The boy was eager to learn and to try everything, and Gareth had to stifle a chuckle when he realized Jamie was copying his every move. Now if he could convince Evelyn to let the boy wear something besides those ridiculous knickerbockers and that straw boater. A velvet suit was no proper attire for a cowboy-in-the-making.

At noon they made their way to the house, pausing on the porch to whack the dust from their clothes and scrape their boots well. The quiet from within sent a shiver through Gareth. Had they killed each other?

The door was propped open to catch the breeze, and he thought he caught a whiff of something burnt. Odd, since Evelyn had proven to be an excellent cook. Shrugging, he ducked and removed his hat as he went under the lintel.

A stranger stood beside the table with a fistful of cutlery. A little red-haired stranger in a dress. Green eyes narrowed into a resentful glare.

"Maddie?"

Her mouth bunched, and she slapped knives and forks down beside plates. Her hair was neatly parted and braided. The braids had been looped up at each ear, and bless him if they weren't tied with ribbons. Ribbons on his Maddie!

Evelyn emerged from the pantry with a pitcher and a plate of biscuits. "Oh, good, just in time." She smiled, but her eyes had a strained look, as if the wrong word might send her right up into the air.

Jamie seemed to read the same sign, for he scooted to his seat without a word.

"We washed up at the pump." Gareth slid into his chair at the head of the table, hardly able to tear his gaze away from his daughter. A snowy pinafore covered her dress, and her face and hands were immaculate, even down to the nails.

When everyone was seated, he said grace and silently asked for an extra blessing on Evelyn for the changes she'd wrought in Maddie.

Forking up a helping of ham, he noticed the black spots on the edges of the meat. Evelyn caught his eye and she inclined her head toward Maddie. His daughter sat with her shoulders hunched, watching him from under her lashes.

"Sure smells good. I'm hungry enough to eat a badger— teeth, claws, and all." He helped himself to a couple of biscuits. When he took a bite from one, all the moisture disappeared from his mouth, absorbed by the incredibly dry fare. Trying not to hurry, he lifted his glass and drank. "Mmm. Good."

Maddie relaxed, and Evelyn sent him a grateful smile. He'd read the situation right.

"Mama? What happened to these biscuits? They're hard and dry." Jamie crumbled the bread on his plate. "And the meat's burnt."

"Jamie, hush. Eat without complaint and be grateful for it." Evelyn frowned at her son. Gareth peeked at Maddie and wished he hadn't. Two tears hovered on her lower lashes.

Maddie never cried. Never. Screamed, threw things, stomped her feet, maybe, but never tears. Her little throat worked, and she pushed back from the table. Scrubbing at her face, she rounded on Evelyn.

"I told you I couldn't do it. Making me wear a dress and cook and clean. What a waste of time." She shoved her plate away and turned to run to her room.

Evelyn reached out and snagged Maddie's arm before she could get away. "Oh no you don't. You can't run away every time you're faced with something unpleasant. You'll sit here and finish your lunch. Jamie, apologize to your sister."

"Sister?" Jamie spoke around a mouthful of ham.

"Jamison! Don't talk with your mouth full. Madelyn became your sister when I married her father. She's taking her first steps in the kitchen, and we can do without your criticisms."

Jamie ducked his head and mumbled an apology. Gareth blinked. Evelyn had certainly taken charge of the children. And Maddie stayed in her seat, even lifting her chin a bit. How had Evelyn managed that?

"This afternoon, Maddie and I are going to work in the garden." Evelyn spread her napkin back in her lap. "Thank you for having Rimfire till the ground for us."

Gareth cut off a bite of ham. "Are you sure you want such a big patch? You'll have to tote water for it this summer."

"The children will help me. That's why I wanted the garden so close to the creek. We'll be able to raise enough vegetables to feed us through the winter."

"Rimfire should be back from town in a few hours. He'll have those seeds you wanted."

"Good. I've got enough to keep us busy until then."

Maddie sent Gareth a pleading look, as if to say, "Get me out of here!"

Evelyn sent him a steady look that said, "Don't you dare."

A smart man would vamoose, and Gareth was known to be a smart man. He rose and reached for his hat. "You finished, Jamie? We've got plenty of work to do. The sty fence needs reinforcing before that sow gets loose."

The boy was off his seat in a flash and headed for the door. He stopped and muttered a thank-you for the lunch before disappearing into the sunshine.

Gareth took a little more time. "Maddie, that was a fine lunch. Learning to cook is a good and necessary skill." He put his hand on her shoulder, but she shrugged it off.

Evelyn rose and began stacking plates. "Maddie, would you go get a bucket of water, please, so we can start washing up?"

With the posture of a condemned man, Maddie got the bucket, banging it against her legs as she trudged outside.

"I can't believe it. What a transformation." Gareth rubbed the back of his neck and tucked his fingers into his hip pocket.

"Only on the outside, I fear." Evelyn put her hands on the base of her spine and stretched. "And we've had several altercations this morning just to get this far."

"Still, it's quite a bit of progress."

Maddie reappeared in the doorway. "Wagon coming, Pa. You want help unloading supplies?"

"Naw. You stay here and help out. Jamie and I can handle things with Rimfire's help."

Maddie's shoulders went limp, and she set the bucket on the table. Keeping her head down, she skirted him with a deep sigh.

Escaping the house, he blew out a breath. A man could only take so many female emotions being pelted at him. He headed for the barn with Jamie on his heels. At least in a barn a man knew where he was and what he was supposed to be doing and saying. Wagon wheels rattled and hooves clopped. His foreman had returned.

Moments later, Rimfire shuffled in under the weight of a bag of grain. "Found a couple more riders for you while I was in town."

"Yeah?"

"They're stowing their gear in the bunkhouse. Then we'll start on those horses." The bag thumped to the barn floor, sending out swirls of dust and burlap chaff. "Should be ready to pull out in three days."

Gareth seized the grain sack, propped it on the edge of the bin, and cut open the top with his jackknife. The oats slid into the grain bin with a rattle. Three days to convince Evelyn that Jamie should go on the roundup. And three days to convince Maddie that she shouldn't.

He wasn't certain which would be the more difficult.

Chapter 5

How on earth did this happen? I thought you were watching him." Evelyn stood in the shadow of the barn and stared in disbelief as a muddy creature blinked at her from under the most vile-smelling coat of slime she'd ever encountered.

"Mama, don't blame him. It was my fault."

She rounded on Gareth anyway. "I told you to watch out for him. Now look. His suit is ruined. And where is his hat?"

"The pig ate it, Mama." Jamie swiped at the muck on his cheeks, causing the malodorous cloud around him to shift.

"I'm sorry, Evelyn." Gareth's grin only infuriated her more. "We were repairing the pigsty fence, and that sow thought we were after her piglets. She let out a bark and barreled into the boards. Jamie went flying, and he landed right in the sty. In the wallow end."

She wanted to check the child over for injuries, but the stench and the viscous coating he wore deterred her. Pinching her nose, she scowled at Gareth. "He could've been killed. That sow has teeth like a wolf."

"Now, Evelyn, it isn't as bad as it looks. I'll take him to the creek and sluice him off. That'll knock back the worst of it. And I had Rimfire pick up some clothes for him while he was in town today. We'll get him kitted out in something more suitable for a cowboy."

Even liberally smeared with pig-muck, Jamie's eyes shone. "Sure enough? That would be great, Gareth. Are they just like yours?"

"He doesn't need new clothes. The ones he has are perfectly serviceable. Or were until you let him fall into the pigsty." Evelyn put her hands on her hips. "Every respectable young man in the East is wearing a velvet suit."

"He's not in the East anymore." Gareth tucked his hands into his hip pockets. "He can't do all the things a boy is supposed to do out here if he's always worried about his clothes. I'd say him falling in the pigpen is a blessing."

"A blessing? He could've been killed. And he can't bathe in the creek. He'll catch his death of cold. He needs a proper bath." And considering the stench, probably more than one.

"Naw, he's man enough to take a dunking in the creek. Besides, if we let him in the house like he is, we'll never get the smell out." Gareth shooed Jamie ahead of him toward the little river. "Bring down some soap and the package I tossed up into the loft. You'll see. He'll be good as new in no time."

Evelyn closed her eyes, willing herself to remain calm. She'd heard the wild yelp clear from the garden and raced toward the sound, sure that her son was killed or maimed. Seeing Jamie flat on his back, spread-eagled in a lake of pig swill, her mouth had gone dry and her heart had taken up residence in her throat. To have Gareth pass it all off as just another day in a rancher's life infuriated her.

A tug on her sleeve. "You gonna get the soap? He's going to need a lot to get that stink off." Maddie spoke to Evelyn for the first time since early morning. "Sure wish I could've seen him land in that puddle."

Evelyn pressed her lips together and went to gather the items Jamie would need. And she'd stir up the fire, too. He'd need a hot drink after bathing in the creek.

This day couldn't possibly get any worse. She'd battled Maddie to a draw, worked in the garden until her back screamed and her hands blistered even through her gloves, and her son had nearly been killed by an enraged sow.

The few scrub trees along the creek bank unfurled pale green baby leaves, a promise of what they would look like come the summer.

"Do you think she'll mind?" Jamie's voice piped up over the gurgle of the water.

"No, I don't think so. Your mother is a reasonable woman. She won't mind at all," Gareth answered.

Evelyn slowed to a stop, still out of their sight. What wouldn't she mind?

"What about Maddie? Will she mind?"

"Why should she?"

"She minds everything I do. I can't seem to do anything right around her."

"Women can be like that, Jamie, hard to figure. Now, shuck those clothes and hop into the water. You smell worse than a dead buffalo. Your ma will be along with the soap soon." A splash, followed by a high squeal that rent the air.

"It's cold!"

Evelyn took her cue and rounded the hillock. "I brought soap, towels, and a change of everything."

"Mama!" Jamie sank down into the water, covering himself. "A little privacy, please?"

Her mouth opened. He'd never objected to her presence at his baths before.

Gareth took the bundle from her arms and turned her around. "Sure enough, Jamie. A man likes privacy when he does his bathing." Sorting out the soap, he tossed it to the boy. "Catch it. You scrub good, and I'll check on you in a minute." He ushered Evelyn away. "Let him be. He's fine. The water's only knee deep."

"I thought I might help him clean up. I'm sure he'll need help washing his hair." She glanced back over her shoulder, but Gareth prevented her from turning.

"I don't think that's a good idea. I can make sure his hair is clean. If you help him, you'll just embarrass him."

"He's never been embarrassed before."

"He's growing up. It's only natural that he'd prefer to wash alone."

She swallowed. "I heard you talking as I walked up. What is it that he's afraid I won't like?"

Squeezing her shoulder, he smiled. "He asked if it was okay to call me Pa."

A shaft of something akin to pain darted through Evelyn. With one sentence, Gareth assumed a place of prominence in her son's life. Jamison Stanford took a step back into the fog of the past, and some of the strings binding Jamie to her seemed to snap.

"You don't mind, do you? I'm pleased as punch about it. I figured after your talk at lunch about Jamie and Maddie being brother and sister, you'd be happy he wanted to call me Pa."

She was, wasn't she? Maybe *happy* wasn't the right word. Whatever it was she was feeling, she forced herself to nod. "It's fine. What about Maddie?"

"You're making a good job of her. She's learning all the things her mother wanted to teach her—cooking, sewing, cleaning, gardening. She'll settle to it now that she knows you won't back down every time she fusses." He trailed the backs of his fingers down her cheek, tucking a stray tendril of hair behind her ear and sending sparks across her skin.

Evelyn stepped back. For the first time, she wasn't altogether sure she was doing the right thing by Maddie, but what to do about it or how to explain it to Gareth was beyond her at the moment. "Best get back to Jamie. He'll be about frozen by now. Make sure you rub him down well. I don't want him to catch cold. I don't know what I'd do if anything happened to him."

⁓

This time Evelyn really was going to kill him. Two whole days had passed since the pigpen incident, and she was still a little bent out of shape about that. If he showed up at the house with Jamie all bloodied up, she'd never let him hear the end of it.

"Tip your head back." Gareth eased the boy over and pressed his bandanna against Jamie's nose.

Jamie obliged, propping himself on one elbow and leaning back. Red blotches decorated the front of his shirt.

Rimfire caught the pony careening around the corral and led him over to where Jamie sprawled in the dirt.

"Piled you up proper, didn't he?" The foreman squatted. "They say no man's a true cowboy until he's been thrown ninety-nine times. You've only got ninety-eight more to go."

"Huh." The boy shook his head, his voice muffled by the hankie.

Rimfire tipped Jamie's chin up, checking the damage. "Every cowboy gets thrown from time to time. The trick is to get right back on and show the pony who's boss. Ain't that right, Gareth?"

"That's right." He looked over his shoulder at the house, willing Evelyn to stay inside. He hadn't told her about putting Jamie up on a cow pony, knowing she'd just worry and fret. "I hadn't counted on old Coffee spooking like that. Wonder what got into him?"

The pony stuck his head down and nudged Jamie's arm as if to apologize. Jamie scooted upright until his narrow shoulders rested against one of the corral posts, and reached out to rub the horse's muzzle. Brown as the bean he was named for, Coffee was the gentlest horse on the ranch. Maddie had ridden him on every roundup but the last, having graduated to a more spirited mount the previous year.

"Has the bleeding stopped?" Gareth peeled the hankie away slowly.

"I think so."

"Then let's get you back into the saddle."

"Do I have to?" The boy's forehead scrunched, and his voice wavered.

Rimfire put his meaty hand on Jamie's shoulder. "Boy, if you don't, Coffee might get the idea that he can pitch off a rider anytime he wants to. What if it was your mama on him next time? You wouldn't want her to get thrown, would you? It's for the pony's own good for you to get back on him. If you don't, he might be ruined."

Jamie's brow smoothed out, and he nodded. "I wouldn't want that to happen. He's a good pony." Scrambling to his feet, he took the reins from the foreman. "Hold still, Coffee.

This is for your own good."

Gareth hid his smile, but he winked at Rimfire, pride bursting through him that Jamie would put the horse's supposed needs above his own fear. A boy to be proud of, to be sure.

Walking to the house a couple of hours later, Gareth put his arm around the boy. "You're going to be a real help on the roundup this year."

The thin chest puffed up, and Jamie added a little more swagger to his walk. "I'm learning, aren't I?"

"You sure are."

They entered together, and Gareth tested the air. Maddie sat beside the window, poking a needle in and out of a piece of cloth. She seemed more resigned to the idea of staying inside and helping Evelyn, though she still wasn't happy about it. It was almost as if she'd become a different person in the last week or so. Instead of storming about the house, expressing every thought and notion, she now sat quiet most of the time or went about her chores without speaking. Gareth missed her chatter. And he missed her dogging his footsteps around the barn and corrals.

His eyes sought out Evelyn. She had her hair twisted up in a pale knot that revealed the graceful curve of her neck and cheek, and immediately his mind went to how she looked with it all down and spilling over her shoulders. She only left it that way for a few minutes each night as she readied for bed. Every time she unpinned her hair and brushed it out, it was all he could do to keep from crossing the room and burying his hands in its creamy softness. Long before he was ready for her to stop, she would set aside the brush and quickly braid it for the night.

"Jamie! What happened?"

Her shocked voice broke him out of his thoughts.

"I got piled up." Jamie grinned, lifting his chin. "Rimfire says I only need to be thrown ninety-eight more times to be a real cowboy."

"Piled up?" Evelyn advanced on her son and knelt before him, turning his chin this way and that. They'd gotten most of the blood off, but his nose was red and a little swollen, and his face bore traces of corral dirt.

"I got bucked off." Jamie stuck his hands in his hip pockets. "But I got right back on Coffee so he wouldn't be ruined."

Evelyn's eyes sought Gareth's as she stood, accusation and questions burning in their blue depths. At the same time, Maddie bolted upright, dropping her sewing on the floor and fisting her hands.

"Coffee? You let him ride my horse?" Red suffused Maddie's face to the point her freckles disappeared. The words came out strained, as if someone were squashing her windpipe.

"He did a great job, too. Got right back on after taking quite a tumble." Gareth put his hand on Jamie's shoulder and squeezed. "Didn't even let a nosebleed hold him back. He's got the makings of a first-rate cowboy."

Jamie beamed up at him. "Thanks, Pa."

Maddie made an odd strangled sound and cleared her throat. "May I be excused? I'm not hungry."

Gareth frowned and shook his head. "You need to eat something. You've been spending too much time in your room lately. Why don't you show me what you're working on?" He pointed to the sewing she'd abandoned.

Maddie handed him the sampler. "It's a Bible verse."

He read the words penciled on the fabric. PSALM 18:2 THE LORD IS MY ROCK, AND MY FORTRESS, AND MY DELIVERER; MY GOD, MY STRENGTH, IN WHOM I WILL TRUST; MY BUCKLER, AND THE HORN OF MY SALVATION, AND MY HIGH TOWER. The reference and the first three words had been stitched over in red thread, a little wobbly and uneven, but readable.

"Looks nice. You've come a long ways. Remember when you tried to fix a button on my shirt and sewed the sleeve to the collar by mistake?" He grinned and tried to ruffle her hair, but she ducked, blinked hard a couple of times, and went to set the table.

⌒

Evelyn set the chicken and dumplings down harder than necessary but easier than her temper would've liked. What was he thinking, putting her son on a horse? Letting him get bucked off. A chill raced through her at the thought of her son flying through the air and landing in a heap in the dirt. She closed her eyes and took a deep breath, trying to settle the quiver in her stomach.

Jamie seemed oblivious to the danger. With each day that passed he became more enamored of Gareth, walking like him, talking like him, even mimicking his gestures.

"Jamie, I thought you might like to stay inside this afternoon. It's been awhile since you spent some time with Chaucer."

"Oh, I can't. Pa and me are going to start loading the chuck wagon, and he said I could help him shoe the team." He shoveled a bite of dumpling into his mouth, dripping gravy on the table.

"It's Pa and I, and hold your food over your plate. You love Chaucer, and you haven't touched it in almost a month."

"Too busy. Gotta help Pa with the forge."

The child's grammar was appalling. *Gotta?* "Is the blacksmith shop really the best place for a child, Gareth?" She tried to modulate her voice, but her lips were stiff, and she hadn't come to terms yet with this morning's accident enough to be calm about the idea of Jamie being so close to all that hot metal.

"He won't learn any younger."

Jamie slid his plate closer and jabbed another dumpling. "I can't wait to go on the roundup. Pa says I can ride herd and help him keep the tally book and everything. He says he's gonna teach me to brand calves."

Evelyn gulped down the bite she'd just taken. "Hold it there, young man. Who said anything about you going on the roundup? Helping with the chores around here is one thing, but herding cattle is a job for grown men, not little boys." She gripped her napkin in her lap and looked to Gareth to back her up.

"Those are my jobs, Pa." Maddie spoke up for the first time during the meal. "If you let him ride herd and keep the tally, what am I supposed to do during roundup? I ain't gonna stay by the fire and cook, that's for sure and for certain." Her green eyes blazed.

Gareth took his time laying his fork down. "Well, Maddie, I kinda thought you'd stay here with Evelyn. She'll need your help around the place, especially with me and Jamie gone."

"Now wait here, Gareth. I don't want Jamie going on that roundup, and that's that." Evelyn glared at him. The thought of her son gone for days at a time, with no one to look after him but a bunch of rough cowboys, riding a horse among wild cattle. . .every muscle tensed, and her stomach rebelled at the very little bit of lunch she'd put in it.

"Evelyn, we've been through this. You've got to let Jamie grow up, or you'll have him so bound by apron strings he'll never be able to do anything for himself." Gareth's jaw had firmed, and his eyes took on a stern light she'd not encountered before.

But her heart quailed at the thought of what could happen to Jamie. "He's not going."

"Pa, you can't take him with you and not take me." Maddie banged her hand on the table. "It's not fair. I'm supposed to be your pard."

"Enough." Gareth pushed his plate back. "I've made up my mind. Maddie, you went along on the roundups before because I didn't have anyone to stay back at the ranch to look after you. You're staying here. And Evelyn, the boy's going. If you won't cut those apron strings, I'll have to."

The fire smoldering in the pit of her stomach flared to blazing life. "Surely there's a compromise we can reach." She grasped at anything she could to keep herself from falling to pieces.

"Not that I can think of." He stood and reached for his hat.

"If you insist on taking Jamie on the roundup, then I'm going along, too." She knew nothing about cattle or horses or roundups, but she'd brave all those and more to watch out for her son.

Maddie rose and came to stand beside Evelyn in a show of solidarity that surprised her, though she tried not to show it. "I think that's a great idea." They waited, tense, for

Gareth's yes or no.

He blew out a big breath. "We'll be gone a whole month. It's no place for a lady."

"I'm tougher than you think. If Maddie has gone along with you before and been fine, I'm sure I can take it." She wasn't sure of any such thing, but he didn't need to know that.

Throwing up his hands, he stared at the pair of them and then at Jamie's eager face. "I'm no match for all of you. We'll all go." Then he said the strangest thing: "Rimfire was right about the dynamite and the henhouse. I sure will be glad when it quits raining feathers."

Chapter 6

She hadn't thought it possible to encounter a rougher ride than the stagecoach that had brought her to Wyoming, but the chuck wagon proved her wrong. Dust covered her hair and face and sifted through her clothing. And the sullen man beside her didn't improve the journey.

Grizzled was the only word that described the cook. Unless it was *silent*. He'd voiced his displeasure at having a woman along on the ride, but when Gareth wouldn't budge on the issue, he'd chosen silence, ignoring her completely. She wasn't surprised at all when someone called him Muley.

The only one who seemed truly happy about the venture was Jamie, who bounced around Gareth and the other cowboys like an exuberant puppy until everyone mounted their horses. He followed Gareth on his pony, all eyes and ears, talking nineteen to the dozen.

Maddie climbed into the wagon with bad grace and took a seat on a sack of cornmeal in the back, pouting because her father had refused to let her ride with the men.

Rimfire rode close to the wagon to talk to Evelyn. "Odd having Mad Dog—'scuse me, Maddie—not riding with us. I remember all of us taking her up in front with us at one time or another when she was real small. Then she rode

Coffee, and finally she had her pick of the remuda. I hope Gareth knows what he's doing with her. I've never seen her so quiet, and when I tried to speak to her, she just buried her head." He scratched his chin. "Do you ride? We'll have to see about getting you a horse."

"No, thank you. I couldn't possibly." The idea of being aboard something with a mind of its own. . .she shuddered.

Jamie rode a brown beast so round the boy's legs stuck out. At least the animal was smaller than the cow ponies the men rode. Seeing him astride awoke all her fears for his safety. How could she possibly protect him when Gareth insisted on letting him do such dangerous things?

The wagon rocked over a ridge and down a slope of prairie. Evelyn gripped the edge of the seat and braced herself against the tilt. She couldn't help but wonder if Muley chose the most difficult route to express his displeasure at her presence.

Rimfire legged his horse away from the wagon, and Gareth took his place. "We're making good time. Should be at the first camp in about an hour. How're you making out?" He removed his hat and wiped his face with his forearm. "Beats me how it can go from so chilly to so hot in such a short time."

Evelyn had to admire the way he looked in the saddle. Lean, supple, rocking slightly with the motion of his horse. Everything about him bespoke capability. A man's man. And a woman's man, too, if she was honest enough to admit it. But stubborn. Why wouldn't he listen to reason regarding Jamie?

She craned her neck to keep the boy in sight. "I'm fine. Will we be near any of my sisters' homes?" If she could just talk to one of them, maybe she'd feel better. Jane would help her be practical, Gwendolyn would champion and encourage her, and Emmeline would soak in everything about the roundup with eager eyes. Her heart ached for them.

"No. I'm afraid we're headed in the opposite direction. They all live south and west of our place. Our range is mostly north and east." He replaced his hat. "I'll take you to visit them later this summer, I promise."

Evelyn busied herself with thoughts of their reunion and all the things she wanted to tell them and all the things she wanted to ask them, trying to keep her mind off what she was going to do about Jamie. And Gareth. And Maddie. All she succeeded in doing was reminding herself how out of control everything was.

By the time they reached the first campsite, Evelyn was only too glad to climb down from the wagon and stretch the kinks in her muscles.

Gareth gathered the riders. "Everyone pair up and fan out. Drive everything this way toward the flat ground between here and the river. Rimfire, you and Charlie will do the groundwork. Start the fires and break out the irons." He was all business, directing his men and planning his attack.

Maddie waited until he'd finished his orders, sidled up to him, and took his hand. "Pa, can't I come, too?" Her round face held entreaty and hope.

He rubbed his hand across the top of her head. "Stay here and help Muley and Evelyn get the fire started. You can tote the water."

Mounting with fluid ease, he galloped away with Jamie in his wake. Maddie stared after him, her shoulders drooping. Evelyn's heart went out to the girl. Neither one of them seemed to have the least little say in what was happening to them. Perhaps that would be their common ground.

⁓

The noise, dust, and smells were incredible. Evelyn had never encountered anything like it. She and Maddie stood on a little rise watching the milling cattle and cowboys.

"Can you explain it to me? What are they doing?"

Maddie pointed. "A couple of cowboys hold the cattle. Two more go in and cut out the unbranded calves, rope them, and haul them toward the fire. The men on the ground bulldog and tie the calf, brand it, notch its ear, and if it's a boy calf, they—"

"Thank you." Evelyn spoke quickly. "I get the idea. How many calves will they brand?"

The girl shrugged. "Depends on how the herd wintered. Hopefully we'll have a good calf crop."

"Thank you for explaining things to me. I'm completely ignorant of ranching life." Evelyn dared put her hand on the child's shoulder, and she was pleasantly surprised when Maddie didn't shrug her off. "I'm counting on you to help me learn."

"Don't know how I can do that if I'm stuck in the house all the time."

She had a point. Evelyn tugged on her lower lip. "How about a compromise? Housework and sewing in the morning, and in the afternoon, you can teach me to ride a horse." What was she saying? She couldn't ride one of those enormous beasts. And yet at the eager light that sprang into Maddie's eyes, the first she'd seen there, Evelyn couldn't back out.

"I'd like that. Can we start right now?"

"Now? I thought we'd wait until we got back home."

The girl squinted up at her. "You aren't gonna chicken out, are you?"

Evelyn's spine stiffened. "I'd never."

"Then why're we waiting? There're plenty of horses in the remuda, and nothing for us to do, since Muley ran us out of his camp."

In far too short a time, Evelyn found herself standing beside a caramel-colored giant of a horse. The animal's feet were enormous and his hide warm and twitching.

"I'm glad Pa brought Buck along. He's the horse I usually ride." Maddie looped the reins over the animal's head and knotted them. "So you don't drop them."

"What do I do first?"

"Come around to this side." She pointed to the stirrup. "Put your foot there, step up, and swing your leg over."

"Astride?"

She shrugged. "No sidesaddles out here. Buck's pretty calm, so he won't care about your skirts hanging down. Won't be much different from a slicker."

The horse was calm? That made one of them. Evelyn bunched her skirt and somehow managed to climb aboard. As promised, the animal barely moved. Her hands closed around the knob in front of her.

"Pick up the reins." Maddie held on to the horse near the bit. "You don't need to do anything just yet. I'll lead him around and let you get the feel of him."

Round in circles they went, out of sight of the cattle and the chuck wagon. Maddie finally stepped back, letting go of the bridle and leaving Evelyn in sole charge of the animal.

She had to peel her hand off the knob—horn—and lift

the reins. Not wanting to show fear in front of Maddie, she forced herself to do as instructed.

An hour later, Evelyn slid to the ground. She had to grip the saddle until she got her sea legs.

"You did great." Maddie's smile rewarded her. "With a little practice, you'll be riding like a cowhand in no time."

Evelyn blew out a breath and stepped back from the horse. "Thank you, but I think it will be enough just to be able to get from one place to another. I'll leave the cows to the men. It would be nice to be proficient enough to be able to visit my sisters."

"You miss them?"

Her throat thickened. "I miss them every day." She blinked and smiled. "But being with you helps that a lot."

Maddie toed the dirt and shrugged, a pink tinge washing her cheeks. "When we get home, you can ask Pa to get out the buckboard. I can teach you to drive the team. Then you could go see your sisters whenever you wanted."

"Really?" Evelyn forgot herself completely and hugged Maddie's shoulders. "That would be wonderful. My sisters will love you."

"I could go, too?"

"Absolutely. Why wouldn't I take you?"

She shrugged again. "I haven't been very nice to you. And nobody else seems to want me around these days."

Evelyn's heart hurt for Maddie. She had to be feeling as if her entire world had gone topsy-turvy with the advent of her father's marriage. Evelyn promised herself she would speak with Gareth tonight. He needed to be made aware of how disconnected Maddie was feeling. "How about we call a truce? We'll forget about all the stuff that's happened up to now and start over."

Maddie shrugged, gave a short nod, and swung aboard the horse, apparently not hampered by her dress at all. "I'll take Buck back to the remuda."

Evelyn's muscles protested every step back to camp. She'd be plenty sore tomorrow, but it had been worth it. *Thank You, Lord, for helping me make some headway with Maddie. Now if I could just make some progress with her father.*

✸

Gareth approached the campfire, weariness coating him like dust. Actually, the weariness was beneath the dust, dirt, muck, blood, smoke, and sweat. His chaps flapped, and his spurs jingled. Jamie all but staggered by his side, dirt-streaked and worn out from his first full day in the saddle.

"How you holding up, cowboy?"

The boy puffed up his chest and put a little swagger into his step. "I'm fine, Pa. I did good, didn't I?"

Gareth patted Jamie's shoulder and a shower of dust sprinkled down. "You sure did."

The men stood, squatted, or sat, balancing tin plates and shoveling hot food into their mouths. Muley stood beside his dutch oven, ladling out beans and salt pork.

No sign of Evelyn and Maddie. Gareth frowned. Where had they gotten to? He cupped the back of Jamie's head and directed him toward the washbasin. "Let's get scrubbed up, then we can get some grub."

The basin sat on a shelf that jutted from the side of the wagon. A bucket of water hung from a rope handle beside it. He poured some water for Jamie and handed him the cake of soap. "Don't forget to scrub your nails good."

A giggle sounded close to his ear. "What did your pa say when he saw it?"

Maddie. Laughing. Gareth smiled in response and leaned close to the canvas. Evelyn's laugh made warmth burst through his chest. "I thought he'd be angry, but he wasn't. He was disappointed, which was much worse."

"I know," Maddie agreed. "I'd much rather Pa yelled at me than gave me that look."

"Exactly. And I couldn't grow my hair back overnight, so my father had a long time to give me that look. As if that wasn't bad enough, he made me go to church and school that way, and he wouldn't let me wear a bonnet to cover it up."

Maddie giggled again. "Did everybody stare at you?"

"Pa." Jamie tugged on his sleeve. "Your turn."

"In a minute, son. Go ahead and get your food. I'll be there directly." Gareth rounded the side of the wagon and eased the canvas cover aside. He had to see if his ears were deceiving him.

In the soft glow of a lantern, Maddie sat cross-legged on the floor of the wagon, and Evelyn sat on the bunk Gareth had fixed for her. With long, deft strokes, Evelyn drew a brush through Maddie's hair.

"Can you put it up, like you wear yours?" Maddie held a book in her lap, flipping the pages, but she stopped and glanced up over her shoulder with appeal in her eyes.

Evelyn's smile was so soft and maternal, Gareth sucked in a breath. "You're a few years away from wearing your hair up." Maddie's brows came down. "But I don't see the harm tonight. I'll have to take my hair down to do it. I only brought a few hairpins along."

She dropped the brush into her lap and reached up to the

knot at the back of her head. Gareth swallowed. Her hair tumbled down her back in a golden waterfall that sucked the breath out of him. Before he knew it, Maddie's hair was piled up on top of her head, and she was looking way too grown up for his liking. She held a little mirror, turning this way and that.

Evelyn quickly wrapped her own hair into a knot. She plucked a pencil off a tablet beside her on the bunk and speared the knot. Miraculously it held. Gareth shook his head. Women were a constant source of mystery.

"Can I wear it up for supper?" Maddie smoothed a stray tendril.

"This once." Evelyn took the mirror and the book. "I'll read you some more of *Sir Gawain and the Green Knight* before bed if you'd like."

"I've never had a bedtime story before." Maddie scrambled to her feet.

"Then it's high time, don't you think?" Evelyn reached over and blew out the lantern. "Let's go get some supper. I'm starved."

Gareth stepped back and hustled over to the washbasin before he got caught eavesdropping. What had come over his daughter?

They emerged from the wagon together.

Rimfire let out a whistle. "You two look fine tonight. I hope this cow camp isn't too rough for such fine ladies." He stood and offered Evelyn a seat on a box, the only decent chair. "Can I get you some supper?"

"Thank you."

A stir went through the cowboys, and more than a few removed their hats and smoothed their hair. Well, well, well.

Gareth hid a smile and returned the towel to its peg.

Evelyn thanked Rimfire, and her eyes sought out Jamie. The boy had wolfed down his meal and now wrestled with his bedroll, dragging it under the wagon where Gareth had told him they would sleep tonight.

"Jamie, come tell me how things went today and what you did."

The boy abandoned the bedroll and swaggered over, his thumbs tucked into his back pockets and his hat perched on the back of his head. Gareth strode over and lifted the hat. "Always take off your hat when you talk to a lady, especially if that lady is your mother." He handed the hat to Jamie and removed his own.

"Evening, Evelyn. Maddie. You sure look nice tonight."

Maddie pressed her lips together and nodded, all her previous joy battened down. He frowned. What had he done? She treated him like a polecat with the plague every time he came near.

She moved to the wagon tongue and sat down. In the group but apart, not like she'd been at the last roundup, laughing and joking with the cowboys and darting everywhere, still full of energy even after a day in the saddle. He missed his little girl. Here, with her hair up and her standoffish manner, she was a stranger.

Jamie squatted beside his mother and began a blow-by-blow account of his day. With each sentence, Evelyn grew paler and her eyes grew rounder.

"And Pa let me brand a calf. It sure bawled. Pa says he's going to teach me to rope. Maybe by next roundup, I can ride a cutting horse and rope calves, isn't that right, Pa?"

"Maybe not the next roundup, but someday, sure." Gareth

accepted a plate from Muley and watched Evelyn as he ate. Her fist had closed around her fork so tight the knuckles showed white. A ripple went through her, and she set her plate aside.

He ate doggedly, waiting for her to say something.

"Gareth, I wonder if we might take a walk?"

He forked in the last bite of his supper and nodded. He caught Rimfire's eye. "Set the night-guard shifts and keep an eye on. . ." He waggled his finger between Jamie and Maddie. Rimfire nodded.

Gareth offered his arm to Evelyn, and they strolled away from the campfire. She smelled like roses or some kind of flower. His heartbeat thickened.

"Maddie sure looks pretty tonight. I couldn't help but overhear you in the wagon while I was washing up. Seems like she's settling in at last, listening to your stories and letting you fuss with her hair and all. Acting like a little girl should."

"I wanted to talk to you about Maddie, and about Jamie."

He stopped, glanced back at the campfire, and decided they were far enough away from prying eyes. He turned Evelyn toward him and put his hands on her shoulders. "How about we don't talk about the kids? It's a beautiful night with a million stars. You should be admiring them. Wish I could."

She blinked. "Why can't you?"

"There's something far more beautiful and captivating right here." He brushed the back of his fingers down her cheek. "Evelyn, I told you I wouldn't rush you, and I won't, but I'd sure like to kiss you right now."

Her lips parted, and her breath quickened. His hand found the pulse under her jaw, pleased that it beat as rapidly as his own. He took her lack of protest as assent and bent his head. The instant their lips touched, lightning shot through him, hot and bright. He might've rocked on his feet, he wasn't sure. His arms went around her, bringing her to him and deepening the kiss.

She let out a little moaning sound that drove him crazy, and her hands stole up his back. And because he'd been able to think of little else but kissing her since the moment he'd spied her in the wagon with Maddie tonight, his fingers sank into her hair, dislodging the pencil and allowing those golden strands to fall down her back and over his arms.

He broke the kiss to catch his breath and threaded his fingers through her hair, soaking in the feel, the smell, the very essence of her. She stared up at him with her enormous blue eyes, and, afraid he'd devour her with kisses if he didn't get ahold of himself, he pressed her head to his chest and rested his chin on her crown.

"Mama?"

She sprang from his arms, her hands going to her hair, fingers flying to get it braided. "Jamie, I thought you'd be in bed by now."

Gareth stifled a groan, fisted his hands, and bit back the words that sprang to his lips. What rotten timing. He'd finally gotten Evelyn into his arms, they weren't arguing about the kids, or even thinking about them, and lo and behold, one of them shows up.

"You all right, Mama? Your voice sounds funny."

Evelyn cleared her throat. "I'm fine. What did you need?"

"I was waiting for you to listen to my prayers. I think Maddie must be waiting, too. She's tossing and turning and bumping stuff around in the wagon."

Gareth relaxed his stance. "Go ahead and get into your bedroll. Your ma and I will be along directly."

The boy scampered back toward the wagon, and Gareth reached for Evelyn once more, but she put her hands against his chest.

"Don't. I–I'm not ready."

"Sure seemed like you were." He tilted his head and tried a smile. "Evelyn, that was about the sweetest, most—"

Her hands flew to his lips. "Stop. I can't. I can't love you, and if you kiss me like that again, I'll forget all the reasons why."

He jerked his head and freed his mouth. "You can't love me? Why not?"

She stepped back, putting way too much distance between them for his liking. "Because it hurts too much. If I let myself love you, what will I do if something happens to you? I've lived through that once, and I don't ever want to go through it again."

She looked like a deer smelling danger, taut and ready to bolt. He tucked his hands into his back pockets and leaned his weight on one leg, hoping to get her to relax so they could talk about this. He couldn't be totally angry with her, since she'd all but admitted that his kiss had rocked her the same way hers had clobbered him. But this notion of not loving because you *might* get hurt?

"I've been through that before, too. I lost a spouse, but I'm not afraid to love again. Maybe I'm better for the experience, value the love more. Don't you think that could happen to you, too? Mightn't love be sweeter now because you know how precious it is?"

She shook her head. "I know how precious and powerful

loving a man is. I wouldn't be able to bear it if I lost that love again. I promised myself I wouldn't fall in love ever again. It's hard enough with Jamie. I can't help loving him. He's my son."

His stomach knotted. "And Maddie?"

"Before today, I would've laughed at the notion." Her fingers twisted together, fisting around the end of her hastily fashioned braid. "But she's wormed her way into my heart. I asked you to come on a walk with me so we could talk about her. I didn't mean for anything to happen between us."

"But it has." He shifted his weight. "And we can't go back. I don't want to go back."

"And I can't go forward. I can't let myself love you. I'd be destroyed if I lost you."

He heaved a sigh. "You know what I think? I think you already love me, you're just too scared to admit it. But I won't press you now. Let's get back and tuck in the kids. I'm on nighthawk duty in about an hour."

When they were only a few paces from the camp, he let go of her arm. "I'll head to the herd. Tell the kids I said good night, and I'll see them in the morning."

He saddled his horse and swung aboard his mount for what he was sure would be a very long night.

ॐ

Would this night ever end? Evelyn turned her pillow over and punched it up. She never should've let him kiss her. Her brains had turned to scrambled eggs at his touch, and his embrace stirred up longings and feelings she was too afraid to examine. From now on, she had to keep her distance, protect her heart. It hurt too much to love, didn't it?

Jamie mumbled and stirred on his bedroll beneath the wagon, and she stilled, concentrating on the sound. She forced herself not to get up and check on him. He'd had such a big day, and he needed sleep.

Maddie slept on a pallet in the bottom of the wagon, her cheek pillowed on her hand. So sweet and innocent looking, so in need of love and assurance.

Evelyn ached for Maddie, realizing that the little girl had already worked her way into her own heart. Without realizing it, she'd come to love Maddie as if she were her own daughter.

Which brought her full circle back to Gareth.

Lord, answering that ad was supposed to be a business arrangement, a way of providing for my son and my sisters. I was going to keep my feelings in check and be sensible. I had everything under control.

She tried to ignore the unraveling feeling trickling through her chest. Daylight would help her make sense of things. Tomorrow would be better.

Chapter 7

The weak light at dawn could hardly be called day. Evelyn awoke to storm clouds, overhead and in the camp. Maddie wasn't speaking to anyone, not even Evelyn. It was as if their closeness the evening before had never happened. Evelyn had no idea what she had done, and Maddie gave her no opening to ask. The child, glaring and pinch-mouthed, boiled like a teakettle.

Jamie ate as if he hadn't seen food in a month and bounced at Gareth's side, waiting for him to finish his bacon and biscuits.

Gareth had a watchful look, an arrow of concern between his brows as he studied his family. Evelyn tried to keep from meeting his eyes, tried to forget what it felt like to be in his arms, to surrender to his kiss and feel his fingers on her skin, his hands in her hair. This morning, everything about him appealed to her.

Stop it.

He looked tired, as if he hadn't slept any better than she. Sleep had eluded her completely until she heard him crawl into his bedroll beneath the wagon after his shift with the herd ended. Restless, dream-filled hours followed. Several times she jerked awake, heart pounding, stalked by the feeling that she'd lost something precious.

Her muscles protested both the damp cold and the time she'd spent on a horse the previous day. If she hadn't been a lady, she would've groaned with each movement.

Gareth rose and tossed the dregs of his coffee cup onto the fire. He glanced at the swollen, gray bellies of the clouds, turning his head when the low rumble of thunder rolled over them. "Time for us to head out. Jamie and I are going to bring in cattle today, so we won't be back until late."

Her mouth went dry. "Perhaps it would be best if Jamie stayed here today. The ground will be slippery if it rains, and he could catch cold if he gets soaked."

"He'll have a slicker to help keep him dry. With the weather getting woolly, we're going to need every hand."

"I can help." Maddie tipped her empty plate into the washtub. "Please, Pa?"

Evelyn didn't know what to hope for. If he said yes, she'd spend the day worrying about all three of them, but if he said no, Maddie would be crushed.

"Thanks, Maddie, but I think you'd be best off here. Evelyn and Muley will need your help getting the tarp set up and stowing all the bedrolls."

"Let Jamie stay. I'd be more help than him with the cattle."

"I'm done talking about this." He leveled a stare her way. "Jamie will ride out with me, and you girls will stay here."

Maddie deflated and sat down hard on the wagon tongue.

Evelyn knotted her fingers at her waist. "Be careful."

"Always." He looked as if he wanted to say something more to her, but he shrugged and turned to her son. "You all set, Jamie?"

"Sure thing, Pa."

"Then let's go, pard."

A scream ripped through the camp. Muley's ladle clattered to the ground and cowboys came running.

Evelyn forgot her sore muscles and jumped up. "Maddie, what's wrong?"

"Everything. Why did you have to come here? You've ruined everything." Two fat tears erupted over her lashes and raced down her cheeks.

Gareth, who had run to her side, frowned and put his hands on his waist. "Madelyn Kittrick, that's enough. You've no call to talk like that."

A sob burst from her thin chest. "I hate you. I hate you all." She whirled and ran toward the creek, the sound of her footsteps failing to muffle her crying.

Evelyn closed her eyes and pressed her lips together. This was exactly what she wanted to talk to Gareth about last night, but she'd allowed him to distract her.

Jamie looked from Evelyn to Gareth and back again, a guilty, confused expression on his little face. Gareth's scowl turned to one of bewilderment, and he started after his daughter.

Evelyn reached for his arm. "Don't. Let her be."

He stopped. "What on earth has gotten into that child?"

"Jamie, why don't you go find Rimfire?" Evelyn inclined her head. "He's over by the horses."

The boy took a couple of steps and turned back, his brows bunched and his hands shoved into his back pockets. "Did I do something wrong?"

She gave him a tight smile. "No, Jamie. Don't worry about it. We'll get it sorted out. You run along."

Gareth removed his hat and scrubbed his head. "Do you

know what this is about?"

Evelyn tugged on her lip, weighing her words. "I think she's jealous, and I can't say that I blame her."

"What? That's ridiculous."

"Is it? From all accounts, you two were inseparable before Jamie and I landed in your lives. You took her with you everywhere and treated her more like a son than a daughter. Then Jamie and I arrive, and suddenly she has to change everything. The way she dresses, her hair, her chores, her manners, her skills. And all the things she used to do with you? Jamie does them now. It's like you don't need her anymore. I'd be more than a little upset, too."

"I never said I didn't need her anymore. I never even thought it."

The hurt in his eyes made her want to hug him, but she forced herself to stand still. "Did you ever tell her otherwise? This is what I was trying to talk to you about last night, that Maddie could use a little of your attention."

He replaced his hat and tucked his fingertips into his back pockets. "I never thought of how she might be taking all of this. I knew she'd have to adjust to things, just like the rest of us. I'd better go talk to her."

At that moment the clouds opened, releasing a torrent of rain and a howling wind that buffeted Evelyn, the more so for being so quick. They went from anticipating rain to the teeth of a severe thunderstorm in one clap. Lightning cracked, striking so close the light dazzled Evelyn. Thunder roared, vibrating the earth, shaking its way through the soles of her feet and right to her core.

"The cattle are stampeding!" Rimfire shouted from the picket line. Cowboys ran, leaping astride their horses and tearing out of camp.

Gareth grabbed Evelyn as another bolt of sizzling lightning scorched the air. "Get Maddie and get in the wagon. We've got to hold the cattle, or they'll scatter all over the range!"

"Where's Jamie?" She clutched his arms, shaking her head to clear her eyes of the rain sluicing down. The place where Jamie's pony had been tied stood empty. Fear closed in around her heart and squeezed all the air out of her lungs.

Gareth shook her. "I'll find him and send him back. Go get Maddie and get under cover!"

He disappeared into the downpour, and Evelyn found herself stumbling toward the creek, calling Maddie's name between rolls of thunder.

Evelyn found the child sobbing on the muddy creek bank, in so much agony of spirit she seemed oblivious to the downpour or the danger. The narrow, chuckling waterway of yesterday boiled and foamed in a brown, menacing snarl, already on the rise.

Half dragging Maddie, Evelyn stumbled back to the camp. She boosted the child into the wagon ahead of her then clambered up, hampered by her sodden skirts. Rain lashed the canvas cover and wind rocked the wagon.

"Get out of those wet things." Evelyn's teeth chattered as she fumbled with the buttons on the back of Maddie's pinafore. "You'll catch your death of cold."

The girl hung her head, water streaming from her braids. She made no effort to help until Evelyn shook her shoulder. "Hurry up. I've still to change, and Jamie will be here soon."

At the mention of Jamie's name, Maddie flinched, but her hands came up to remove her wet clothing. Evelyn snatched up a pair of rough towels and began rubbing the little girl down. "Wrap this around your hair and get into dry clothes."

Once dry and re-dressed, Evelyn pulled Maddie close, sat down on the bed, and wrapped a quilt around their shoulders.

All she could do was wait. And pray. Pray that Jamie would come soon, that Gareth would be safe in the teeth of the worst thunderstorm she'd ever seen. Her mind raced, worrying about Jamie and Gareth, and remembering all the times she'd waited and prayed for Jamison to come back to her. But he hadn't, in spite of all her prayers.

⁓

Evelyn jerked awake. The thundering of her heart filled her ears, and her right arm was numb and heavy. Blinking, she found Maddie's head pillowed on her shoulder. Gently, she eased herself from under the child and sat up. The last thing she remembered thinking was that she mustn't fall asleep before Jamie returned.

Jamie.

Had he come back while she slept?

Opening the back flap of the wagon cover, she poked her head outside. A soft rain fell, puddling and running, but the worst of the storm appeared to be over. How long had she been asleep? She rubbed her eyes.

Muscles still stiff, she creaked her way to the ground and skirted puddles, hurrying to the canvas tarpaulin Muley had erected over the campfire. Three cowhands squatted there, cupping their hands around their coffee mugs. Water dripped from their hats and chaps. Muley poked the fire under a steaming cauldron of stew.

"Have you seen Jamie?" She ducked under the shelter.

"I fell asleep and missed his return. I hope he got into dry clothes."

Muley shrugged and spit into the grass. "Haven't seen him."

One of the cowboys stood, his hat bumping the canvas overhead. "Last I saw of him, ma'am, he and Gareth were trying to corral a bunch of steers and turn 'em back. Lightning struck right in the middle of the herd, and every last bovine scattered."

"What time is it?" She instinctively glanced at the leaden sky, but the heavy clouds hid the position of the sun.

Muley slid his watch into his palm. " 'Bout two."

Two o'clock? She'd slept for more than six hours, her sleep-deprived night before catching up with her.

And Jamie hadn't come back. Anger burned hot and bright in her middle, but not at her son. Gareth had promised to send him back to the camp where he would be safe. She'd had enough of her husband discounting her fears and ignoring her wishes. When she saw him again, she was going to blister him, and no mistake.

"Rider coming." Muley spat again.

Out of the obscuring rain, a dark form emerged.

"That's Coffee. Jamie must be coming in."

Relief coursed through her. Her son was safe.

Instead of stopping at the picket line, the animal charged into camp, jerking and skittering. One of the cowboys ran out into the rain to grab the bridle.

Her heart clogged her throat.

The saddle was empty.

Chapter 8

I'm going, Rimfire, and that's all there is to the discussion."
Evelyn tugged on a pair of gloves. Maddie led two saddle
horses through the drizzle. "I can't sit by and do nothing
when my son is out there somewhere on foot, maybe injured."

"You don't know that for sure. Maybe the pony just got
loose. He's probably riding double with Gareth right now,
headed back to camp."

"And you don't know that for sure." Evelyn fumbled
with the stirrup, trying to remember everything Maddie
had taught her while her thoughts raced across the prairie to
wherever her son was.

"The boss will kill me if I let you ride out on the search."
Rimfire contradicted his words by giving her a boost into
the saddle. "If you're determined to go, then follow the creek
upstream. Thataway you can always get back to us here. Don't
try to cross the stream. It's running a banker."

Her horse sidled, tossing its head and stamping. Maddie,
already mounted, lifted her reins. "Let's go."

"Be back here before dark!" Rimfire's shout carried after
them as they galloped away.

Evelyn clung to the saddle horn and a fistful of wet
mane. Her horse followed Maddie's like a coal car behind an

engine. As they rode, her mind settled into one long string of "Please, Lord" prayers, and she tucked her chin into the collar of the enormous slicker Rimfire had given her. Rain pelted her and streamed off the wide brim of the hat the foreman had insisted she take. And how glad she was he'd insisted on the headgear. Her bonnet would've soaked up the rain and turned to a sopping mess.

Maddie plunged on, checking over her shoulder from time to time to see that Evelyn still followed. Clad in a pair of Jamie's overalls and checked skirt, she rode like a cowboy.

"Thank You, Lord, for Maddie's abilities. I'd be lost without that little girl."

They traveled forever. Her hands and feet went numb from the cold, and her backside ached from pounding the saddle. And the rain never quit, though it varied in intensity. At last, Maddie pulled her mount to a halt.

"We're going to have to turn back if we want to get to camp before nightfall." Her freckles stood out on her pale, wet face.

"Can't we go a little bit farther?" The idea of returning to camp without her son terrified Evelyn.

"Maybe one of the other riders has already found them and brought them in." The girl raised her voice to be heard over the rain.

A spark of hope lit in Evelyn's chest. Maybe Jamie was safe beside the fire, listening to Muley's growling and filling up on hot stew. "All right. We'll turn back."

Maddie wheeled her horse expertly, and Evelyn let her horse have its head, hoping it would follow and grateful when it did. She cast one last look over her shoulder toward the hills rising before them, and a flicker of gold caught her eye.

"Maddie, wait."

Standing in her stirrups, Evelyn stared hard through the rain and growing gloom. There it was again.

"I think I see a fire."

Maddie rode up beside her, squinting and swiping the water from her face. "If Jamie was hurt bad in a fall, Pa would camp and make a fire, I bet."

Weakness trickled through Evelyn's limbs. Jamie might be too injured to move. Her mind froze, and she kicked her mount, yanking him around and urging him toward that flickering light much too fast for the wet, slippery ground. Maddie joined her, leaning over her mount's neck and slapping him with the ends of her reins.

The tiny glow in the distance grew larger, until Evelyn could make out the flames of a campfire under a rough shelter. All her attention focused on the slicker-covered pallet beside the fire, and she almost forgot to pull her horse up.

She was off her horse and kneeling beside the makeshift bed before she realized it wasn't Jamie's broken body under the slicker.

Gareth lay, pale and tense, his hands fisted and dried blood crusted to his cheek.

"What happened?" She lifted the edge of the slicker. His left leg, lashed to two sticks and bound with strips of blanket, had swollen up like a balloon.

"Evelyn?" His voice rasped. "How'd you get here? Did Rimfire come?"

"No, it's just me and Maddie. Oh, Gareth, what happened?" A powerful fear and concern for him swept over her, nearly toppling her, followed by a wave of love. She loved this man, and it was too late to stop it. And here he was injured and maybe dying, and how would she survive if God took him from her?

"Where's Jamie? Is he with you?"

"I'm here, Ma." The boy staggered in with an armful of twigs and sagebrush. "Pa's horse stepped in a hole and broke its leg. He landed on Pa's leg and twisted it some. Pa had to shoot the horse." The brush clattered to the ground, and he dusted off his sleeves. "When I was rigging this shelter and getting Pa onto that bed, lightning scared Coffee, and he ran off." Jamie squatted beside the fire, poking up the blaze and adding fuel that hissed and smoked.

"You made this shelter and started a fire? All by yourself?"

Jamie shrugged and nodded. "Wasn't hard. Pa told me what to do." Right before her eyes, her son shed a layer of little boy and put on a cloak of capable young man.

Evelyn bit her lip, tugged off her gloves, and removed her hat. "Maggie, you're going to have to ride back to camp and have Muley bring the wagon. Your father can't ride."

Maggie wrapped her horse's reins around her wrist and knelt beside Gareth's bed. "I'm staying with Pa. Jamie can ride back for the wagon."

Jamie was on his feet in a flash. "I'll go. I can do it, Ma."

She didn't miss the fact that he was calling her Ma and not Mama as he always had. He was so confident, so eager to go, she hardly recognized him. He'd grown up overnight. No, not overnight, she corrected. He'd been growing up and maturing since the day they arrived in Sagebrush; she just hadn't wanted to admit it. Something shifted inside her, illuminating a dark corner of her heart. Her tight mother's grasp of her son loosened a notch, and though it would cost her, she knew she needed to let him do this. And she knew that God would take care of him, as He always had. Gareth had the right of it, modeling for her son the truth that God was in control, that He was sovereign. It wasn't her job to try to hold the universe together.

"All right, Jamie. If you follow the creek, you can't get lost. Take my horse." She couldn't resist giving him a hug before he mounted, but she forwent a kiss. "Be careful, son."

"I will, Ma. Don't worry."

She watched after him until she could no longer hear the plopping hooves of his mount or see him through the rain. Blinking and gathering herself, she ducked under the shelter, edging around Maddie, who was adding twigs to the embers. They'd need to scout for more fuel to keep the fire going until Muley arrived.

Kneeling beside her husband, she touched his shoulder. "Gareth, where else are you hurt?"

His eyes opened, and his hand came up and captured hers. "Other than some bruises, just the leg. It's not broken, only wrenched."

"You're sure?"

"Sure as I can be. Now, would you explain how you two happen to be riding around in the rain? What was Rimfire thinking?"

"He said you'd be mad, but he couldn't stop us, not once Jamie's pony showed up without him. Maddie led the way, and I followed."

Gareth shook his head. "I knew you'd be worried sick when Jamie didn't come back. You must've been terrified when Coffee trotted in alone."

"Terrified just about covers it." Though the world was drenched in rain, Evelyn's mouth was dry as the inside of a flour sack. But she wouldn't give in to the fear. She would trust.

Maddie edged close, dug in her pocket, and withdrew a handkerchief. She dabbed the cut on Gareth's cheek. "I didn't mean what I said, Pa. I don't hate you."

He reached out and tweaked her braid. "I know, kiddo. I wish you'd come to me and talked it out, but I can see where you couldn't. I can be awful thick sometimes." He cupped her head in his big palm. "Why don't you tell me what's on your mind. It'll distract me from this bum leg of mine." He edged upright and braced himself against the rocky outcropping that formed the back wall of the shelter. Maddie scooted into the corner of his arm.

"I was so mad." Maddie jerked her head toward Evelyn. "Letting Jamie ride my horse and call you pa. He did everything with you that I used to do, and I had to stay behind. I couldn't figure out what was so wrong with me that you had to get a new kid to replace me."

Gareth rubbed his chin on the top of her head. "Oh, Maddie, I wasn't replacing you. There's not a blessed thing wrong with you, and I don't want you to ever feel that way." He squeezed her tight.

"I was awful bad. Mean to Evelyn and Jamie and you. I thought you didn't love me anymore. I was all mixed up. Then I figured if I learned all that stuff Evelyn was trying to teach me, maybe you'd love me again."

Gareth's eyes met Evelyn's over Maddie's head. Regret filled his expression. "I never stopped loving you, Maddie, and I'm sorry I didn't show you better."

"I know things can't go back to the way they were, but couldn't I ride out with you sometimes?"

"You bet. We'll work out something. I've missed having you with me."

She snuggled into his side, careful of his leg. Gareth held out his other arm to Evelyn, and she sat beside him, resting her head on his shoulder. The security of his embrace, the warmth of his cheek on her hair, the steady beat of his heart under her palm reassured her.

"Jamie will be all right, won't he?"

"Sure he will. He's quite a boy. Building this shelter, starting the fire, wrapping my leg. A grown man couldn't have done better. That's quite a boy you have."

"We have. That's quite a boy *we* have."

His arm tightened. "That's right. We have quite a family. A son and daughter to be proud of."

The rain slackened while they waited, and Evelyn's thoughts chased one another. Gareth dozed off and on while Maddie gathered wood, fed the fire, and checked on her horse.

Alone under the shelter, Evelyn rested against Gareth's shoulder.

"I'm proud of you, Evelyn."

His words drew her away from her scampering thoughts. "You are?"

"You're quite a woman. I don't think there's anything you can't do when you put your mind to it. Taming my wild daughter, coming along on a roundup, or riding out in the teeth of a storm to find your son. Nothing seems to daunt you."

"You're wrong there, Gareth. I might seem efficient or capable, but inside, I'm a mass of insecurities and knots. But I'm trying."

He brushed a kiss across her temple that sent a shiver up her spine and made her scalp crinkle. "You've come a long way since you first got here. I know you worry, but you try not to show it."

"I've lived with fear for so long. Trying to control everything so I wouldn't be hurt, forgetting that God is sovereign and that worry is the opposite of faith." She picked up a pebble and closed her hand around it. "I held everything in a closed fist—like this. When God wanted to remove something, He had to pry my fingers apart, and that hurt." She opened her hand. "I'm learning that if I hold things on an open palm, not only does it hurt less if He has to take something out, but my hand is also open to receive something He wants to give." She pressed her lips together and added two more pebbles. "Like you and Maddie. He's been waiting for me to open my hand and heart to receive you both as His gift to me."

Gareth made a low rumbling noise in his chest and raised her chin so he could look into her eyes. "And have you?"

Waves of love for this man crashed through her, welling up and surging, filling her with warmth. She couldn't speak, so merely nodded.

"Finally." His mouth quirked in a smile before his head descended, and he claimed her lips in a kiss that scorched her enough to dry out all her clothes. He tore his lips away and rested his forehead on hers, taking deep breaths. "I love you, Evelyn Kittrick."

"I love you, too."

He chuckled. "Trust you to finally admit it when I'm laid up with a twisted knee, stranded on the prairie in the teeth of a thunderstorm, and smack in the middle of spring roundup."

She tucked her head under his chin and wrapped her arms around him. "Don't worry so much. We've got all the time God gives us."

~

Three months later, Gareth walked toward the house without a trace of a limp, Jamie swinging from one hand, Maddie from the other. Evelyn sat on the front porch sewing, the wind teasing her pale hair and putting some color in her cheeks. Contentment swelled his heart.

Stepping up onto the porch, he released the kids' hands and bent to kiss his wife. She smiled up into his eyes. "What have you three been up to?"

"Maddie was swinging upside down from the hay hook in the barn, and Jamie was busting broncs for me."

The reproving, playful light that he loved came into her eyes. "You're a tease, Gareth Kittrick."

"Actually, we were getting something for you."

Maddie and Jamie each pulled a bunch of wildflowers from behind their backs and handed them to her. "Here you go, Ma." Jamie thrust his bundle at her.

"These are for you, Ma." Maddie's cheeks pinked, and she added her flowers to Jamie's. The tender look that invaded Evelyn's eyes told Gareth she cherished being called ma by Maddie more than a million prairie blossoms.

"Thank you." She buried her nose in the bouquet. "I have something for you, too, Maddie." She handed the flowers to Gareth and shook out the fabric on her lap. "It's a divided skirt, so you can ride astride."

Maddie's mouth opened, and her eyes shone. Without warning, she hurled herself into Evelyn's arms. "Thank you, thank you, thank you."

Evelyn's eyes locked with Gareth's, and he mouthed a thank-you of his own. Seemed like it had finally quit raining feathers.

LADY-IN-
WAITING

Chapter 1

This mail-order bride venture wasn't turning out at all like Jane Gerhard had planned.

"How far is it to the next place?" She glanced at the sky, wishing the thin sunshine held some warmth. The wagon hit a rut, jostling her against the driver.

"Coupla hours by road to Garvey's." Reverend Cummings slapped the reins. The breeze ruffled his long whiskers. He continued to scowl as he had since he'd first picked up the four sisters in Sagebrush that morning to deliver them to their prospective grooms.

Jane glanced over her shoulder at the ranch buildings receding into the distance, the Kittrick ranch where they'd left their oldest sister, Evelyn, and her son, Jamie, with Evelyn's new husband and daughter. How many times on the journey from the East had they talked about what a blessing it was that the sisters would all be neighbors, helping, supporting, comforting one another in this cross-country move? But none of them had counted on the vast distances in this territory so far from the Massachusetts coastal town they'd grown up in. Now she would be two hours from her sister.

And if Garvey's ranch was the next on their journey, she would be the next to marry. Harrison Garvey, her soon-to-be husband. Her insides squirmed like kittens chasing a ball of ever-unraveling yarn.

I wish his ranch was last.

Not that she was afraid, exactly, or wanted to put off getting married. She'd long dreamed of being a bride, of having a husband and house of her own to care for, though she had never expected it to actually happen. No, she wasn't afraid. She just didn't want Harrison Garvey to be disappointed when he realized he was getting the plain sister. If she was last, he wouldn't have Gwendolyn and Emmeline to compare her to right off.

Evelyn, Gwendolyn, and Emmeline all possessed striking blond hair and brilliant blue eyes. Thick lashes, slender figures, beautifully curved lips. Their fair skin and delicate features were the epitome of feminine beauty and the picture of their departed mother.

Then there was Jane. Mouse-brown hair, eyes that were neither brown nor green, short, with a figure more curvaceous than willowy, and a chin that could only be described as stubborn. Jane was the plain sister, the one who melted into the background. The one who worked hard to be useful, since she couldn't be decorative.

Shrugging, she tried to turn her mind to more productive thoughts, like what her new home would be like. Evelyn's had been a log structure, sturdy and solid, with a wide, inviting porch. Would Mr. Garvey live in a log cabin? Scanning the stark prairie spreading in every direction, she couldn't imagine where logs could be found for any structure, though when she'd put the question to Reverend Cummings, he'd jerked his chin to the mountains far in the distance and said, "Up there."

Her thoughts returned to her groom, as they had nearly every minute since receiving his proposal by mail. Harrison Garvey. She ran quickly through the list of things she knew about him. Twenty-eight, four years her senior. Originally from Columbus, Ohio. In need of a wife.

Not much to go on. But then again, what did he know about her? Twenty-four, a spinster from Massachusetts, in need of a husband.

A familiar ache returned to her chest. It was all well enough telling oneself to be practical, but Jane knew, in spite of what her sisters thought, that she possessed feelings, fears, and dreams that weren't remotely practical, things she kept squashed way down inside, things that only came out in weak or stressful moments.

She tugged her shawl around her shoulders and surveyed the landscape. The terrain rolled in gentle hills covered with tall, waving grasses, showing a hint of spring green in their strawlike stems. To the right in the distance, blue-purple hills rose toward a pale, cloudless sky, reminding Jane of her Creator and sustainer. Her mind prayed her most frequent prayer these days:

God, go before us. Sustain us, and bless our new marriages and homes. Smooth the way for us where You will, and help us over the rough patches. Remind us of Your goodness and our need of Your strength.

"Reverend Cummings?" Gwendolyn stood in the jouncing wagon, grasping Jane's shoulder for balance. "Can't you tell us anything about the men we are to marry?"

The preacher's scowl deepened. "I told you you'll find out soon enough."

"But what are they like? Tall, short, lean, stout, learned, ignorant?"

Jane hid a smile. Gwendolyn and Emmeline had been the most enthusiastic about the prospect of moving to Wyoming Territory and becoming mail-order brides, and Gwendolyn had speculated almost constantly about what their prospective husbands would be like.

"What does it matter now what they're like?" the reverend asked. "You're here and you're bound to marry them. You should've asked these questions before. All you need to know at this point is that they're good, God-fearing men." He hunched his shoulders, braced his elbows on his knees, and clamped his lips shut, an odd trait in a preacher to Jane's way of thinking. The pastor of their church in Seabury had been well known for his ability to talk the leg off a Yankee mule.

Gwendolyn blinked, started to say something but subsided, her brow puckered and her arms crossed.

The reverend had a point. They should've found out more about the men they were to marry, but there hadn't been any time. With money running out, the eviction notice hanging over their heads, and post–Civil War men in Massachusetts scarcer than honest politicians, when an answer to their advertisement in the *Matrimonial News* had come, they'd acted swiftly.

After an eternity of jostling and fretting, a dark dot appeared on the horizon.

"Garvey's place." Reverend Cummings unbent himself enough to speak.

Jane studied her hands and tried to quell the fluttering in her chest. The dot resolved itself into black squares that eventually turned into buildings. The vast wooden barn and corrals were easy to see. It was the smaller structures Jane couldn't identify.

"What is that?" Emmeline asked, disregarding her manners and pointing between Jane and Reverend Cummings.

"Soddy."

"Pardon?" Jane asked.

"Sod house."

She swallowed. "The house is made out of dirt?"

"Yes." He drew out the *S* sound in annoyance.

She ignored his rudeness by focusing on the notion that she was supposed to live in the dirt like a gopher or a mole. A prayer made it as far as her lips.

"Oh, Jane. I'm so sorry." Emmeline squeezed her arm.

They pulled to a stop, and from the wagon seat Jane could look directly onto the low roof. Grass grew on the roof of her house? Her knees trembled.

A short, bald-headed man came around the corner. He was so bow-legged, he couldn't have stopped a pig in a lane, and he limped badly. His mouth split in a grin that showed several gapped teeth, and his eyes looked like raisins tucked into a sour-cream pie. He couldn't possibly be her groom. Twenty-eight had come and gone for this man a few decades ago.

"Welcome, welcome. I'm Lem Barton. Which one of you lovely ladies is Harrison's bride?" His smile and welcome eased the knot under Jane's breastbone. His gaze passed from one Gerhard girl to the next and settled on Jane. The grin widened, and he dropped one eyelid in a quick wink. She sensed she and this wizened old man would be friends.

"Barton, no time for palavering. Where's Harrison?" Cummings clambered to the ground. "Bags?"

While Emmeline and Gwendolyn sorted out the luggage, Jane accepted Lem's help alighting.

Lem didn't seem affronted by the reverend's gruff manner. "Now, now, parson, you've surely got time to introduce me to the young ladies. Harrison's working the kinks out of a new horse." He poked his gnarled thumb over his shoulder. "You'll see him yonder. He's anxious to be getting on with the work, but he's had to hang about here waiting for his lady to arrive."

All eyes turned to the hill on the far side of the wagon. A horse and rider stood atop the rise, silhouetted against the early afternoon sunshine. Jane swallowed, and her heart sounded much like the hoofbeats thudding the earth when the rider started down the slope.

When he reached the house, he pulled up in a swirl of dust and swung easily out of the saddle. Lem came forward to take the reins of the snorting, skittering horse. "What's the verdict?"

"He's coming along." Harrison tugged off his gloves while Jane tried to regain her composure. At the sight of her soon-to-be husband, her heart had taken a dive. Broad shoulders, well-muscled arms, long, straight legs, and a confident air. He swept off his hat to reveal coffee-colored hair and eyes to match. He was one of the best-looking men she'd ever seen.

What a shame.

He shook hands with the preacher and tucked his gloves into his belt before turning to Jane and her sisters. He studied each one briefly, and Jane braced herself for the disappointment she knew would come when he realized he was stuck with her instead of one of her beautiful sisters.

His attention focused on her, and a hollow place opened in the pit of her stomach. *Stop staring and shilly-shallying.* She offered her hand. "Mr. Garvey, I'm Jane. I'm very pleased to meet you."

Would he mind the calluses on her hands? Would he think her ill-bred and unladylike? She needn't have worried, for he only touched her hand for an instant. A jolt shot up her arm and scurried through her veins. He blinked, and something flashed in his dark eyes. Had he felt it, too? Surely, these flighty flutterings would subside in a moment, and she would return to her normal, practical self.

He didn't return her smile. "Ma'am." His eyes flicked between her sisters and herself, and her heart sank. She lowered her gaze to keep from seeing his disappointment and busied herself with straightening the fringe on her shawl.

Her trunk landed with a thud in the dirt. "I'm in a hurry, Harrison. Let's get this done." Cummings reached under the wagon seat for his Bible.

No music, no flowers, no friends, and only her younger sisters to support her. At least she had a little idea of what to expect, for the ceremony mirrored Evelyn's only hours before. Trembles raced down Jane's legs and made her knees wobbly. Her wedding looked nothing like the beautiful ceremony she'd dreamed of in that twilight time between waking and sleep when her handsome knight would ride out of the mist, declare his undying love, and carry her away with him to his castle.

You're going to be practical about this, Jane Gerhard. Pull yourself together and be sensible.

She squared her shoulders and lifted her chin. In a steady voice, she promised to love, honor, and obey Harrison Garvey. When it came time for Harrison's vows, she swallowed and dared a look at him. He had a straight nose and firm chin with just a hint of shadow showing. His dark hair had a bit of a wave and curled at his collar. Her eyes went to his mouth. Straight, not too full, and with a determined set. Everything about him seemed so...solid. Other than her father, she'd not spent much time in a man's company, and this man she was in the process of marrying exuded masculinity and strength.

Yet the clasp of his hand was warm and gentle, and his thumb moved disconcertingly across the back of her knuckles in a gesture that comforted her out of all proportion.

Before she was ready, the reverend closed his Bible and pronounced them husband and wife. "I forgot at the last ceremony, but if you want to, you can kiss the bride."

Jane's gaze collided with Harrison's, and his eyes darkened, but he made no move. Did he want to kiss her? Did he *not* want to?

Lem nudged his arm. "Go ahead, boss."

Harrison's hands came up to cup her shoulders, and he brushed a quick kiss across her cheek. He pulled back, blinked slowly, and bent his head again, this time kissing her lips.

So this is what kissing is like. It's very nice.

She was just getting the hang of it when Lem cleared his throat. Harrison broke away, and the older man grinned. "My turn, boss."

Jane registered the rasp of the old man's stubbly whiskers as he pecked her cheek.

"We're awfully glad you've come, ma'am." He clasped both her hands between his. "You'll be the saving of the place, I wager."

She struggled to find her voice, still affected by Harrison's kiss. "Please, call me Jane." What did he mean? How could she be the saving of the place?

Reverend Cummings stuffed his Bible into his pocket. "Time to go." He made a herding motion toward Gwendolyn and Emmeline. "Daylight's burning." He leaped aboard the wagon, stopped, and dug in his inside coat pocket. "Almost forgot. Letter for you." He passed a thick envelope to Harrison, who scanned the return address, scowled, and tucked it into his back pocket.

"We'll just be a minute saying our good-byes." Emmeline's voice sounded as if she was damping down tears, and linking her arms with Jane's and Gwendolyn's, she drew them a few paces away. The hard lump in Jane's throat almost choked her.

"I feel like we'll never see each other again." Emmeline squeezed Jane's hand. "It wasn't supposed to be this way." She whispered the last sentence.

"I know, but there's no help for it."

"How are we supposed to manage all alone?" Gwendolyn asked.

"We're not alone. God is with us, and we will see each other. We're not *that* far apart. We are neighbors, after all." Jane hoped her voice sounded more certain than she felt, because as the older sister, it was her duty to set the example. If she acted bravely, they would, too. She hoped. If they started crying, she would surely follow suit.

"How can you sound so calm? We might be neighbors, but the neighborhood we live in is bigger than the state of Massachusetts." Gwendolyn's hands flew out in a wide arc. "We might as well be living in different countries."

"Stop it. There's nothing we can do about it now. Evelyn's married"—Jane swallowed—"I'm married, and you two will be married before the day is out. We have to make the best of things. I'm sure we'll be able to visit one another from time to time."

Emmeline hugged Jane. "Your husband is very handsome, like Evelyn's."

He was. So handsome, he must've been expecting someone more his caliber than Plain Jane.

Gwendolyn embraced Jane, too, hugging her neck so hard it hurt.

Jane swallowed against the lump in her throat. "I'm going to be fine, and so are you two. Remember, God has led us this far. He'll be our refuge and strength."

As the wagon rumbled out of sight, she repeated that truth to herself.

༄

Harrison rubbed the back of his neck. He'd expected some of the tension to bleed away once he said his vows, but his muscles remained taut. His bride wasn't at all what he'd expected—though he didn't know exactly what he had expected. In truth, he hadn't spent much time thinking about it. Once her acceptance of his proposal had arrived, he'd known a sense of relief and shelved the issue. The ranch begged all his time and attention, and he didn't have time to waste speculating about what his bride might be like. Time enough to cross that bridge when he got to it.

Now his new wife stood only a few paces away saying good-bye to her sisters. One thing was for certain, he hadn't expected to be so attracted to her. Her intelligent eyes— greeny-brown like forest moss—drew his attention, and though she was a bit on the short side, she had a figure that would turn any man's head. He could still feel her hand in his, small and yet strong. Her cheek had been so smooth when he'd given her that chaste peck after the ceremony, he hadn't been able to resist following it up with a kiss on the lips. He wasn't sure who was more surprised, his bride or himself. And he had to admit, it was a very nice kiss.

"I think you got yourself a good one, boss." Lem eased onto the bench beside the front door and stretched his bad leg out.

"Time will tell."

"Hope she settles in."

Harrison couldn't take his eyes off her, not even when Cummings started grumbling about time-wasting. The girls embraced. As an only child, Harrison couldn't imagine what they must be feeling, but he didn't like the sadness on Jane's face. He'd known her less than half an hour, so why did he want to put his arms around her and tell her everything would be all right?

He rubbed the back of his neck again. He'd been out in the wilds of Wyoming Territory for far too long. Cut off from all feminine company and influence. That's all it was. Any woman would elicit such a response from him.

And yet the other two hadn't. They looked too fragile, and he'd never been drawn to pale hair and eyes. Pretty enough, but it was clear Jane was the pick of the litter.

He stuck his hands in his back pockets, and his fingers brushed the envelope. A thrust of satisfaction shot through him. At last he'd have something to report, something his father would hardly expect.

As always, the sense of sand running through his hour-glass seized him. Shifting from boot to boot, he went through the chores he still hoped to accomplish today.

Lem rubbed his leg and scratched his chin. "She'll add a bit of brightness about the place. Wonder what your father will say. With the deadline coming, I bet he figured you'd be admitting defeat and heading home soon. This will catch him sideways."

Jane held her sisters' hands after they boarded the wagon, and she walked beside them a few paces as they rolled away, still clinging to their fingers. When she halted, she hugged her arms at her waist and stared after them until they disappeared.

Harrison hardened his jaw. "Father should know better. I'm no quitter."

Lem pushed himself upright. "Hope she isn't too lonely out here. I'm thinking those girls expected to live a tad closer to one another. By the time the last one is delivered, they'll be spread out more than thirty miles."

"That's not far out here." Harrison ignored the tickle of unease scampering across his skin. Should he have been more forthright about the distances involved? Would she settle in? What if she didn't?

"No," Lem agreed, "but considering where she's from, it's a fair stretch of the legs. She's a city girl."

When she brushed tears from her cheeks, the tickle of unease became a poke. What he didn't know about dealing with women would fill several books.

She walked toward the house, and he looked over to Lem for guidance, but his friend and employee was headed around the corner of the soddy like his hair was on fire.

Harrison glanced up at the sun, calculated the length of his chore list, and was surprised to realize he didn't want to leave her in spite of all he needed to do today. "Would you like to see the house?"

An uncertain light came into her eyes as she considered the soddy, but she swiped at her cheeks once more and squared her shoulders. "Yes, please."

Relieved that she seemed to be getting ahold of herself, he nodded. He guessed he could spare a few minutes to show her around.

Chapter 2

Jane sniffed back the tears and swallowed against the hard lump in her throat. It was all well and good telling her sisters that everything would be fine, that God was with them, but it was another thing altogether to act accordingly after being stranded in the middle of nowhere with complete strangers—one of whom she was now married to.

Harrison lifted her trunk as if it weighed nothing, his muscles stretching his faded chambray shirt. "This way."

She lifted her two valises and followed him as he ducked under the lintel. Her first impression of the interior of the soddy was that it was dark. Her second was that it was dank. An unmistakable musty smell came from the walls. For Jane, who prided herself on her housekeeping abilities, the task of keeping anything clean in a house made of dirt staggered her mind.

"It isn't much. I'm sure it's not what you're accustomed to at all, but you'll get used to it. It's warm in the winter and cool in the summer." He let her trunk come to rest on the hard-packed dirt floor beside a plank table. "There's just the one room, but we're outside most of the time anyway."

Jane tugged the grosgrain ribbon on her bonnet and slid the hat from her hair. The entire structure couldn't be much more than twelve by twenty, with a low ceiling of poles and grass matting with sod overlaying the whole. A stove, the table with four chairs, a metal bed, and a chest of drawers took up most of the space. Crates, barrels, and boxes lined the walls.

"Those are what's left of the winter stores. We don't get to town too often, so we stock up." He motioned to the rear door. "Water comes from the creek out back, and there's a lean-to for fuel." Scrubbing his cheek, he shrugged. "We mostly burn cow chips."

Cow chips? *Manure?* Faintness crept over her, and the already close walls seemed to crowd in around her.

"If you're not too tired from your trip, I can show you the rest of the place."

She almost beat him to the door. Breathing deeply of the cool spring air, she tried to quell the panic sloshing in her chest. Harrison strode toward the immense barn, and she hurried to catch up.

"Have you lived out here long?" Perhaps the soddy was a temporary structure until he could build a house. That was it. Building a real house must be part of his summer plans. Surely she could camp out in the soddy for a few weeks until a proper house could be erected.

"Two and a half years."

Her heart landed hard against her stomach. He'd spent two long winters in that dirt mound?

"Lem came west with me, and before that we both worked in my father's company in Ohio. Reed, the other ranch hand, has been here about a year. He'll be riding in tomorrow, most likely. I sent him over to the fort with a few head of cattle."

They reached the barn, and he pulled wide the door. He breathed deeply, his eyes lighting with what she thought must be pride. What an odd thing to be proud of, a great cavernous barn.

"Biggest in the territory." He pointed right then left. "Milk cow over there, stalls for horses on the other side. Hay storage for winter here in the middle." A few wisps of hay littered the floor, while the barn roof soared overhead. "We have to do quite a bit of haying and feeding out in the winter. I learned that the hard way my first year. Getting cows through a winter out here takes quite a bit of feed, and I lost so many it set me back quite a ways. Last summer we cut and stacked hay and piled this barn to the top, but the herd survived."

Jane's feet crunched on the graveled floor. Sweet dry-grass smells mingled with dust, grain, and animal, and a stiff breeze swirled through the open doorway, stirring her skirts and ruffling her hair.

"Over here is Butterscotch." Harrison leaned against a partition and reached over to scratch the rump of a cow the exact color of her name. She turned her head, blinking huge, liquid black eyes fringed with long lashes. Her jaw ground contentedly.

"Probably the only Jersey cow in the Territory. She's a grand little milker, though she's dry at the moment. Due to calve any day now. I'll double my milking herd soon if she has a heifer."

Jane tentatively touched the warm hide. Butterscotch shifted her weight and swished her tail.

"After she calves, she'll need milking twice a day. I have to say, I'm glad you're here to take over the chore. Lem doesn't complain, but with his bum leg, getting up and down off the milking stool is pure torture."

Milk a cow? Her? Jane stepped away from the animal, clenching her hands. Still, how hard could it be? She gave Butterscotch one last look and hurried out after Harrison.

They stopped beside a small, square sod structure. Netting strung on posts created an enclosure on one side, and within, nearly a dozen rusty-brown hens clucked and scratched. In their midst, a rooster strutted, his head cocked, regarding them with one beady eye. His magnificent tail, iridescent green, plumed higher than his red-combed head.

"You'll want to watch out for Napoleon. He'll peck you every chance he gets." Harrison threaded his fingers through the wire and watched the birds. "The hens are gentle enough, don't seem to mind when you gather the eggs, but that rooster will come at you." He pointed to a twig broom leaning against the coop. "But if you carry the broom with you, he'll run the other way." He reached for the door to the sod structure. "We've set a couple of hens in here."

The door groaned when he tugged it open. Ducking inside, Jane wrinkled her nose at the pungent odor. Droppings littered the floor, the roosts, and the edges of the nesting boxes. When was the last time anyone cleaned out this henhouse?

"These two are each sitting on a nice clutch of eggs. The flock should double this year if we don't lose too many to coyotes, hawks, or some such. Feed's in a barrel in the barn. And always make sure you close the gates and doors." He scuffed some scattered straw on the floor. "It's not the tidiest in here. I've had a hard time keeping up with everything since the spring rush of work is on us."

Milk cows, feed chickens, live in a dirt house? What else could she be expected to do? She followed him into the sunshine once more. "What are in the other buildings?"

"That's the bunkhouse." Harrison gestured toward a sod hut identical to the house and glanced at the sun again.

"And that one?" She pointed to a long, low sod building set well away from the rest.

"That's the house." He frowned and tucked his hands into his back pockets.

"The house?"

"There's materials to build a house—boards, windows, nails, paint—all of it."

"But, why—"

"I'd best get back to my chores." He turned away, heading toward the soddy, where his horse stood dozing in the sunshine.

She followed, wondering what she'd done or said to provoke that reaction. Why have house-building materials and not use them? Why get mad when someone asked? A quick glance over her shoulder at the storage shed revealed no answers.

As they approached the soddy, weariness swept over Jane. Too many new things, too much to process. They came to an awkward halt before the door, barely acquaintances, and yet married for better or worse. Her mind shot back to the wedding, and she touched her lips, remembering the warm tingle of their bridal kiss.

"That's about it, I guess. The creek's out there where the trees are. There's a cold store down there for the milk and butter when we have them."

A movement caught his eye, and she followed his gaze.

A pair of pointed black ears and a long black tail stood above the prairie grass near the barn. He smiled for the first time, just a fleeting one, but a smile all the same, and her heart did a flip. He had dimples. Two adorable creases dented his cheeks for an instant and momentarily erased the burdened light in his eyes. "That's the cat."

Jane looked closer. Green eyes stared at her through the tawny grass. "Does she have a name?"

He shrugged. "We just call her the cat. She showed up a couple of weeks ago. Probably escaped from a wagon train. She hunts rats and mice in the barn at night, and she does just what she pleases the rest of the time. And if she gets near the rooster, there's a dustup. She doesn't seem to like people too much. A law unto herself. I'd advise leaving her alone unless you want to get scratched or bit." He checked the angle of the sun and resettled his hat. "I'd best get back to work."

"Thank you for showing me around." How formal they sounded, husband and wife, yet strangers.

He shifted his weight, reached for his horse's reins where they trailed on the ground, and looped them around the animal's neck. The way he studied her, unsmiling, made her skin quiver. He was weighing her up, but was he finding her lacking? Was he sorry?

"I won't be back until suppertime. Lem's around somewhere, so if you need anything, just holler. He and Reed fend for themselves in the bunkhouse, taking turns cooking. I'll see you this evening." Harrison swung into the saddle, touched the brim of his hat, and put the animal into a lope.

As he galloped away, Jane wanted to sink into the prairie grass and give free rein to the tears welling behind her eyes.

She was alone on her wedding day, and her husband acted like he couldn't get away from her fast enough. He must be disappointed; why else would he ride away only minutes after they were wed?

Though she'd braced herself for such a reaction, a spark of hope had remained—fanned by the clasp of his hand during the ceremony and his gentle yet fervent kiss—that perhaps he hadn't minded so much about her plain features.

Jane cast one last glance back over her shoulder to where her new husband had vanished, picked up her hem, and headed into the house.

～

Harrison topped the rise and pulled his gelding to a halt. The animal was really coming along, the best of the three young horses he'd acquired this past winter. He swung his leg over the horse's neck and dropped to the ground, sweeping the horizon and the ranch spread below him. In the hours since he'd left the house, he'd pulled two cows out of quicksand created by the spring-swollen river, delivered one calf who'd decided to enter the world backward, and ridden more miles than he wanted to remember. And he still hadn't managed time over the forge to repair a broken branding iron, nor had he sharpened the knives they'd need during the roundup.

Smoke drifted from the soddy chimney. Jane was down there waiting for him. His new wife. Guilt twisted his gut. He should've stayed, but work had beckoned, and her eyes had been full of questions about the unbuilt house—questions he hadn't wanted to answer.

Everything had seemed so simple when he first saw that advertisement. A mail-order bride would solve several of his problems. He'd get someone to help with the household chores, someone to ease a little of the burden around the ranch and free him up to spend more time on the range, and as an added bonus, he'd get to mark something off his father's list of demands—though not the way his father anticipated, he was sure.

But now, with his decision a reality, he wondered if he'd made a mistake. She wasn't just an idea anymore. Jane was a flesh-and-blood woman with feelings and expectations. She was a reality more complex than he'd bargained for.

He swallowed, hard.

Digging in his pocket, he withdrew the letter Cummings had given him and squatted in the grass to read it.

Smoothing the pages on his thigh, he scanned the familiar handwriting.

Harrison,

Have you given up on this nonsense yet? I had hoped a second long winter in the primitive conditions of Wyoming Territory would have cured you of this ranching bug. Only a few months before the deadline. You should have a fairly good idea if you're going to make it or not. And if you know you're going to fall short, then end this farce now by coming back to Columbus.

Harrison grimaced, shaking his head. Every letter began the same: give it up and come home.

The factory continues to prosper, though Peterson isn't the manager you are. New orders pour in every day.

I still can't fathom why you would turn your back on such a successful business, on an inheritance I've given my life's blood building up for you, for this pipe dream. The conditions you describe are appalling. I can't bring myself to even discuss them with my friends and business associates. Why are you still living in a dirt house when I sent more than ample supplies—at considerable cost and aggravation, I might add—to build a proper dwelling?

Harrison flicked a glance toward the sod structure housing the building materials. Rolled up in a trunk under his bed lay the plans, along with stern instructions from his father to see the house was erected as soon as possible. It was a disgrace for a Garvey to be living in a rabbit hole. Taking a deep breath, he resumed reading. His eyes lit on a name that made his gut clench.

I dined with the Norwoods this week. Sylvia is still waiting for you to come to your senses, though I fear her patience (and her mother's) is wearing thin. Last week Sylvia was seen walking out with one of Rankin Booth's sons, and Mrs. Norwood went to considerable pains to tell me of all the invitations her daughter has been receiving of late. If you're not careful, you'll lose that girl to someone else. She's too beautiful a woman and has too much of a dowry behind her to go unclaimed for long.

Sylvia Norwood. The little black barn cat had nothing on Sylvia when it came to claws and stalking. The Columbus socialite had set her sights on Harrison years before—or rather Harrison's family fortune—and nothing he did seemed to convince the woman he wasn't interested in her. At least a part of his reason for fleeing Columbus could be laid at Sylvia's feet.

But not all of it. The rest came from within himself, this burning desire to be his own man, to be free, to make his own way. Here, on his own property, away from the city and boardrooms, the factory and the demands, he felt a solace and completeness like nowhere else. Working with his hands, bending his back and making something solid out of a wilderness, pitting his strength and will against whatever challenge rose up to meet him, this was what he'd dreamed of since he was a small boy.

And it was almost within his grasp.

I can only hope and pray that once you return, you'll have gotten this wildness out of your nature and will embrace the role you were born to. But if you continue to be stubborn and insist on the full three years, I can't stop you.

Rutherford Garvey

Never "Dad" or "Pa" or even "Father." He always signed his letters "Rutherford Garvey." Harrison refolded the pages and slipped them into the envelope. If he was stubborn, at least he had come by it honestly.

He swung aboard his horse and pointed the animal's nose toward the ranch. He could put in a couple more hours before dinner and perhaps formulate a response to his father's letter. His father was going to have a conniption when he found out Harrison had married. And a mail-order bride at that.

Chapter 3

Jane surveyed her new domain. Though the bed had been spread up, one couldn't exactly call it tidy, and the ugly wool blanket covering it made her wrinkle her nose. Dust covered every surface, and boxes, crates, and cans tilted along the perimeter of the room.

She pursed her lips. What this place needed was a good cleaning and organizing. Well, she wasn't afraid of hard work. Refusing to be daunted, she rolled up her sleeves. If Harrison was going to be gone until supper, she had some time to get unpacked.

And to poke around a little to see what she could find out about her new, if absent, husband. A twinge hit her conscience that she might be prying, but she laughed it off. In a one-room house barely larger than her bedroom back in Seabury, it would be difficult to keep any secrets from each other.

She paused, realizing anew that she was indeed married, and to a man she barely knew. Her muscles tightened. Perhaps unpacking should come first. Her valises sat on the bed, and her trunk took up a fair portion of the available floor space. Time to get to work.

Opening the top dresser drawer, she knew a glimmer of

hope. Half the space lay empty. And in each of the lower three drawers, his belongings had been placed to one side.

He'd made room for her things.

He'd made room for her.

That thought warmed her heart even as her cheeks warmed at the intimacy of laying her clothing next to his and organizing her toiletries near his shaving mug and razor on the dresser top. A small mirror hung over the dresser, suspended from wire tacked into a roof brace. She studied her face, wishing once again she could be classically beautiful like her sisters. But her own ordinary face looked back at her, pale brown hair and greeny-brown eyes.

With earthen-block walls, there were no shelves or hooks, so she left her books and bonnets in her trunk. The one thing she did take out was her sewing basket. At least she'd have her knitting and her reading to occupy her hands and mind in the evenings.

She drew in a deep breath. Perhaps she'd best leave the rest of her belongings in the trunk and concentrate on putting a meal on the table. Cooking she could feel confident about. At least he had a proper stove with an oven and water reservoir. She propped the soddy doors open for more light and headed to the fuel shed.

Wrinkling her nose, she kicked a few of the dried cow-pats into a bucket. Ugh. What she wouldn't give for a hod or two of coal or a few sticks of wood. Getting the fire to light was no easy task, and she managed to fill the soddy with smoke before she got the dampers adjusted correctly. She prayed the haze would dissipate before Harrison returned.

An examination of the stores turned up basic staples and a few pleasant surprises. She could work with these, and perhaps her wedding dinner wouldn't have to be plain fare after all.

৵

Harrison headed for the house as the last of the sun's rays slipped below the horizon. His heart beat a quick tattoo.

The smell of hot biscuits and frying meat drifted toward him as he approached the soddy. On the doorstep, he scraped his boots as best he could and whacked some of the dirt and sand from his clothes.

Jane turned from the stove at his arrival. Her glance meshed with his. A flush colored her cheeks, and several wisps of hair curled at her temples. An apron covered her skirts, and his eyes were drawn to the bow in the back, so perky and feminine. When he realized he was staring, drinking in the contentment of not coming home to an empty house to prepare his own meager supper and fall into bed, he forced himself to look away. Her presence wasn't the only change in the soddy. A handful of grass-flowers stood in a glass of water on the windowsill, and a colorful patchwork quilt covered the straw mattress.

Jane flipped the ham in the skillet as if she knew her way around a stove, and he swallowed as his mouth watered.

"Smells good."

She smiled and took a pan full of golden brown biscuits from the oven. "Sit down. I'll have this on the table in a jiffy."

The table had been scrubbed and was set with stoneware dishes and steel flatware. He usually ate right out of whatever pan he cooked in. Glancing down at his work-stained clothes, he realized how accustomed to bachelor life he'd become. "I'll just wash up first." He ducked out the back door to scrub up at the washstand there. He grinned. Married half a day and already things were changing for the better. He returned just as she set the final dish on the table, and he didn't miss the surprise in her eyes when he held her chair for her.

"Thank you."

He took his seat and spread his napkin in his lap, a ritual he hadn't performed in so long it seemed foreign. And because he couldn't resist the impulse, he held out his hand to her. Though she raised her eyebrows, she hesitantly placed her fingers in his. Warm, strong, small fingers. She was so tiny his hand swallowed hers up. Her fingers quivered, and she sucked in a breath as if trying to calm herself.

"I'll say grace."

Comprehension entered her forest-colored eyes, and she bowed her head.

"Lord, I thank You for Your leading, and for bringing Jane here. I ask Your blessing on our union, and I pray that You'll help me to be a good husband to her. I thank You for this food, and I thank You for the hands that prepared it." His fingers tightened around hers. "Amen."

"Amen," she whispered then busied herself dishing up his food and hers.

He almost closed his eyes again when he bit into a biscuit. So light it almost floated off his tongue, and perfectly cooked. His efforts at biscuits usually resembled granite lumps. Slowly he chewed, savoring every bite.

"Is it all right?" Her fork poised over her plate.

"That's the best biscuit I've ever had."

She exhaled and smiled. "I've never used this particular brand of fuel before. I wasn't sure how they would turn out."

"I'd say you did a fine job."

All through dinner she kept glancing past his shoulder, a pensive expression in her eyes that puzzled him. The lamplight picked out highlights in her hair and lashes and turned her skin to gold. Everything about her intrigued him, from the softness of her skin to the gentle curve of her cheek. Baby-fine hair wisped along her slender neck, and his fingers itched to touch it.

She stared at her half-eaten meal. "I hope you don't mind. I unpacked a few of my things and put them in the dresser."

He shook his head. "Jane, this is your home now. You can do whatever you want."

She swallowed and nodded, and when he reached for her hand again, she scooted her chair back. "I made dessert."

What had her so skittish? She was as jumpy as a jackrabbit with the hiccups. His attention went to the pan she set on the table. When was the last time he had peach cobbler?

"I thought, since it was our wedding day"—a delightful blush deepened in her cheeks, and her lashes swept downward—"that we should have something nice to celebrate. I couldn't manage a cake, so I made this."

As she lifted a square of syrupy, fruity goodness onto his plate, he realized how much she must've given up when she agreed to marry him. All the things a girl wanted in a wedding, all those things Sylvia Norwood and her mother had gushed about all the time—flowers, music, food, fancy clothes—Jane had missed out on all of those things. Instead, she got a wagon ride with a cranky preacher, a rushed ceremony with a total stranger, and an afternoon spent alone wondering if she'd overstepped her bounds by unpacking her bags.

Not knowing what to say, how to apologize or even if he should, he dug into the cobbler and tried to justify his actions. She knew what she was getting into becoming a mail-order bride. If she wanted all the fancy trimmings of a wedding, she should've stayed back east, right? The justifying didn't work. His conscience still jabbed him.

When he'd mopped up the last delicious crumb from his plate, she took it and started the washing up. Her movements were jerky, and more than once, something slipped from her hand to plop into the water. Finally, it dawned on him why she was so on edge. She finished the dishes, threw out the dishwater, and wiped her hands on her apron, all while trying to avoid looking at him.

He checked the clock on the dresser, rose, and put his hands on her shoulders to stop her bustling. She flinched, but he kept a gentle hold on her.

"Jane."

He lifted her chin to look into her eyes.

"You know this is going to be a real marriage, right?"

Though her eyes widened, she nodded, staring at his chin as if unable to look him in the eye. A tremble rippled through her.

"It's going to be all right."

An adorable blush started at her neck and crept upward, and she tried to lower her face, but he resisted gently. He brushed a tendril of hair off her temple, reveling in the soft strands that tangled around his fingers. "I know you're nervous, but everything will work out. We're married. Nothing that's going to happen tonight is wrong between a husband and wife."

"I know. I don't—" She swallowed and closed her eyes as

if summoning her courage. "I don't know—"

Slowly drawing her into his arms, he rested his chin on her head, hiding his smile. She fit his embrace perfectly. He waited, and after a moment her arms came up to wrap around his waist, tentative and shy, but courageous, too, since he could feel her tremors and could only imagine how difficult this must be for her.

She was so strong and yet fragile, so tender, and yet he sensed the steel in her. She was everything he could've asked for in a wife, and so sweet his heart pounded, and he cautioned himself to go slowly, to not scare her. He brushed a kiss across the top of her head, said a prayer for wisdom, and led her to their marriage bed.

⁓

"How long will you be gone?" Jane folded a shirt and two extra pairs of socks together, and Harrison took them to stuff into his saddlebags. They'd been married less than a week, and already she couldn't imagine her life without him— though he spent nearly every daylight hour working. All the love she'd been holding on to for such a long time had found a place. Her whole world now revolved around her husband.

He shook his head. "Depends on how much the cattle have drifted. I could only afford to hire a handful of extra riders, so roundup might take a month or better." He glanced up from his list. "We'll be as quick as we can."

Reed Foster knocked on the open soddy door. "Boss, we're all set." Sunshine flashed on his reddish-yellow hair and made every one of his hundreds of freckles stand out. Barely out of his teens, he was Harrison's other full-time ranch hand. The three lounging beside the packhorses in front of the soddy were temporary hires, men who had ridden in together looking for work.

Harrison hoisted his bedroll and saddlebags and strode out into the sunshine. Though Jane wanted to sag onto the side of the bed and wallow in her sorrow, she forced herself to smile and follow him. She wouldn't make a spectacle of herself, especially not in front of his men. If only their good-bye wasn't so public, she might be able to do more than just wave and ask him to take care.

Lem tightened the ropes on one of the packs and stepped back, rubbing his chin. "Sure wish I were going with you, boss."

Harrison secured his belongings behind his saddle. "I do, too, but I'll feel better if you're here looking after things. There's plenty that needs doing."

Jane felt the scrutiny of the men. Reed, who had returned safely from Ft. Laramie with laden packhorses, was no trouble, frank, open, and sunny. But the other three were older, harder men, unlike any she'd encountered in Massachusetts. She wouldn't mind at all when they left for the roundup. She only wished Harrison didn't have to go with them.

"Let's move out." Harrison swung aboard his saddle and waited while the men followed suit. Saddles creaked, horses sidled, and bits jingled. They formed up with Harrison in the lead, and Jane swallowed against the lump in her throat, blinking hard. She would *not* cry.

Turning away, she entered the soddy. She needed to get to work, her favorite outward antidote for inward turmoil. Clacking dishes and cutlery together, she barely registered the sound of hoofbeats. A shadow blocked the light from the open door, and she whirled.

Harrison. He crossed the room in two strides and swept her into his arms. "I forgot to kiss you good-bye." He suited actions to words, crushing the breath out of her while filling her heart brim full.

He was gone as abruptly as he'd come, and she sagged onto a chair, sighing. Surely he must care for her at least a little. Perhaps eventually, he might even come to love her as she longed to be loved. As she loved him.

Everything was perfect. She only hoped her sisters were as blissfully happy as she was right now.

Chapter 4

The first order of the day was to get the soddy thoroughly cleaned and organized, which entailed enlisting Lem's help and moving everything out onto the grass.

"I'm not spending another night in this gloomy place until I have something between me and the dirt." Jane stood on one of the chairs and held the stretched canvas so Lem could nail it to the rafters. "Dirt sifts down onto everything, and this morning, a spider dropped smack on the table." She shuddered. "The canvas should stop a lot of that, and it brightens the place up. This afternoon, I'll need you to bring me the ash bucket from the bunkhouse and a couple of wheelbarrows of that clay you used on the chimneys."

"What do you want that for?" He spoke around the nails clamped between his teeth.

"I'm going to plaster the walls in here. Clay, ashes, and a little hay for a binder. That will lighten things up and seal out the dirt." She grappled with another fold of tough fabric. "If it works, maybe we can do the same in the bunkhouse."

"I wouldn't mind something between me and the dirt wall, that's for sure, but it seems like an awful lot of work. You're going to tucker yourself out."

"One of my mother's favorite expressions was 'Nobody ever died of tired.'" Jane smiled. "I want everything as nice as I can make it before Harrison gets back."

The plastering took two days of backbreaking toil. Every muscle ached from mixing the clay, toting the buckets, slapping the mixture on the walls, but when she had finished applying two coats, the inside of the soddy looked fresh and clean. Even Lem had to agree it sure spruced the place up. He helped her haul things back in, following her orders as to where to place the furniture.

"Glad you'll be sleeping inside tonight. I don't know why you wouldn't use the bunkhouse. I offered to sleep in the barn." He grappled with the bed frame.

"I didn't mind. I've never slept outside before, and besides being a little chilly, I wouldn't have changed a thing. The stars were amazing." She pushed the table under the window beside the door, where it would get the most light. "Would you nail together a few crates to make some storage cupboards?" She set the chairs under the table, lining them up just so. "I want to unpack my books, and I'd dearly love to get the foodstuff up off the floor."

"Harrison won't know the place when he gets home."

She certainly hoped not. Making their bed, spreading her patchwork quilt over the mattress and plumping the feather pillows before tucking them into linen shams, her thoughts returned again to her husband. Where was he right now? Was he safe? Did those rough men he hired follow his orders? When would he be home?

"This is the last of it. Where should I put them?" Lem stood in the doorway gripping two fancy leather suitcases.

She tapped her chin. "I found them way back under the

bed. A mouse or something has already been chewing on them, which is a shame, since they're so nice." She surveyed the room, which, while it was now much brighter and neater, didn't abound in extra space. "Put them here on the bed for now."

"I'll fetch some water for coffee. I think we've earned a break." He picked up the bucket by the door and limped away.

Jane spooned coffee into the pot and poked up the fire before she unlatched the first suitcase. If she could consolidate the contents, she could nest the suitcases one inside the other safely in one of the trunks.

Opening the case, her eyes fell on a beautiful broadcloth suit, snowy shirts, and several silk ties and handkerchiefs. Her fingers brushed the navy silk as a hundred questions leaped to her mind. How had her husband, who wore homespun and buckskin and denim every day, come to own such fine clothing?

She quickly opened the second suitcase, expecting more of the same, but was surprised when papers and books filled the space. Letters, photographs, books on raising cattle, on farming, and several history books. Rolled up along one edge were large sheets of paper that proved to be blueprints for a house. In one corner of the drawings, bold and scrawling, someone had written, *Stop being so stubborn and build the house. I won't have you living in the dirt. Rutherford.*

Curious.

A picture caught her eye. A beautiful young woman with soft, creamy shoulders rising from an evening gown, and dark ringlets piled high stared back at her with large, luminous eyes fringed with heavy lashes, a saucy tilt to her bow-shaped mouth. Jane turned the photo over.

Something to remember me by, Harrison darling. I won't wait forever. Sylvia.

Who was this gorgeous creature? She must know Harrison very well to call him "darling." Jane studied the face in the portrait, a green feeling sloshing in her middle. Sylvia. An unusual name for an unusual face. Her own name, Jane, was as plain as pudding. Her father had insisted on medieval monikers for each of his daughters, and where her sisters had received beautiful names, Evelyn, Emmeline, Gwendolyn, she'd been given Jane. Plain old Jane.

Another photograph, this one of two men, lay in one corner of the suitcase. The younger one was clearly Harrison in city clothes with his hair brushed neatly. He stood behind an older, seated man with piercing eyes and an uncompromising set to his jaw. Her fingers curled around the frame as she studied her husband's face.

A shadow fell across the doorway. "That's Harrison and his father." Lem set the bucket of water on the table and ladled some into the coffeepot. "Two more stubborn individuals, I don't know that I've met."

"Help yourself to some cornbread if you like." She waved to the pan on the table before returning the photographs to their place and latching the case. A heavy feeling, as if she'd been prying into secrets, pressed on her chest, but her curiosity about the man she married shoved it aside. She had so many questions that needed answers.

When the coffee boiled, she poured them each a cup and sat opposite Lem at the table. "Tell me about Harrison. You've known him a long time, haven't you?"

He took his cup, blew across the steaming, dark liquid,

and sipped. "Since he was a kid. I worked for his family back in Ohio, and when he wanted to head out west, I tagged along."

She cradled her cup and breathed deeply of the rich aroma. "I want to know everything about him. How he came to be in Wyoming, why he wanted a mail-order bride, what his childhood was like. He's got a suitcase of city clothes and another full of books on how to raise cattle and live on the prairie. He's got the plans and materials for a house, but it's sitting in a pile in a sod storage shed. Nothing seems to fit."

Lem chuckled. "All those things are tied up together. One thing you need to know about Harrison is that he's a strong man. Not just physically, though he could work most men to a standstill every day of the week. He's strong inside. When he sets his mind to something, he doesn't quit until he's accomplished it. Gets it from his father, Rutherford Garvey."

"Rutherford?" The one who had written the dictatorial note on the blueprints.

"Yep. That's him. Rutherford Garvey owns a factory in Columbus. They make sewing stuff. Pins, needles, thread, trimmings."

"The Garvey Sewing Company? That's Harrison's family?" Everyone woman who had ever sewn on a button had heard of Garvey's. "How on earth did he wind up out here?"

"Stubbornness mostly. All his life Harrison has wanted to be his own man, make his own decisions, and all his life his father has tried to hem him in, force him to be the man his father wants him to be. Rutherford had the boy's whole life planned out from the minute he was born, right down to the kind of girl he should marry and where he should live."

Jane set her cup down carefully. "The kind of girl he should marry?"

"That's right. Rutherford had a real beauty picked out for Harrison. Sylvia Norwood. A face to rival one of those Greek statues. Everyone expected them to announce their engagement, but Harrison bucked against the old man's maneuvering. He wanted to make his own way in the world. I don't know where he got the notion, but since he was a kid, he's wanted to farm and raise cattle. That's where the contract came in."

"The contract?" Jane could hardly concentrate, she was so stunned.

"Yeah, old Rutherford finally decided Harrison wouldn't settle down until he got this ranching lark out of his system, so the old man drew up a contract. He would loan Harrison the money to get started out here, to buy cattle, build the barn, hire hands. Harrison would have just three years to pay it all back with interest and show a profit. If he doesn't, then he agrees to return to Ohio and work for his father in the family business. Rutherford put all kinds of clauses in it, I guess. I haven't seen them all. Harrison doesn't talk about it much. I do know Rutherford heard Harrison was living in a soddy and shipped that house out here. Harrison won't build it though, because he doesn't want to incur more debt. He won't build it until he can buy the materials outright from his father. I don't imagine that will be anytime soon, since everything he's got is going into fulfilling the contract. It's due soon."

Her mind reeled. What kind of man was so ruthless as to treat his son this way? "And will Harrison make it?" She suddenly wanted him to succeed, to show his father he wouldn't be ruled, that he would be his own man.

Lem shrugged, his face sober. "I don't know. The first year out here was a rough one. We lost a lot of cattle over the winter, and that set him back. Since then, he's worked himself nearly to a frazzle every day trying to make it up."

"What about this Sylvia Norwood? Is she waiting for Harrison to get ranching out of his system and come home?"

"Doesn't matter much now, does it? Harrison's already married." Lem refilled his coffee cup. "You could've knocked me over with a gesture when Harrison said he was answering that advertisement. I don't think the notion ever hit him until Parker brought the paper over. They talked about it a long time, and I guess Harrison figured if he got married, that would be one less hold his father could have on him. Though he wrestled with the idea for a while, especially since he would need to pay your expenses out here, I guess he thought having a wife to do some of the chores would help him get the ranch. He could spend a lot more time on the range if someone was keeping the home fires burning, so to speak."

Jane studied the red and white checks on the tablecloth, heat swirling in her ears and cheeks.

"You're the right sort for here. I can't see that fancy Sylvia lasting a day in a soddy, much less slapping clay on the walls or feeding chickens or the like. No sirree. You're just what Harrison needs to help him meet that contract. I reckon he knew he'd need someone strong and healthy to share the load, who won't expect pampering. Someone plain and sensible."

Lem had no notion that his words hit like hammer blows, smashing all Jane's fragile dreams. While she'd known

Harrison hadn't married her for love, she had cherished the hope that love might grow between them. But if he'd only married her to spite his father and to have someone to do the chores, what hope did she have of happiness with him?

That night she curled on her side, pressing a pillow to her middle. She wanted to cry for her lost dreams, but the tears wouldn't come. Sylvia's beautiful face mocked her. Had Harrison loved her? Had she refused to follow him west? What was she, Jane, going to do?

Her hand drifted to the empty side of the bed, and mortification coursed through her. She'd responded wholeheartedly to Harrison's advances. What must he think of her behavior? She'd assumed he was at least beginning to care for her, but if he only saw her as a scullery maid, cook, and gardener, then their coming together had nothing to do with tender feelings.

She drew a shuddering breath and clutched the pillow with more force.

The only thing she knew to do was to work hard. Perhaps if she helped Harrison get the one thing he wanted above all others, he might come to care for her a little bit, to see her more as a woman than as a hired hand.

But unless or until he did, there would be no more intimacy between them.

꙳

Harrison let his weight up off the calf, and it sprang away with a bawl of protest. The smell of singed hair, smoke, cows, and hot metal swirled around him like dust. He shoved the branding iron back into the coals and swiped his forehead with his sleeve.

"Here come a few more." Reed coiled his rope and prepared to cut out another calf. "Do you want me to spell you?"

"No, I'm fine." He motioned the boy toward the bunched cattle. Digging in his shirt pocket, he withdrew his tally book and pencil. The calf crop, though decent considering the winter they'd been through, wasn't near what he'd hoped for, not nearly what he needed it to be. He blew out a breath and prepared to tackle the calf bucking at the end of Reed's lasso.

The new men were working out all right, though they kept to themselves. He'd been lucky to hire them, considering he couldn't afford to pay top wages and he didn't even have a chuck wagon. But these fellows hadn't seemed to care, only wanting to find work. Harrison looked forward to the day when he could afford to keep a full crew on year-round.

By nightfall of the twenty-third day, they'd finished. They'd ridden every corner of his range, they had branded every HG calf they could find, and their supplies were running low.

Fletcher, the leader of the trio of temporary hands, let his saddle plop into the dirt beside the campfire. Reed stirred yet another pot of beans and rice, squatting on his heels, his face and hair illuminated by the flames. Harrison stretched out on his bedroll and went over his figures again. No matter how many times he added it up, he was still going to be short.

"Come and get it before I throw it out." Reed ladled out for everyone and piled his own plate high. The boy had lost weight, like Harrison had himself, over the course of the roundup. They could both use a rest.

But judging from the bottom line in the tally book, a rest was just what they weren't going to get. Harrison had worked too hard, come too far to fall short this close to the end. As he shoveled the bland food into his mouth, he racked his brain for a way to make up the deficit.

"Be good to get back to the ranch tomorrow, huh?" Reed flopped beside Harrison. "Bet you're looking forward to some good cooking. I thought you were crazy when you said you were sending off for a bride, but those cinnamon rolls she gave us before we left. . . It was enough to make me think about getting hitched myself."

Harrison smiled. He *was* looking forward to getting back to Jane, but a twinge of apprehension feathered across his chest. The time was coming soon when he'd have to explain to her about his situation, about the contract with his father and all that went with it. He should've told her in his letter, so she would know what she was getting into, and he certainly should've told her when they met, but he'd taken one look into those hazel, trusting eyes and couldn't. If she knew about his life back east, she might start badgering him to give up the ranch and return to civilization.

"How'd the tally go? I've seen you scowling at that book." Reed set his plate on the ground and stretched his boots toward the fire.

"Not as good as I'd hoped. We'll have to find a way to make up the difference."

"Like how?"

"Dunno. I'll have to think on it."

"Sure hope you come up with something. I'd hate to see you lose everything after coming this far." Reed took his plate and Harrison's now-empty one and headed to the creek to wash up.

Harrison's hand clenched into a fist, and he pounded his thigh. He wasn't going to lose this ranch. There had to be a way.

Chapter 5

Harrison paid off the three temporary hands, broke camp, and with Reed and the packhorses in tow, headed home. Finally, near midday two days later, they topped the last rise, and his ranch spread out before him. Pride of ownership, the pride of knowing he'd worked by the sweat of his brow to build something out of nothing, welled up in his chest. He was so close to fulfilling his dream.

He frowned and pulled to a halt. Something was different.

"What's that?" Reed pointed with the hand that held the packhorse leads.

A large square of broken ground lay between the soddy and the creek. At least an acre? Gray-brown earth, tilled and harrowed smooth. Two figures bent over the dirt. Lem and Jane. He kicked his horse into a lope, leaving Reed to bring the packhorses.

Down the slope, around the soddy, and to the edge of the plowed dirt he rode, and the whole way he remembered his parting kiss and anticipated Jane's welcome.

Jane straightened, pressed her hand to the small of her back, and leaned on her hoe handle. He swung down from the saddle and strode across the broken earth, ready to embrace her, but her expression changed from surprised relief to. . .something else. Something wary and. . .hurt? He stopped a few paces away.

She swiped the back of her wrist across her forehead. Was it his imagination, or did she look thinner? "Welcome home."

Harrison blinked at the cold tone. Every day, several times a day, while they had been apart, he'd remembered the ardor of her embrace and looked forward to taking up where they'd left off. And now she looked every bit as self-contained and remote as the moment she'd climbed down from Cumming's wagon.

Lem shouldered his shovel and sauntered over. "Boss. What do you think?" He waved toward the expanse of dirt. "When your wife does something, she does it thoroughly. She said she wanted a garden patch, and she's had me digging for the past week." He stuck his spade into the earth. "With all she's planting, I don't reckon you'll need to buy much in the way of supplies this fall. You'll probably have enough to sell at the fort."

Jane pushed a strand of hair off her cheek. "That's my hope."

Why wouldn't she look at him? Was she shy in front of Lem? Relief trickled through him. That must be it. She just didn't want to show affection in front of an audience. Later then, when they were alone. He almost chuckled. He could wait.

Lem turned his attention up the hill where Reed plodded down with the packhorses. "I'll go help the kid."

As he shuffled away, Harrison stepped closer to Jane. "I missed you. You look tired. The garden is a surprise. Not that you're planting one, but the size. Are you sure you can keep up with such a large plot?"

Her back straightened. "Don't worry about me. I'm strong, and I can take care of a garden. How was your roundup?" She whacked her hoe blade into a stubborn dirt clod.

"Fine. Well, not as fine as I'd hoped. Not as many calves as I would've liked, though the herd seems to have wintered fairly well. All that extra feeding out we did helped." A pungent odor drifted up from the dirt, and he realized she was incorporating fertilizer into the soil. She'd need it, since the dirt out here wasn't the best for gardening.

"Are you hungry? I can leave off here for a bit and fix you something." Chop, chop, chop. She sounded as if she didn't care one way or the other.

Baffled by her remoteness, he shook his head, though his stomach gurgled at the thought of a decent meal. "I'd best see to my horse."

She never looked up, just nodded and continued working the soil.

Entering the barn, Harrison shrugged. Women were indeed a mystery, though he hadn't thought Jane the moody type.

Reed and Lem worked at the far end of the barn, slipping packs off and stowing equipment. Lem opened one of the packs. "She's worked herself to a standstill every blessed day you all were gone." He sorted the branding irons and hung them on hooks on the wall. "I rode over to Gareth's and got a plow and team to turn most of that field, or I swear she'd have done it all with a hand spade. As it is, she's hoed it over twice and planted most of it by herself. She had me ride clear into Sagebrush for seeds, too. I offered to take her with me to Gareth's. Figured she'd want to see her sister, but she said she'd go next time, that there was too much to do before you got back from the roundup. Never seen a woman work so hard."

Reed coiled a length of rope. "Guess she'll fit in with the boss pretty well then. He works from dark to dark himself."

"How was the calf crop?"

"Boss said it was fine, but his face was awful long every time he counted things up."

Harrison cleared his throat, and they both jumped. "Be sure to give those horses a good rubdown and feed now."

"Sure thing." Reed got busy, but Lem limped over to Harrison.

"You got time for a little walk? There's something I want to show you."

Harrison removed the saddle from his mount and led him into a stall. "Let me take care of this fellow first." He curried the animal while Lem doled out feed and made sure the water bucket was full.

"Look in here." Lem pointed into Buttercup's stall.

He looked over the partition into the eyes of the most perfect little jersey calf he'd ever seen. A smile tugged at his mouth. Big kneed, round-bellied, moist-nosed, the little heifer was the picture of bovine beauty.

"She came about a week after you left. Hard calving though. Breech. Your missus helped with the birthing, though you could tell she was scared to death. Kept talking to Buttercup like the old girl could understand every word while I delivered the calf. And Jane's been down here every day teaching the calf to drink from a bucket. She's taken over the milking, too, though I had to teach her how."

As he emerged from the barn, Harrison checked the

garden plot, but Jane had disappeared. A wisp of smoke trickled from the soddy chimney.

"Boss, that Jane is a wonder, but I'm worried about her."

Lem had his attention. Maybe he could give Harrison a clue as to why Jane was so distant. "She's not ailing, is she?" Was she homesick? Missing her sisters? Maybe he could take time out to let her visit one of them. But when? Work piled up every day as it was.

"No, that's not it. At least I don't think it is." He scrubbed his jaw and hitched his suspenders. "She found your city clothes and papers and things when she was cleaning out the soddy, and she started asking questions. I didn't think much about it, since it isn't exactly a secret, and I told her about the contract with your father. She also found a photograph of Sylvia Norwood and asked about her."

Harrison grimaced. He'd much rather have told Jane about his past himself, and he'd very much rather she had never known about Sylvia at all. They strolled in the direction of the chicken coop.

"How did she take the news?"

"That's just it. I thought everything was fine. She didn't seem upset at all, just a little quiet, but considering all the work she'd put in on the house that day, her being quiet and tired made sense. But ever since that day, she's about killed herself working. Look in here." He opened the henhouse door.

Pristine white greeted his eyes. The roosts and nesting boxes had been scrubbed and scoured, and the dirt walls whitewashed. A layer of fresh hay covered the floor, with not a feather or dropping to be seen.

"Look at the pen." Lem pointed to the fenced yard.

Raked clean, pans of mash and water immaculate. Even the birds looked cleaner. And fresh netting surrounded a smaller pen inside where two hens and more than a dozen chicks scratched and pecked.

"She rakes it every morning and hauls the droppings to the compost heap, and she's treated all the birds with delousing powder. You should see those crazy chooks. The minute she steps into the coop, they all squat down to be petted. Even that old rogue Napoleon eats out of her hand and almost purrs when she picks him up."

The rooster tilted his head and regarded them with a beady eye. His tail feathers shimmered in the sunshine as he strutted.

"And I don't know if you noticed, but the barn's cleaner than it's been since we put it up. No loose hay, no tools out of place, and every last piece of leather has been soaped and polished. She had me haul the manure pile to the garden and harrow it in, and bless me if she didn't strike out across the creek to gather cow chips, some for fuel and the rest for fertilizer. I've had to chase her out of the garden or the barn in the evening. If I didn't, I think she'd work all night."

"Why?" He scratched his head. "Not that I'm not pleased with the improvements."

"Beats me. I thought you might know. Maybe she was just filling in time. She seemed to miss you something fierce."

Harrison smiled. That was good to know. Her cool reception of him had set him back a bit. "Then I guess she'll taper off now that I'm home."

He couldn't believe the transformation inside the soddy. Clean, organized, and homelike. Little touches that said a woman lived there—everything from curtains at the window to the pretty shams on the pillows. A couple of rag rugs covered the floor, and she'd managed a set of shelves for the books he'd never unpacked. Her own books stood beside his, and atop the dresser, a chessboard and pieces stood perfectly ranked. How long had it been since he'd indulged in a game of chess? A feeling of contentment, of knowing himself blessed, settled around his heart.

She stood at the table, kneading dough. Though he needed a shave and a bath, and he wore the marks of three weeks out on the range, he didn't care. He needed to feel her soft skin and recapture the bond he'd felt with her the moment he'd said his vows. He needed to fill the void created when he'd ridden away from her more than three weeks ago.

"Careful." She turned her shoulder to his offer of an embrace, punched and rounded the pale ball one last time, and set it in the pan to rise.

He pushed his hat back, contentment giving way to puzzlement. "Jane, what's wrong?"

"Nothing."

"Lem says you've done nothing but work the whole time I was away. I think you could slow down for a few minutes to at least say hello."

She took a deep breath and folded her hands at her waist. "Hello. Welcome home. Your dinner will be ready in about half an hour."

"There something interesting about the floor?"

Her chin jerked. "What?"

Impatience at the change in her made him brusque. "You keep looking at the floor. Is there something interesting there? Most folks look at each other when they talk."

She raised her lashes, and he found himself staring into

her pretty eyes, mostly brown at the moment, and still with that hurt look in the shadows.

"Is something bothering you?" If she'd just tell him what was wrong, he'd fix it, but he wasn't a mind reader.

"No. There's nothing bothering me. I've just got work to do." She turned away and grabbed a skillet, clanking it onto the stovetop.

He shrugged. "I'll go clean up then."

Women. What was a man supposed to do?

❦

Not a word about the improvements. Jane blinked hard and sliced ham into the skillet. What good did it do to work herself to a nubbin if he didn't even notice? Her gorge rose a bit, and she swallowed. Only halfway through the day, and already she wanted nothing more than to crawl into bed and sleep, to forget for a while that her husband had only married her to spite his father.

Harrison sat up to the noon meal and tucked into the food as if he hadn't had a decent meal in weeks. He looked thinner, more worn. She dished out another helping of ham and beans for him and added another slice of bread.

"Are you pleased about the garden? I've put in beans, peas, corn, turnips, carrots, and potatoes. Oh, and onions."

He nodded. "The garden's fine."

Something stirred under the bed, and he jerked around. His hand closed around the broom by the door.

"Don't. That's just Boadicea." Jane rose, scraping her chair on the dirt floor.

"Boadi—who?" His forehead wrinkled.

"The cat. Actually, it's cats now. Come and see."

She knelt beside the bed and lifted the edge of the quilt. He followed suit, but tentative, as if he expected a cougar to leap out. Instead, over the edge of a box, two green eyes blinked, and a rumbly purr rolled out accompanied by some squeaks and mewls.

"They're waking up. I found them one morning in the barn, and she was spitting and yowling, trying to keep a coyote away from them. I brought them into the house to keep them safe, though Lem warned me she might move them out again. But she didn't. I think she was just starved for some attention, and she knows I won't hurt her babies. Aren't they sweet? There are three of them." She reached into the box and withdrew a black kitten with four tiny white feet and a white vest. "I named the mama Boadicea. It just seemed fitting, since she was so fearless defending her babies." The kitten curled in her hand, and she raised it to her cheek, nuzzling the fur and crooning.

"First the rooster and now the cat. Is there anything you can't tame?" His voice rumbled in his chest like the cat's purr and sent a shiver through her. He reached out and stroked one of the kittens in the box, and she found herself longing for him to touch her that way.

She swallowed and returned the baby to its mother. "If you don't want her in the house, I understand. Lem said they would take them into the bunkhouse."

"Do you want them to stay?"

She stroked Boadicea's head. "Yes. She's good company."

"Then she can stay." They returned to the table, and Harrison knew he couldn't put things off any longer. "Jane, we need to talk."

She rested her hands in her lap, trying to keep her composure.

"Lem says he told you about the contract between my father and me for this land."

"Yes. It came as quite a shock. I wish you'd told me yourself." Though she tried not to sound accusing, she winced at the chiding in her tone.

He pushed his plate away. "I should have. I meant to, but there never seemed to be a good time. But I don't want you to worry. I'll meet the contract demands if it kills me. I've worked too hard for this and sacrificed too much."

"Including Sylvia Norwood?" The words were out before she could stop them. She hadn't been going to mention Sylvia at all, but the image of the beautiful woman he could've married had stalked her dreams for the past three weeks. The Sylvias of the world were crystal chandeliers, while the Janes were the tallow candles. One beautiful, fragile, exquisite; the other utilitarian, ordinary, and plain.

His forehead bunched. "Sylvia? You saw her picture. Can you imagine her living out here? It would be a disaster."

But he could imagine her, Plain Jane, living here. Jane wanted to pick up the pot of coffee and dump it on his insensitive, practical, blind-as-a-mole head.

Harrison went on. "My father might think he has the upper hand, but he's going to get quite a shock when I write and tell him I'm married."

I bet. He'll be horrified when he finds out Harrison Garvey of Garvey Sewing Company married a nobody because she could work hard and survive living in a dirt house in the middle of nowhere. Somebody stupid enough to believe that her husband might come to care for her.

"What happens if you can't meet the contract?" She was proud of herself for sounding so calm when inside she hurt more than she'd ever thought possible.

"I will." His hand fisted on the table.

"But if you don't." She kept her voice firm.

"The contract stipulates that if I don't meet the demands, I will return to Columbus and take up my position in the family business."

Return to Columbus. Return to Sylvia? What about her, Jane? If he left Wyoming Territory, would he leave her, too? She was part of his life out here, not back east. If he returned to the world of business, power, and the company of socialites as beautiful as Sylvia, surely he wouldn't want a wallflower like Jane holding him back. Would he seek a divorce? What about the scandal? What about her sisters?

Her weary mind refused to contemplate a future in Columbus with Harrison or a future in Wyoming without him, so she changed the subject. "If the calf crop was less than you expected, how are you planning to make up the difference?"

His lips pressed thin, and he shook his head. "I'm not sure. I can't sell cattle. Keeping the herd up is part of the contract. I've cut expenses to the bone. I can't run the ranch without Reed and Lem, and they're taking less than standard wages as it is. What I need is cash."

"What do you have to sell?"

"That's just it. I don't have anything. I wouldn't make enough over the next few months hiring myself out to make it worthwhile, and I can't afford to be away from here that long. And I've got to cut hay for this winter."

An idea sparked. "Do the other ranchers around here cut hay?"

He shook his head. "No, most of them just let the cattle

fend for themselves. I learned the hard way that winters here can decimate a herd, and I promised myself I'd never be caught out like that again. There were plenty of ranchers who came knocking last winter though. I could've sold a barn full of feed." He sucked in a deep breath.

"Exactly. What if you cut and stacked hay, not just for your herd but to sell? Your neighbors would buy hay if it was available, wouldn't they?"

"They might. They just might." A smile spread across his face, bringing out those devastating dimples. "I could send Lem to make the rounds, see who would be interested. And Reed can keep an eye on the cattle while I cut and stack hay." He bounced out of his chair, grasped her hands, and pulled her to her feet. "That's brilliant, girl."

He hugged her, lifting her from the floor, but when he bent his head to kiss her, she turned her face so his lips just brushed her cheek. Though she longed to stay in his embrace, to savor his kisses and more, she forced herself to ease out of his arms. "I'd better clear the dishes."

Late that night, when he reached for her, she rolled onto her side away from him and feigned sleep. If he succeeded in winning the ranch, then she might be willing to risk her heart again, but until then, she had to be on her guard.

Chapter 6

Harrison pulled the whetstone from his pocket and ran it along the curved blade of his scythe. Bits of grass and dirt clung to his sweaty skin, and he swiped a rivulet from his temple. His shoulders burned, his muscles aching from the constant motion of swinging the scythe, and all around him the smell of fresh-cut grass rose up. Swallows darted over the hay field, feasting on the bugs stirred up by his passing.

Across the creek, Jane toiled in the garden, surrounded by knee-high corn plants. She toted yet another bucket of water. Cold, chilly spring had given way to hot, dry summer. Enough rain fell to keep the grass fairly green and thick, but her garden needed more. Her first crop of peas had come up like hair on a dog, and she'd spent hours shelling and drying them.

His chest pinched. He needed to send Lem to town to get Jane some canning jars, but he didn't want to spend the money. Every precious dime needed to be saved. The deadline, only four months away, stalked his dreams and pressed on his shoulders every waking minute.

As did his concern for Jane. She remained as remote as ever, and if he wasn't so dead tired every night that he could hardly muster the energy to fall into bed, he'd break down those walls and find the loving, generous girl he knew lived inside her, the girl he'd married.

Returning the stone to his pocket, his fingers brushed the latest letter from his father. He pushed his hat back on his head, set the scythe on the ground, and eased himself down to the warm grass. He unfolded the letter and squinted when the sunshine glared off the white pages. Short and right to the point, it opened with a bang:

Married? What were you thinking, son? Who is this girl? What am I supposed to tell the Norwoods? To say you've put me in an awkward situation would be an understatement. I can only ask again, what were you thinking? I've half a mind to come out there and see for myself just what you're up to.

Harrison sighed and shook his head. He couldn't imagine his father jolting across the prairie aboard a stagecoach. He'd never make good on that threat. As to what to say to the Norwoods, his father could hold his own with the Norwoods or anyone else he came in contact with. Harrison wasn't worried there. It was his father's own fault if he'd made promises on Harrison's behalf. He should've known better.

You sent no word on the progress of the house. I imagine now that you're married—I still can't believe it—your new wife will want the house put up as soon as possible. Any woman who'd be happy living in a dirt house can't be a suitable bride for you, though at this late date in the contract, building the house seems like throwing good money after bad. Still, if you build it, I can sell the property for more money once the deadline passes.

His father's lack of faith in him was galling. And his sideways swipe at Jane set Harrison's teeth on edge.

The house. His eyes strayed to the shed where the building materials lay under canvas shrouds. A fetter and a promise, an obstacle and a goal, a blessing and a curse. Someday, when the land was his, when he could pay his father for the building materials, he would build that fine house, but until then, knowing it was there waiting in the dark shed, it taunted him, accused him of being a poor provider.

He shoved the letter back into his pocket and picked up his scythe. Enough time wasted.

࿓

Jane poured the last of the bucket of water onto the thirsty corn plant and straightened her aching back. Pressing her hand to her temple, she tried to still the dizziness. The sun baked everything, and she could well believe the nation's Independence Day was less than a week away.

She toted the empty bucket back toward the spring. Only half a row to go and she could be done with the watering for today. She'd have to remember to move the stick—her memory stick, she called it—to remind her where to start watering tomorrow. Dividing the garden into six parcels, one for each day, helped her keep up with the weeding, thinning, watering, and picking.

Boadicea stalked down the row, her tail erect. She stopped when she reached Jane and rubbed against her ankles. Jane lifted the animal into her arms and cuddled her, loving the hearty purr and the sleek fur. Gone was the wary, skinny, combative feline she'd first encountered. Satisfied, she set the cat down. "How are the babies?"

The triplets had quickly outgrown both the box and the soddy and spent their days prowling around the ranch buildings and wrestling one another in the high grass. The wagon rattling out of the barn drew her attention, the hay-rack jostling and tilting over the ruts created by so many trips to and from the hay field. Lem slapped the lines on the team's rumps and waved to her.

She followed his progress back to the piles of hay he and Harrison had raked together yesterday and beyond to where her husband, with what seemed tireless strokes, sliced swaths of long grass into rows. With such a favorable response from the surrounding ranches, he had hope that he might be able to make up the difference between his resources and the contract's bottom line. But it was taking everything they all had. From before sunup to well past sundown, he drove himself. And she and Reed and Lem worked alongside him, as driven as he to achieve his goal.

Jane refused to let herself hope, though. Until the deed to the ranch was in Harrison's hand, there was always the chance they would fall short, that he would leave her.

She picked up her bucket and headed toward the house. Halfway there, she stopped, holding her side, low down. For days, off and on, she'd experienced twinges and aches in her abdomen, some sharp, some persistent. Shrugging it off as the result of toting so much water from the creek, she rubbed the spot and resumed her journey. Her favorite part of the day was fast approaching, and she wanted to be ready for it.

Harrison moved steadily, but he glanced at the angle of the sun frequently. His favorite time of day would be here soon. Step. Slash. Step. Slash. Keep up the rhythm, keep moving forward. Every swipe, every row, haycock, load, and stack meant he was closer to reaching his goal.

Another check of the sun, another glance toward the creek.

There she was.

His heart tripped. With a basket over one arm and a brown earthenware jug in the other, Jane crossed the stubble. Her bonnet hid her face from the merciless sun, but he knew when she arrived she would slide it off her silky hair so she could survey the landscape.

He waved across the field to Lem, who forked hay into the wagon. The older man waved back, flung his pitchfork into the pile of hay beside the team, and limped toward Harrison.

They arrived at the same time. Harrison reached for her basket while Lem took the jug. As anticipated, her bonnet slid off, and she swept the terrain. "I can't believe how much you've gotten done."

She said it every day, but every day it made his heart swell. Peeking under the napkin in the basket, he found his favorite sugar cookies. He took one, letting the sweet, sugary goodness melt on his tongue.

"We're going to have to start stacking in the field, boss. The barn's full." Lem took a long drink from the jug and swiped the back of his hand across his mouth. "I can't get so much as one more blade of grass in there."

Harrison traded him the basket for the jug and shook his head. "I don't want to stack it out here on the range. That's asking for trouble. We'll put the horses in the barn and stack hay in the corral. That way none of the cattle can get at it, and it will be handy for when the buyers come."

"We sure could use an extra hand or two. Stacking's a two-man job." The older man rubbed his hip. "Having to climb on and off that wagon is wearing me thin."

Familiar guilt settled in Harrison's gut. Lem couldn't swing a scythe all day. With his bum leg, he couldn't get the proper leverage. And yet, he was right. He wouldn't last long climbing on and off the hayrack like he'd have to do if he were stacking the hay.

"I wish I could afford to hire someone to help us, but I'd just be paying out in wages everything we were earning selling hay." Harrison took off his hat and tunneled his fingers through his hair. "Maybe I can help stack after I'm through cutting for the day."

Lem grimaced and shook his head. "You can't cut all day and stack all night. You'll kill yourself. I'll manage somehow."

"I can help." Jane twirled her bonnet string around her finger. "The garden work is well ahead. If you'll show me what to do, I'm sure I can manage."

Harrison's immediate response was to say no. She had enough to do with her own work without doing his, too. And yet, what other choice did he have? "It's hard labor. Lem would pitch down the hay from the rack, but you'd have to rake it smooth and walk it down tight."

"I can do it." She straightened her spine and tugged her bonnet into place.

The stubborn light in her eyes made him smile. The

newest member of the Garvey family just might be the most determined of them all. He couldn't deny the relief her offer gave him. "I'll let you help on one condition. If it's too much for you, you'll say so. No standing on pride. And I'll rope Lem in on the decision, too. If he thinks it's too much for you, he has the authority to stand you down and take your hay rake away."

She tugged her sunbonnet into place and took the now-empty basket and jug. "I'll just take care of a few things at the soddy, and I'll be ready when Lem brings the next load."

Harrison followed her with his eyes, thankful for her and puzzled by her. Lem nudged his elbow.

"She's a fine woman. Reminds me of my wife."

Harrison's head swiveled to the older man. "I didn't know you were married."

"It was a long time ago. My Deborah passed away when you were just a youngster, before I came to work for your dad. She was a hard worker, always looking to my comfort. Her passing left a big hole in my life. I always felt bad that I never told her how much she meant to me. I think she knew, but I never said it. I guess it was the way I was raised. I took her for granted and didn't realize what a treasure I had until she was gone."

Harrison didn't know what to say. He picked up his scythe and slipped the whetstone from his pocket once more.

Lem shrugged, hitched up his pants, and took a couple of steps away before pausing. "I'd hate to see you make the same mistake I did, son."

Chapter 7

Jane adjusted the kerosene lamp, slipped out of her wrapper, and eased her aching body into the tub. A glance at the clock told her Harrison wouldn't be in for another hour yet, so she had plenty of time for a good soak.

And a good think.

For the past month, she'd been too busy and too tired to think, but a rare rainy day had put a halt to the haying and endless garden work and allowed a respite. Harrison, ignoring the chance to rest, had donned his slicker, saddled up, and gone out to check on his herd, spelling Reed and giving him his first day off in weeks.

She rested her head against the back of the tub and closed her eyes. They were so close. Ranchers had already started sending hands to buy winter feed, wagonload by wagonload. With each purchase, Harrison added to his reserves, making notes in his ledger. If she could just hold out until the deadline, this endless round of toil would ease off. Harrison would've won his ranch, and her future here with him would be secure. She would be safe to let herself love him.

Raising her hand to the lamplight, she studied the hard-earned calluses. Though she couldn't remember a time when her hands had been soft and beautiful, they'd never been this rough and work-worn. In spite of wearing gloves, the daily toil with the hay rake had raised blisters. She'd had to keep her hands hidden from Harrison until new calluses formed, though with as little as she saw of him these days, it wasn't difficult. He left before sunup, returned after dark, ate whatever she left for him in the warmer, and fell into bed.

Not that her days looked much different from his. Early mornings she hurried through her housework and cared for the cows and chickens, picked whatever was ripe in the garden and spread it to dry between layers of weighted cheesecloth, and then it was off to the corral to stack hay, walking in endless circles, spreading what Lem pitched from the hayrack. In the evenings she pulled together a simple meal for herself and Lem, who helped her put up whatever foodstuffs she hadn't gotten to from the garden that morning, and then to bed to fall asleep before Harrison came in.

Today, in spite of the rain, she'd done laundry. Lem had protested that she should rest, but she pointed out that since they couldn't work outside this was the perfect opportunity to catch up on other chores. Now garments hung drying from lengths of rope stretched across the soddy, shirts lay over the backs of chairs, and her delicates draped over the foot of the bed.

In the midst of all this splendor, she let the hot water soothe her aches. Boadicea rose from the quilt, stretched, and wrapped her tail around herself, regarding Jane with accusing eyes. Or at least they seemed accusing to Jane's tender conscience.

"I know. But how am I going to tell him? And when? He's never here." The suspicion nagging at the back of Jane's mind for weeks now had become a certainty. She counted backward to her wedding day, to that first week of happily wedded bliss. Almost four months. Guilt tightened her chest. The timing couldn't be worse. Her desire to linger in the warm water waned.

Scrubbing quickly, she got out, dried, and donned a nightgown and wrapper. Placing her hands on her abdomen, she couldn't deny the thickening at her waist. It was time to acknowledge that she was carrying Harrison's child. She drew a shuddering breath, not knowing whether to laugh or cry and too tired to do either.

How would a child affect Harrison's plans? They had never spoken of starting a family, and since their first week of marriage, it hadn't even been a danger. He'd apparently taken her touch-me-not demeanor to heart. That and they were both too exhausted every night to do anything more than collapse. A baby was the last thing on Harrison's mind right now, and the very last thing he needed to worry about.

She couldn't tell him. He'd forbid her to work on the haying. Not that she would mind never picking up a hay rake again, but he needed her. Harrison was focused on his goal, throwing all his effort into winning the ranch. He didn't have the time or energy to be burdened with anything else.

Thunder boomed as she climbed into bed and scooted over toward the wall. Boadicea protested with a meow and settled herself near Jane's feet. Jane pressed her hand against her stomach. A tiny fluttering under her palm made her freeze. Had she imagined it? Lying perfectly still, she waited. . .

There it was again. Like butterfly wings. Faint, but insistent.

Her throat tightened. Nothing in her marriage was right.

Her husband, who was supposed to be her gallant knight and rescuer, needed her hard work but didn't love her, was even now riding through a downpour to check on his herd instead of snuggled beneath the covers with her, and what should've been the most exciting and happiest news she could share with him was now her secret burden to bear.

Lord, I feel so alone.

Sleep dragged at her eyes, and her last thought was to wonder if the wait to be loved would ever end.

⌇

The rain finally slackened off, just in time for Harrison to make it back to the barn. Soaked to the skin, hungry, and more tired than he could ever remember being, he stripped the saddle from his wet horse. Mechanically, he rubbed the animal down with a grain sack and fed him.

Not a glimmer of light shone from the soddy. Jane must be in bed already. His heart sank. He'd hoped that with a day to herself with no outside chores, she might've been rested enough to at least stay up until he got home. He headed toward the bunkhouse to check in with Reed and Lem. His boots squelched with each step along the path.

Warm lamplight spilled over him as he knocked and opened the door. The smell of hot coffee and biscuits made his mouth water and his stomach rumble.

His two hired hands sat at a plank table playing dominoes. Reed stood as Harrison entered and removed his drenched hat.

"Evening, boss. Everything all right with the cattle?" He motioned for Harrison to take his chair and perched on the end of his bunk.

"Right as can be. With all this rain you'll have to watch the trouble spots along the creek over the next few days and make sure none of them bog down."

Lem tipped his chair back and snagged a tin cup. "Coffee's hot."

Harrison helped himself, inhaling the warm fragrance. He stripped out of his slicker and pulled the chair up to the stove. "Sure hope things dry out quickly."

"The rain isn't all bad. The grass will grow, and we could use the break." Lem ladled up a plate of stew and biscuits. "Tuck into this. Jane brought it over this afternoon, so it's edible, not like Reed's cooking."

The kid shrugged. "I never claimed to be no cook. I can only make beans and rice anyway." He picked up a lariat and twisted the rope until it creaked. "We got all the tools sharpened and went over the wagon and all the harnesses. Everything's tight."

"You've done well, both of you. I know I've asked a lot, and there's still plenty to do, but I never would've gotten this far without you."

Lem grunted and laced his fingers on his belly. "Or Jane. Best thing you ever did marrying that gal. I don't know how she does it. Even today, instead of resting like she should've, she was scrubbing laundry, mine and Reed's, too. Said a rainy day was the perfect day to catch up on other chores."

Harrison's fork stopped halfway to his mouth. "Laundry?"

"Yeah, and she had me string a couple of ropes for her so she could hang clothes up to dry."

"Boss, two riders from the Circle M passed through with word that their foreman wants to buy some feed. He says it's plain foolishness to pay for grass, but the ranch owner says better safe than sorry. They'll take a couple of tons, and they'll send the wagons and hands to load it."

Harrison managed a smile. Word was spreading.

"That will help, won't it? Will we still be here ranching come spring?" Reed tossed the rope onto the bed. His blue eyes held the same worry Harrison knew lingered in his own.

"If hard work and praying can do it, we will."

Letting his chair fall back onto all four legs, Lem inclined his head to Reed, who nodded. "Boss, me and Reed have been talking, and there's something we want to say."

Harrison stilled. Lem's sober face and tone sent a chill racing through him. If they quit, he'd lose the ranch for sure. *Please, Lord, don't let it be that.*

"We know you've been about killing yourself trying to meet your dad's demands, and we know every penny is precious. So we have a proposition for you. Me and the kid have been talking it over, and we've decided we don't want any wages for the next little while."

"What? No. Absolutely not. You can't work for nothing."

"Sure we can. And it wouldn't be for nothing." Lem eased his suspenders over his shoulders. "If you lose this ranch, we lose our jobs. Neither of us has forgotten how you brought us out here and gave us jobs when nobody else would. Since the accident that mangled up my leg, I had to quit the factory. But you still thought I could be useful, and that means a lot to me."

Reed nodded. "And you didn't listen to all the folks who told you I was too dumb to work. You taught me to read and write, which nobody'd ever been able to do before, and you gave me a job and your trust. I ain't forgetting that."

Harrison studied his hands, humbled to his core. "I don't know what to say." Their wages, though modest, added back into the total would go a long way toward reaching their goal. "When this is over, I'll pay you both back. I promise." He held out his hand to shake Lem's then Reed's.

"We ain't worried about that."

Harrison knew a lightening of heart as he made his way to the soddy, something that hadn't happened in quite a while. He had the best crew in Wyoming Territory.

As quietly as he could, he eased open the door and slipped inside. Jane had left the firebox open on the stove, and pale orange light illuminated the lines of drying clothes. Boadicea's green eyes glowed from the end of the bed.

He let the cat sniff his fingers and stroked her furry cheek. She rumbled a purr, stood, and walked to the door to be let out. Navigating the clotheslines and the still-full bathtub, he got ready for bed.

The minute he slid between the sheets, Jane turned toward him, as she always did when she was asleep. His arm went around her, and she tucked her head under his chin. The pillow she clamped to her middle pressed against his side, and her soft breathing feathered across the base of his neck.

He brushed a kiss across the top of her head and closed his eyes, his muscles relaxing by increments. She might remain aloof during the day, but at night, she slept in his arms. He yawned, his thoughts already evaporating into sleep. But one notion persisted. The minute the ranch was his, the instant he could finally relax and think of something besides that contract, he was going to start courting his wife like she deserved. He was determined to find that sweet, spontaneous, loving girl he'd caught a glimpse of the first week they were wed.

Chapter 8

Jane walked another round on the haystack, careful of the edge now that she was several feet off the ground. The wheatgrass slipped and slid under her feet, seeds and chaff floating around her, sticking to her skin and clinging to her clothes. Sweat trickled between her shoulder blades.

Lem pitched the last forkful of hay from the wagon and stopped to swipe his handkerchief over his face and neck. "Sure wish that rain would come back. Hot enough to fry a stove lid."

She let the heavy rake fall from her fingers and shaded her eyes. Harrison was a tiny dot on the hillside across the creek, a perfect picture of how far her heart felt from him. Her hand started for her waist, but she stopped, not wanting Lem or anyone else to guess her secret.

She dropped to her seat and slid off the partially formed haystack, her feet thudding on the baked earth. The shade cast by the barn beckoned her, and she straggled to it, aching from head to foot and fighting a wicked headache. Lem hefted the water jug from under the wagon seat and toted it to where she leaned against the barn wall.

"Here, take a few sips of this. Not too much now. Don't want you getting sick."

She tilted the earthenware jug and let the lukewarm water trickle into her parched mouth. Though she wanted to gulp it down, she heeded Lem's advice. Her bonnet slid off her hair, and she welcomed the breeze on her face.

"Who do you reckon that is?" Lem stepped around the wagon, shaded his eyes, and squinted. A plume of dust followed a dark carriage.

Jane blinked. Heat made the landscape shimmer, and she wondered if she was seeing things. As the vehicle grew larger, sunlight glinted off glass. A carriage with glass windows? Out here?

Lem let out a chuckle. "Awful fancy rig. Somebody got lost. Must've made a wrong turn at Saint Louie." He took the jug from Jane and wet his handkerchief, swiping the damp cloth over his reddened face. "Looks like Harrison sees it, too."

Her husband was headed down the far hill, scythe over his shoulder. It almost appeared as if he and the carriage were on a collision course. She shook her aching head. The heat was making her giddy.

Blinking away odd, black spots on the edges of her vision, she took the jug from Lem, but it seemed too heavy for her leaden limbs, and she dropped it. "I'm shorry." She cleared her throat. "I'm sorry." But she made no move to pick up the container, and the water glugged onto the parched ground.

Hooves clattered, harness jingled, and a horse snorted. Jane took all this in, keeping her eyes closed against a wave of dizziness.

"That you Barton? Where's Harrison?" An imperious voice forced her eyelids open, and she stared into a face that seemed acutely familiar, though her mind didn't seem to be working well and she couldn't place him. "Is this her? The girl he married?"

The gray-haired man, immaculate in a dark suit, climbed from his coach. He pointed with his cane. "Where is that son of mine?"

"Mr. Garvey?" The name slipped out between her stiff lips, and she had just a glimpse of Harrison rounding the corner of the corral when the ground rushed up and smacked her in the head.

~

Harrison pulled his chair closer to Jane's bedside and bathed her face with a cool, damp cloth. When she'd fainted, he'd died about a hundred deaths, and his heart still *whumped* erratically. Fear stalked him, armed with spears and arrows of guilt.

This is your fault. How stupid could you be? You had no business letting her help with the haying.

"Where is that doctor?" His father smacked his cane-head into his palm.

"It's a long ride into Sagebrush, and the doc might've been out on his rounds." Harrison brushed baby-fine wisps of hair off Jane's temples. Her skin was so pale and clammy. "Thank you for sending Lem in your carriage."

His father waved aside the thanks. "How is she?"

"I don't know. I wish she'd wake up." He wrung out the cloth and placed it against her forehead. Hours had passed since Lem had pelted it to town, and she hadn't so much as flickered her eyelashes.

His father grunted and pursed his lips, making his mustache poke out. "This is utter nonsense. Look at this place." He waved toward the clay-plastered walls and canvas ceiling. "What kind of hole is this to live in? It's a wonder you aren't all sick in bed. I wish you'd listen to reason. And another thing. . ." He levered himself up from the table. Hampered by the small space, he could only pace two steps before having to turn around. "I don't like it that you've ignored my letters. I haven't heard from you in weeks, not since you told me you got married. What was I supposed to think? Regular communication, you promised. I don't like being ignored. Now I arrive to find you looking like a scarecrow, down to skin and bones, and that girl beyond the brink of collapse. And what for? Hardheaded mule."

"Not now. We'll talk about all that later." Harrison glanced out the open doorway at the gathering dusk. Pushing himself upright, he stretched his back and worked the kinks out of his shoulders, stiff from bending over the bed. Digging into the matchbox, he withdrew a match and scratched it on the heel of his boot. Raising the glass on the lantern, he touched the flame to the wick, inhaling the pungent kerosene-smoke smell. "I need to go take care of the stock. Will you sit with her?"

"Of course." His father leaned his cane against the table and took Harrison's chair. "I'll be right here."

Harrison headed toward the barn in the fading light. The cow had to be milked, the animals fed and watered, but the whole time he worked, his mind was back in the soddy. If Jane didn't recover, he would never get over his guilt. Driving her so hard. And for what? A few acres of land?

He knew a flash of anger. Why hadn't she told anyone she didn't feel well? Why had she pushed herself so hard? She'd promised to tell him if the work was too much for her.

His conscience shoved him. Hard. Jane wasn't to blame for this. It was his fault. And the minute she woke up, he was going to tell her so, beg her forgiveness, and make plans to return to Columbus. Life here was too difficult, even for his redoubtable Jane. His shoulders sagged, and he leaned against Buttercup's warm flank. Though he hated to admit defeat, he would, for Jane's sake.

At least his father would be pleased at getting his way.

He set the entire bucket of milk into the calf pen, not wanting to bother with straining and storing it. The calf could enjoy it instead.

Emerging from the barn, he drew in a deep breath, contemplating the faint stars emerging as the sunlight faded. He loved this ranch, this wide-open land, and it would be a wrench to lose it. But the truth was, he loved Jane more, and he would give it all up to have her love. He only hoped he got the chance to tell her.

Chapter 9

Why couldn't she seem to open her eyes? She frowned and tried again, this time rewarded by a sliver of lamplight before her heavy lids fell again. She ached. From the top of her head to the soles of her feet, everything hurt. And her brain felt as if someone had wrapped it in wool. She moistened her lips, or tried to, but her mouth was so dry she only snagged her tongue on her chapped lips.

What time was it? She needed to get up. She needed to get to work, to help Harrison keep his ranch, so maybe he would love her. Feebly, she tried to move aside the quilt, but firm, gentle hands stopped her.

"Here now. You need to lie still and rest."

A strange voice. With every ounce of energy, she forced her eyes to open, but they didn't seem to want to focus.

"Harrison?"

"He's gone to stretch his legs. We're waiting for the doctor, and Harrison's been glued to your side for hours. I thought he needed a break. He hasn't left you except to do the chores since you first passed out."

"Thirsty." A desert fire raged in her throat, rasping her voice.

Awkwardly, he held her head up a bit and pressed a tin cup of water to her lips. Thankfully, she gulped the refreshing liquid until no more remained.

"Is that sufficient?"

She nodded and closed her eyes, fatigue rolling over her in waves.

"What time is it?"

"About two in the morning. The physician should arrive any time."

"Who are you?" she whispered.

"I'm your father-in-law, Rutherford."

Jane bit her chapped lip but couldn't stem the rush of tears that leaked from her eyes. She hiccuped on a sob.

"Here now. Here. What's wrong? Are you in pain?"

"This is all my fault."

"You can't help being ill." He patted her hand, rough and tender at the same time, this man she'd labeled a dragon to be battled in the quest for Harrison's ranch and happiness.

His gentleness seemed to open the floodgates where she'd stored up so much fear and pain and sorrow. Tears ran into her hair, and she couldn't muster the strength to wipe them away, nor could she seem to stop them.

"Do you want me to fetch Harrison?" Rutherford pressed a handkerchief into her hand, his voice gruff.

She shook her head. "No, please." Here she was supposed to be helping Harrison reach his dream, proving to him that she was a good helpmeet, and look at her. A bedridden, sobbing mess, not only failing to help him but taking him away from his work all afternoon and evening to care for her. What kind of impression was she making on his father?

She pressed the handkerchief to her lips. "He must be so

disappointed in me." The words came out all broken, half-stifled. "I'll never earn his love now." Her heart cracked wide open.

"What kind of nonsense is this? Harrison isn't the least disappointed in you. That boy is besotted, judging from the letter he wrote me just after you married. He filled page after page about you. I couldn't have been more pleased. That's half the reason I came all this way. I wanted to meet the woman who could make my son wax lyrical."

She blinked, smearing tears with the back of her hand. "You're mixed up. He wouldn't wax lyrical about me. Sylvia Norwood maybe, but not Plain Jane."

"What's Sylvia got to do with anything? Proper little baggage. Everything has worked out perfectly. I couldn't have planned it better." He rubbed his hands on his knees, smiling like a cat with canary feathers decorating its whiskers. "I know my son better than he thinks I do."

"What do you mean?" The tears abated in the face of her curiosity. If only she had the strength to get out of bed, or even to lift her head off the pillow.

"My son is as stubborn as his father. I knew if I crammed Sylvia Norwood down his throat, she would be the last woman he'd marry. And I was right. Not only did he not marry Sylvia, he found himself a bride all on his own." Rutherford cackled and slapped his leg. "Yep, I know Harrison. I'm tickled to death he defied my wishes and came out here to make his own way. Seems to be a family tradition. I did the same with my father. Do you think he owned a factory? No he did not. He owned a fleet of barges on the Ohio River, and he expected me to take over for him, but I struck out on my own, built my own empire. And I wanted Harrison to do the same."

Trying to make sense of this incomprehensible man, she asked, "But what about the contract?"

"What good would it do him if he had it too easy? If he had too much money too soon, it would ruin him. He needed to fight, to prove to himself that he could do it, that he didn't need family money to reach his dreams."

His reasoning baffled her, but she was too tired to sort it out. Her eyelids fell, and she rushed toward sleep.

⁓

The doctor arrived just before dawn, yawning and blinking. Harrison greeted him at the door and brought him to Jane, who still slept soundly.

Rutherford jerked awake from dozing in a chair. He'd refused to go to the bunkhouse to sleep, though Harrison had encouraged him to.

"Tell me what happened." Dr. Iverson shrugged out of his jacket and rolled up his sleeves. "How long has she been asleep and what brought on her faint?"

His eyes were so piercing, Harrison was taken right back to his schoolboy days, caught in some prank or other. "She passed out yesterday just after noon. We were putting up hay, and I guess the heat got to her."

"She woke up a few hours ago, cried her eyes out, and fell asleep again." Rutherford rubbed his bristly cheek.

The doctor frowned. "All of you go out. I want to examine her."

Once on the other side of the door, Harrison couldn't stand still. He paced the grass, and while he paced, he prayed:

Lord, please let her be all right. I'll get her out of here as soon as possible, just let her wake up and be fine. I have so much I need to tell her.

Lem brought a pot of coffee and plate of biscuits from the bunkhouse.

"How is she doing?" The worry in the old man's eyes bespoke his affection for Jane. "It's my fault. I should've noticed she was ailing."

Harrison bit into a biscuit and grimaced. What had he made these out of? Damp wool and sawdust?

"She's still sleeping. Doc kicked us out so he could take a look at her."

After what seemed half of forever, the door finally opened. Doc stood there, wiping his hands on a towel.

Harrison wheeled. "How is she?" His heart acted like a jackrabbit with a coyote on its tail.

"You two need to talk. She'll tell you."

"She's awake?"

"She is. And my prescription is for the two of you to get things straightened out between you. She's got some odd notions that need disabusing. Beyond that, she needs bed rest and building up. She's underweight and overworked in addition to being overwrought. No more fieldwork and not much of any kind of work for at least a month."

"But she'll be fine?" He hardly dared hope.

"Eventually, if you go carefully." Dr. Iverson smiled. "What are you standing there for? She's waiting." He stepped aside and Harrison took a deep, steadying breath before entering the soddy.

༞

The time had come. Jane pushed herself up against the pillows, so weak her limbs shook. Harrison closed the door and leaned against it, crossing his arms. She needed to get in first, before he said anything.

"I'm sorry. The last thing in the world you needed was to be pulled away from your work to tend to me. And now you have the added expense of the doctor. I'm sure I'll be fine in a day or so." She swallowed, trying not to sound as pitiful as she felt. "This won't set you back from meeting the contract, will it?"

"I don't care about the contract. My father can have the place. I won't need it."

"What?"

Harrison left the door and came to her side, dropping to his knees and taking her hand. "Jane, I'm not keeping the ranch. That contract has done nothing but drive us apart. When you first came here, you were so happy, and you made me happy. You filled a place in my life and heart that I didn't even realize was empty. Then Lem told you about the contract and you changed. All that joy and hope disappeared." He lifted her hand and brushed a kiss across her fingers. "I want the old Jane back. The one I married. And I won't have her killing herself to help me get a ranch. It isn't worth it."

She stared at the quilt. Was he really willing to give everything up, everything he'd worked for, just for her? She raised her eyes to examine his face.

"Jane, darling, I love you. I think I've loved you from the minute you first set foot on this ranch. Look at this house." He swept his arm to encompass the small room. "You took a hovel and made it a home. You bring light and joy wherever you go. You're loving and giving, and so sweet it makes my chest hurt. My father said you called yourself Plain Jane."

He squeezed her fingers. "I don't ever want you to even think that again." His hand came up to touch her cheek. "You are the most beautiful woman I've ever met. I could willingly get lost in your beautiful eyes. I want to spend the rest of my life proving my love and earning yours."

Afraid to hope, yet unable to deny him, she leaned into his caress. "You love me? Me, Plai—" His hand stopped the words.

"I love you, beautiful, sweet, adorable, strong, amazing, Jane Garvey." Gently, but insistently, he gathered her into his arms. His lips found hers, giving and taking, healing and renewing. Love for him overwhelmed her. This was what she had waited for all her life. When he broke the kiss, she rested her cheek against his strong chest, thrilling to the erratic beating of his heart.

"Harrison, there are a few things you should know."

"What?" He brushed a kiss across her hair.

"I don't want you to give up the ranch. We've got so much invested here. All your dreams."

"Not all. My dreams are bound up in you now."

"Well then, my dreams are here. I want to stay. To see this through." She cupped his stubbly cheeks and stared into his eyes, willing him to understand how important this was to her. When he still seemed unconvinced, she said, "I want our baby to be born here, on his father's ranch."

His eyebrows rose. "Baby?"

She nodded, her throat too thick for words.

He exhaled on a half laugh, blinked, and shook his head. "You're sure?"

"Yes, the doctor confirmed it."

He was off the floor and resting beside her on the bed

before she could blink. His arm went around her, and he cradled her close. Reverently, he placed his hand on her abdomen and kissed her temple. "Ah, Jane, I didn't think I could love you more, but you're proving me wrong. I think I've been waiting for you my whole life."

She wrapped her arms around his neck and leaned into him. "Me, too."

⁓

When they broke the news to Rutherford, he couldn't stop grinning. "How about that? A grandchild. Your mother would be so proud if she could see you now." He tapped his fist against the edge of the table.

Jane sipped chicken broth from a cup, resigned after much haranguing and negotiation to being on bed rest for the next couple of weeks. Harrison hovered, anxious and loving by turns.

Rutherford dug inside his suit pocket and withdrew a long envelope. "This is yours, son. My gift to you and Jane. It's the deed to the ranch. Enough of this standoff. I'm tickled to death at the start you've made here. Now it's time to bury pride and be done with that foolish contract. I only cornered you into signing it because I knew you'd get your back up and determine to make good on it."

Harrison froze. "Are you serious?"

"Never more so. The place is yours. Though you can do me one more favor."

"What?"

"Get that house out of storage and get it built. I don't intend to sleep in a dirt house when I come to visit my grandchild. Jane,"—his eyes twinkled—"Harrison has been

179

too stubborn to accept my gift of a house, but I know you're smarter than he is, and you'll see reason. I'm giving you that house, and I'm trusting you to convince him to get it built before the snow flies."

She leaned her head against the pillows, tickled at the outraged expression on her husband's face that quickly turned to sheepish pleasure.

"I think I can manage that."

Late that night, cradled in her husband's arms, Jane sighed.

"What's that for?" Harrison smoothed her hair back from her face and brushed a kiss across her brow.

She savored the security of his embrace. "All my life I dreamed of a gallant knight who would come and sweep me off my feet, carry me away to his castle, and love and cherish me forever."

"Huh, too bad you got stuck with me."

She levered herself up to look down into his eyes in the glow of the lamplight. "How can you say that? You are a gallant knight. You brought me all the way to Wyoming Territory to your castle on the plains, made me fall in love with you, then made me the happiest woman alive by loving me back. You're a wonderful husband and provider, and you're going to be a wonderful father. What more could a woman ask?"

He caressed her cheek and let his hand drop to cup her shoulder through the thin lawn of her nightgown. "Jane Garvey, you're amazing. I knew it the first time I saw you, and you've been surprising me every day since. I can hardly wait to see what you'll do next. If I'm a knight, you're my lady." He brought her down for a gentle kiss.

She snuggled close, wrapping her arm across his flat stomach and pressing her swelling abdomen against his side. As her eyes drifted closed, she envisioned her knight holding a little lord or lady in his arm, his other encircling her waist, and a smile curved her lips. Her wait for love had finally come to an end.

SHINING
ARMOR

Chapter 1

Would her soon-to-be husband be a knight or a dragon? In just a few moments, she'd find out. A cluster of buildings in the distance grew larger, as did the ball of anxiety in her middle.

Gwendolyn Gerhard twisted a piece of string around her index finger, unwound it, and wound it again, all the while jolting and jostling in the wagon next to the crankiest preacher she'd ever encountered.

Reverend Cummings hunched over, his elbows on his knees, his face set in a scowl. Had he ever heard of the joy of the Lord? At least he wasn't talkative. Not that she would've minded getting a little information out of him, but every time he opened his mouth, crabbiness flowed out.

Her sister Emmeline rode in the wagon behind her, taking in everything about their surroundings. After Gwendolyn got married, Emmeline would have to go on alone to her own wedding without the benefit of any of her sisters in attendance. Though she didn't seem worried. Of all the Gerhard girls, Emmeline had most embraced the notion of coming west as a mail-order bride.

Gwendolyn wound the string again, noting the ridges it caused in her finger. The shock of leaving her two oldest sisters just moments after each of their weddings hadn't quite worn off. This morning when they set out from the town of Sagebrush in southeastern Wyoming Territory, they had all been single women. Now Evelyn and Jane were married, Evelyn had acquired a stepdaughter in addition to her son Jamie, and Jane was living in a dirt house.

That might've been me. After all, the selection of husbands had been a bit haphazard, with each sister picking a name from the list of four who had answered their advertisement. If she had chosen Gareth or Harrison instead of Zebulon, she might now be the mother to an angry young hellion of a girl or residing in a sod hut. According to Cranky Cummings, she was next on his mail-order-bride delivery route, and who knew what fate awaited her there? Of the four applicants, she knew the least about hers. Where her sisters had all received letters, she had only a telegram.

SENDING TRAIN AND STAGE FARE. STOP. COME AS SOON AS POSSIBLE. STOP. WARMLY, ZEBULON PARKER. STOP.

At least he'd included the word *warmly*. Not exactly a love letter to melt a girl's heart but better than nothing.

In spite of the shocks of reality, she couldn't quite bring herself to be downhearted. For the first time in her life, she felt as if the doors had flown wide open. Living with a widowed father and three older sisters was like having three mothers. One or all of them usually had some correction, suggestion, or instruction regarding her appearance, her posture, or almost anything else she could name. With Evelyn a Civil War widow, the house had been somber and structured most of the time. And her father, while giving them all a deep appreciation for medieval history and classical literature, had often been distant and distracted, living in some castle in Camelot in his head and only surfacing to the real world periodically.

Of course, Camelot was a fine place to escape to. How often had she dreamed of Sir Gawain or Lancelot riding to her rescue, scaling ramparts, slaying dragons, laying siege to her heart? A man who would want her for the rest of her life, who would offer love, laughter, and a life together?

She pressed her palm against her skirt pocket, crinkling the telegram. Being a mail-order bride had little to do with the romance of her girlish fantasies, yet she couldn't help hoping—dreaming—just a little, that she was traveling to meet her knight.

The buildings were growing uncomfortably and excitingly near. A lump lodged in her throat, and her heart beat double-time. Pressing her lips together, she tried to sort out the structures ahead. A barn, sheds, and outbuildings, and oh, praise be, a house.

A two-story, wooden clapboard house. She threw a quick glance over her shoulder at Emmeline, who grinned back. No soddy or log cabin for Gwendolyn. She'd have a proper house, with a wide porch that wrapped around two sides, glass windows, and gables. There were even saplings planted in the yard and a picket fence with a gate. Though the barn and outbuildings bore some signs of age, the house looked surprisingly new and well kept.

Several figures moved between and around the buildings. Which one was *him*? She swallowed. Soon, she'd meet her intended, her knight in shining armor. *Please, Lord, let him be a knight and not a dragon.*

Reverend Cummings pulled the wagon up in front of the house with a grunt. "Parker's place."

A long, sloping ramp led to the porch—the boards even newer than the house appeared to be, still yellow and filling the air with a sawdust-and-pine redolence. A hundred questions popped into Gwendolyn's head, colliding and bouncing off one another. She gathered her skirts and her courage and climbed from the wagon on the side away from the house. Emmeline joined her, clutching Gwendolyn's hand with chilly fingers. The wagon box was so high, they could barely see over it. Movement caught her eye. The men working near the barn and in the corral all headed their way.

Cummings rounded the back of the wagon and unpinned the tailgate, muttering and grumbling.

The men, six in all, approached and formed a half circle around the wagon, staring and shifting their weight. She searched each of the faces, praying for a glimpse of recognition, hoping she would know Zebulon Parker when she saw him. But though she surveyed each one carefully, nothing special happened, not on their faces or in her heart. They were just men.

Some looked away from her scrutiny, some reddened and shrugged, and one grinned and raked her with his gaze. Though handsome, with black hair and mustache and glinting green eyes, he wore an insolent expression that diminished his good looks. *Please, Lord, don't let this be him.*

She'd been saying a lot of "Please, Lords" over the past few weeks.

The screen door squeaked. A man's voice—she couldn't see him over the heads of the other men gathered around—

broke the silence. "What're you doing standing around? I'd think, heading out on the range like you are tomorrow, there'd be plenty to keep you boys busy."

The men parted, and Gwendolyn sucked in a breath.

Broad shoulders, lean hips, long legs, and brilliant eyes so blue they seemed to sparkle, even from this distance. She grabbed hold of the side of the wagon and peeked over the edge at him.

"Oh my," Emmeline whispered. "Do you think that's him?"

He strode across the porch, scorned the ramp, and leaped to the ground in a lithe movement. "Padre, what brings you out this way?"

Cummings dragged a trunk toward himself, cocked an eyebrow at the girls as if to ask "is this the right luggage?" and at their nod, hefted it from the wagon box. "I don't have time to palaver. I brung your bride. Let's get this wedding over and done with."

The blue-eyed man laughed and shoved his hat to the back of his head, revealing a forelock of reddish-brown hair. "Right. Tell me another while you're at it." His thumbs went into his belt loops. "Seriously, it's been awhile since you've been through. On your way to Dellsville? Need a place to stay, or are you going to try to make it before nightfall?"

"I *am* on my way to Dellsville. I don't need a place to stay, and I'm serious about the wedding." The trunk hit the dirt. "One of these two. Not sure which. You'll have to ask them which is which. Where's Zeb? He knows all about it."

"You can stop kidding around, Cummings. We're not much in the mood for it around here. I don't know anything about a bride, and you can't talk to Zeb. He isn't here."

Gwendolyn bit her bottom lip, gripping the side of the

wagon box until her hands ached. Obviously this young man couldn't be her intended. Odd that she should feel a little swoop of disappointment when she didn't even know the man. But where was Zebulon?

Grimness stole over the young man's face, and his voice lowered. "Zeb passed away two weeks ago."

This brought Cummings to a halt. His perpetual scowl deepened. "I hadn't heard." He adjusted his jacket and scratched his chin. "His heart?"

"We've known for a while that he could go at any time, but it's still a shock."

"Too bad, but the wedding can go on just the same."

The man's hand shot out in a throw-away gesture. "What wedding? Make sense, man."

The reverend motioned toward Gwendolyn and Emmeline. "Come around here. Which of you is supposed to marry a Parker?"

Emmeline's grip on Gwendolyn's arm made her fingers tingle, but Gwendolyn rounded the wagon. "I am." She hoped her voice didn't sound as small and bewildered as she felt. If it was true that her intended had passed away, where did that leave her? "Zebulon's dead? Are you sure?"

The tall young man's gaze raked her from bonnet to boots. "Don't you think I'd know if my own grandfather was dead?"

She flinched at his harsh tone and the cloud of grief in his eyes. "Of course. I'm so sorry for your loss—wait. Your grandfather?" Her voice squeaked. "Zebulon Parker is— I mean was—your grandfather?" Her mind cartwheeled.

"Just who are you, anyway?"

The reverend nudged the trunk out of his way and

reached for a valise. "This one yours, missy?" He hefted it. "Zeb asked me to wait around Sagebrush until these gals arrived. I watched Zeb send the telegram myself, six weeks ago. I thought he looked poorly then but figured he'd just had a hard winter. She's one of those mail-order brides, her and her sisters. Zeb fetched her out from back East. Massachusetts, I think it was."

The cowboy jammed his fists on his waist and widened his stance. "That's ridiculous. Granddad would never send away for a bride. What kind of hoax are you trying to pull, Cummings?"

"No hoax. Gareth Kittrick, Harrison Garvey, Zeb, and Joe Barrett all worked it out together. One bride apiece. All sisters."

His narrowed eyes angled toward Gwendolyn then back to the preacher. "We've been bitten by this particular bug before, remember? And we all lived to regret it, though some not as long as others."

"It's true as I'm standing here. Lightning don't strike twice. This one won't be like Edith. Let's get to the marrying."

"Maybe you didn't hear me, Reverend. There's no marrying, because there's no groom. Zeb's dead, remember? You can just take this"—he jerked his thumb toward Gwendolyn—"this woman back where she came from."

"Then you marry her. I'm due in Dellsville, and you ain't my last stop before then. Won't take but a few minutes to say the words, and I can be on my way."

The scowl on the young man's face could've started a fire. "Whatever scheme you and Granddad and this money-grubbing female have cooked up, count me out. I'd rather be shot like a rabid coyote than marry a mail-order bride, especially a gold digger who would come all this way to marry a man three times her age."

Gwendolyn blinked, her ire rising to replace her bewilderment. It appeared knights in shining armor were singularly lacking on the Wyoming plains. She marched over to him and poked him in his well-muscled chest. "Sir, I'll admit to being flummoxed at this turn of events, but at least I haven't resorted to wild accusations or name-calling. For your information, I wouldn't have you if you were hung from top to toe with diamonds."

Matt Parker couldn't have been more stunned if she'd walked up and slugged him. For such a dainty-looking female, she had some grit, standing up to him that way. He stepped back and resisted rubbing the spot where she'd jabbed him. "Fine then. We're agreed. Nobody's getting married here. You can put those things back in the wagon, Cummings. The lady isn't staying."

Reverend Cummings got an even more mulish set to his jaw. "She surely is. I told Zeb I would pick her up, deliver her here, and see to the ceremony. He promised her a wedding, and a wedding is just what we're going to have."

"But how? Thankfully, a dead man can't get married, no matter what promises he made or what plans this finagler dreamed up." Matt ignored the indignant gasp from the girl.

"Zeb might be dead, but you ain't. You can hold up your granddad's end of the bargain. And don't give me that look. You'll keep his word, because there's no other help for it. I can't take her on with me, so get that notion out of your head."

Stepping between them, the girl glared from Matt to the reverend. "I'm not staying." She pushed her bonnet back, revealing hair the color of ripe wheat that curled around her face and looked as if it wanted to romp free of the pins holding it high on the back of her head. When she turned the full force of her gaze on him, he couldn't help but notice the deep, purple-blue of her eyes, like the east sky just after sunset. "But I'll have you know, I came all the way from Massachusetts in good faith." She waved a piece of paper under his nose. "I have a telegram inviting me to come and asking me to hurry. I'm not in the habit of trapping men into marriages they don't want, nor am I after anyone's money. It's shameful of you to cast aspersions on my character when you don't even know me." She turned to the preacher. "Please return my things to the wagon."

Matt's men had stepped closer, eyebrows raised, smirking and elbowing one another. Having them witness this little set-to wouldn't do much for his authority around the place. "Don't you boys have something else you should be doing?"

"Nothing more interesting than this." Jackson tugged off his gloves and stuck them into his belt. "If you don't want her, boss, I'll have her. She's a looker. I wouldn't mind coming home to a pretty filly like her every night."

Matt scowled. "Watch your mouth, Jackson."

"Matt?"

The soft voice pulled his head around.

Betsy. He'd forgotten clean about her. "Be right there." Leaping to the porch, he held the screen door open. "Can you manage, or you want some help?"

"I've got it, I think." She wheeled herself through the

opening, clunking down over the threshold. "Whoa, a bit bumpy."

"I'll fix that for you as soon as I can." Why hadn't he thought to ease that threshold when he built the ramp the other day? He added that task to his already gargantuan to-do list. At least the chore would keep him close to the house. With Granddad gone and Betsy confined to this contraption, he couldn't stray far from home these days.

"I know, Matt. Don't worry so much. We're all adapting as fast as we can." Her sweet smile ripped through his gut. How could she be so calm, so brave and accepting? How could a barely fifteen-year-old girl be so mature? He wanted to yell, scream, kick something, demand God tell him why. Why would He afflict such a gentle creature as Betsy with a disease that robbed her slowly of even the ability to walk? Why had He taken Granddad so suddenly, just when Matt needed him the most?

"Matt?"

He shook his head, clearing his thoughts, and let go of the door. It slapped, bounced, and settled.

She maneuvered her chair awkwardly toward the ramp. "Oh, hello, Reverend Cummings. How are you? Is your lumbago better?" Just like her to ask after someone else's ailment instead of dwelling on her own. Cummings grunted and kept rootling around in the wagon.

Matt guided her chair down the ramp and along the path to the gate. "Betsy, are you sure you should be outside? You aren't supposed to tax yourself, remember?"

"Don't fuss. I'll be fine." She extended her hand to the two women. "Hello, I'm Betsy, Matt's sister."

Matt held his breath. Folks could be so cruel, assuming

just because someone was in a wheelchair, she must be an idiot who should be in an asylum. If this woman who claimed to be Granddad's bride so much as sneered, he'd pack her into Cummings's wagon like a bag of feed and send her on her way before she could say "rags to riches."

When she smiled with real friendliness at his sister, his breath snagged in his chest. In one thing at least, Jackson was right. She was a looker. But then again, Edith had been, too.

"How do you do? It's a pleasure to meet you. I'm Gwendolyn Gerhard." She took Betsy's hand. "I'm so sorry about your grandfather."

"I've been looking forward to meeting you." Betsy let her head rest against the wheelchair's high back. "I'm only sorry Granddad can't be here. I know he would've loved meeting you. He was really anticipating your arrival."

Matt rounded the chair. "What do you mean you've been looking forward to meeting her? You knew she was coming?"

Betsy swallowed and nodded. "Granddad told me he was sending for someone." She toyed with the end of her braid, the coppery-red hair gleaming in the sunshine. "He said not to mention it to you just yet, that he would do it when the time was right. I guess he didn't get around to it before. . ." She let her words trail away.

Matt ground his back teeth. So this was real and not a hoax. Cantankerous, foolish old man. "Just what was his game? Didn't he learn anything from Edith? Why would the old man want to get married again?"

A peal of laughter caused every head to turn Betsy's way. "You didn't think Granddad brought her out here to marry *him*?" Again she laughed, such a rare sound these days, he wanted to bottle it. "He brought her out here for you. Said you weren't getting around to the job quickly enough, that Edith had soured you on women, and he didn't like the way you were headed." She grasped Matt's hand. "You aren't going to send her away, are you?" Her eyes pleaded with him. "I've been holding on, just waiting for her to arrive."

He'd been hard pressed to ever deny Betsy anything, and now with her trapped in that chair for the rest of her life, he found it even more difficult. But marriage was asking a bit much of a man.

Cummings thumped one of the girl's bags onto the porch. "Now see here, Parker. I'm in a hurry. I can't take the girl with me. I've got to take her sister out to Barrett's range, and you know he can't board her there. And Dellsville is no place for a decent woman. I'm supposed to be preaching a funeral service the minute I can get there, and daylight's wasting. Let's get to the marrying."

"I am not marrying her."

Every head turned their way, and Matt realized he'd all but shouted the words. Diamond-hard light glared in Cummings's eyes, and Matt had a feeling fire and brimstone might pour out of his mouth at any second. Not too many men cared to defy Cummings, who—it was whispered— had been a companion of John Brown's and contributed personally to giving Bleeding Kansas its nickname.

Jackson left his place among the drovers and sidled toward the girls. Though a good cowhand, he had a well-earned reputation as a skirt chaser, and the sight of him ogling the sisters tightened Matt's muscles. He stepped between his hired hand and the women.

Cummings crossed his arms. "I can't take her on with me." Aware of the stares and anticipation hanging in the air, he found himself looking at the woman. Gwendolyn. What kind of an outlandish name was that? She clenched her fists and chewed her lower lip. She looked so vulnerable, standing in this circle of men like a filly being auctioned off.

"Reverend Cummings?" Betsy eased her chair forward. "When will you be coming back through this way?"

He scowled, his bushy eyebrows thrusting outward. "Six weeks, give or take. I have some business to transact over in Medicine Bow, and then I'll have to make my regular circuit. Why?"

"I thought, maybe, Gwendolyn could stay here until you come back. There's a spare bed in my room, and we could all get to know one another. Then, if it didn't work out for her to marry Matt, you could pick her up on your way back through here." Betsy lifted her face toward Matt, her eyes filled with appeal. "Please, Matt, can't she stay, at least for a little while? She would be company for me."

He found himself giving in, all the while deriding himself for being a fool.

Chapter 2

That's settled. I'll see you in six weeks or so to sort this whole thing out." Pointing to Emmeline, Reverend Cummings motioned toward the wagon seat. "We're squandering daylight, so no dillydallying."

Emmeline ignored the cleric grouch and gripped Gwendolyn's hands, drawing her away from the crowd. "Gwendolyn, what are you going to do? What happens in six weeks when the reverend returns? Where will you go?"

"I don't know." Her eyes stung, her windpipe constricted, and she clutched her elder sister's hands as if they were her only lifeline in a tossing sea. While she hadn't expected hearts and flowers, she certainly hadn't expected to be treated like a leper in the place that was supposed to be her new home. The Parkers acted as if she were goods received on approval. *We'll try her out for a few weeks, and if we don't like her—and I expect we won't—you can take her back where she came from.*

"Hurry up!" The reverend slammed the tailgate shut.

Emmeline hugged her tight. "You're the smartest one of us all. You'll think of something." Her whisper did little to bolster Gwendolyn's confidence, and within moments, she found herself watching her sister disappear with the preacher. Emmeline waved and looked back until dust and distance obscured her.

Blinking and swallowing against the lump in her throat, Gwendolyn reminded herself that she had vowed to embrace the adventure. The reminder didn't work, and a tear slipped over her lower lashes. She swiped at it, aware of the stares. Nobody seemed to know what to say or where to look now that a stranger had been tossed into their midst like a rock in a pond.

At last, Betsy broke the silence. "Matt, why don't you bring the luggage in, and we'll show Gwendolyn the house?"

Her words broke him free of whatever had him trapped… probably shock, if her own reaction was anything to judge by. "Good idea. You men, get back to work. Those chores aren't going to do themselves." He hoisted her trunk. Her valise sat beside the gate, but when she picked it up, Betsy reached for it.

"I'll help. Set it on my lap." She reached for the bag, laughing. "Really, I can do it." Plumping the carpetbag, which wasn't all that heavy, onto her knees, she grabbed the wheels on the chair.

Gwendolyn relaxed a bit at this show of friendliness and took hold of the handle across the back of the chair. "I tell you what, you carry, and I'll push."

Aware of Matt's scrutiny, she maneuvered the chair carefully up the ramp and into the house. She stopped just inside the door, stunned.

The front room was crammed with furniture, settees, chairs, tables, lamps. Rugs lay over the top of one another, and bric-a-brac crowded shelves and tables. Heavy drapes blocked out the sunshine, and from what she could tell in the low light, dust cloaked every surface.

A narrow aisle led between the furnishings, and Matt

stalked ahead, through a doorway in the far wall, refusing to offer any explanation as to the condition of the parlor. "This way."

Maneuvering the chair after him, Gwendolyn arrived at what she sensed was the hub of this home. Stark in comparison to the ornate parlor, the kitchen contained plain furnishings and an immense black stove. Dirty dishes sat on the table and counter. And a bare, glass-paned window let in light.

"We just finished lunch." Matt's defensive tone flicked her, but he continued. "Betsy isn't up to much housework, and I've been busy. I didn't exactly know we were going to have company." He trod heavily on the last word, emphasizing the temporariness of the situation. Her trunk landed with a thud on the floorboards. "You'll bunk with Betsy through here."

Gwendolyn shot Betsy a quick glance and was rewarded by a warm smile. Someone at least was glad she was here. Sharing a room with Betsy would be like sharing with Emmeline back home.

"You're going to love it here." Betsy gripped the valise handle. "When Granddad said he was sending for someone, I was so happy. I've always wanted a sister."

Matt stiffened. "Hold it right there, young lady. I am not getting married, so don't get any ideas. This is a mess of Granddad's making, and it's going to take some time to sort out, but six weeks from now when the reverend returns, you and I will be on the porch waving good-bye to this whole problem, understand? Anyway, you heard her. She wouldn't have me if I came dipped in diamonds."

Gwendolyn's ire flared. "Would you stop referring to me as a mess and a problem? It's not my fault your grandfather didn't explain things to you, or that he isn't here to do so now." She crossed the room and planted herself squarely in front of him. "If I had my druthers, I'd have been out of here so fast you wouldn't have seen me for dust." She snapped her fingers under his nose.

He blinked, taking a step back.

Betsy giggled. "You sound a little like Granddad standing up to Matt that way. I'm so glad you're here. Let's get your things put away, and don't mind him. He hates change of any kind, and things have been changing around here rather rapidly."

"I do not."

"Yes, you do."

He carried her trunk into the bedroom, and Betsy followed with the valise, both of them bickering in a way so familiar to Gwendolyn, a giant aching loneliness for her sisters swept over her. Though she chafed at her sisters' strictures, she missed them and would've given anything at that moment to have them here to boss her around.

"Are you coming?" Matt stuck his head through the doorway. She stopped woolgathering and entered the bedroom.

A chest of drawers stood between two iron bedsteads, though only one bed was made up. A china ewer and bowl painted with lavender flowers sat atop the dresser. A thin, limp set of curtains hung at the window. A feed store calendar adorned one wall, the only nonutilitarian object in the room. A chill went through Gwendolyn.

Matt slid the trunk toward the foot of the unmade bed. "Betsy can tell you where to find clean sheets and such, and you can unpack some things, but don't settle in too deep. As soon as I can make arrangements, I'll get you on your way back to where you came from." He took the valise from Betsy's lap and set it on top of the trunk.

Gwendolyn bit back the sharp reply that rose to her lips. He didn't have to keep reminding her that he planned to throw her out like used dishwater. "Very well."

"I'll help. It's going to be so nice to have another girl to talk to." Betsy noticed the ribbon holding her braid was coming loose, but when she tried to tie it, her fingers stumbled. Frowning, she tried again, but the shiny ribbon slipped from her grip. "Fiddlesticks, I'm all fumble-fingered today."

"Maybe she could leave the unpacking until later. You're tired." Matt stepped forward and tied the ribbon for her, his voice gruff. "You need to rest. You know the doctor said your symptoms get worse when you're tired."

Betsy submitted, and relief passed over Matt's face. He patted her shoulder awkwardly, and she smiled, covering his hand with her own for an instant. Gwendolyn tugged her bottom lip as she left them alone and returned to the kitchen.

A man like Matt, capable of such tenderness toward his sister, would make someone a wonderful husband. He clearly cared about Betsy, was protective of her. Somewhere under that gruff, contrary, dragonish exterior, there might be a knight in shining armor with a chivalrous heart.

But how did one go about exposing it?

❧

Matt lifted his sister from her chair and eased her down on top of the covers. "You take a good nap." He brushed the red curls on her forehead. "I'll be close by when you wake up."

Betsy grabbed his hand. "Matt, she's nice, isn't she? And pretty. Did you see the way she took my hand and looked right into my eyes? Like I was a real person."

"You *are* a real person, and I'll clobber anyone who says different." He gave a mock growl, but he knew just what she meant. How many times over the years had people's eyes just slid right over Betsy? First the leg braces and canes, and now the wheelchair. Even the ranch hands were uncomfortable around her, not knowing what to say or do.

In that, at least, he couldn't fault their visitor. She'd certainly spoken to Betsy with more friendliness than she'd directed his way. Not that he could blame her. He hadn't been exactly cordial himself.

"It's been a long time since I had a girl to talk to." Betsy sighed, her eyes beginning to drift shut. "I really couldn't talk to Edith. She acted as if I wasn't even there." Her words slowed as she fell asleep.

Maybe, for the time being, having Gwendolyn here wouldn't be all that bad, not if she could bring a little happiness into Betsy's life.

He shook his head and left the room, easing the door almost closed so he could still hear if she called out. One glance into the crowded parlor brought him back to reality. No way was he going to be made a fool of. Women like Edith and Gwendolyn were only after one thing by marrying a man they didn't even know, and if that little miss thought she was going to sink her claws into him the way Edith had done to his father, she had another think coming.

When he returned to the kitchen, he stopped in the doorway. Gwendolyn stood at the dishpan, up to her elbows in soapy water.

"What are you doing?"

She glanced over her shoulder. "Is that rhetorical, or have

you never seen anyone wash dishes before?"

Leaning against the doorframe, he crossed his arms. "Got a little vinegar to you, don't you? And quite a vocabulary. You don't look old enough to have been a schoolteacher." He didn't know why he felt compelled to taunt her, unless it was to show her he wasn't fooled by her pretty ways and willingness to help out. Edith had been a new broom that swept clean, too. Before the rot set in.

"A schoolmaster's daughter." Cups sloshed through the soap and into the rinse water.

"And what does he think of you moving out here to marry an old man?"

"Like your grandfather, my father is dead, and fairly recently, too. That's why I, along with my sisters, was forced to advertise for a husband. We were being evicted from our home in Massachusetts at the boarding school where my father taught. I didn't know Zebulon Parker was a grandfather. I didn't know anything about him except that he lived in Wyoming Territory and was—I thought—looking for a wife. There wasn't time to learn anything else about him. We had no other options open to us. His telegram and the letters from the other three men were godsends, or so we thought."

He didn't miss the wry twist to her voice, but he wasn't going to rise to the bait. He wasn't anyone's godsend, thank you very much, nor did he want to be. "You didn't ask any questions or try to find out anything about the man you thought you were going to marry? No exchange of photographs, no letters. Not even an inquiry into his financial situation? You might've been jumping out of the frying pan and into the fire." Nobody would be that naive.

Surely she'd probed Granddad's prospects before agreeing to marry him.

"My correspondence with your grandfather was by telegram only, and long telegrams cost more than I had to spend. I assumed that if he had the money to pay for my train fare, he couldn't be on his beam ends, and if he was a friend to the other gentlemen who wrote to my sisters, he must be all right. All we asked was that the gentlemen be God-fearing and live close together. Reverend Cummings assured us of the God-fearing part, though we're coming to realize a bit too late that our interpretation of close together doesn't exactly match those of the ranchers out here."

He marveled that she didn't even try to hide her penniless state. Well, she wasn't going to get her hands on any Parker money, no matter what Granddad might've promised her. He glanced over his shoulder toward Betsy's bedroom door. His sister had taken an immediate shine to Gwendolyn, something she didn't normally do. Of course, she didn't have much of a chance to meet folks out here.

"I appreciate the way you've treated Betsy, but I've cautioned her, and I'll caution you again. You're not staying. Don't encourage any of her fancies. She's got a head full of romantic notions, and I don't want to see her get hurt."

Her hands stilled, and her shoulders drooped. Guilt at his harshness plucked his conscience. She had to be boneweary, coming all the way from Massachusetts to Sagebrush, bumping across the prairie in Cummings's wagon since before daybreak, and then landing in the middle of the Parker woes where all her plans had burned to cinders.

Before he did something stupid like apologize for telling the truth, he wheeled and headed up the narrow stairway to the top floor. He braced himself before the door to the bedroom across the hall from his. This room, like the parlor, went unused, tainted by the memory of Edith. He thrust those thoughts aside and entered. Her stamp was everywhere in the ornate furnishings. A four-poster bed with velvet drapes, dressing table, fly-spotted and dusty mirror, rugs—he should've tossed out the lot when Edith scarpered.

Ignoring the oppressive, cloying feel of the room, he crossed the carpet and pulled open the wardrobe. A set of plain sheets lay on the top shelf, but he pushed them aside and withdrew the set of bed linens farther back. Fine, expensive, snowy material with fancy stitching on the pillow slips. He might not've given her the warmest of welcomes, and he might have no intentions of letting her stay, but the Parkers could show a bit of hospitality to the stranger in their midst.

He returned to the kitchen where she had finished washing the dishes and now leaned over the table, wiping it down. The nape of her neck caught his eye, vulnerable, soft, with wisps of golden hair teasing it. He swallowed. She'd removed her jacket, and to his way of thinking, her blouse fit her just fine. She straightened, and he wrenched his gaze away, chagrined to be caught staring.

"You can make up your bed with these." He held out the bundle of bedclothes. "I'd best go see about fixing that threshold." Thrusting the sheets at her, he stalked out the back door toward the barn. What on earth had come over him? He was acting as if he'd never seen a pretty girl before.

Chapter 3

S o legend has it that's why the Knights of the Round
Table wear green sashes, in honor of Sir Gawain's
adventure with the Green Knight." Gwendolyn finished buttoning up Betsy's shoes for her and pushed herself
up from the kitchen floor. Betsy insisted on doing as much
as possible for herself, but this morning the buttonhook had
refused to cooperate.

"That's the most wonderful story. How do you know all
these tales?" Betsy brushed her hair, slowly separating it into
three hanks to braid.

"I've heard them for as long as I can remember. Tales
of Guinevere, Arthur, Lancelot, St. George. Father was a
medieval scholar and professor, and my sisters and I just
mopped it up." She quickly made Betsy's bed and straightened
up the room for the day. "I used to dream of a knight coming to my rescue, saving me from the dragons and declaring
upon his sacred honor his everlasting devotion to me." She
laced her fingers under her chin and batted her eyes.

Betsy snickered. "Can you imagine Matt clanking around
the ranch in a suit of armor?"

Gwendolyn grimaced and shook her head. She affected
a gruff, deep voice, one hand on her hip, the other pointing

at the window. "Hark, fair maiden, hast thou not been forbidden to settle thyself in at this castle? What is this I espy? Draperies?"

More laughter from Betsy as they relived the moment yesterday morning when Matt had caught them hemming pretty yellow fabric to adorn the kitchen panes. The fuss he'd kicked up over something so innocuous had baffled both the girls, but Betsy had declared the whole enterprise her idea, and he'd collapsed his protests like a stepped-on bellows.

"What is going on in here?" Matt eased the half-open door aside.

Gwendolyn jerked around, lost her balance, and grabbed for a chair back to steady herself. How much had he heard? She fought to keep her color down.

Betsy covered her mouth, but helpless giggles escaped. Matt's cheeks creased in a rare smile, and he laughed. The rich, mellow sound did strange things to Gwendolyn's insides, and she forced herself upright, smoothing her skirts and hair. He tugged on Betsy's newly-fashioned braid. "It feels good to hear you laugh again, Bets. What's so funny?"

"Gwendolyn." Betsy's shoulders quivered, light dancing in her brown eyes.

"We were just talking." Gwendolyn hustled to the stove, chagrined to be caught giggling like a schoolgirl. "I'll have breakfast ready in two shakes."

A breeze fluttered the curtains at the kitchen window, but she hid her grin. He really had been grumpy about them. But what harm could it do? Aside from that chock a block full parlor, the other rooms in the house were rather stark and uninviting. Surely a few womanly touches wouldn't hurt anything.

Matt washed up and sat down at the head of the table. Gwendolyn turned the bacon and cracked a couple more eggs into the skillet. The warm, inviting smell of biscuits curled through the room when she opened the oven door. Neither Matt nor Betsy had complained that she had taken over the meals, and Betsy tried to help as much as she could.

"Ah, perfect." She whipped the biscuits onto a platter and set them on the table then slid the eggs and bacon onto plates before placing them in front of Matt and his sister. She took her own chair and bowed her head.

Matt offered his hands to each of them and bowed his head. A flutter started just under Gwendolyn's heart, the same way it did every time they happened to touch, and she chided herself to keep her mind on the blessing.

His simple prayer of thanks warmed her as it always did. There was something so straightforward about Matt. Hard-headed, but straightforward. He hadn't budged on the idea of her staying, but at least he no longer looked at her as if she might steal his wallet.

As he tucked into his food, she observed him from under her lashes. Square jaw, straight nose, and that thick, slightly wavy reddish hair that just begged her to touch it. His muscles moved under his worn, blue shirt when he reached for the jar of honey, and a light dusting of ruddy hairs sprinkled his forearms and the backs of his strong hands.

His lips, which could be hard and uncompromising one moment and soft and smiling the next, drew her attention. Then there were his eyes. The same shape as Betsy's. Brilliant blue and slanted a bit at the corners, often filled with care or concern when he looked at his sister and consternation or confusion when he looked at her.

What would it be like to have him look at her with tenderness, or even just friendliness?

"Do I have dirt on my face?" He sat back and rested his knife and fork on the edge of his plate.

She blinked and looked away. "Um, no. I'm sorry. My thoughts were wandering." And into a region she should keep them well away from. "What are your plans for the day?" She helped herself to another biscuit, though she hadn't finished the first—anything to cover up being caught staring like an infatuated twit.

"I thought I'd slap another coat of paint on that fence today." He resumed his breakfast.

Betsy, who had been quietly pushing her food around on her plate, frowned. "Isn't it about time for the spring roundup? Shouldn't you be out on a horse somewhere?"

He shrugged. "The boys are handling it. They rode out a couple of days ago."

Her brow scrunched farther. "This is because of me, isn't it? You're staying here because you're afraid to leave me now that I'm stuck in this chair and Granddad isn't here. You should've gone with the men. You always go on the roundup." Tears filled Betsy's eyes, a surprise to Gwendolyn, for she had a feeling Betsy fought hard to always be cheerful and staunch. "I don't want to be a burden to you, Matt. You have a ranch to run, and you can't do it from inside this house."

"You aren't a burden, so get that notion right out of your head. I've got plenty of work to keep me busy around the ranch, and I have a whole crew of men to help me do it. I just feel like painting today, that's all." Matt frowned.

Betsy sat back, letting her fork clatter to her plate. "Matthew Parker, you're lying. You hate that picket fence.

When Edith insisted on it, you called it the most nonsensical contraption ever to hit Wyoming Territory. 'A maintenance headache that serves no useful purpose.'" She tugged a handkerchief from her sleeve and dabbed her eyes, her lip quivering. "And you're lying when you say I'm not a burden. I can't even button my own shoes." Tossing the handkerchief into her lap, she backed her chair up and turned, bumping into the table leg and rattling the dishes before rolling toward her room.

Matt shoved back his chair to go after her, but Gwendolyn touched his arm. "Leave her be."

His shoulders slumped. "What did I say? She was so happy just awhile ago, giggling and laughing with you. Now she's crying. Betsy never cries."

Gwendolyn tugged on her lip, unsure how far to go. "I don't know her as well as you do, but I suspect she might cry more often than you think; she just doesn't want you to know it. She would rather stifle her feelings than ever cause you hurt. I suspect she's already regretting tearing up in front of you."

"She's not a burden." He sat back, an indignant scowl creasing his brow.

"Well, she is and she isn't." She rose to clear the table. Clearly they'd all lost their appetites. "It's true there are plenty of things she can't do for herself, and it's also true that because you love her, you don't consider doing things for her a hardship. From the little bit Betsy has told me, her illness has been advancing gradually for the past several years?"

He relaxed a little and leaned forward, turning his coffee cup in circles on the tabletop. "It started a few years back as a bit of weakness, then numbness, and now she can't feel much of anything in her lower limbs. The sickness is affecting other places, too. Her fingers won't always do what she tells them to. At first, she could get around with a cane, and she still went to school, but as things got worse, the doc switched her to leg braces and crutches. Just a couple of weeks ago, the day before Granddad passed away, in fact, she had to go into the chair. We knew it was coming, but that didn't make it any easier. Then Granddad died, and since then, I've been afraid to leave her. I've been working around the house so I can keep an eye on her, and I'm doing all I can to make things easier for her."

"Like building the ramp?"

"Yes, and moving her clothes out of the top drawers in her dresser and putting her brushes and fripperies on that low table in her room so she can reach them. I just wish there was more I could do."

"I know."

"No offense, but how could you possibly know what it's like?" He raised one eyebrow, drained his coffee cup as he stared at her over the rim. Scraping back his chair, he rose and brought his dishes to the dishpan.

She shaved some soap chips into the pan and lifted the kettle from the stove. "My father had something similar, though not until much later in his life. He was in a wheelchair for the last five years, since I was about Betsy's age. I'm just glad the school kept him on. So often people seem to think if someone can't use their legs, they can't use their brain either. They get cast aside or relegated to the poorhouse. I'm thankful that didn't happen to him and he was able to keep teaching right up until the day he died. His work was his life."

A few lines in Matt's forehead cleared. "So that's why you were so natural around Betsy right from the start. I guess I don't need to tell you how cruel folks can be, just through pure ignorance sometimes. Last time I took Betsy to town, I promised myself I'd never do it again. Several folks said right out in front of her that I should send her to an institution back east." His lips hardened.

He stood so near, her concentration wavered. The care of an invalid was a huge burden to shoulder alone. She had shared the task with three sisters, and it hadn't been easy. His troubled eyes scanned the horizon through the curtained window, and his compassion for his sister touched her heart and gave her courage.

"Matt, Betsy is right in one respect. You do have a ranch to run, and if you neglect it to care for her, she's going to feel terrible, not to mention see right through your feeble smoke screen." She smiled. "That picket fence is already whiter than a summer cloud. It needs a new coat of paint like the sky needs more blue."

"I know, but what can I do?" He shrugged. "She needs me." Sinking onto his chair once more, he rested his forehead in his palms. His plight and his posture made her offer easier to voice.

"Of course she needs you, but what about me? I can take care of her while you're working. I've had plenty of practice, and even though you harbor doubts as to my motives in coming out here, I promise you I'd never do anything to hurt Betsy."

He appeared to wrestle with her words, his shoulders stiffening and his back straightening. "I don't have any right to ask it of you. It's not as if we were married or anything."

That reminder stung, but she forged on. "You're not asking for anything. I'm offering."

For a long moment, he studied his hands, and she was afraid he would refuse her, but then his muscles slackened and he sat back.

"It surely would take a load off my mind." He raised his head and smiled at her for the first time, his eyes captivating her. "I could pack and head for the cow camp today. And Pete and Mike would be here if you got into trouble. They stayed behind to take care of the livestock and chores." She could see his mind was already racing with things he needed to do, but then he stopped. "You're sure? I don't have to go. And roundup lasts for at least two weeks, but closer to three. That's a long time. Maybe I should just ride out there and check on them and come right back."

"Nonsense. You need to be where the work is, and Betsy and I will be fine. As you say, there are two ranch hands here if we need anything, and it's only for a couple of weeks."

"This sure would help me out of a bind."

She grinned, warmed through to be able to help him. "Then it's decided."

He headed toward the back door, plucking his hat off the peg beside it. He halted with the door half-open, tilted his head, and regarded her. "I appreciate the help, but it doesn't change anything. This is only a temporary situation, until roundup is over. Then I'll see to getting you a return ticket back east."

Gwendolyn ground her teeth and considered hurling the wet dishrag at his retreating back. Stubborn man. She was foolish to entertain any hope he might come to care for her and want her to stay.

‿

Matt joined his crew at the cow camp, fitting himself into the roundup with the experience gained from punching cows since his early teens, first in Texas and then in Wyoming Territory. Cattle bawled and churned the dust, men shouted, dogs barked, the smells of smoke and burnt hair filled the air. After being chained to the house for so long, he relished the labor, the wide-open skies, and the camaraderie of the cowboys.

By nightfall, every muscle ached, but it was a good ache. The calf tally looked promising so far, and his skill with his rope had not gone unnoticed by his crew. Not even Jackson could beat him when it came to throwing a loop.

In spite of how well things had gone today, an unnamed guilt sat heavily on his shoulders. As he waited for supper to be ready, he unrolled his bedding and sat down to sort it out. Snatching up a stem of wheatgrass, he broke off little pieces to aid his thinking. Being back at work felt good, and yet, as he thought about it, the guilt stemmed from those feelings and got all mashed up with thoughts of Betsy. It wasn't fair that he could ride away from the house, rope, flank, and flop calves all day, walk his own land if he so chose, while Betsy was bound in that chair, her world hemmed by a picket fence and her body wasting away before an ever-advancing illness. How soon before the sickness forced her into a bed and finally took her very life? His gut twisted at the thought. He'd already lost so much—his mother when Betsy was born, his father when Edith exploded all their lives, and Granddad just over a fortnight ago. When God took Betsy, who would he have left of his own?

Which thought sent his mind racing to Gwendolyn. Was he right to leave her in charge of his precious little sister? What did he really know about her? Heart-joltingly pretty for sure. She admitted she had no money, that she had nowhere to go.

All courtesy of Granddad. It was just like the autocratic, bossy old man to try to maneuver Matt into getting married. He'd certainly harped on it often enough, but Matt had resisted, not willing to put his neck into that noose. Edith had sickened him on the idea of marriage, especially to a high-stepping easterner.

But Betsy really liked Gwendolyn, which made him even more wary. This was a temporary situation. When Gwendolyn went back east, it might break Betsy's heart. And how could he be a party to that?

"Vittles!" The cook, a Russian, pronounced it "wittles" and clanged on an empty pot. Cowboys scrambled to grab tin plates and get in line for their chuck. Matt held back, waiting his turn. As the men squatted with their full plates, he took his own serving from the cook.

Jackson lounged on his bedroll near Matt, scooping the beans and bacon into his mouth. "Surprised to see you out here, boss. Thought you'd be at home with that pretty gal." He gave a knowing leer, and several of the younger men chuckled and elbowed one another. "She as nice as she looks? Nice for you to be holed up in that house with just a kid sister to chaperone."

Matt lowered his fork and studied Jackson. "What I do isn't any concern of yours, Jackson. Miss Gerhard is our temporary guest, that's all."

Shrugging, Jackson took another bite. "Still, she's mighty

pretty. A fellow could hardly be faulted for making the most of the situation. I know I wouldn't mind letting her warm up my bedroll, even if it was only for a little while."

Matt's jaw tightened, and his fingers gripped his fork so hard the skin showed white over the knuckles. A stillness passed over the group, as if everyone held their breath, waiting to see what his reaction would be.

Jackson seemed to pick up on the fact that he might've gone too far and shrugged. "Well, you know what I mean. No offense or anything."

Before Matt could answer, the cook lifted the lid on one of the pots.

"Sucamagrowl's done. Bring your plates."

Again a scramble for this camp delicacy. Sugary, vinegary aromas mingled in the air as the ranch hands held out their plates for the sweet dumplings—a rare treat, and one that Jackson hustled to get in line for. Matt forced his muscles to relax, grateful for the distraction, and took the chance to confer with the foreman, Melton.

"The cattle look to be in good shape."

Melton—whether this was his first name or last name, Matt didn't know and had never felt comfortable asking—nodded, his primary form of communication. The toothpick he kept permanently clamped in the corner of his mouth twitched a fraction.

"How're the men working together? The new men fitting in all right?"

Another nod. Granddad, a talker if there ever had been one, had questioned Matt's choice of ranch foreman on several occasions for his lack of conversational skills, but not even Granddad could fault the man's cow sense. Or his ability to get the most out of a crew.

"Walk?" The foreman discarded his toothpick and dug another from his pocket.

"Sure." They rose and headed for the rope corral, where their mounts grazed.

When they were well out of earshot of the men, Melton stopped and looked at the night sky, breathing in as if testing the weather. A horse stamped and swished his tail, his teeth ripping through the grass.

"That yellow-haired gal, she taking care of the little girl?" Concern colored his question.

Matt went still. Melton had never given the slightest indication that he even knew Betsy existed, much less asked after her health. "That's right."

"Good idea. Good you're back to work. Best if the men see you leading from the front." The toothpick switched sides. "Men haven't talked of much else besides that gal. Taken with her, especially Jackson."

It was the longest speech Matt had ever heard Melton make. While he loathed the men's curiosity, he couldn't really blame them for wondering. It wasn't exactly a usual situation. "She's pretty enough, I guess." Though *pretty* seemed a weak word to describe her.

"She after money?"

"She's made no bones about the fact that she's broke." The willing way Gwendolyn had pitched in around the house and the easy manner she had with Betsy had distracted Matt from the crux of the issue, but Melton's question brought it home again. Edith had made them all gun-shy, and with good reason. "I'll send her on her way as soon as I can."

"What about your sister?"

Matt rubbed the back of his neck. "I don't know. I'll have to think of something. Betsy can't stay alone. It was all right when Granddad was here." A fresh pang of grief seared his chest. "I miss the old codger."

"Natural."

"We fought hammer and tongs every day of my life. He could get under my skin worse than a cactus spine. Stubborn, bossy, hardheaded. His passing leaves a big hole, you know?" He shoved his hands into his pockets. "I feel stuck, no matter which way I turn."

For a long time, they stood looking at the stars, listening to the horses cropping grass and the lowing of cattle as they bedded down for the night.

Finally, Melton stirred himself. "Man has to be careful around women. Be they stepmothers, sisters, or wives." He strode away into the darkness, but his brief words lingered in the night air, a reminder and a warning. Matt shouldn't let his head be turned, or he'd find himself in a pickle.

Chapter 4

Gwendolyn tightened the kerchief covering her hair and handed Betsy a cloth. "If ever a room needed some attention, this parlor takes the prize." She swiped her finger through a layer of dust. "You're sure Matt won't mind?"

"If he does, I'll take the blame. Matt never talks about this room, and he mostly avoids it, uses the back door. But this parlor is hideous and a reminder of a time we'd all like to forget. Nobody's touched anything in here in almost a year. The sooner it's cleaned out, the better, to my way of thinking."

Both Matt and Betsy had alluded to past trouble, but how it connected to this overstuffed room remained a mystery. Gwendolyn didn't want to pry, especially since Matt had made it clear that hers was a temporary stay, but curiosity as to how an ostentatious parlor had come to be in a simple ranch home this far from civilization nagged at her.

She threaded her way to the front windows and pulled aside the heavy drapes, coughing and waving her hand in front of her face when a cloud of dust erupted from the velvet folds. Turning, she examined the room in better light.

"We need to remove at least half of this furniture, and the rest needs to be arranged so you can maneuver. A garter snake couldn't edge his way through here without bumping into something."

Betsy dusted figurines and china pieces while Gwendolyn shoved tables out of the way, rolled up rugs, and planned the new arrangement. "Any idea where we can put the extra furniture?"

"There's a storage area under the eaves. Pete and Mike will carry things upstairs for us."

"Perfect. Let's figure out what stays and what goes, so they can move it all at once."

Hours later, the girls surveyed the results. Though the front porch shaded the windows from the bright glare outside, enough light came in to glint off the newly polished surfaces. More than half the furniture had been relegated to the attic, and Gwendolyn had placed what remained into an inviting arrangement that left plenty of room for Betsy's chair.

"There. That's a good job done. It will be so much easier to care for, and you can be comfortable in here." Wiping her hands on her apron, she glanced at Betsy, noting her pale face and the way she rested her head against the chair back. "I'm tuckered out. We deserve a rest."

Betsy lifted her head and tried to appear less tired. "You're the one who did all the work. I just dusted a little. How about if we sit on the porch for a while?"

Gwendolyn fetched shawls for them both and a lap rug for Betsy, since the spring wind was still a bit fresh. Easing herself into the rocker beside the wheelchair, she tugged the kerchief from her head.

"You have beautiful hair. I wish I had golden curls." Betsy flicked her braid. "Better than this old carroty color."

"How can you say that? You have lovely hair. It glows like burnished copper." Gwendolyn fingered the end of Betsy's braid where it lay on her shoulder. "Two of my sisters have yellow hair like me, though mine's the curliest. Jane's hair is a soft, smooth brown that shines like silk. I always wanted raven-black hair or glorious red like yours. I guess we always want what we don't have."

"You must miss your sisters."

The ache that was never far below the surface rose afresh. "I do. We all thought we'd live closer together and be able to see one another often, but we didn't count on the distances out here. I can't help but wonder how they're getting along with their new husbands." At least they all had husbands. Neither Gareth nor Harrison had shouted in front of everyone that they weren't getting married, or that they would ship their mail-order bride off at the first possible moment. She crossed the ends of her shawl over her chest. "But having you here makes everything so much easier. I don't know what I would've done otherwise. I'm used to having someone to talk to. If you weren't here, I guess I'd just have to talk to myself." She laughed.

Betsy's eyes, so like her brother's, sobered. "I wish Matt wasn't so stubborn about you staying. I can't tell you how much better things are with you here. I feel like we've known each other forever."

Gwendolyn reached over and squeezed Betsy's hand. "I feel the same way."

"Then we should figure out a way that you can stay. You do like Matt, don't you?"

She did. And if she was honest with herself, she could easily come to love him, stubbornness and all. He had proven he could be caring and chivalrous, and he was a good provider. He put the needs of others ahead of himself. As if all these qualities weren't enough, just the sight of his handsome face and physique was enough to give her heart palpitations.

"I like him. And I'd like to stay." She recognized the longing in her voice, the unspoken desire to be Matt's wife and not just his temporary guest cum housekeeper. How had it happened so quickly? She was wise enough to know she had been ripe to fall in love, but the fact that it was actually happening and she couldn't seem to stop it surprised her.

"Then we have to get Matt to change his mind. He needs someone like you. He just doesn't know it yet. Granddad would've liked you, too. And you'd have liked him. He and Matt were very alike. So alike that they fought over just about everything. But that never bothered me, because I knew they each cared for the other one so much. They'd start out discussing something, and before you knew it they were pacing and jabbing the air, and then they'd start yelling. Finally, one or the other would throw up his hands and walk away." She chuckled. "That famous redheaded temper, I guess. But under it all, they loved each other, and they would work it out eventually. I know Matt's grieving something terrible. He thinks he's hiding it from me, but I can tell it hurts. I don't think he's ever really gotten over Father's death, especially since they were on the outs when he died."

Gwendolyn turned her face into the quartering breeze and let it blow the hair back from her temples. Her father's passing was recent enough to still ache. "Sometimes grief is so personal and deep, you can't share it. Everybody grieves differently. My sister Emmeline couldn't keep her sorrow at my father's death bottled up. She had to talk about it, to cry and grieve aloud. When she asked why I didn't cry, she quoted Shakespeare: 'Give sorrow words. The grief that does not speak whispers the o'er-fraught heart, and bids it break.' But I couldn't talk about it. Sometimes sorrow is too deep to express, especially when it is new. Perhaps that's why Matt doesn't give voice to his grief."

Betsy nodded. "See, you understand him so well already. Surely there must be some way to convince him to let you stay." She fisted her hands, resting them on her frail legs.

"If he's as stubborn as you say he is, I don't see how we can change his mind."

"We're two fairly smart women, aren't we? Between the two of us, we'll figure it out." The girl smiled. "Now that I have a sister, I don't intend to let you go."

Matt rode toward the ranch, weary but content. After seventeen days of hard work, the new Circle P calves were all branded, the herd tallied, and the crew worn out. He rubbed his rough chin, conscious of his cow camp dishevelment.

He shrugged and grimaced. Nothing a bath, shave, and clean clothes wouldn't fix. Why should he care how he looked? He'd never cared before.

"Sure will be nice to have a bed instead of a bedroll." Jackson rode beside him. "And the sight of some feminine beauty would sure be nice. You must be eager to get home."

Weary of Jackson's digs, Matt legged his horse into a canter. Though after the first night in camp Jackson had minded his words to keep them just this side of insolent, he still managed to reference Gwendolyn at least once a day.

Not that Matt's mind wasn't already centered on her

most of the time. He couldn't believe how often she traipsed through his thoughts, how often he wondered what she was doing or how she was caring for Betsy, and what sort of financial compensation he would have to offer her. At the very least, he owed it to her to pay her passage back east, and she deserved something for her trouble and the way she'd pitched in to help him out of a bind.

And yet, the idea of her departure brought him no joy. Not like he'd anticipated. And more than once, he found his thoughts straying to the mind-boggling notion of what it might be like if she actually stayed. Not for himself, of course. Only to help out Betsy.

At least having Gwendolyn to think about managed to distract him from some of his grief and kept him from brooding on Granddad's death.

The house and barn came into view, and his horse picked up the pace of its own accord. Matt's heart picked up the pace, too. A smile tugged his lips, and instead of riding to the barn, he headed straight for the house.

Tying the reins to the picket fence with a quick jerk, he opened the gate and started up the path. With the warmup to the weather, he wasn't surprised to see the windows open to catch the breeze, but he'd have to be extra quiet if he wanted to surprise them. A thump and giggle reached him.

"Good thing the picture will cover that mark. You can't hammer a nail worth anything." Betsy's laugh wrapped around him. He'd missed his little sister something fierce, worried about her the whole roundup, but she sounded happy. Creeping up the ramp, he eased to the open front door to peer through the screen.

Across the parlor, Gwendolyn stood on a chair with her

back to him, her arms stretching up to hold a nail over the fireplace. Her posture caused the hem of her skirt to come up several inches, and he glimpsed snowy petticoats and a very trim ankle in a high-buttoned boot. Her apron strings nipped in her shapely waist, and glory, her hair hung down her back in a curtain of golden curls. The sight snatched the breath from his chest and turned his mouth to a desert.

The chair wobbled, and Betsy squealed, reaching out to grip Gwendolyn's leg. Before he could open the screen, Gwendolyn grabbed the mantel, and the hammer clattered to the floor.

"Botheration," she muttered, steadying herself.

"Are you sure you should do this? Maybe we should wait for Matt. Or call Pete or Mike to help." Betsy eased back, holding something in her lap.

"I can do it. I just hadn't counted on a teetering chair." Gwendolyn flipped her hair over her shoulder in a motion that captivated Matt. So feminine. Had she gotten prettier since he was away? "Never let it be said Gwendolyn Esmeralda Gerhard was daunted by a mere nail. My motto is *Excelsior*, and my course is onward. I want this done before Matt gets home." She lifted the hammer and gave the nail a couple of whacks. "There. Now hand me that picture, young lady."

She hefted the frame—a painting?—and eased it along the wall until the wire caught on the nail. Leaning back, she studied it, straightened it, and put her hands on her hips. "There. What do you think?" She had her attention on the picture and didn't turn when Matt drew the screen door open and stepped in, his finger pressed to his mouth to still Betsy's squeal.

When he stood right behind Gwendolyn, he made his

voice as gruff and stern as possible, "What are you two doing?"

At his words, she whirled, arms flailing, and his hands shot out to grab her. The chair teetered, and she gripped his shoulders to steady herself. "Matt!"

A feeling of inevitability swept over him, and without thought, he tightened his grip on her waist and eased her from the chair. But somehow, she didn't make it all the way to the floor. Instead, he held her against him, wrapping his arms around her waist. Forgetting everything around him, he found himself staring into her wide, violet eyes. Her arms wound around his neck in a move that felt way too good for his peace of mind. She blinked, her lips parting.

"You're back."

Her smile slammed into his heart and got it beating again, and bless him if she didn't squeeze his neck.

Kiss her.

The notion came out of nowhere, but once it arrived, he could think of nothing else. His eyes zeroed in on her pink lips, so close to his. He halved the distance between them before he realized what he was doing.

Betsy's chair squeaked, reminding him of her presence and the folly of what he was thinking about. He glanced over to see his sister trying to back out of the room. She stopped. "Welcome home, Matt." Her innocent expression couldn't hide the glee in her eyes.

Reluctantly he released Gwendolyn, letting her feet reach the floor. He tried to ignore the empty feel of his arms and the regret at not getting a taste of those sweet lips as she stepped away and smoothed her hair. He turned from her purply-blue stare, trying to gather his scattered wits.

"What have you two been up to in here?" He scanned the

room that had been off-limits for even conversation for the past year. Though some of the furnishings were the same, it was as if all traces of Edith had been removed. Open, bright, and without the clogging clutter, he might even be able to sit in here without feeling as if Edith might spring out from behind the drapes.

Betsy rolled her chair closer. "You aren't mad, are you? If you are, it was all my idea. But if you're not mad, then we thought it up together." She gave him a gamine grin. "Do you like it? We've worked so hard. And look." She turned the chair left and right. "Plenty of room for my chair now."

He rested his hand on his sister's shoulder, noting the color in her cheeks—cheeks that had a bit of roundness to them again. How could he be mad when Betsy looked better than she had in months? "It's nice."

"We were just putting on the finishing touches. Isn't it beautiful?" She motioned toward the painting. "Gwendolyn brought it all the way from Massachusetts."

Gwendolyn had laced her hands and laid the sides of her index fingers against her lips—those soft, pink lips. He dragged his mind back to what she was saying.

"My sister Evelyn painted it. It's of the shore near Seabury where we lived." She took a deep breath. "I can almost hear the waves hitting the beach. I can't remember a time when I didn't know the sight and sound and smell of the sea. Sometimes, when I close my eyes, I imagine I'm walking along the rocky shore, leaning into the breeze, gulls keening overhead. I knew becoming a mail-order bride meant leaving the sea, but I never knew I would miss it so much."

The wisp of homesickness in her voice jarred Matt, as did her reference to being a mail-order bride, reminding him that her stay here was temporary, that soon enough she'd be on the train back to her beloved ocean. High-stepping easterners only caused trouble, changing everything to suit themselves then running off without a backward glance once they'd bled a fellow dry—and broken his foolish heart.

She still had a wistful smile on her face when she asked, "What do you think, Matt?"

He hardened his voice to bring them all back to reality. "What it looks like to me is that you're settling in. I told you there was no point in unpacking that kind of stuff. You'll just have to take it down again." He avoided looking at either of them, knowing he'd see hurt and confusion at his harsh tone. But the sooner they accepted the truth, the easier it would be on all of them. "I'd best see to my horse."

⁓

Gwendolyn sank onto the settee, staring after his departing form. All the happiness, the hope of belonging and companionship she'd built up during his absence, evaporated like a snowflake on a hot griddle.

Betsy pressed her lips together and narrowed her eyes, watching Matt through the screen as he untied his horse and led the animal toward the barn. She fingered the end of her braid, a sign Gwendolyn had come to recognize as meaning she was deep in thought.

"Well, that didn't go too well, did it?" Gwendolyn ran her fingers through her hair. It was finally dry now from the early-morning washing she'd given it, and she pulled a ribbon from her pocket. With the dexterity of long practice, she divided and braided the heavy curls, winding and tying the ribbon. She coiled the braid, slid her hairpins from where she'd tucked them along the edge of her collar, and jabbed them into the knot of hair to secure it.

"Actually, it went better than you think." Betsy grinned. "If he wasn't starting to care about you, he wouldn't have reacted so strongly. I saw the way he was looking at you, like he was a starving man and you were the last cookie in the jar. I just wish my chair hadn't squawked when it did. He looked like he wanted to kiss you senseless."

Gwendolyn shook her head, convinced she was already senseless. The way he'd held her for an all-too-short eternity. . . Her blood zinged in her veins. She hadn't been able to resist winding her arms around his neck, and the instant it flashed in her head that he might actually kiss her, she realized she wanted nothing more. She was afraid to put too much stock in what Betsy said. The way he'd backed away, and worse, the wary look that had crept into his eyes were more reliable than anything his fanciful sister might read into his actions.

"We'd best get supper started." She rose and picked up the chair to return it to the kitchen.

"And get some water heating. Matt's going to want a bath." Betsy followed.

Gwendolyn had just slid the pan of corn bread into the oven when the back door opened and Matt came inside. He hung up his hat and began dipping water from the reservoir into a bucket to carry upstairs for his bath. She wiped her hands on her apron. "The bread should be ready in about half an hour. If you're all right, Betsy, I'll be back in a few minutes."

Returning to the parlor, she picked up the hammer from the mantel to take it back to the barn. It was nice to be able to leave the house for a while without worrying about Betsy being alone. She let herself out onto the porch and walked toward the barn. The prairie rolled away from her in all directions, the only trees a few stunted individuals clinging to the creek bank. In the northern distance, lavender hills rose. What had Cummings called the tallest one? Laramie Peak?

She breathed deeply of the grass-scented air. Hanging Evelyn's painting had made her a bit homesick, both for her sisters and for the sea. How often had they rambled along the shore together, watching the waves roll in like a great ocean heartbeat? What would her sisters advise her now about Matt? What if he really did send her away? Where could she go? Jane's place was much too small, and Evelyn's cabin housed four already.

Lord, I don't want to go. I want to stay here. Betsy needs me, and though he isn't ready to admit it, so does Matt. He's everything I could ask for in a husband.

She chuckled.

Except that he doesn't want to be married. What made him so skittish, and how can I change his mind?

She could almost feel his arms around her again, and she knew without a doubt that she wanted him to hold her like that again. Soon. She wanted him to want to be married to her.

Entering the barn, she let her eyes adjust to the dimness. The tools were kept in a room on the far side next to where they kept saddles and such. Her footsteps crunched on the dirt floor, and the smells of hay and livestock wrapped around her. The men must've stowed their gear and headed to the bunkhouse for supper. She entered the toolroom, grateful for the small window high in the wall that let in some light. A neat row of tools hung along the back of a wooden workbench, and she placed the hammer back where she'd gotten it.

"Evening."

She whirled, clutching her throat, and found the cowhand who had been so insolent her first day here blocking the doorway. A quick glance told her nothing about him seemed to have changed in the intervening days. He wore the same intent expression, his gaze roving over her from hair to hem and back again.

"Good evening." She gripped the edge of the workbench behind her.

"Didn't expect to see you here."

"I was just returning something."

He stretched, gripping the top of the doorframe and leaning a bit into the room. "You're sure a sight for this cowpoke's weary old eyes. Don't believe I've ever seen a woman as pretty as you." His smile made her shiver.

"I need to get back to the house, if you'll excuse me." She waited, but he didn't move.

"There's no rush. I imagine you've been cooped up while we've been gone, what with looking after the cripple. That can't be very pleasant for a woman like you. I'd think you'd be looking for something a little more—shall we say, stimulating?" He studied her, letting his eyes linger far too long on certain parts of her anatomy. "My name's Jackson, by the way."

She crossed her arms at her waist and tried to ignore the prickles dancing across her skin. "I'm sorry, but I really do have to go. I left something in the oven."

He moved to the side of the doorway but not quite enough for her to get by. "I bet you're a fine cook."

The way his eyes glittered in the dusky light made her think of a gull. Dark, beady, watchful eyes, waiting for an opportunity to snatch up any morsel that happened to land in its path. He'd positioned himself so she would have to brush against him to get out of the toolroom, and his smirk said he knew it.

"Jackson?" A voice she didn't recognize came from behind him. A man with graying hair and a grizzled beard stepped from the gloom.

Jackson straightened and stepped back. "Melton. I was just"—he broke off—"you know."

The older man removed a toothpick from his mouth and stared hard at Jackson until the cowhand fidgeted and finally ducked his head and left.

Relief coursed through Gwendolyn, and she blew out a breath.

The man returned the pick to the corner of his mouth, clamped down, and spoke around it. "Trouble?"

"Uh, no. Everything's fine." She had no desire to try to explain Jackson or his behavior. "I'd best get back to the house, Mr. . . . ?"

"Melton. Circle P ramrod." He jerked his head toward where Jackson had disappeared. "Best stay away from the men, ma'am." With a tip of his hat, he was gone, as silently as he'd come.

"Stay away from the men?" she muttered on her way back to the house. "I'd love to stay away from that Jackson for the rest of my life."

Chapter 5

Everywhere he turned, she had invaded his life. In the week since he'd returned from the roundup, Matthew's world had been subtly and not-so-subtly altered. First it was the parlor, the painting over the mantel, the new curtains in the kitchen. Now it was cushions on the chairs, a chess set on the sideboard, and now, of all things, a flower garden along the picket fence.

Matt hooked his thumbs into his belt loops and stared at the scraggly plants in the newly dug soil. Yarrow, Indian paintbrush, Queen Anne's lace. Weeds, every one of them. What did a body want with extra work like tending flowers when there was plenty to do with the vegetable patch and looking after the house? Not to mention the fact that in just a couple of weeks, Reverend Cummings would be back through here, and she'd be on her way somewhere else.

"Stop scowling." Gwendolyn passed him with a sloshing bucket of water, pouring around each plant carefully before moving on. "What harm can a few flowers do? It pretties up the place a bit." Her shrug and ultra-innocent expression made him want to smile.

Grasping for a hold on his irritation, he tugged the kerchief from his neck, removed his hat, and wiped the sweatband. "You realize you've planted a row of weeds."

"Wildflowers," she corrected. "I didn't notice any nurseries around here where I could get roses and pansies. I had to make do." She bent to touch the ivory blossoms of a Canada milk vetch and trailed her fingers over a tiny cluster of harebells. "Aren't they pretty?"

Pretty. If anything in this yard could be called pretty, it was her. The afternoon sun bathed her face, bringing out honey strands in her hair and the smooth surface of her skin. He busied himself with retying his kerchief to keep from reaching out to stroke her cheek. What was the matter with him?

"What's going to happen to them when you leave here? I don't have the time to weed and water them, even if I wanted to, which I don't."

Her happiness at the flowers faded, and she gave him a reproachful glance that lanced his gut. More and more, the thought of her leaving gave him a hollow feeling under his heart. He had to remind himself why she couldn't stay, and it seemed she needed the reminders, too. Everywhere he turned, she was going against his orders not to settle in. He decided to change the subject.

"Where's Betsy?"

"Reading in the parlor. She's enamored of Chaucer's *Canterbury Tales* at the moment."

"One of your books?"

"Yes. My father used to read it to us in the evening, and we'd discuss it bit by bit. Even Jamie, my nephew, joined in, though he preferred Mallory's tales of King Arthur. He even had a stuffed dog he named Glastonbury Tor." Her smile flashed, and there was a faraway, remembering look to her eyes. "I miss Jamie. I wasn't yet ten when he was born, and I was sure Evelyn produced him just so I would have someone to play with. I wish I could see my sisters for just a little while, so I could make sure they were all right."

"You sound like a close family."

"Very. We've never been apart like this before. Every time things have been hard, we've always had each other to lean on. When Mother died, and when Evelyn lost Jamison in the war, when Father passed away. Then when we were being evicted from our home." She watered another weed. "Hard times remind you of who you can count on. God and my sisters have always been faithful. Our adversity brought us closer together."

"Adversity doesn't always bring people together. Sometimes it tears them apart." Sadness coated his words. Adversity, distrust, deceit, despair. He'd felt them all over the past year.

Her brows inched together. "But you and Betsy have a beautiful relationship."

"It's not Betsy I was thinking about."

She smoothed her hands over her hair, trying to tame some of the wispy curls that escaped the knot on the back of her head. Remembering the way her hair fell down her back in a glorious cape of curls when she was hanging that picture in the parlor, he swallowed. What would it be like to bury his hands in her hair, to let those curls twine around his fingers? He found himself stepping closer to her, close enough to touch, close enough to see the purple flecks in her blue eyes.

Her pulse beat in her throat. "Betsy told me how you used to argue with your grandfather."

He pulled his attention back to what she was saying. "We did. But neither of us was much for holding a grudge. Flare up and forget about it. Granddad knew just what to say to get my back up. He loved a lively debate. There for a while, after my father died, I wondered if Granddad would ever care about anything enough to argue again. He just sort of drifted for a few months. Then one morning he lit into me about something, and instead of getting mad, all I could do was grin. That made him madder, and he really erupted. It was nice to have things back to normal."

She fetched a sigh. "I wish I could've met your grandfather. He sounds like quite a character."

"That he was. I still can't figure his sending for you, but—" Matt just stopped himself from saying he was glad she'd come. Was he glad? She'd lifted his load considerably, and there was no denying she was the prettiest thing he'd seen in a long time. Fun, cheerful, and easy to talk to as well. He couldn't resist reaching out to tuck a stray curl behind her ear, and it just seemed so natural to let his fingers trail down her cheek. Softer than a sage leaf. Before he really knew what he was doing, he'd bent his head to brush his lips across hers. He pulled back to gauge her reaction.

Her eyes widened, and she looked so bewildered he had to kiss her again. Everything he'd been dreaming about since the day she arrived, all the questions he'd been asking himself about how soft and sweet she'd be got answered in that kiss. His arms came around her, and he angled his head to deepen the kiss. After her initial gasp of surprise, she delighted him by kissing back. The bucket fell from her hand, *thunking* to the ground and splashing his boots.

Reluctantly aware that they were standing in the yard

in full view of anyone on the ranch, he ended the kiss and stepped back. Her lips were rosy pink, and a delicate coral color graced her cheeks. He had a sense of having taken a giant step across a line he'd drawn in the sand. There could be no going back to a time when they hadn't kissed. But did he want to go back? Maybe things would work out, maybe he could trust her after all.

She tucked her lower lip in and studied the horizon, clearly bemused. He smiled. She was so adorable, he wanted to kiss her again, just to fluster her.

He picked up the bucket she'd dropped. "I best be getting into the house. I've got some paperwork to finish. If there's one thing I hate, it's keeping track of the accounts."

"What kind of accounts?" Her voice sounded distracted, as if she was having a hard time gathering her thoughts.

He shrugged. "Wages, expenses, taxes, herd tallies, bills, sales receipts. Sometimes I feel like I'm drowning in paperwork. My father was the one who used to take care of it all, but over the last year, it's fallen to me." They walked up the path, and he could almost imagine she really belonged here.

"There's so much more to running a ranch than I ever thought, especially one as prosperous as this place appears to be." She paused halfway up the ramp and put her hand on his arm. "I'm pretty good with figures. If you'd like, I could help you." She turned the full force of those blue eyes on him. Her lips parted, expectant.

He glanced down at her hand on his forearm. Warning bells jangled in his head, and he flashed back to another time, another woman. A woman who barged into their lives and destroyed so much. A woman with a powerful attraction, who used her feminine wiles to trap and disarm. A woman who had caused catastrophic harm.

A woman who had offered to help with the bookkeeping.

Plucking her hand from his arm, he hardened his features. What a fool he'd been, letting her charm him, lowering his defenses, letting history repeat itself.

"The finances of this ranch are none of your affair. You can forget whatever notion you have of getting your hands on any Circle P property, and that includes me."

He dropped the bucket onto the dirt and stomped into the house. Brushing off Betsy's cheerful greeting, he marched to his room.

～

Gwendolyn stood still, as shocked as if he'd struck her. A chill rippled across her skin, followed hard by a wave of anger. Her hands fisted. How dare he? How dare he kiss her one moment and accuse her of trying to steal from him the next? Of all the hard-headed, mule-stubborn, moody men, he took the biscuit.

Her breath came fast, and her heart thundered in her ears. She wanted to scream, to throw something, to give vent to the frustration raging inside. Knowing she couldn't go into the house, couldn't face him until she got her feelings under control, she turned toward the gate. Halfway there, she stopped and went back to the door.

"Betsy," she called through the screen, "I'm going for a walk." She tried to keep her voice nonchalant and light, though she couldn't quite hide a tremor. "I'll be back."

The crooked branches of the stunted cottonwoods along Sagebrush Creek beckoned her, and she strode toward them, arms swinging, feet hitting the dirt with force, trying to expel the anger Matt's accusations had aroused. As she walked, she fought a mental battle with him, crossing verbal swords. His behavior was inexcusable.

But, oh my, how he could kiss.

She touched her lips, still sensitive, and tears pricked her eyes. *Oh, no you don't. You're not going to cry over that despicable louse. From this moment on, he isn't the only one counting the days until Reverend Cummings returns to free you from this untenable situation. Matthew Parker is no knight in shining armor. He's a dragon, through and through.*

She waded through the waist-high grass until she reached the stream bank and the cottonwoods there. She leaned against the rough bark of a tree trunk. The water flowed slowly here, sluggish and sleepy in the growing dusk. A bird called from the tall grass on the far bank, and the wind skittered through the leaves, as unsettled as her thoughts.

The anger trickled away, leaving her tender. An overwhelming rush of loneliness, of longing to see her sisters, swamped her, and she slid down until her back rested against the tree and she could draw her knees up. Wrapping her arms around her legs, she pressed her forehead into her knees.

Lord, where do I go from here? I don't understand any of this. You led us to Wyoming Territory, You gave us all husbands, except me. I have no family, no husband, no home, nothing. I have nowhere to go when I leave this place. I can't trust anyone or anything here, not even my own feelings. What can I do?

She squeezed her eyes shut, and a memory flashed across her mind. Jane's cross-stitch sampler that had hung in the parlor at home, stitched with her favorite Bible verse:

The LORD is my rock, and my fortress, and my deliverer; my God, my strength, in whom I will trust; my buckler, and the horn of my salvation, and my high tower.

Gwendolyn raised her face, letting the breeze cool her hot skin, and contemplated the verse that had been a part of her life since she was a little girl. How many times had she flown past that sampler with only a cursory glance? And yet, the truth of the verse seeped into some hitherto unlit corners of her heart, illuminating her lack of faith in a God who had never failed her yet. Her heart might've been broken by Matthew Parker, but God had not abandoned her. He had a plan, and she could trust Him.

Perhaps He had needed to remove from her all that was dear and familiar in order to show her how she needed to rely on Him. Perhaps that had been His purpose all along for each of the Gerhard girls. He wanted to be her high tower, her rock and refuge. He wanted her trust.

Swallowing hard, she leaned back until her head rested against the tree. "All right, Lord. I choose to trust You. I don't know what is going to happen to me, but I know nothing happens that is not in Your control. Nothing surprises You. If it is Your will that I not stay here, then I'll go where and when You direct. If Matthew Parker isn't Your will for me, then I accept that."

As hard as the words were to say, there was tremendous freedom in them as well. As stubborn and confusing as Matt Parker was, he was beyond her ability to sort out. She closed her eyes, listening to the murmur of the water and the sighing of the wind until she slipped over the edge of sleep.

Chapter 6

"What is wrong with you? You're as cranky as a badger with a blister." Betsy dished up the half-burnt bacon and beans—her attempt at cooking the evening meal.

Just like a woman to sulk and stay away. Matt poked at the food. Beans weren't his favorite, burnt or not, and his appetite was nil, thanks to Gwendolyn's duplicity.

"I'm not cranky. I've just got a lot on my mind."

"Like what? Maybe I can help." Betsy wheeled her chair to her place and held out her hand for the blessing.

He mumbled through the words and released her fingers.

"It's nothing for you to worry about." He glanced at the clock and the angle of the shadows on the ground outside the back door. Gwendolyn should've been back by now. Where was she?

"If it concerns you and Gwendolyn, then I think I will worry about it, thank you very much. You do realize you're making more of a hash of your relationship than I made of cooking dinner?"

"We don't have a relationship." Being chastised by his younger sister wasn't on his to-do list this evening.

"Perhaps that's the problem. You're like the man who got

bitten by a mustang, and now he hears hoofbeats everywhere. Gwendolyn isn't Edith."

"I never said she was."

"No, you just treat her like she is. I don't know why she'd ever want to marry you with the way you act, so suspicious and snarly."

"I'm not snarly." He paused, modulated his voice, and took a deep breath. "And who said she wanted to marry me? She's waiting for Cummings to come back the same as I am, so she can leave. Until that time, I have every right to be suspicious. Do you know what she asked me? She asked if she could help with the bookkeeping."

"And?"

"Do you remember what happened the last time we let an outsider look at the accounts? She fleeced us like a flock of sheep."

"How many times do I have to say this? Gwendolyn is not Edith. Her innocent offer of help was just that, innocent. Did you know she kept the household accounts for her family for years, even though she was the youngest? She has a knack with ledgers and figures. It's perfectly natural that she'd offer to help."

He wasn't ready to let go of his wariness, though his sister's logic and information put a dent in the wall of his suspicions. Had he jumped to the wrong conclusion? Had he misjudged Gwendolyn's offer? Had he been wrong about her all along?

If he had, if he'd kissed her and held her and then thrown her sincere offer back into her face. . . Shame wriggled through his chest. What kind of a beast must she think him?

"Matt, I'm getting worried. She said she was going for a

walk, but she's never been gone this long before."

Glancing at the clock, he pushed back his plate. "Do you know where she might go?"

Betsy shook her head. "She goes to the rise just east of the house sometimes. Pete and Mike put a bench up there for her. But I can see the bench from my bedroom window, and she isn't up there. Maybe she needed to walk off her temper. She might've gone farther."

He rose and plucked his hat off the peg by the door. "You'll be all right while I look for her?" Though what he'd say when he found her, he didn't know.

"I'll be fine. Go."

"The rise east of the house, you said?"

"That's the only place she's mentioned walking before."

"I'll start there."

Matt left the house, his long strides eating up the ground. Betsy's assertion bored through his brain. *Gwendolyn is not Edith.*

He supposed he'd best practice his apologizing.

⁓

Gwendolyn awakened, confused at first, memory trickling back as she straightened and rubbed her stiff neck. The sky, no longer a pale, hot blue, now showed streaks of rose and gold and gray. The breeze had died away, and the stalks of grass and sage bushes stood still. She'd been gone way too long. Betsy would be worried.

Scrambling to her feet, she brushed the dirt and grass from her skirts. A hank of hair slid over her ear, and she tightened a couple of hairpins.

A rustle in the grass off to her right caught her attention.

Jackson rose from the grass, grinning. "Hello, Gwendolyn." Her name rolled off his tongue like syrup.

Her heart quickened, as did her breathing. A glance over her shoulder told her no one from the ranch complex could see her here, down over the creek bank. She could just make out the roof of the house, a hundred yards away beyond the rise.

She gripped the tree trunk behind her, the rough bark biting into her skin. Jackson had always had a too-familiar gleam in his eye, but now that gleam burned white-hot. Her mouth went dry. "I should be getting back to the house."

"There's no hurry. It's a nice evening." He stepped closer, edging aside a sage bush, crushing the stems beneath his boots and releasing their herbaceous scent.

"Really, I'm overdue. It must be well past suppertime." She edged around the tree, hoping to put it between herself and Jackson, but he moved like quicksilver, his hand clamping down onto her wrist.

"I said there was no hurry." He loomed over her, the last rays of the sun glinting in his dark eyes. "Why do you skitter away every time I get near you?"

Because you remind me of a snake? "I'm sure Matt and Betsy must be expecting me now."

"Why do you care about them? The cripple is useless, and Matt's a real dog-in-the-manger. He doesn't want you himself, but he doesn't want anyone else to have you." He bared his teeth in a sneer. "I sure enjoyed sticking it to him on the roundup, digging at him about you." Grinding the bones of her wrist together, he jerked her toward him. "He's so almighty arrogant, walking around here like a little plaster saint, but I know better." He laughed. "Bet you didn't know he was cheating on his old man with his stepmama, did you?"

Gwendolyn gasped. "No."

"Why do you think his dad killed himself?" Jackson flung his arm toward the creek. "Ended it all right here. Shot himself and landed in the water. Heartbroken."

"Let go of my arm."

"I don't think so. I've bided my time, but I'm tired of waiting." He brought his face within inches of hers. "I saw you, you know. Out in front of the house. I knew you two had something going on, just like him and Edith. Those were some kisses you were giving him. I figure one man's as good as another to you, just like one woman's as good as another to him." He shifted his hold on her, gripping her upper arms and hauling her up against his chest. She struggled, sucking in a breath to let out a scream, but before she could, his hard lips came down on her mouth, stifling any sound.

The disgusting touch of his lips on hers made her want to retch. So different from Matt's kiss. Jackson wanted to punish, to take, where Matt's embrace had been safe, a giving and a receiving, everything a kiss should be.

Pinned against the tree as she was, she couldn't even draw back her leg to kick him. Her struggling seemed to fire him up, so she went limp in his arms, hoping to surprise him into dropping his guard long enough for her to break free.

The instant she drooped, he raised his head, a triumphant laugh escaping him. "I knew you'd give in."

As he shifted his grip, she steeled herself to slap his face, but before she could raise her now-free arm, a roar split the air. Jackson was flung away from her, and the sound of a fist hitting a jaw cracked.

Matt stood over Jackson's sprawled form, gasping, his

hands clenched. Without a word, he bent and grabbed two fistfuls of shirt, hauling Jackson to his wobbly feet. Another punch sent him reeling into the dirt, his lip split and his nose bleeding.

"Jackson, get up to the bunkhouse and draw your pay. You're through here." Matt's chest rose and fell rapidly, his hands fisted at his sides.

Gwendolyn clutched the tree for support for her shaky knees. Blinking, trying to catch her breath, she couldn't help the rush of gratitude and something else, something stronger, that overwhelmed her. Matt stood there like an avenging angel. . .no, like a knight in shining armor, defending her honor against a scoundrel.

She crossed to him, holding out her hand as Jackson scrambled to his feet and backed up. "Matt, thank you. I'm so glad you came when you did."

He turned cold eyes to her for a brief second before swinging back to watch Jackson's retreat. "Are you? I don't know why. I'd think you'd be disappointed, having your little rendezvous interrupted. I want you off this property, and I'm not waiting for Cummings to come back for you. You can either leave with Jackson, or I'll take you to town first thing in the morning."

A strange, this-can't-be-happening icy shudder rippled through her. He'd gone from knight in shining armor to fire-breathing dragon—again. She swallowed.

"Matt, I didn't have any rendezvous with that. . .that animal." She pointed to a quickly retreating Jackson. "He caught me by surprise."

"That's not what it looked like to me."

"Then you're wrong. And if anyone should know what

it feels like to be wrongly accused, it's you." Jackson's taunts about Matt rang in her ears. But she couldn't—wouldn't—believe them.

"What are you talking about?" The question jerked from him, deepening his scowl. "Never mind, I don't want to know." He jammed his fists on his waist. "I almost fell for it. Betsy *almost* had me believing I'd made a mistake, that I'd misjudged you. I was all set to apologize, to ask you to stay." A bark of mirthless laughter shot out. "What a fool I am." He turned on his heel and marched up the hill toward the house.

ॐ

When Matt reached the house, he knew he couldn't go in, couldn't face Betsy's questions until he got himself under control. Glancing over his shoulder through the growing dusk, he spied Gwendolyn approaching, bold as polished brass in the noontime sun. He ground his teeth. When was he going to learn that women were nothing but trouble from a man's first breath to his last?

The bunkhouse door opened and Jackson emerged, saddlebags over his shoulder and a defiant set to his jaw. Melton edged out after him and, seeing Matt by the picket gate, strolled his way, hands in pockets. He came to a stop a few feet away, dug a toothpick from his pocket, and went to work on it, silent as usual.

Gwendolyn didn't come to the front yard, instead disappearing around the back of the house. The kitchen door slapped shut.

Matt waited, watching Jackson head to the corral and lasso his horse, saddle up, and ride away. Though he should've been relieved, his heart felt like it had been replaced with a fistful of horseshoes, cold, heavy, lifeless.

"Good riddance." Melton slipped a rifle bullet from a loop on his belt and used the point to clean under his fingernails. "Madder'n a skunk-bit coyote. Busted nose, too."

Matt flexed his hand, wincing at his bruised knuckles. "He deserved it."

" 'Magine so. Wanted to punch him myself a time or two. Had to hold the boys back just now. Wanted to tenderize his hide, spouting off about you and that girl. And Edith."

Matt flinched. "What did he say?"

"Claimed you were dallying with that gal. And the real reason your daddy kilt himself was because he caught you and Edith together."

Closing his eyes, he took a deep breath. "It's not true."

"Figured."

This must've been what Gwendolyn meant about him knowing what it was like to be falsely accused. But he'd seen what he'd seen. Her in Jackson's arms, not struggling, not fighting him in the least.

"Don't usually give advice, but you and her need to talk. Deserves to know about Edith. And you deserve to be rid of Edith and her trouble. Weighing you down. Holding you back." Melton placed the cartridge back in his gun belt and shifted the toothpick. "Plain she's not like the other one and that you're in love with her."

Matt's mind rebelled at the thought, even as he embraced it.

"If I had to believe Jackson or that gal, I reckon I'd choose the gal. Shame to let her get away." With that, Melton turned and sauntered back toward the bunkhouse.

Matt gripped two of the pickets, hanging his head. His gut muscles clenched. The scene by the riverbank played itself over and over in his mind. Had he made a mistake? Was she telling the truth, that Jackson had caught her unawares and forced his attentions on her? Was he being unfair by lumping her in with Edith without giving her a chance to explain? Would she believe him if he told her the truth, and would she forgive him if he did?

The last thing he wanted to do was dredge all that up again. And yet, he wanted to be free of Edith and all the hurt she'd caused. He wanted peace and a chance to be happy. And he wanted to hold Gwendolyn in his arms, with no suspicions or accusations between them.

Edith's ivylike vines had imprisoned him for far too long, binding his thoughts and actions. Guilt, disgust, anger, bitterness, and no matter how he slashed at them, they grew back with longer thorns and stronger boughs.

And at first, he'd seen Gwendolyn the same way, trapping, scheming, plotting. But now, when he thought of her, there were no entangling thorns or entrapping vines. Gwendolyn meant wildflowers in the breeze, sunshine and light, laughter and hope.

His heart craved some hope. It had been a long, dry spell.

Chapter 7

You can't leave." Betsy reached out her fragile, pale hand and stopped Gwendolyn from putting another folded garment into her valise.

"I have no choice." She choked back the tears that wanted to fall. No way was he going to see how he'd hurt her. She refused to cry. This very day she'd promised to let God be her refuge and tower. Well, she would. If it killed her. No more trusting in men.

"But where will you go?"

"Evelyn's, I suppose. After that, I don't know."

"This is ridiculous. If you're going, I'm going with you."

Gwendolyn stopped cramming things into her luggage and sagged onto the side of the bed. "You can't. Matt needs you here."

"He needs you here, too; he's just too dumb to see it."

Weary beyond anything she'd felt before, Gwendolyn wrapped her arms around her waist. "I can't do this anymore. I'm fighting shadows, wild accusations, and half-spoken thoughts. I'm left to imagination and supposition. He doesn't trust me. How can I win against something I can't see, someone I don't even know? Nobody will talk about this Edith woman and what she did. At first, I didn't want to pry, and then I was afraid to. It was almost as if she were still here, still holding sway. I have so many questions, but Matt's locked everything up behind a wall of prejudice I can't break down."

The bedroom door eased open. She raised her eyes. Matt stood in the doorway, his expression sad and watchful. Jumping to her feet, she began packing once more, blinking hard and commanding herself not to cry.

"Matt, this has gone on long enough. Either you tell her about it or I will." Betsy backed her chair up to make room for him to enter.

"You don't have to preach anymore, Betsy." He sounded weary, beaten down. "Gwendolyn, we need to talk."

Gwendolyn's heart went out to him, captured by the sorrow in his blue eyes and the way his shoulders drooped, but she steeled herself, not wanting to get hurt further. He stepped aside to allow her to pass through the doorway and motioned for her to head toward the kitchen.

"Can we go outside? I have a few things to say that I'd rather Betsy not hear." He held the back door open for her.

Instead of stopping in the backyard, with its washtubs and clothesline, Matt grabbed her hand and took off walking, heading away from the house and the creek to her favorite rise a few hundred yards from the buildings. He followed the path her feet had created on multiple trips up the hillside. The long twilight held, but a few stars peeked from the eastern sky.

When he finally stopped, he let go of her hand and walked a few paces away. She waited, running her fingertips across the airy fronds of wheatgrass stalks. She was finally going to get some answers, but her heart quailed at the thought that they might not be the answers she wanted to hear.

He stood with his thumbs in his belt loops, legs braced apart, staring out over the prairie. The wind rippled through the grass and fluttered his shirtsleeves. She couldn't help but step closer and only just refrained from putting her hand on his back to offer solace. Fear of being rebuffed kept her from touching him.

"I owe you an apology. Several of them, actually." His voice rumbled in his chest, as if the words had to work hard to come out.

She took his elbow and tugged gently. "Come sit." Leading him to the little bench Pete and Mike had built for her, she braced herself and told herself not to hope. She turned so she could see his profile, put her hands in her lap, and waited.

He took a deep breath and plunged into his story. "Three years ago, right after we moved here from Texas, my dad made a trip down to Denver to buy cattle. He left me and Betsy and Granddad here to look after things. Betsy wasn't so bad then. She could get around with a cane most of the time. We had a little cabin, just a couple of rooms. Betsy slept on a bed in the front room and me and Granddad and Dad had bunks in the other room. It wasn't much, but we were happy. We'd saved and worked hard to get started ranching here, away from the divided loyalties and backlash of the war in Texas. A place where we could start over."

He had a faraway look in his eye, and his voice held a touch of longing.

"Dad came back from Denver with a herd of cattle, a half-dozen ranch hands, and Edith, his new bride." His hands fisted on his thighs. "She was about ten years older than me and about as ready to rough it on a ranch as she was to sprout wings and fly. Fancy clothes, fancy talk, fancy manners. Real handsome, and Dad was head over heels. At first she gushed over everything and played nice, but the rot set in pretty quickly. She hated it here, hated the people, the prairie, the animals. The cabin appalled her, even though Granddad and I moved into the bunkhouse with the ranch hands to make room for her and all her belongings.

"The first thing she demanded was a new house. Dad tried to put her off, get her to wait awhile so we could build up the herd, but she wouldn't let up about it. Finally, he gave in, had all the materials freighted out here, and hired builders. For a while she seemed happier, picking out wallpaper and paint and rugs and such, supervising the construction. When it was finished, Granddad and I moved in with them and Betsy again. She wanted to go to Denver on a shopping spree to furnish the place, but Dad told her the house had cost more than he'd anticipated, and she could only decorate a couple of rooms. The rest would have to wait until we had cattle to sell. She pored over the catalog and spent right up to the limit."

That explained the parlor.

He seemed to read her mind. "Yeah, the parlor. And one bedroom upstairs. The places Edith was most likely to be. The rest of the house looks like the kitchen and Betsy's room did when you first got here. No decorations, nothing soft or pretty. We weren't even allowed into the parlor, not that any of us wanted to be in there. We weren't good enough."

She held her tongue, not wanting to interrupt him. The longer he spoke, the easier the words seemed to come.

He pursed his lips and shifted on the bench. "You know

Granddad and I used to argue about pretty much everything? We knew it didn't mean anything, flare up and be done with it. But Dad was different. He never argued, just kept everything bottled up inside. And the more Edith complained, the more silent he got. She whined she was wasting the best years of her life in this forsaken place and wanted him to leave the ranch. He'd tell her his life was here and that she'd get used to it after a bit. She just needed to 'settle in.'"

Gwendolyn flinched at this phrase that she'd come to loathe. No wonder he'd said it to her so often.

He glanced her way. Grim lines bracketed his mouth. "A few months after the house was finished, Edith started acting strange. I couldn't put my finger on it, but she seemed to be there every time I turned around. Watching me, paying compliments, using any excuse to be close. At first, I didn't want to believe it. I mean, she was my stepmother. But after a while, I couldn't ignore it. I ended up putting a lock on my door." A dusky red crept up his neck. "I was afraid she'd come into my room one night.

"I couldn't talk to Dad. He defended her at every turn. In spite of how unsuitable she was for the life here, he was in love with her. Then one day when I was coming in off the range, I forded the creek down where I found you today. I stopped to water my horse, and. . .I'd made up my mind to have it out with Dad about Edith. I knew she was giving Betsy a rough time, though Betsy didn't say anything, and I'd had enough of Edith's maneuvering." A shudder rippled through him.

"I was just getting ready to mount up and head for home when I heard someone crying. It was Edith, huddled in the grass, bawling." A grimace twisted his lips. "I wanted to ride away and leave her there. I wish now that I had."

Gwendolyn squeezed her laced fingers together. Pieces of the puzzle began to fall together, creating a picture of tension, conflict, misery, and mistrust. Poor Matt.

"Like a fool I squatted down beside her. I wanted to make sure she wasn't hurt. She threw herself into my arms, crying about how miserable she was, about how she'd never loved my father, she'd just wanted to get out of Denver." He shook his head, shrugging. "I didn't know what to say to her, and I tried to get loose, but she held on tight. Then she came at me, trying to kiss me." He swallowed.

"I shoved her away and tried to leave, but she came after me, saying she was in love with me, that her marriage was a mistake. When I wouldn't give in to her, she got ugly, screaming and calling me names. Then she went all quiet. I don't know how to describe it. It was like she went cold inside, her eyes kind of glittered. Then she said real loud, 'We'll have to tell your father. I can't go on deceiving him like this. He deserves to know we're in love.' I know now that she'd seen my dad coming down the bank. I was so stunned I couldn't move. And then she kissed me again." He rubbed his hands down his face. "I'll never forget the look on Dad's face. I pushed her away, and she fell down. Dad turned around and headed back toward the house. Edith started laughing, and I went after Dad, to explain."

Gwendolyn's chest squeezed as if caught in a vise. Biting her lip to keep back the questions, she kept her eyes glued to his profile in the fading light, his chiseled lips, straight nose, stubborn chin. She loved every plane and angle of his face, and her heart ached for what he'd been through.

"He didn't believe me. I suppose he couldn't bring himself

to. I guess it was easier to believe his son had betrayed him than to believe his own judgment had been so flawed. I knew I couldn't stay here. Dad left the house, and I went upstairs to pack. When I came down, I went to say good-bye to Betsy and Granddad. I prayed I wouldn't run into Edith, because I don't know what I would've said or done. Then I heard the shot."

Gwendolyn took his hand between both of hers. "Matt, I'm so sorry. You don't have to say any more."

"I do. I have to tell you the rest of it, so you can decide what you want to do." He studied the horizon. "I've never forgiven myself for not trying harder to convince Dad of what really happened. I should've gone to him the minute I first suspected what Edith was up to. I should've cut and run when I found her crying by the creek."

"This isn't your fault, Matt."

"I never thought he'd do something like that."

"Is there any chance that it was an accident?"

"I don't know. That's what folks assumed, and I never told anyone until today what really happened between the three of us, though I think some of the ranch hands suspected."

"What happened to Edith?"

He heaved a sigh. "Dad had turned over the ranch bookkeeping to her pretty early on, because she asked if she could help. By the time we found Dad's body downstream and got back to the ranch house late that night, she'd cleaned out the cashbox and disappeared. We found out she rode straight to Sagebrush and withdrew every last cent from our account there. Last I heard, she was back in Denver, married again."

"And Betsy knows none of this?"

"How could I tell her? She was just a kid, still is, and she has her own problems. I didn't want to disillusion her about our father, and I didn't want her ever to have any doubts about me. I never even told Granddad, though I think he suspected there was more to the story. Then he died, and Betsy got worse." He gave a rough laugh. "And before I could hardly draw a deep breath, you landed on my doorstep out of the blue." Giving her hands a little shake, he released her and stood, pacing the area in front of the bench. "A mail-order bride I didn't order. I thought you were like Edith, grasping, conniving, finagling your way into an old man's affections, coming out here to see what you could bilk him out of."

Gwendolyn moistened her lips, for the first time seeing things from his point of view.

"Every time you tried to help, I accused you." He stopped pacing. "I thought history was repeating itself. But gradually, you were winning me over. The way you took care of Betsy and the house, the way you never asked me for anything or complained that the house wasn't big enough or that you were lonely. You seemed to get joy from such simple things, like those ridiculous weeds you planted today." He chuckled. "I was falling in love with you, but I was still fighting it."

Her heart swelled, and her breath snagged in her throat.

"Then, I went and ruined it by throwing your offer of help with the bookwork back at you." He closed his eyes, turning his face toward the darkening sky. "Then I found you with Jackson, and it looked like all my suspicions were being proved. I was so angry, I wasn't thinking right."

She rose and went to his side, touching his arm. His eyes opened, and he looked down at her. "You do believe me, right? That it was Jackson forcing his attentions on me?"

His hands cupped her shoulders. "I do. I of all people should know what it's like to be falsely accused. Jackson and Edith sound like two of a kind. But I don't want to talk about them anymore. Gwendolyn, I want to start over. I'm tired of fighting how I feel about you." He shoved his hat to the back of his head and starlight illumined his eyes. "I love you, and I don't want you to leave. I regret every harsh word I ever said to you. Please say you'll forgive me and that you'll stay." His grip tightened. "Tell me that when Cummings comes back, you'll marry me. I don't want to live without you."

Tears burned the backs of her eyes. "Oh, Matt, I love you, too." She went into his embrace, wrapping her arms around his waist and pressing her cheek into his chest. The thundering of his heart and the harshness of his breathing matched her own. Now that she knew the whole story, forgiveness came easily. She raised her face to stare into his eyes. "I've been waiting forever for you to ask me to stay."

He lowered his lips to hers, and her eyes fluttered closed. Gathering her even closer, he kissed her with all the ardor and passion her heart could hold. As starbursts of happiness broke behind her eyelids, she knew she'd found her knight in shining armor after all.

ON A WHITE CHARGER

Chapter 1

F ire!"

Reverend Cummings's shout jarred Emmeline almost off the wagon seat. He'd been silent for hours, ever since ordering Emmeline to say her good-byes to her sister at the last ranch and get into the wagon. A greasy, black cloud of smoke billowed into the late afternoon sky ahead of them. The wagon bucked as Cummings urged the team into a gallop, and she gripped the seat to keep from being hurled to the ground.

"What's burning?" The wind whipped the words from her mouth, and she clenched her teeth to keep from biting her tongue as the wagon jolted and swerved.

"Looks like Barrett's place!"

Her heart, lodged in her throat from the wild ride, dropped. Barrett's place. Joseph Barrett. The man she was supposed to marry. Today.

The prairie thundered by in a blur, all her attention focused on the smoke ahead. She held on tight, fighting to keep her seat, but she spent half her time airborne, the other half wincing as her backside smacked the bench.

Buildings rushed toward them, a long, low sod affair open on one side, surrounded by fences and gates, and a small board structure engulfed in flames. Sparks and gouts of fire shot skyward, and clouds of angry smoke bellied up and out as if from a steam engine smokestack. Ash filled the air, choking and hot.

Two men—or one man and a near-grown boy to be precise—ran from a watering trough to the house with buckets, sloshing ineffectively at the raging flames. Steam hissed with each dousing, but the crackle of the hungry inferno made a mockery of their efforts.

The wagon slewed to a stop safely back from the fire, and the horses hung their heads, heaving and panting. Cummings raced toward the men, his rusty black suit coat flapping and his spindly legs churning. Emmeline found herself clambering down and running after him. She bunched her skirts in her hands, and her feet pounded the ground.

Without waiting to be asked, she grabbed the pump handle. Water gushed out of the spout into the half-full trough. Reverend Cummings plunged a bucket into the water and hauled it up. The other two barely seemed to notice she was there. After half a dozen more trips, when Emmeline's arms burned with the unaccustomed effort of wielding the pump handle and her throat and eyes stung from the smoke, Reverend Cummings put his hands out to stop the man and the boy.

"Give it up. It's gone." He wheezed, coughed, and sank onto the edge of the trough.

The bearded man pitched one last bucket of water through the open doorway onto the angry red flames and with slumped shoulders tossed the bucket aside. The younger man let his bucket fall to the ground, where it tipped and ran its contents over the dry ground, puddling around his boots before disappearing into the earth. His back, ramrod straight, was toward Emmeline, and his posture shouted anger, as did his fisted hands. Hair as orange as a carrot showed at the nape of his neck under his hat brim when he bowed his head.

She let go of the pump handle. At that moment the slanted roof cracked and plummeted into the house. Glass broke, and the fire gave a muted *whump*. Heat blasted through the doorway, baking her cheeks, and bits of ash and cinders floated in the air, borne on the breeze.

Digging her handkerchief from her pocket, she swiped at smoke-induced tears. She coughed and cupped her hand under the few trickles still dribbling from the waterspout. A few sips and her throat cleared a bit.

The young man turned sharply and kicked the bucket by his feet. It rocketed into the side of the trough. "Is this enough? Is this enough to make you see reason?" His angry eyes—green as new grass—sparked with all the heat of the house fire behind him. "We're lucky they did it during the day instead of burning us in our beds."

The bearded man put his hand on the boy's shoulder, but the boy shrugged it off, moving a few paces away.

"What are you going to do about this?" The kid spat the words out as if they tasted bad.

"Sean—"

"Never mind. I know what you're going to say. Don't even start with all that claptrap about turning the other cheek. You've been doing that for months and all it gets you is another slap." He stared at the sky, as if imploring the heavens for strength or patience or both, and stalked away down the fence line.

Emmeline pressed her lips together and swallowed. She

felt as if she'd been pitchforked into a play halfway through and didn't know the script. The boy made the fire sound deliberate, but who would set fire to someone's home on purpose? She rubbed her arms to ward off the sudden tremor that raced across her skin.

The bearded man stared at the flames, his face streaked with soot and sweat. He removed his hat, revealing hair the color of newly spaded earth, rich and dark; swiped at his forehead with his sleeve; and drew a deep, raspy breath before turning to Reverend Cummings.

"Thank you for helping."

"I wish we could've saved it." Cummings rose, staggered a bit, and steadied himself. Emmeline had the feeling fighting that fire was the most physical exertion he'd had in months. She grabbed the tin ladle hanging on the fence post beside the trough and filled it from the pump. He took it from her with barely a glance but nodded his thanks. When he'd downed it—his Adam's apple bobbing furiously—he coughed and handed it back to her.

"Barrett, this here's your bride." Cummings righted his suit coat and smoothed his lapels. "Call the boy back to witness the ceremony."

Emmeline jerked. In the rush of pitching in to help with the fire, she'd clean forgotten about her reason for being here. This smoky, sweaty man before her was her fiancé.

Her now-homeless fiancé.

༄

The day Joe Barrett had been waiting for now for weeks, and this had to happen. He turned his back on the fire to study the woman who had traveled hundreds of miles to be his bride.

In the thick of trying to save his home, he'd barely registered that she was there, hauling away at the pump handle.

Now he studied her face and features, comparing them to the mental image he'd carried since first responding to her advertisement. Her letter had given him a few hints, but the reality—though disheveled from her exertions—was better than his daydreams. Yellow hair framed her face and slipped from under the edge of her bonnet. She'd stuck a brave sprig of wildflowers onto her hat sometime that day, and they'd wilted just a bit. Inside the rim of her bonnet, white lace set off the creaminess of her skin.

He closed the distance between them, noting her eyes, light blue and fringed with surprisingly dark lashes. She barely came to his shoulder, and when he stood in front of her, he noted the spattering of freckles across her nose and cheeks.

"Emmeline." He spoke her name, his heart bumping a bit. Now that he was faced with a real-live woman instead of a name on a letter, his blood raced and his breath hitched. A bit of his loneliness slipped away just looking at her.

"I'm so sorry about the house." Her eastern accent took him right back to his younger days, growing up in Boston.

"I'm sorry, too. It's not much of a welcome for you."

Cummings dug into an inner pocket. "No time to waste, Barrett. Let's get this done so I can move on."

Emmeline dabbed her throat with a lacy bit of handkerchief and gave a slight shrug. "He's got to be in Dellsville tonight, and he's rushed us—my sisters and I—all day. He's in an awful hurry, and he won't quit harping until we do as he says." Though she smiled, Joe caught a glint of exasperation in her eyes that bespoke the truth of her words.

Joe lowered his voice. "Old Cummings is a rough stick, and a might crotchety at the best of times. But he isn't as bad as he seems. More bark than bite."

"That's good, because he's been barking all day." A mischievous glint lit her blue eyes, and a smile curved her pink lips.

"I best call Sean back." Putting his fingers to his lips, Joe let out a whistle. Emmeline jumped and gasped, but the sound caught up to the boy in a flash and had him loping back.

Sean. A burden and a blessing all at once. Also responding to Joe's whistle, Shadow, one of his dogs, crested the brow of the hill and trotted at Sean's side, her shaggy black-and-white fur shimmering in the sun. The stock had been brought in close to the house, in anticipation of Emmeline's arrival, and was now grazing less than a half mile away, though out of sight of the house over the hill.

"I'm sorry to have to rush you like this, but I don't actually mind getting the ceremony done quickly. We can't leave the livestock unattended too long, and this"—he waved toward the smoldering ruins of his house—"brought us both running."

Sean arrived, hands in pockets, shoulders hunched, so much hurt and anger and frustration bound up in his scowl. "What?"

"This is Emmeline, Sean. The reverend's in a bit of a hurry, and I need you to witness our marriage."

His orange eyebrows shot toward his hat brim. "You can't be getting married now? Where's she going to live? The house is. . ." He waved to the dying flames.

Joe ran his hand over his whiskers. "There's the wagon. We can live in that until we can rebuild the house. It'll be crowded, but we'll be outside most of the time." He shot Emmeline a glance, apprehensive about how an eastern woman would take to the idea of living in a wagon for the summer.

Sean tugged his sleeve and pulled him a few steps away. As tall as Joe's own six-foot- two-inch frame but lacking the bulk of a grown man, Sean radiated disapproval. "I knew this mail-order bride idea was a harebrained scheme when you first mentioned it, and the house fire makes it even more so. Now isn't the time to be getting married. You should be putting your effort into protecting what's yours. It has to be Randall, and he isn't going to stop. You're going to have to fight him, to stand up for what's yours."

"You know my views on that, Sean. Nothing I own is worth killing a man for. You can't go off half-cocked, making accusations you can't back up with proof. We have Orla Randall's word that he'll leave us alone."

Sean snorted. "You might have the old man's word, but that don't extend to his son, and you know it. You're blind if you think he isn't behind all this. If you don't fight back, Blake will either run you off the range, or he'll shoot you in the back some night when you're on watch. When are you going to grab a gun and fight?"

"Sean." Joseph dragged his hands down his face, weary of this argument. "I swore I would never pick up a gun against my fellow man ever again, not after all I went through in the war. I'm not willing to kill over some grass and some animals."

A dark look, one that made Joseph sad and caused him not a little worry, passed over Sean's face. "You might not be willing to kill for them, but are you willing to die for them? Because that's what's going to happen."

Chapter 2

The wedding took only a few minutes, and Cummings all but hurled her baggage onto the ground before picking up the reins and hurrying the team away down the west trail. Emmeline stood beside the trough next to her new husband, watching the last link—however cranky and temporary—with her sisters disappear in the rattling wagon. The prairie suddenly seemed bigger and emptier. A quick thrill followed hard on the shock. She'd done it. She was here in Wyoming Territory, married and living on a real ranch.

Hooking her pinkie through a strand of hair blowing across her face, she surveyed the place that would become her new home. Netting-like fence stretched between wooden posts, forming smallish pens around the long, low shed that was open on one side. She hadn't seen fencing like that on her sisters' ranches, but perhaps this was something new.

Sean, his face seemingly set in a permanent scowl, shoved his hands into his pockets and headed back the way he'd come, taking the dog with him.

"We'll follow as soon as I hitch up the wagon." Joe had to holler after him, but Sean didn't break his stride or relax his hunched shoulders.

When would she meet the cowboys? On her sisters' new ranches, the ranch hands had come to the wedding—though at Jane's wedding there had only been the one older man present. Joseph's hired men must all be out working.

A pair of horses dozed in the corner of one corral, the only livestock evident.

Joseph headed toward the smoldering house and put his boot against a blackened upright, giving it a shove and sending it toppling into the ashes. "Not much of a welcome for you, I'm afraid."

"You couldn't help it, Joseph." She glanced at her possessions sitting on the ground where Cummings had left them. "You said there was a wagon?"

"Call me Joe. And the wagon's behind the shed. I'll hitch up the team, and we can load up your things. It will be a bit cramped, but we spend most of our time outside anyway."

While she waited for him to return, she opened one of the valises. Her sketch pads and pencils were jumbled from Cummings's rough treatment, and several of her colored chalks had broken, but a safe familiarity trickled through her as she touched them. The wind fluttered one of the pages, and she lifted the sketchbook out of the valise and flipped through the pages. A smile formed at the various drawings of cowboys and knights, cattle and castles, cow ponies and chargers. Closing the book, she hugged it to herself. Now, instead of just reading about and dreaming of cowboys, she was actually married to one.

Joe led the two horses from the corral around the back of the low, three-sided shed. How soon before he taught her to ride a horse? She imagined herself skimming over the ground on a fleet mount, the wind streaming through her hair, racing the sun. Since it was still early spring, surely she'd arrived in time to see a real cattle roundup. Her mind filled with everything she'd read about cowboys and ranch life. With every passing moment the trappings and conventions of school life in Massachusetts fell away.

A rattle caught her attention. Joseph led the team, hitched to what appeared to be a wooden house on wheels. It even had a stovepipe jutting through the curved roof. Not quite as long as a farm wagon, it had a window in each side, and as he turned the team, she spied a door in the back. The wagon looked for all the world like it belonged in a gypsy caravan. It only lacked the gaudy paint job like she'd seen on similar vehicles back east. Surely her new husband wasn't a gypsy?

"I'm glad I stocked the wagon yesterday. Plenty of food and supplies to last a few months. At least those didn't go up with the house." Joseph came around to load her things. "I'll help you up inside."

"Where did you get a wagon like this? Did you buy it from a gypsy?"

He laughed. "No, it came with the ranch." He helped her up the small set of stairs hanging from the back.

She stepped into the wagon, glad it was tall enough she could stand erect. A narrow aisle ran down the center with a bunk on each side, covered with rough, woolen blankets. At the far end, near the front of the wagon, a small sheet-metal stove stood on squat legs. Bags of flour, cornmeal, and beans crowded each other, and a case of canned goods blocked the aisle.

Joe joined her, stooping to keep from hitting the ceiling. "We'll have to make room for your things. For now, I'll just put them on a bed. Each of the bunks lifts up, and there's storage underneath. I'll clear out one of them for your use when we get to the camp. I hadn't figured on you coming out on the range with us all summer, but with the house gone..." His voice was pleasantly rumbly and deep, sending a shiver through her. He hefted her trunk onto one of the bunks. Surveying the cramped space, he tugged on his beard. "This isn't exactly the honeymoon you must've hoped for, but I'm happy you're here. I've been looking forward to your arrival ever since I got your letter." He patted his shirt pocket. "I'm glad I carried it with me, otherwise I would've lost it when the house burned down."

Heat swished in her cheeks at the mention of a honeymoon, and she sought a safer topic. "How long will it take to get the house rebuilt?"

He leaped out of the wagon and picked up her last bag. "It won't happen right away, I'm afraid. I'll have to wait until the fall sale to have enough cash for lumber and hardware." His dark brown eyes regarded her, as if judging how she would take this news. "I know it isn't what you're used to, being from the East Coast. We'll try to take it easy on you."

A whole summer in this wagon, out on the range. She bit her lip, trying to quell her excitement as she stepped out of the wagon and closed the little door. This was going to be the best summer of her life. She'd be an experienced cowgirl in no time. Would they have a sidesaddle, or would she have to learn to ride astride? Would she see any Indians? She should've bought one of those wide-brimmed hats. Her bonnet would never do out here. Perhaps he had an extra she could borrow. A thousand images popped into her head, fueled by her curiosity with all things western.

"I'm sure I'll be fine."

She found herself giving in to the desire to talk as they rattled out of the yard, conscious that for the first time in her life she needn't worry about one of her older sisters reminding her to hold her tongue. "I can't tell you how long I've looked forward to this. Wyoming Territory is nothing like Massachusetts. There, houses and people are cheek-by-jowl, and everything is so. . ." She didn't know how to explain it. "Constricting, I guess. Everyone seems to watch everyone else and feels free to judge their behavior. And the buildings block out the view and seem to press in on you. The only place you can see any distance at all is down at the shore, looking over the sea." She spread her arms wide, as if to embrace all of this openness, unable to contain her excitement and joy any longer. "I've dreamed since I was a little girl about living on the frontier. I fell in love with stories about Daniel Boone and Davy Crockett, then Kit Carson and Jim Bridger. I read everything I could find on wagon trains, the Oregon Trail, cattlemen and ranching and branding and roping and everything. I nearly wore out my edition of *Harper's* when an article on cattle drives from Texas appeared in print. I think it's so romantic, cowboys on horseback riding night herd, singing to the cattle. I never imagined I'd be married to a real cowboy."

He stiffened beside her. "You think cowboys are romantic?"

"Oh, yes. When your letter arrived from Wyoming Territory, I knew God was answering my prayers. I can't wait to learn to ride a horse, and I want to learn to herd cattle. I want to learn to cook over a campfire and a hundred other things. I want to be a real westerner."

He was silent for a while, and she studied him from the

corner of her eye. The smell of smoke clung to his brown shirt and tan pants. The legs of his trousers disappeared into high-topped boots with long earflaps. Strong hands held the reins, and his broad shoulders stretched his suspenders. She hadn't expected him to be bearded, though the effect wasn't unpleasant. His letter had said he was thirty-one years old, but there was something about his eyes—so dark brown it was hard to distinguish the iris from the pupil—that bespoke a hard-won wisdom beyond his years.

Flicking the reins, he shifted on the seat. "I didn't know you were so interested in cattle ranching. Before we get to the campsite, there's something you should know, and I hope you aren't too disappointed when you see the setup. You see, I'm not exactly a cowboy—"

"Oh, I know. You're the ranch owner, not a mere cowboy. But you do work the range. I've read all about it. I'm eager to meet the rest of your hands. It must take a lot of men to cover so much ground and tend so many animals. Where was Sean going? He can't be too far away if he was walking. Though I thought that was curious, since I'd read that a cowboy never walks when he can ride. Where was Sean's horse? Are we going to catch up with him and give him a ride?"

"Emmeline, if you'll just let me explain—" He broke off as a strange sound drifted toward them.

"What on earth?" She braced her hand against his shoulder to maintain her balance, unable to believe what she was seeing. "What are those animals doing on your land? This is a lot of nerve. You'll have to run them off."

A river of woolly backs flowed over the brow of a low hill, baaing and bleating. A dog barked, and behind the short-legged, barrel-shaped beasts, two men walked with long crooks.

"Those sheepmen have invaded your range."

Joe pulled the horses to a stop. "Emmeline, I've been trying to tell you. I don't have cattle. Those are my animals. *I'm* a sheepman."

⌇

Two hours later, Emmeline eased onto the chair Joe had placed beside the campfire for her, still dazed. She rested her limp hands in her lap and stared into the coals.

From the other side of the fire, Joe watched her, as did the boy, Sean. A third man, one of Joe's—her mind still balked at the idea—*shepherds* sipped coffee, his hands wrapped around his cup to ward off the evening chill. Pierre, Joe had called him. An older man, quiet, slim, with a French accent.

All around her in the deepening night, fuzzy pale humps lay on the ground or stood quietly. Moonlight bathed their dumpy bodies and glinted off marble-like eyes. Those eyes, with their strange horizontal pupils, eyes that didn't engender trust, that gave her a shivery unsettled feeling, as if they might go berserk at any moment. She could pick out a faint grinding noise, the occasional click of teeth, as hundreds of sheep chewed their cud. Every so often a bleat or baa punctured the night calm.

Sheep.

Hundreds of them.

This wasn't just a bad dream or a cruel joke. It was real. She was married to a sheepherder. Everything she'd read told her that sheep were the bane of the open range, a blight on the land that caused untold devastation to the grazing, making it unfit for cattle. Real ranchers despised sheep and sheepherders, and in her heart, she'd joined their crusade against the woolly animals and their minders. Now she was—*gulp*—one of them.

Emmeline jumped when something wet and cool nudged her hand. The shaggy black-and-white dog sat before her, a silly grin on her face with her ears cocked and head tilted just a bit as if to say, "Hey, you're new here. Want to be friends?" Her pink tongue lolled, and she swiped it toward Emmeline's fingers.

"That's Shadow." Joe poked the fire, sending gouts of sparks upward as the coals settled. "I'm hoping for some nice litters of pups from her. Good sheepdogs are highly prized, and Shadow's one of the best."

Emmeline reached a tentative hand toward the dog's broad, smooth head, touching the silky ears and almost smiling when the dog closed her eyes and leaned into the petting. Emmeline had never had a dog before. The school had forbidden pets in the masters' houses. Now she found she had several dogs, with more on the way. Perhaps there was no great loss without some small gain.

Joe had pointed out a large white dog on the perimeter of the flock when he'd first helped her from the wagon. She'd barely been able to take in his words through the fog of shock swirling in her brain.

"That's Shep, and he's the guard dog. His job is watching out for wolves and coyotes. He's not a pet, so don't try to touch him. Once I introduce you, he'll leave you alone." Joe snapped his fingers and the shaggy white dog loped over, stopping a few paces away and lowering his head, sniffing and eyeing Emmeline. "Shep." Joe commanded the dog to come closer. Shep came, and after a close examination that had Emmeline wanting to back away, he shook himself and trotted back to his job.

Another dog, black and white like Shadow, now sat beside Joe on the far side of the fire. His bush of a tail stirred the grass when Joe patted his head. "This is Robert Burns, but you can call him Robbie. He's Shadow's mate, and a first-rate sheepdog. I got them as puppies from a Scotsman who was trailing his flock north to the Big Horn Basin."

The Frenchman rose and tossed the dregs of his coffee cup out onto the grass. He stretched, yanked at his suspenders, and flicked back the hank of salt-and-pepper hair that had fallen over his forehead. "Robbie only has room in his heart for one master. But Shadow, she loves everybody. I will take ze first watch tonight, and I will wake ze boy when it is his turn."

"I'm supposed to take the midwatch." Joe frowned, the campfire casting shifting patterns of light and dark on his face.

"No, no, not tonight. Sean and I can handle it. You should stay in camp wiz madam." He nodded toward Emmeline. "I am sure ze madam would appreciate it."

The madam would appreciate it if her husband had told her about the sheep before she prattled on like a nitwit about cowboys and horses and all. She forced a polite smile in Pierre's direction.

Sean, who had ignored her all evening, went to the back of the wagon and jerked down a bedroll. "Guess me 'n' Pierre will be sleeping outside all summer." He pressed his thin lips together.

Emmeline stopped stroking the dog and gripped her fingers in her lap. The boy's hostility rolled from him like the waves of heat from the burning house had. She couldn't tell if he was angry at her, Joe, or the whole world. Shadow whimpered and put her head on Emmeline's knee, staring up at her with dark, imploring eyes to continue petting.

"Nothing unusual in that, is there?" Joe kept his voice calm and reasonable. "The only time you slept in the wagon last summer was when it rained. I thought you liked sleeping outside."

The boy scowled. "I like having a choice."

"We don't always get to choose, Sean. And sometimes what we think we want isn't what's really best for us."

"Like you'd know what was best for me. You can't even figure out what's best for you. Sitting here, when we should be tracking down the varmints that burned your house. You know who's responsible, and you know he's laughing at you right now. Instead of going after him, you're sitting here like a lump, hoping that if you ignore the problem, it will go away." Sean walked with jerky steps around to the far side of the fire, and just outside the ring of light cast by the glowing coals, he shook out his blankets. Shadow wriggled, whined, and headed over to join him.

A thousand questions rippled through Emmeline's head. Sean had all but declared Joe a coward. What would her new husband do about that? Sean might only be a boy, but according to all her reading, calling another man a coward was a good reason for a gunfight, or at the least a fistfight.

Instead of calling the boy out, Joe rose, tossed his stick onto the fire, and came to stand before her. Emmeline's muscles tightened. He held out his hand. "We'd best turn in.

Lambing is going to start soon, and we'll be rushed off our feet."

His voice, though tired, was as mild as a spring breeze. He didn't appear angry at all. She swallowed. Was Sean's assessment true? Was Joe a coward? Her mind thrust away that idea. He couldn't be.

Taking his hand, she rose, still numb from the shocks coming at her one by one today, how far from her ideal her reality was turning out to be. He led her to the back of the wagon and helped her inside. A match scratched and flared, illuminating the cramped space as he lit the lantern hanging from a hook in the center of the ceiling.

Time. I need a little time. Everything is happening too fast, and I need time to think it all through. She pressed her hands to her middle and plunked down onto the edge of one of the bunks. "Can we talk?"

He moved aside a sack of cornmeal and sat on the bunk opposite her. Gently he took her hands, leaning forward until his elbows rested on his thighs. "I'd like that. You've been mighty quiet tonight."

Warmth slid up her cheeks at his nearness and the rasp of his rough hands on hers. The smell of smoke still lingered faintly on his clothes, but it was mixed with the scent of soap and outdoors—and sheep. She took a shuddering breath. "It's all so different from what I imagined." She couldn't hold his gaze, instead staring at their hands, his so dark and work-worn and hers pale and small by comparison. "I feel like a fool, going on like that about cowboys and the West." Her throat tightened.

He squeezed her fingers. "I should've explained things in my letter, though I never thought you'd care. Since we didn't have a real courtship, it's expected that there are a lot of things we still need to learn about each other."

A trapped feeling wrapped around her, and she swallowed. She needed to put some distance between them, however small, and withdrew her hands, scooting away until her back rested against the side of the wagon. She drew her legs up onto the bunk and tucked her feet under her skirts. "Perhaps now would be a good time to get started on that learning. I have a hundred questions."

A soft smile crossed his face. "I'm not surprised." Settling back as if he had all the time in the world, he said, "Ask away."

"Sean seems to think you know who burned your house. If you know who did it, why aren't you chasing them down and bringing them to justice? Why haven't you notified the local sheriff or marshal or whoever the law is out here? Shouldn't you be forming a posse or something? Strapping on your six-guns and chasing down the varmints?"

He blinked, grinned, and let loose a laugh. "You've been reading too many dime novels. I'm not Wild Bill Hickok, and this isn't Abilene. I can't go gunning after every man in Wyoming Territory who hates sheepherders. I'd run out of bullets."

Her temper flared at his amusement. "Well, what *are* you going to do about it then? Sean seemed to think you weren't planning on doing anything." Again the fear that she might've married a coward nudged her heart. Here she was on her wedding night, and instead of the gallant, brave knight of the range of whom she'd dreamed, she had a pacifist, a man prepared to just swallow any insult or attack.

"I'm not going to do anything tonight, that's for sure."

Disappointment cracked her heart. A sheepman *and* a coward? What had she done? Considering the man from behind the shield of her lashes, she knew she wasn't ready to be his wife, wedding ceremony notwithstanding. He was nothing like she'd imagined, nothing like she'd built up in her mind. When she'd first gotten his letter, she'd spun such dreams. It was almost as if she'd known him forever. But the man before her bore little resemblance to those dreams. A sense of betrayal settled onto her shoulders. Drawing a deep breath, she studied her hands in her lap. "Joe. . ."

"Emmeline, I know things aren't exactly what you expected, but I hope you can adjust to me and my way of life without too much hardship. I've been waiting a long time for you to get here, and I know that if you give me a chance, you won't regret marrying me. We can have a good life together, build up this ranch into something to be proud of, and along the way, I hope we can come to truly care for each other."

She dared a glance at his face and had to look away from the hopeful, eager light in his dark eyes. "Joe, everything is just so different from what I expected, I'm going to need a little time. I'm not prepared to. . ." She battled down the embarrassment fluttering higher and higher in her chest. ". . .to live with you as man and wife just yet. I think we should get to know each other better first." Though what good that would do, she didn't know. She only knew a little about him, and that was more than enough to make her realize she might've made a huge mistake in marrying him.

Chapter 3

The next morning, Joe took care not to make much noise as he rose and dressed, conscious of the woman sleeping on the far side of the curtain he'd hung around her bunk the previous night. As he tucked his shirt into his trousers and eased his suspenders over his shoulders, he tried to shrug off the disappointment at her pronouncement that she wasn't ready to be his wife in every sense.

A part of him could appreciate that. . .or tried to. She'd suffered some serious blows to her dreams. But he had, too. Finding himself wed to a woman enamored of cowboys had been a shock, not to mention the loss of most of his worldly goods in the house fire.

But what hurt the most was the disenchantment in her sky-blue eyes as she realized he wasn't prepared to grab a gun and go after whoever had torched his house. She hadn't been able to hide the fact that she thought him at best weak, at worst a coward. The fact that she sided with Sean in his assessment of Joe's character pierced his pride like a cactus spine.

Emerging into the dawn, he breathed deeply. Shadow rose from her place under the wagon and wriggled toward him, head low, tail waggling so hard her hindquarters danced.

Robbie, ever alert at the edge of the flock, trotted over to sniff his hand. The dog shook his head hard enough to make his ears slap, and the shake went through him from nose to tail. Joe grinned at the execution of this morning ritual.

He stroked Shadow's head and ran his hand along her shiny, black-and-white back. Robbie submitted to a single pat before heading back toward the flock, which was already rising, methodically cropping grass with insatiable appetites.

Joe stretched once more, working the stiffness out of his back. He'd tossed on his bunk for hours, wondering if he'd made the biggest mistake of his life, sending for an eastern bride with a head full of ridiculous notions and expectations. The idea had seemed not only feasible but downright sensible when Zeb Parker and Harrison Garvey had approached him about it. Of course, they'd caught him at a weak moment, when he was feeling particularly lonely as the winter wind gusted against the door. Sean and Pierre weren't much for conversation, and the starkness of their bachelor existence had been nudging Joe for a while. The thought of someone feminine and soft in his life had greatly appealed.

He glanced through the still-open door of the wagon at the curtain surrounding her bunk. She probably slept peacefully behind the drapery, dreaming of dashing cowboys, stampedes, and gunfights over sacred honor.

With a shrug, he turned away to pile sticks and twigs together in the ash circle left from last night's fire.

Pierre lay in his bedroll, his shock of graying hair just visible above the blankets. The Frenchman kept mostly to himself, but he was a good shepherd.

Putting more twigs on the fire, Joe could just make out Sean's silhouette on a little knoll about a hundred yards away.

He sat hunched with a blanket over his shoulders, staring down at the flock. Remembering the young man's fury from the previous night, Joe scrubbed his beard and pressed his lips together.

"What am I going to do with him, girl?" He spoke to Shadow as he filled the coffeepot from the water barrel fastened to the side of the wagon. "He's like a lit match in an ammunition bunker."

Joe frowned at the black memories that surfaced at the comparison. When would those dark days stop haunting his thoughts? The war and those horrible times were all behind him, and he had no intention of ever living that way again.

He foraged among the camp supplies until he found the can labeled Arbuckle's Ariosa Coffee. Prying off the lid as quietly as possible, he got the coffee into the pot and onto the fire. A few rustles and bumps from within the wagon told him Emmeline must be stirring.

Sean strode into camp a few minutes later, sniffing the aroma and rubbing his eyes. He nudged Pierre, who sat up and rubbed his eyes. Scratching his chest through the wrinkled front of his shirt, the Frenchman yawned. Joe started to say good morning, but Pierre's mouth snapped shut and his eyes widened at something behind Joe.

Wheeling, Joe caught sight of his bride on the top step of the wagon. The breath disappeared from his lungs, and he froze, mesmerized.

Her hair. He couldn't take his eyes from it. Falling in a glorious ripple, strands of gold and yellow and a hint of red glinted in the morning light. Not straight and not curly, it swayed in perfect waves from crown to waist. She beckoned him closer, and he unstuck his feet to walk over to her.

"I hope you don't mind." She kept her voice low. "It's so cramped in the wagon, I keep bumping into things when I try to put my hair up. Is it all right if I come outside to do it?"

"Yes," he croaked. How he resisted reaching out to touch those soft, silky strands, he'd never know. A wave of possessiveness swept over him. "I'll bring a chair around to the back of the wagon so you can have some privacy."

He wanted her away from Sean and Pierre's eyes. As her husband, that glorious sight should be his alone. He brought her a chair, and when she sat, tilting her head to the side to brush her hair with long, steady strokes, he crossed his arms and leaned against the wagon to watch.

"Did you sleep well?"

"Once I finally got to sleep, yes."

She spoke around a mouthful of hairpins jutting from between her pretty lips, and he couldn't help but notice the faint pink to her cheeks and the way she kept her lashes down.

Much too quickly, she had her hair twisted into some kind of fold on the back of her head, removing pins from her mouth one by one and inserting them until she had it all firmly secured. Not until then could Joe seem to draw a deep breath.

He carried her chair around the wagon as she put her brush away. Sean poked the fire and tested the coffeepot to see if it was hot yet.

"Lambing started this morning. No trouble so far that I could see. Couple of sets of twins and a couple of large singles."

"Any trouble during the night?"

"A few coyotes sniffing around, but Shep ran them off pretty quick."

Joe poured out the first cup of coffee and took it to Emmeline. She gave him a quick peek, accepted the cup, and blew across the top.

"Thank you."

He couldn't help noticing that she looked fresh as the morning, and a spark of hope and longing lit in his chest. If she could just get over this infatuation with cowboys, everything would be perfect.

She seemed impervious to the effect she had on him, her eyes darting to the sunrise, to the fire, and out over the flock on the green hillside. A sip of the dark brew had her blinking.

"I usually have mine with milk and sugar. Black coffee will take some getting used to."

"Sugar I can help you with." He dug in the trunk beside the wagon. "Milk will have to wait a bit. With lambing just started, ewe's milk is still a day or so away."

"Sheep's milk?" She turned the full force of her blue eyes on him. Her nose wrinkled.

He smothered a smile at her astonishment. "Sure. People have been drinking sheep's milk since Adam and Eve. Makes a fine cheese, too, so I hear."

She accepted the sugar crock and dipped out half a spoonful. "No, thank you. I'll make do with just sugar."

Sean rolled his eyes. "Are you going to cook breakfast?" He sloshed coffee into a cup and eyed Emmeline as if to say "Why are you even here?"

"Sean." Joe lifted a cloth-wrapped bundle from the food locker. "We've been a bachelor household for a long time, but I'm sure you haven't forgotten all the manners your mama tried to teach you. Emmeline is a lady and my wife, two very good reasons for you to show her some respect." He kept his tone mild, but he gave Sean a steady look to let the boy know he was serious.

With a shrug, Sean drained his cup. The sound of hoof-beats drew Joe's attention away from any further reprimand.

Blake Randall.

Though the rider was still too far away to see his face in the early morning light, Joe would know that black horse anywhere. Loping along on graceful legs, that stallion was the pride of the Rocking R Ranch.

Randall rode through the edge of Joe's flock, scattering ewes and wethers without care. Shadow lowered her head and emitted a deep growl. Her hackles rose, and her lips pulled back, baring her teeth. Joe snapped his fingers and flattened his palm toward the ground. Shadow lowered herself until her belly touched the ground, but her body remained tense.

Joe didn't blame her. Blake Randall had a disturbing effect on man and beast.

⁓

A real-live cowboy at last. Emmeline couldn't stop staring at the young man on the black horse. From his wide-brimmed hat to his tall leather boots, he was the epitome of everything she'd imagined a cowboy should be. He wore a bandanna knotted at his throat, a leather vest, and a confident smile.

His horse pranced, tossing its head, causing the sun to flash off the bright metal of the ornate bridle. The saddle creaked pleasantly, and the bit jingled in time to the impact of hooves on the dry ground. Emmeline couldn't help but compare the image before her—the perfect picture of a true westerner—with her homespun-clad, soft-spoken husband.

Joe stepped forward. "Blake. You're out early."

The cowboy didn't dismount. "Pa sent me over." He shrugged. "That cranky Reverend Cummings came through our place just after dark last night and said your house went up in smoke. A real shame. Any idea what happened?" He cocked his head, his horse sidling. He didn't sound particularly sorry, more bored than anything.

Shaking his head, Joe put his hands into his pockets. "No. We were tending the flock and saw the smoke. By the time we got there, it was too late to save anything."

"Like I said, that's a real shame. Cummings said he'd brought you a bride, too." His encompassing glance took in the campsite and stopped on Emmeline. With graceful fluidity, he dismounted and swept his hat from his dark hair, his smile flashing. "He didn't mention how pretty you were." He dropped the reins and advanced, holding out his hand.

Though this was a breach of eastern etiquette—not waiting until the lady offered her hand first—Emmeline reciprocated, a flush of pleasure at his compliment rushing to her cheeks. She tried to quell the blush, but easy coloring was the curse of being so fair. Her sisters, though fair themselves, had teased at how easily Emmeline's skin colored, whether angry or happy.

"I'm pleased to meet you, Mr. . . . ?" She raised her eyebrows and smiled into his gray eyes.

Joe cleared his throat. "Sorry. Emmeline, this is Blake Randall. Blake, this is my wife, Emmeline Barrett. Blake and his family own a spread just west of here. His father, Orla, is my friend."

Her new married name sounded strange to her ears, and the possessive tone to Joe's voice didn't escape her. Blake engulfed her hand in his gloved one, gave it a quick squeeze, and let go. "A pleasure, ma'am." He turned back to Joe.

"Pa wanted me to tell you that if you need anything, you just have to ask. Supplies, blankets, anything. Why he wants to let stubby-legged, walking vermin ruin the best grazing is beyond me, and I've told him so many times." His lip twisted, and he flicked a glance toward the flock. "Mangy beasts. Not worth the aggravation of driving them to the market. But I'm still willing to buy every last one of them. When you're finally ready to sell, I'll pay top dollar then run them all off a cliff."

Emmeline stiffened. Run the animals off a cliff? Just who did this young man think he was? Not that she had any love for sheep, but to just kill them all? She waited for Joe's response, hoping he'd throw this arrogant neighbor out of his camp.

But it was Sean who leaped into the fray first. He thrust out his chest, strode over to stand in front of Blake, and poked him in the shoulder. "We're not selling, and you can't drive us out. I don't care how many shanties you burn or how many of our sheep you try to kill. We're staying. This is our land, bought and paid for. If you think you can drive us off, you've got another long think coming." His chin jutted, and his hands clenched so hard he shook. Rearing back with one skinny arm, Sean prepared to launch a punch.

Blake responded in kind, his huge hands balling and his muscles tensing as he reared back.

Lightning quick, Joe's hand covered Sean's fist and held it, spinning the boy around. The speed and ease with which he deflected the boy amazed Emmeline. He interposed his body between the two combatants.

"Enough. Sean, get back to the flock and check on those lambing ewes. Blake, I apologize. Please thank your father for his offer of assistance. We're doing fine for now."

Sean's hot glare and red-suffused face reminded Emmeline of a kettle ready to explode. He quivered, his narrow chest rising and falling, before spinning on his heel and stomping toward the sheep. Emmeline let out her breath. She wasn't used to being around men much at all and certainly had no experience to prepare her for yelling and brawling. Yet she couldn't deny the thrill that shot through her. This was more exciting than a dime novel.

Pierre set his cup beside the fire and headed after Sean without a word.

Blake removed his gloves, finger by finger. His gray eyes were cold as sleet. "My ma said to tell you that if you need a place to leave your bride until you get your house rebuilt, she could stay with us. Ma would like the company, and we've got plenty of room."

Emmeline waited for her husband to answer. Would he take this opportunity to send her away?

Joe shook his head. "I appreciate the offer, but we'll be staying here. Mrs. Barrett is prepared to spend the summer months in the camp with us. I'm sure by this fall I'll be in a position to rebuild the house."

Blake tucked his gloves into his belt. "You're making a mistake. Why not sell out now? If you wait too long, you might not have anything worth selling. Pa isn't going to be around forever to protect you, you know. His heart's mighty fragile." His eyes narrowed. "Once he's gone, you might find yourself in a tight spot."

"We'll be fine."

"Don't say I didn't warn you." Blake mounted his horse. He nodded to Joe, touched his finger to his hat brim, and she couldn't quite be sure, but he might've winked her way. He certainly smiled broadly. Lifting his reins, he galloped away. Shadow wriggled to her side and put her broad forehead under Emmeline's hand.

"Are you done?"

Joe's question jarred her out of her daydreams. "Pardon?"

"Did you look your fill at that cowboy?" His voice held a tone she'd not heard before, something sharp and weighted.

"Was I staring? I'm sorry." She stroked the dog's head. "Would he really run all these sheep off a cliff?"

"That's the cattlemen's favorite way of destroying a flock. Cheaper than wasting bullets. I heard up in the Bighorn Basin they ran a flock of two thousand off a cliff in one go."

"Two thousand?" She gasped. "Did those men go to jail?"

"No. The law is on the side of the cattlemen. Even if they do investigate, nothing ever comes of it." He grabbed a handful of last night's leftover biscuits. "I'll take these out to the boys." Stalking away across the short-cropped grass, he looked so strong and capable. He hadn't backed down from Blake Randall, nor had he gone out of his way to provoke him.

Joe Barrett was a puzzle.

Like squirrels, her thoughts raced and chased one another, over and around, through and back. If only she could talk to her sisters, to see how she was supposed to handle this. Though she had always chafed at their restrictions, she now longed for their advice. Emmeline tried to imagine what they would say. Evelyn would tell her to get her foolish notions about knight-cowboys out of her head and start thinking sensibly about being a married woman. Jane would tell her to get busy in camp, straightening up and making herself useful instead of mooning after things she couldn't have. Gwendolyn would put her arm around Emmeline's shoulders, give her a squeeze, and whisper that she should make the best of things, because things always turned out pretty well, didn't they?

Pinning her shoulders back and raising her chin, she resolved to take all their imagined advice. She was a married woman now, and she would make the best of things, and she would start by making breakfast and tidying up the camp.

Chapter 4

Easy, girl." Joe straddled the ewe and held her immobile, allowing her knock-kneed youngster to dart in to suckle. "Stand still and feed your baby. You'll both feel better if you do." Every time the lamb had tried to nurse, the ewe had sauntered away, oblivious to her maternal duties. Now the lamb's tail flicked and swished in contentment. Hopefully, this pair would get the hang of things quickly and be able to operate without assistance.

"They're coming thick and fast." Sean wiped his hands on the grass and observed a large pair of twins, wet and slimy, being nuzzled and licked by their mother. "Like opening a floodgate."

His first hostility-free words to Joe since the confrontation with Blake Randall almost a week before. Joe let go of the sheep and stepped away, pleased when she stood still, eyes at half-mast, chewing her cud while the lamb finished its meal. On the other side of the flock, Pierre watched another lambing ewe, ready to step in and help if necessary.

"At this rate, the flock will double in a week." A satisfied feeling settled into his chest, the first in a long time. In spite of setbacks, they were making a success of sheep farming. *Thank You, God.*

Joe scanned the campsite, spying Emmeline coming their way with Shadow at her side. His new wife had spent the past several days learning the rudiments of camp life, and the dog had been her constant companion. When Emmeline wasn't trying her hand at campfire cooking or organizing the wagon, she sat on a hillside well away from the sheep with paper and pencils.

She hadn't mentioned cowboys or cattle again. With all the lambing going on, Joe hadn't had much time to spend with her. Though around the fire at night she engaged in conversation and appeared to take in everything with intelligent eyes, she still maintained her distance, ducking behind her curtain in the wagon before he went to bed. He took his turn on watch each night and had to force himself to concentrate on the flock. His mind strayed to her over and over, trying to figure out a way to bridge the distance between them.

Instead of walking away from the flock, she edged closer, holding a book in her arms. A pencil jutted from behind her ear. So far, she'd kept her writings to herself, though he had a powerful hankering to see what she spent such time on.

Her blue eyes, a little wider than usual, darted from sheep to sheep as if she expected one of them to attack her. Shadow stopped at the edge of the flock and lay down as she'd been taught, and Emmeline inched between woolly bodies. Most of the sheep moved out of her way, but one barrel-shaped ewe stood her ground and even stamped her foot, protecting the speckle-faced lamb she'd birthed early that morning.

Emmeline froze, her shoulders squeezing together as if she wanted to make herself small.

"What's she doing?" Sean snorted. "She think that ewe's

gonna bite her or something?"

"Go easy. She's not spent much time with animals before."

"Why'd she come all this way and marry a shepherd then? She should've married a shopkeeper or something." Sean, who was young enough to have little tolerance for anyone who wasn't just like him, sauntered away with his hands in his pockets.

Joe headed toward his bride, slow and easy, as one had to be around sheep. She glanced up at him, and her hand smoothed her hair. A bit of color came into her cheeks, and he smiled. Watching the ebb and flow of her blushes was an activity of which he never tired.

The lamb seemed to sense his mother's distress, for he set up bawling, jutting his pink tongue out with each bleat. He shook his head and ducked under his mama's belly, seeking some milky comfort.

"Easy there, old girl. Nobody wants to hurt your baby." Joe soothed the ewe with his voice. She cocked her head, regarding him with one eye, and seemed to shrug before lowering her head to crop grass.

"So it's really true. Sheep do know their shepherd's voice."

"There are a lot of Bible passages that I understand so much better now that I'm a shepherd. God wasn't wrong in comparing his people to sheep. We need the Good Shepherd, or we're all goners." He tucked his fingers behind his suspenders. "This is the first time you've come out into the flock. Did you need something?"

She shaded her eyes against the glare of the sun. "Just to talk. I was wondering if you could teach me about the sheep. It's getting awfully boring being alone all day, and if you're intent on being a shepherd, I'd best resign myself to the idea."

Joe pursed his lips and stroked his beard. Not exactly a joyous embracing of his chosen profession but better than seeing her mooning around camp mourning the loss of her girlish fantasies of cowboys and cattle ranching.

A low grunting groan caught his ear. He scanned the flock until he located the birthing ewe. "You're just in time. Roll up your sleeves. You can set your book over there." He motioned to the canteen and lunch pail a few yards away. "Then come back and see a lambing."

ༀ

Watch a lambing? Emmaline's mouth went dry. She still wasn't comfortable being surrounded by so many of these unfamiliar animals, but she wasn't about to back down from the challenge she saw in her husband's eyes. All week she had felt him watching her, and to her mind it seemed he was almost daring her to get over her disappointment and reconcile herself to her new reality.

She stowed her sketchbook with his belongings and rejoined him. The sheep moved out of her way as she walked through them, but she was glad to get back to Joe's side. He was like a safe harbor in all this sea of wool. He knelt beside a ewe that tucked her front legs under her body, then her back legs, and flopped over on her side.

"They're much bigger than I thought they would be." She knelt beside him. "Though the only sheep I've ever seen before are pictures of lambs in my Sunday school children's quarterly."

"An adult ewe will run about one hundred fifty pounds, with the rams a bit larger. They looked bigger almost a month ago before we sheared them."

The ewe's sides strained and her legs stiffened with her labor. Her eyes had a faraway look, as if she were barely aware of their presence.

"Shearing. I forgot about that."

"Each sheep gives us between eight and ten pounds of wool, and we pack it into bales. The Wyoming Woolgrower's Association helps out by sending wagons to transport the bales to the railhead. After it's shipped east and sold, I get my cut. The money will be banked in Sagebrush. Same for when we sell the wethers this fall. Once those payments are deposited, I can think about rebuilding the house and making some improvements to the ranch."

"The wethers?"

He glanced at her. "You know the difference between a bull and a steer?"

"Of course." She wasn't that green.

"Same thing for sheep. A wether is a castrated male sheep."

He stroked the ewe's flank. Before long, a slimy yellow nose appeared under her tail, followed by a bulbous head with the ears laid back against the neck.

"Hmm. . .no feet." Joe positioned himself better behind the ewe. "There should be a pair of hooves sticking out under that chin. He spoke so softly, Emmeline could barely hear him. "I'll have to help her out."

With a tenderness she'd never seen in a grown man before, he worked his fingers alongside the lamb's neck and gently eased out first one bent leg then another. The ewe seemed to sense when everything was as it should be, and in just a couple more pushes, expelled the lamb onto the grass.

"It's not moving. Is it dead?" Emmeline bit her lower lip.

The ewe gave a mighty strain.

Joe tossed a look over his shoulder. "Wipe its nose and face, will you? Make sure it's breathing."

"Me?"

"Yes, you." He bent over the ewe again, palpating her abdomen. "There is at least one more lamb in here, and it looks as if it's coming out tail first. I can't deal with both right now, so I need you to care for that lamb."

Emmeline reached out to touch the lamb, grimacing at the blood and birthing matter clinging to the soggy creature. Swiping at the tiny nostrils, her heart pounded in her ears. What if it didn't breathe? It was so small and helpless. Suddenly she wanted the little lamb to live more than she'd thought possible. As the seconds ticked on, she massaged the tiny rib cage and fondled the ears, oblivious to the mess. *Come on, baby. Breathe.*

All at once, the lamb jerked. Its chest convulsed, and its head flopped. The little sides began to rise and fall in a sweet rhythm. Emmeline let out a breath she hadn't known she was holding and resisted the urge to snatch the baby up and cradle it.

"It's alive. It's breathing." With growing confidence she stripped mucus from the lamb.

"Good. He'll have a twin soon." And sure enough, within a matter of minutes another lamb lay on the grass. The ewe rolled to her chest and made a peculiar chuckling sound deep in her throat. Joe dragged the lambs around to where she could nose them. "Best to get them acquainted right away. Some ewes don't have any idea what it means to be a mother, but this ewe's an old hand at raising lambs. She shouldn't have any trouble."

"Look at them. They're perfect." Emmeline couldn't explain the feeling of accomplishment filling her, though her part in the birthing had been small. "Are all these sheep going to lamb?"

Joe rose and helped her to her feet. "No, not all of them. But a lot." He smiled down on her, and her tummy did a strange flip. "You did a fine job with that lamb. We'll make a shepherdess of you yet." He drew a rough square of toweling from his back pocket and handed it to her to wipe her hands on.

A shepherdess. Her? A sense of possibility drifted through her mind, and strangely, the idea of becoming a shepherdess wasn't quite as far-fetched as she'd thought.

Joe led her back to where he'd set his gear and gave her his canteen. Sipping, she studied him. The wind ruffled his hair, and he squinted against the sunshine, studying the landscape. He seemed so content, so in tune with the animals around him, as if he couldn't possibly be anything other than a shepherd. She stoppered the canteen and placed it under his jacket to keep it in the shade.

"Is that a sketchbook or a journal you carry with you?" He pointed to her leather-bound book.

"A bit of both, I suppose. I jot down my thoughts and sketch whatever takes my fancy."

"Do you ever show anyone your sketches?"

"Only my family. I've never let anyone else see my drawings." She picked up the book and held it to her chest, crossing her arms over it.

His lips twitched. "I'm your family now." A teasing glint lit his brown eyes.

Heat blasted into her cheeks. Of course he was. But was

she ready to share something so private with him?

The light faded from his expression, and resigned lines formed around his eyes. "It's all right. I won't pry. You don't have to show me if you don't want to."

Chiding herself, she loosened her arms. "I don't mind. As long as you don't laugh. I've had no formal training, and some of it is quite amateurish."

"I won't laugh." He folded his long legs and patted the grass beside him. "Maybe it will help me understand you better."

With an odd combination of reluctance and eagerness she handed over the book.

✦

The color ebbed and flowed in her cheeks in a way that set his heart racing. He didn't know when he'd seen a more expressive face. She would never make a poker player.

"Have you been drawing a long time?"

"As long as I can remember, though I've only had this sketchbook for a couple of years."

He opened the cover and ran his finger over her name inked onto the endpaper. "Emmeline Charlotte Gerhard" and the date, "Christmas, 1871." "I didn't know your middle name was Charlotte."

"All of us girls have old-fashioned names, my father's choice. What's your middle name?"

He shrugged. "It's kind of. . ."

"What?"

"My given name is Joseph Ambrose Barrett III."

Her eyebrows, several shades darker than her hair, arched. "You're the third?"

"Yup. I come from a long and illustrious line of Barretts.

Some of whom still live not far from where you grew up. My family hails from Boston."

"Really?" She smiled and grasped his hand. "I suppose I'm so familiar with the accent I didn't even notice. We probably know some of the same places."

He had to pull his gaze away from her face, for her sudden delight had him wanting to touch her skin and kiss her pink lips. Instead he flipped to the first drawing, a tall-masted ship on a storm-tossed sea. The detail amazed him. "This is really quite good."

She shrugged, but her eyes glowed.

He turned another page and stopped at the drawing of a beautiful woman looking into a mirror. A tapestry lay loose in her lap, and the mirror had been turned so the woman could see the scene outside her window. Reflected in the mirror was a river, a castle in the far distance with pennants flying, and a handsome knight on horseback coming down a winding road. "What's this?"

"I used to draw some illustrations for my father to use in his classes, especially for his primary students who had never studied medieval history or literature before. He thought it helped them understand the legends better. This one is from Tennyson's *Lady of Shalott*. That's the lady, and that's Lancelot." She touched the knight on horseback. "She could only view Camelot through that mirror, for if ever her sight truly fell upon the outside world, she would die. In the end, her desire to really live life—however briefly—instead of only experiencing it secondhand via the mirror won out. She left her tower, got into a boat, and drifted downriver toward the castle in search of Lancelot."

Flipping through the pages, he learned more about her

from her drawings than perhaps she realized. He stopped at a sketch of three women that had to be her sisters. She'd written their names beneath their oval-shaped portraits. He studied them, comparing Emmeline to her siblings. She most resembled the one named Evelyn, though her eyes slanted just like Jane's, and her mouth curved like Gwendolyn's.

Her hand came out to touch the corner of the page, and she blinked.

"You must miss them. Are you very close?"

She nodded. "Very. Evelyn and Jane are older, and Gwendolyn is younger. We've never been apart before, not even when Evelyn married. Her husband, Jamison, was a soldier, and she lived with us during the war. Jamison didn't come home, so she and her son Jamie stayed with us. Then Papa died, and we had to move. When you and the others answered our advertisement, we had no idea of the distances out here. I suppose we thought ranches would be like farms, that we could just about see one another's homes from our front porches. Instead, I'm almost a full day's ride from Evelyn. Even Gwendolyn, who is the closest, is hours away."

The forlorn note in her voice tugged at his heart. He reached down and squeezed her hand. "We'll visit your sisters as soon as we can. It's the busy season for all of us, but there will be time. Out here, a day's ride is nothing."

Another page showed a boy of perhaps six or seven, a mop of dark curls and big, dark eyes. He wore a suit with a white collar and a straw boater. "Is this your nephew?"

"That's Jamie." Her mouth curved in a smile. "He's so sweet. I wonder how he's getting along with his new sister. Evelyn had no idea Gareth had a child, but then again, she didn't tell Gareth about Jamie either, so I suppose they're quits."

Joe laughed. "They treed themselves quite nicely, didn't they? I guess you weren't the only Gerhard sister surprised by what she found at the end of the trail then."

She turned the page. "This is Papa."

The picture of her father showed him in a room filled with books and papers with a huge carved desk and with heavy drapes on the windows. A well-appointed room, not as rich or ornate as the Beacon Hill mansion he'd grown up in, but certainly better than a shanty or a wagon on the Wyoming prairie.

He perused the rest of the drawings in the sketchbook. An entire page had been devoted to drawing hands in various positions and another of eyes. Then at least a dozen pages covered with medieval motifs: coats of arms, pennants, armor, weaponry. He turned to the back of the book to see what had occupied her mind most recently and wasn't at all surprised to see pages of cowboys and horses, cattle and ranch scenes.

Joe closed the book and handed it back to Emmeline, conscious that he wasn't her idea of heroic, sketch-worthy material. No girl so enamored of high adventure and romance would dream of shepherds and sheep.

Emmeline brushed her hand across the tooled leather cover. Lambs bleated and ewes answered, and a soft breeze swept across the grass and fluttered her blue skirts.

Sean and Pierre patrolled the sheep, and not far away, the twin lambs he and Emmeline had delivered staggered up and butted around their mother's udder.

Sunshine warmed the air, redolent with the smell of spring grass and sheep. This was the life. So far away from the strictures of his upbringing and the horrors of war that had changed him forever. He breathed deeply of wool and sheep and lambing. Not everyone liked the smell of sheep, but he'd never found it offensive. Cows smelled, too, but no cowboy ever complained about it, though they wasted plenty of breath on how odiferous sheep were to them.

Emmeline seemed not to mind. Sean passed by a few paces away, and she shaded her eyes to look up at him. He watched the sheep, at seventeen already an experienced shepherd, the image of his father at that age. Without a word or glance their way, he wandered toward the north.

"Is he always so angry?"

Joe sighed. "He wasn't always, but over the past year, he's become more so. He's not one to take an insult, real or perceived, and he's very protective and possessive. As you saw, he and Blake Randall get along like matches and dynamite. He's sure Randall is behind the burning of the house."

"How did Sean come to work for you? He's young to be on his own."

A familiar pang smote Joe's chest. "I met his father during the war. He was my best friend. Folks laughed that a Boston Brahmin and a wild Irishman would be such pals, but we didn't care. I was holding his hand when he breathed his last after taking a bullet. We were at a place called the Wilderness, and before he died, Seamus made me promise I'd take care of his wife and son."

She rolled her pencil over the cover of her sketchbook and said nothing, just listening. It felt so good to have someone to talk to, he couldn't seem to stop.

"When the war ended, I went back to Boston. My family was glad to see me, but when they found out I wanted to help an Irish woman and her son from East Boston, they pitched a fit. I went to Seamus's home as soon as I could and found seven-year-old Sean trying to hold body and soul together all by himself. His mother was in the last stages of some kind of wasting disease, and the boy was barely scraping by. I brought him home with me, but my parents would only consent to making him a servant." Joe shook his head, remembering the epic row and accusations that had marked his last night in his parents' home.

"I wasn't about to make the son of the man who had saved my life on more than one occasion into a boot boy or footman. I left that next day and haven't been back. Sean came with me, and for the last ten years, we've been together. I worked for a farmer in Pennsylvania for a while, and after that I had my own little farm in Indiana. Then I got a flyer about the opening of Wyoming Territory, and we sold the farm and headed out here a couple of years ago. When we arrived, we found Pierre wanting to sell his land and sheep, so we bought him out."

"So you've been like a father to Sean. That poor boy, losing both his parents at such a young age. He's blessed to have had someone like you to step in and not only care for him but care about him."

"I don't know that he'd agree with you, especially lately. It seems the longer we're out here, the more his anger and bitterness grow. You saw him with Blake Randall the other day. If Sean's not careful, he's going to instigate a range war that he can't possibly win."

"But why? There's nothing out here but grass and open space. Isn't there enough room for everyone? Why do cattlemen hate sheepmen so much? I've read a little bit, but all the haranguing doesn't seem to make sense with what I see."

"Cattlemen in Wyoming Territory think sheep ruin the

grazing for cattle because they crop it so short to the ground. Our flock grazes down about forty acres per week, and then we move to a new area. Most of the land out here is open range, meaning any rancher can run his stock on it. Because all stock, cattle, or sheep, need water, most of the grazing is done along creeks like the Sagebrush." He waved toward the stream just to the north. "The land I actually own is the quarter section I purchased from Pierre, but the land I use is many hundreds of acres more. This is true for all the ranchers around here, and since we're all using the open range together, clashes are inevitable. When Pierre owned the flock, because he was alone and a foreigner, he came in for quite a bit of abuse. The only rancher who doesn't give us trouble is Orla Randall, Blake's father. For whatever reason, he's let it be known that he won't stand for anyone bothering us. Since he's the most powerful rancher in this area, things have been fairly peaceful, though Blake doesn't share his father's views. He'd like nothing better than to rid the range of all sheep and shepherds. I do worry about what will happen when Orla isn't around, or Blake decides to openly defy him. Some of the other cattlemen in the area have harassed us from time to time but nothing major. We make sure to never leave the sheep alone, and there are usually at least two of us handy all the time. And we have the dogs."

"Do you think the house fire was part of the harassment?"

He shrugged. "It couldn't be proved either way, though if I wanted to run somebody off a ranch, I'd start by burning the house."

"So it might've been Blake or another of the cattlemen?"

He stroked his beard. "It might've been. Nobody was at the ranch. With lambing starting, we were all out with the sheep. It might've been an accident."

"Do you think that's what happened?"

"I'd rather think that than that one of my neighbors was capable of such hatred." He shifted, wrapping his arms around his knees. A ewe stalked by followed by a set of triplets. "She had three last year, too."

Emmeline regarded him skeptically, as if she couldn't tell if he was trying to pull one over on her or not. "How can you tell? There must be a thousand sheep here, and you recognize one ewe from last year? They all look the same."

He chuckled. "Not a thousand. About half that, though the flock's growing every minute right now. And yes, a shepherd knows his own sheep. Each one is an individual, and over the last few seasons, we've gotten to know them. When we first bought Pierre out, we didn't know anything about sheep, but he agreed to stay on to help us get started. I don't think he has any place to move on to, so he's just stayed."

"Why did he sell in the first place? Was it the trouble from the cattlemen?"

Joe shrugged. "That was probably part of it, but mostly he needed the money. He got himself into trouble over at the fort. Gambling."

The triplets, a couple of days old now, gamboled and frolicked around their mother, giving little crow-hops and bleating to one another.

"They are quite possibly the cutest things I've ever seen." Emmeline flipped open her sketchbook and removed the pencil from behind her ear.

"God sure gave them more than their fair share of charm."

With quick strokes, Emmeline captured the vignette. His

heart swelled. She was putting a sheep into her sketchbook. How long before she might draw a shepherd there, too? Fine hair teased her temples and the curve of her neck as she bent over her work. He looked away, swallowing hard, wishing she hadn't put the brakes on their relationship and hoping their time together today counted as getting to know each other better.

"I should wander through the flock. Do you want to come with me, or do you want to stay here?" He rose and offered his hand.

"I'll come." She fitted her hand into his, and he helped her to her feet. He slung the canteen crossways over his chest and picked up his staff. Perhaps he and Emmeline weren't so far apart as he'd thought. Surely if they continued to spend time together and talk, she'd come around to his way of life and be content here. He took her hand and tucked it into his elbow, leading her through the sheep.

Chapter 5

Three months into her marriage Emmeline hardly recognized herself as the naive daydreamer who had set out from Seabury with her sisters. Lambing had come and gone, and now she spent every day out with the sheep. . .and her husband. Looking back on her first days out here made her insides curl up in shame like the legs of a dead spider. Her initial disappointment that her husband wasn't a cowboy-knight of the range now seemed silly. The more time she spent with Joe, the more she saw his fine qualities of patience and intelligence. As she watched him care for his livestock and handle both the aloof Pierre and the volatile Sean, she was coming to redefine her notion of what constituted manly strength.

She labored over trying to capture that gentle strength on paper. Every chance she got, she filled the pages of her sketchbook with portraits of Joe with his flock. But she didn't show them to him, afraid of revealing how quickly he'd come to dominate her every thought. On the last page of the sketchbook, she drew the familiar lines of his face and wrote a Francis de Sales quote that she felt summed up Joe perfectly:

Nothing is so strong as gentleness, nothing so gentle as real strength.

She felt as if her mind were shedding a too-tight skin, as if her boundaries and awareness were expanding in new and exciting ways. Having to abandon long and fondly held ideas wasn't easy, but a new reality overlaid the storybooks and sensationalized serials that had formed her opinions of the west, and at the center of that new reality was Joe Barrett.

He was quiet, kind, and helpful, always taking the time to explain what he was doing with the sheep and why, and always including her, never talking down to her or making her feel embarrassed when she asked questions or made mistakes. He was just about perfect, and she knew she was in love with him.

But how did she go about telling her husband that she had changed? How did she let him know she was willing to be not only his companion but his wife in every sense? She couldn't just blurt it out. Could she?

Emmeline checked on Shadow and the puppies. Six black-and-white squirming bundles, now almost ten days old, snuggled in a blanket-lined box under the shade of the wagon. Shadow lay beside the box, her head on her paws. The birth of the puppies had caused much joy and consternation. Joe was thrilled at such a healthy litter but not so thrilled that Robbie Burns had gone on strike. The dog seemed to think if Shadow was on vacation, he should be, too.

"How far will we go today?" Emmeline shook out a dish towel and folded it to pack away.

"About ten miles. We'll camp where the Washout flows into Sagebrush Creek. The grass should be pretty good there, and there'll be plenty of water." Joe doused the morning fire with the dirty dishwater, pouring carefully so as not to scatter the ashes. "Sean and Pierre are already getting the flock moving." He leveled a stare at Robbie. "In spite of some people's refusal to work." The dog yawned, his ears pinning back and his tongue lolling.

He helped her finish loading, saving the pups for last. Shadow whimpered and paced along the side of the wagon, even hopping up onto the seat to check on her babies.

"Are you going to ride up here with me, girl?" Emmeline stroked Shadow's silky coat with one hand, while plucking her already sticking blouse away from her skin with the other. Moving the sheep in this heat wasn't an easy proposition, and Joe could really use the dogs, but he'd been trying to give Shadow time to recover from what had proven to be a rather difficult birthing. However, the minute Joe picked up his staff to head toward the sheep, Shadow leaped from the wagon seat and bounded to his side.

"Are you sure, girl? I could use your help. If you pitch in, maybe that silly old Rob will, too." Joe caressed the dog's head, his hand ever gentle despite his broad shoulders and well-muscled arms. Hatless, his brown hair shone in the sun, in need of a trim. He glanced up and caught Emmeline staring. "Are you sure you'll be all right driving?"

She swallowed and pulled her thoughts away from how handsome her husband looked this morning. Bending to cover her blush, she picked up the reins. "After a week of lessons, I should hope I'd be able to drive this team. You're only going to be walking anyway."

Joe grinned and winked and reached up to pat her hand. A tingle shot through her at his touch. "I have a notion you could do anything you set your mind to. Your driving the wagon will be a big help. It's usually Sean's job, and I can use him on foot better. Give a holler if you get into any trouble."

By midafternoon, Emmeline was heartily sick of the sight, sound, and smell of sheep. This was the first major trek they'd made with the flock. Up to this point their progress had been gradual as the flock grazed off an area, but now the grass on the upper plateau was playing out, getting sparser in the summer heat. Joe wanted to move the flock down into the river basin to the better pastures. The sheep, used to lazy living, balked at passing up grassy tidbits. The wethers stalked to the front of the flock, stopped to graze, and caused a pileup of ewes and lambs. Lambs seemed to become separated from their mothers with annoying frequency, panicking and bleating. Anxious mothers answered back, searching for their offspring. Keeping the group together and all moving in the same direction took the skill of all three men and the dogs.

A headache formed behind Emmeline's eyes, and a fine grit of dust stirred up by thousands of sharp hooves hung in the air and sifted into her hair and clothes. After a while, the animals either got the hang of moving as a flock or else wore themselves out for anything other than doing as the shepherds wanted. The men didn't break for lunch, because once they had the sheep moving, they didn't want to stop them until they reached their destination.

The puppies whined under her feet. She'd stopped once, midmorning, for Shadow to feed them, but they were hungry again. "I know, babies. This new campsite had better be worth all this fuss." Though Joe claimed the grazing near the river would be better than where they had been, her untrained eye hadn't been able to tell. It all looked like grass to her.

The land grew rougher the farther they went, with rocky outcroppings and jagged rises. Sagebrush Creek, which had been slow and lazy farther downstream, now rushed through narrower channels, shaded by the only trees to be found on the prairie—brushy, twisted, gnarled scrub, nothing like the maples, chestnuts, and oaks of Massachusetts.

When Joe finally threw up his arm for her to halt, she slumped, pressing her fingers to her eyes to still the throbbing. Too much sun, heat, and noise. If only she could stretch out under those trees and take a nap.

A plaintive yip from the box beneath her seat got her moving. Clambering down, stiff from sitting for such a long time, she lifted the puppies up and over the wagon side, transferring them to the shade under the wagon. Shadow, released by Joe from herding duties, wriggled and nudged the fuzzy babies, licking and checking. Their little yips and yelps of reunion made Emmeline smile in spite of her headache. The little mama flopped onto her side in the grass and the puppy noises, beyond a few satisfied grunts and whimpers, ceased.

Emmeline assessed the new campsite. Sagebrush mingled with wildflowers and prairie grasses, covering the ground right up to the creek. The grayish-green fragrant bushes perfumed the air and made Emmeline think of turkey stuffing at Thanksgiving. She shied away from that memory, knowing if she dwelled on it for long, as tired as she was right now, homesickness and loneliness for her sisters would overwhelm her, and she might break down and cry.

Joe and Sean and Pierre spread out, and Shep nosed around the area. Emmeline had taken Joe at his word and steered clear of the watchdog. He patrolled an area well beyond the flock, his only goal to stop predation and protect his master's sheep.

The flock made its way down the banks to the water,

spreading out along the edge to slake their thirst. Emmeline brushed the clinging hair from her forehead and decided they had the right idea. Taking a bucket from the wagon, she set out upstream.

Once under the shade of the trees, her headache eased some, and the knot between her shoulder blades relaxed. Unaccustomed to driving a team, she was grateful for the walk to loosen up stiff muscles. Meadowlarks sang and chirped in the tall grass, and a breeze fluttered the leaves overhead. When she reached a quiet place along the water's edge well upstream from the sheep, she plunged her hands into the cool water and doused her hot face. Further tension seeped from her, and she closed her eyes, breathing deeply of the warm summer air and letting the water drip dry on her skin.

"Well, well, well, we meet again."

Emmeline's eyes popped open, and she stumbled away from the water. She knocked against the bucket and sent it clanking into a tree trunk.

Blake Randall sat on his black horse, wrists crossed on the saddle horn and a playful grin on his face. "Sorry to startle you."

She pressed her hand to her chest, chagrined to be caught with her face dripping. Groping for a handkerchief, she tried to gather her scattered wits.

"Mr. Randall."

"Blake." He swung down from his horse. "I was watching you all from up there." He pointed to a ridge some distance to the south.

An uneasy feeling trickled down the base of her neck. He'd been watching them? Aware that she was some distance from the flock and well out of earshot of any of the men, Emmeline retrieved the bucket and scooped up some water. "I should be getting back."

He took the bucket from her hands. "My ma would pin my ears back if I let you carry this all the way back to camp."

"Please, I don't want to be a bother. You must have a lot to do today."

"It's no bother. I want to talk to Joe anyway." His voice lost its light, bantering tone, and his face settled into grim lines. "He's asking for trouble bringing his sheep back here, especially after last year."

"Last year?" She hurried to keep ahead of his horse tromping behind them, breathing down the back of her neck. "What happened last year?"

"Hasn't he told you? He lost a mess of sheep. Night raiders hit his camp and shot a bunch of his animals."

"Shot them? Why?"

"Because they're mangy sheep, that's why. And this is the best summer grazing for fifty miles in any direction. The cattlemen aren't going to sit still while a flock of knot-headed mutton ruins it." His strides lengthened. "Especially now that word's gotten around that Barrett won't defend himself. He never even shot back when the raiders came, just stood there by the wagon and let it happen. He's lucky the raiders were under orders not to shoot any men or he'd have met his Maker that night."

"He just stood there?" Emmeline stopped, and the horse shouldered her out of his way to keep following Blake. She tripped but managed to keep her footing, though the world spun in her head. "He didn't fight back to protect what was his?"

"Nope, he held his men back, too, that Frenchy and the

kid. The dogs put up more of a fuss than he did." Disgust dripped from his lips like kerosene from an overturned lamp. "Anyone as spineless as him shouldn't even be in Wyoming Territory, much less trying his hand at ranching." He spit on the ground and then seemed to remember both his manners and who he was talking to. "Sorry, ma'am. It just sticks in my craw when a man shows yellow."

"Surely he must've had a reason. No man would just stand there and let someone destroy his property and kill his livestock." Her mind boggled at the notion, and fear, fear that her husband *was* a coward, too afraid to stand up for himself, barged into her mind. Her mouth tasted of ashes. She'd been living in a fool's paradise, choosing to ignore Sean's allegations about her husband, choosing to consider Joe reserved and thoughtful, not cowardly. But here stood Blake Randall confirming her fears. She started walking once more, barely taking in anything around her until they approached the edge of the flock.

Movement caught her eye, and a pale, shaggy canine slipped through the brush. Silently, Shep edged nearer, head low, back rigid, on a parallel course. When she stopped, Blake did too, and the dog crouched and bared his teeth, growling deep in his throat, his eyes honed in on Blake. The cowboy froze. Sean jogged down a slope of prairie, his staff in his hand and a scowl on his face. His red hair blazed in the sun, as did his green eyes.

"Call off your dog, Irish." Blake stood tensed and completely still.

"What are you doing here?"

Blake handed the bucket to Emmeline, moving deliberately, and fingered the gun strapped to his hip. "Call him off, I said."

"Sean, please. Blake isn't here to cause any trouble."

"Trouble's what he's going to get if he hangs around these parts for long. Joe can do what he wants, but I'm not standing still for any more harassment from the likes of this jughead. And the name's Sean O'Hara, not Irish." Sean gripped his staff, his legs braced in a defiant stance.

"Youngster, I'm getting tired of you. Either you call off that dog, or I'll shoot him in the head." His hand closed around the butt of his pistol.

"Shep." Fingers snapped, and Emmeline turned. Joe stood a few paces away. Though he had a watchful look in his eye, he stood relaxed. "Sean, why don't you go unhitch the team and water them." Though his words sounded like a suggestion, his tone said, "No arguing."

The guard dog looked as disgruntled as Sean when Joe motioned him away. Blake let his hand fall away from his gun, and the tightness in Emmeline's chest eased, though a waterfall of regret cascaded through her because of what Blake had revealed about her husband.

"What brings you to my camp?"

"Wanted a word. What's the idea of bringing your sheep down into the bottoms? Didn't you get the message after last summer? Sheep ain't welcome here." He tucked his thumbs into his waistband and stuck his chest out.

Joe pressed his lips together and took a deep breath. "It's open range. The grazing is good here, better for my flock than the upland, and this creek won't dry out."

"That's just why the cattlemen want that grazing. If we don't fatten our cows up enough during the summer, they won't make it through a tough winter, and we're counting on the grass here in the creek bottom. Every cattleman I know is planning on grazing his herd through here. If your sheep get to it first, it'll be ruined for cows, not just this summer but clear till next spring." He jammed his fists on his waist. "I'm not a man for violence, but I can't see letting my herd starve to death this winter just because you wanna take it easy on those flea-bitten bleaters from Hades. There'll be trouble if you don't head back where you came from. And I'm not the only cattleman who thinks so. There's plenty around here who won't be content to just tell you to go. They'll do what they did last year, only worse."

Emmeline sent up a silent prayer that Joe would prove Randall wrong, that he'd tell the brash cowboy to get lost, that he wasn't going to be bullied any longer. Anything to show he wasn't afraid.

"I have your father's word that we'll be left in peace. He wasn't happy about what happened last year and offered to make restitution when he discovered some of his own ranch hands had played a part. I'd hate for him to be disappointed again."

"Maybe you haven't heard, but Pa's ailing pretty bad. I'm in charge of the ranch now. If he doesn't recover, you'll find yourself in a world of hurt. Night raiders will descend on this place like wolves on a wounded buffalo."

"I'm sorry to hear about your father, but I don't want any trouble, Blake."

"Trouble will come, whether you want it or not if you don't get these sheep out of here."

Emmeline let the bucket drop to the ground, disgusted at the rancher and ashamed of her husband. "Blake Randall, don't you threaten us. If this is open range, then anyone can

graze their livestock on it, be they cows, horses, sheep or. . .
or. . .camels." If her husband wouldn't stand up for them,
then she would. "If you or your cowpuncher friends think
you can storm in here and hurt our sheep and we'll stand
by and do nothing, then you've got another think coming.
Those animals are our property, we're not breaking any laws,
and you don't know the first thing about sheep if you think
they'll ruin the grazing."

Joe put his hand on her arm, but she shrugged it off.
"I'm not through. I don't understand you, Joe Barrett. Why
won't you fight back? Why won't you protect what's yours?
I've seen your guns in the wagon. Sean's told me what a
good hunter you are, a dead shot, he claims, and yet you
stand there like a buffoon, letting ignorant men storm over
you. Well, I'm not going to stand by and do nothing, even if
you are."

Her husband blinked. "Emmeline, take it easy. There's
no call to—" But she didn't have time for his waffling.

"Mr. Randall, if you and the other cattlemen would
use the sense God gave a goose, you'd see that the sheep
actually improve the grazing for the cattle, eating a lot of
plants the cows won't and clearing the way for better grass
to grow. I've only been here a few months, but I've already
learned that much about sheep. If you took two minutes
to talk to experienced shepherds like Joe or Pierre instead
of treating sheep like vermin and shepherds like pariahs,
you'd learn for yourself how wrong your assumptions are."
She poked him in the chest. "But if you think all shepherds
are cowardly or won't fight back, you're wrong, because this
shepherdess isn't afraid of you. Next time you come in here
making threats, the guard dog won't be the only one you

have to watch out for."

Scooping up the bucket, she marched past them both, scattering sheep out of her way. Tears stung her eyes. Though she hadn't wanted to believe it, her husband was a jellyfish.

Chapter 6

Are you going to back down again? Because if you are, I'm through." Sean jabbed at the fire. "I'd rather be a dead lion than a live dog, and I don't care what sort of promise you made to yourself. That kind of thinking might work in the ballrooms of Boston, but it won't fly a lick out here."

"I sink perhaps ze boy is right zis time. If what Monsieur Randall said is true and his father is near death, zey may not stop at killing a few sheep. Zey may not stop until we are all dead. We must fight back or flee." Pierre's droopy gray mustache sank farther at the corners of his mouth.

Joe rubbed his forehead, conscious that Emmeline had not emerged from the wagon. The look of disgust on her face when she'd passed him sat like a burning cactus patch in his middle. How could he make her understand his reasons for not taking up his guns without revealing to her all the horrible things in his past he constantly battled to forget?

And how was he going to keep everyone safe if he didn't shoot back? Especially Emmeline.

He had to admire her grit. She hadn't backed down an inch, reminding him of Shadow guarding her pups when Shep got too close. The thought of night raiders swooping down on the camp, shooting and hollering, turned his blood cold.

"I think we need to keep two men on watch at all times. It will mean going short on sleep, but there's no help for it." He tossed the dregs of his coffee onto the fire. A hiss and puff of steam rose from the coals. "Keep Shep or Robbie with you, too. For now we'll leave Shadow in camp with Emmeline."

"What about guns?" Sean bounced to his feet. "What good is it going to do us to be wandering around out there if we're unarmed? We'll just make fine targets to shoot at."

Pierre rummaged in his pack. "Joe, you can decide for ze boy, but I am a man grown." He pulled out a wicked-looking pistol. "I have respected your decision not to go armed, but now I sink ze time has come. I will go down fighting." He thumped his narrow chest.

"I'm a grown man, too, not a boy." Sean shifted his weight from foot to foot.

"You're barely seventeen."

His shoulders shot back and his chin up. "You require the work of a man, and I deliver it. You've taught me how to handle a gun. You're asking me to stand watch like a man, so I have the right to be equipped for the job."

In that moment, with the flickering campfire bathing his face in light and shadow, Sean looked so much like his father, that a giant fist gripped Joe's ribs and squeezed. This was madness. Why wouldn't the cattlemen just leave him and his little flock alone? He'd tried reasoning with them, ignoring them, and avoiding them, but they were relentless.

He jammed his fingers into his hair while his stomach did a Texas two-step. "All right. You can go armed. But you don't shoot first, understand?" He stared hard at Sean, who stood tall and stared hard right back, growing up before his eyes.

"I understand."

Joe rose, his feet leaden, and went to the wagon. He knocked lightly to give Emmeline some warning and opened the door. He needn't have bothered knocking. The curtain around her bed was tightly closed.

All the progress they'd made, the growing closeness, destroyed in a few minutes. And how did he go about rebuilding? If her face and her actions were anything to judge by, she'd lost all respect for him. But if he did as she asked and gave in to the anger, if he strapped on guns and took the war to his enemy, then he'd lose all respect for himself.

He raised the mattress and bunk where he slept and moved a couple of items to get to the one he wanted. Lifting the heavy parcel, made heavier by the responsibility it contained, he let the bunk down quietly. No sound from behind the curtain.

When he returned to the fire, Pierre had gone, taking his gun with him. Sean paced with Robbie Burns at his heels. Unwrapping the burlap and twine, Joe withdrew one of the rifles. Reluctant to let it go, he resisted when Sean grabbed hold of it, but finally gave it up. "Be careful, stay sharp, and don't shoot unless you have to. The dogs will alert you if anyone is around."

"I'll be careful."

"One of you come and get me about three or so."

Sean's glance fell on the other rifle. "You best load that and keep it close."

Though he'd hunted game with that gun many times and

not worried about it, the gun took on a sinister look and feel as Joe inserted bullets he prayed he wouldn't have to use against another man.

Please, Lord, don't make me have to shoot another human being. I swore I would never take up arms against my fellow man again, but I can't let anyone hurt Emmeline. In the morning, I'll have Sean escort her to one of her sisters' places so she'll be safe. Please keep all of us safe through the night, and show me what I'm supposed to do. I never thought about what might happen if Orla Randall couldn't control his son, or I never would've brought Emmeline here. . .

The prayer continued as he doused the fire, checked the picket lines tethering the horses, and lifted the box of sleeping puppies up into the wagon. "C'mon, girl." He jerked his head to Shadow. She rose to follow but hesitated since she'd never been allowed into the living quarters of the wagon before.

"It's all right." He wanted her close to alert him if anyone started prowling around camp. If he was to be any use on watch in the middle of the night, he had to get some sleep, but he didn't want to be totally unguarded. Laying the gun alongside his bunk, he eased his suspenders off his shoulders and slipped out of his boots. Removing his shirt, he stretched out on his blankets. Nothing stirred behind the curtain. Would there be time in the morning to explain his motives to Emmeline before he sent her to one of her sisters? Would she understand? Would she despise him for a killer rather than a coward if she knew all he'd done? Or would it be best to get her away as quickly as possible and explain everything after the dust settled?

Night sounds surrounded him, and he identified each one: the breeze rustling through the grass, the croak of a frog from the creek, the night call of an owl. He strained to hear any noise coming from the flock's bed-ground. If Orla Randall didn't recover. . .

᠁

Smoke filled the air, men shouted, and bullets whined. Chunks of earth exploded skyward under the impact of cannon fire. Joe clutched his rifle, crouching, running through the trees. Each round from the artillery sent a shockwave reverberating through the forest, and each concussive blast bombarded his chest and left it feeling hollowed out.

Swiping the sweat from his brow, he strained to see through the trees, smoke, and running men. His objective lay a hundred yards up the hill in a small clearing. He dropped to one knee to catch his breath and survey the situation.

In a flash, he was transported from the woodland battle at the Wilderness to a hiding place in the loft of a ramshackle barn. He lay flat out on his belly in the musty straw, all his attention focused on the gap in the trees down the road. Seamus lay beside him, and his best friend and sergeant nudged his arm and passed him the spyglass. "They're coming."

A part of him knew he was dreaming, for it was a scene, a memory that had visited him many times before. He could taste the gunpowder in the air, smell the coppery blood soaking into the ground, feel the heaviness of his rifle in his hand. It was all devastatingly real. And he knew how it would end.

A line of gray-clad soldiers marched down the road, two mounted men in front carrying tattered flags. Joe forced his heart to slow down and steadied his breathing. Their mission was clear. His squad was in position. A dozen men, all with the ability to shoot fast and straight, were positioned along the road, and the instant the enemy was all in view, they were tasked to cut them down. Joe, as the officer in charge, would fire first, the signal to open the battle.

Not that it would be much of a battle. These men were footsore, half-starved, and worn to the fraying point by the punishing Northern army. They had very little ammunition and almost no will left to fight. And yet, the major had ordered no prisoners to be taken. If they were to bring an end to this war, they had to stay aggressive and not give the enemy any chance to recover.

A single wagon followed by a single cannon brought up the rear of the procession. Joe studied them through his field glass— haggard faces, tattered clothing. Ribs showed on the horses, and several of the men wore dirty bandages.

He squashed any feelings of remorse, any feelings at all, lowering the glass. His orders were clear. This was war. He had a job to do.

Easing his rifle up, he drew a bead on the soldier with the most gold braid. He fired, and the massacre began. Confederate soldiers dropped onto the road as gunfire burst from the trees and tall grass. Seamus's rifle barked beside Joe's head, but it sounded far away.

Then he was running through the trees, once more at the Wilderness, only this time, Seamus was ahead of him, dodging and weaving through the trees, racing to outflank the enemy. Everything slowed down, and the edges of his vision blurred. Seamus shouted something to Joe, but the words were garbled, muffled by gunfire. A Confederate soldier appeared around a pine trunk, raised his rifle, and aimed at Joe. Seamus charged, knocking Joe off his feet. A single rifle shot split the air, drowning out every other sound as Joe fell. A red splotch formed on Seamus's breast, and he staggered backward, lurched, and dropped to the ground. Joe tried to scramble to his feet, to race toward his friend, tried to catch him as he fell, but his legs refused to move. He shouted for Seamus to hold on, not to leave him, to be strong for his wife and son, but his tongue became wooden, his voice stopping up in his throat until he could only make a garbled, sobbing groan.

❧

A horrible, agonized sound jarred Emmeline awake. Immediately alert, she sat up. The sound came again. Joe. Was he hurt?

She flung the curtain aside, swinging her legs over the edge of her bunk. Something stirred at her feet. The dog. Shadow whined and pressed her nose into Emmeline's hand. Joe thrashed and groaned on his bunk. Moonlight from the window over his bed revealed his sweat-drenched grimace.

"Joe." She reached for him. "Joe, what is it?"

He flung out his arm, knocking her hand aside. "Seamus, no!" The blankets twisted around his legs, and his chest heaved. "No!" The long, haunting cry sent a quiver through Emmeline. She realized he wasn't hurt, only dreaming, but this wasn't a normal dream. Whatever nightmare held him, it was strong.

"Joe, it's a bad dream. Wake up." She shook his shoulder. Shadow whimpered and tried to worm around Emmeline's legs. Knocked off balance, she toppled onto Joe. His breath shot out of his throat, and his arms closed around her.

Her cheek pressed against his bare chest, and his heart thundered in her ear, nearly drowning out his harsh gasps.

"Emmeline?" The question ripped from his throat in a raspy whisper.

Pushing herself upright, she shoved her hair out of her face. "Joe, are you awake? You were having a nightmare." She fumbled for the lantern and matches. Yellow light bathed the interior of the wagon as she lowered the glass over the wick. "Are you all right?"

He nodded, his throat lurching. Her eyes strayed to the curling brown hair covering his broad chest. She'd felt its softness against her cheek moments ago, breathed in the manly scent of his warm flesh. Heat congested her face, and she knew she was blushing fiercely, but she couldn't look away. Hopefully the low light hid her blatant curiosity.

Joe didn't seem to care or even notice. He drew his hand down his face. "It's been a long time since I had that nightmare."

His voice sounded so lost, as if he still wandered in that terrible dream, that Emmeline found herself perching on the side of his bed, grasping his hand. "Perhaps if you told me about it, you would feel better?"

He sat up, his breath still ragged. "It's always the same dream. The war. Seamus dying. I suppose today's events brought it back. You woke me up before the worst part."

Pain saturated his words, and she remained still, clasping his hand, waiting.

"Seamus—Sean's father—and I saw a lot of action, but neither of us was ever wounded. We never even got ill. It was as if we led a charmed life." His voice became far away, remembering. "We were part of an elite squad tasked with making life difficult for the enemy however we could. We rode light and fast, living off the land, destroying rail lines, telegraph poles, blowing up ammunition depots. And ambushing enemy troops. That was our specialty—ambush.

I can't tell you the number of men we killed." His fingers tightened around hers. "At first, it turned my stomach, but after a while it was as if I became numb to all the killing." He sucked in a breath. "Then Seamus was killed. He saved my life, shoved me out of the way of a bullet. I watched him die, and I shot the man who killed him. And I felt nothing. I couldn't even seem to mourn, not then. Nothing mattered, not his life, not mine, and not the lives of the men I killed. I just kept on killing. Every day for weeks and months, I shot men. And I felt nothing. No remorse, no fear, nothing."

Tears burned her eyes. She had been greatly sheltered from the war when it happened, since she was but a child at the time, and afterward the subject had been taboo in their household out of respect for Evelyn. She'd never heard any firsthand accounts like this, nor had she realized that Joe's memories lay like a festering wound in his breast, a wound that needed drawing out.

"Then the end of the war came. When we got word of the surrender, I was deep in the South. We'd been burning houses and fields, pushing to the ocean. When the news came, men all around me celebrated, whooping and cheering. But I couldn't seem to feel anything. Not joy, not relief. I just wandered the streets in Charleston in a fog. I don't even know how I got there, but I found myself in a church, on my knees at the rail. Then something inside me broke, like an axe hitting a rain barrel. Tears ran down my face and splashed onto the floor, and in that instant, I wasn't numb anymore. Pain like I'd never known." His hand pressed against his chest. "It was as if I could feel the bullet that took Seamus's life. All that time of not feeling anything caught up with me."

Her throat thickened, and she blinked hard.

"I swore that day I would never pick up a gun against my fellow man again. I know you've wondered why I've been so reluctant to fight back against the cattlemen in the area, why I don't protect my property with a gun. It's not because I'm afraid I couldn't kill another man but because I've had my fill of it. I'm afraid if I shoot another man, I'll go back to that place of not caring, of not feeling, and I won't be able to stop killing."

The tears Emmeline had been fighting spilled over her lashes and tumbled down her cheeks. "Joe, I'm so sorry. I had no idea."

He seemed to become more alert, as if shedding the last bits of his nightmare. Leaning close, he stared into her eyes. His hand came up to touch her face, catching the tears with his thumb. The gentle caress of his fingers against her cheek sent a warm feeling through her middle like the first drink of hot cocoa on a cold day. Awareness of his state of half-dress and her own thin nightgown pricked her mind, but she didn't care. He was her husband, and he was laying his soul bare before her.

She didn't know who moved first, but the distance between them closed ever so slowly until their lips touched, soft as a whispered prayer. His arms tightened around her, and his hands came up to bury themselves in her hair, releasing it from its loose braid to cascade over her shoulders like a shawl. He kissed her again, stealing her breath, and she kissed him back, tentative at first then with growing ardor. Sunbursts shot through her, and her skin suddenly felt too tight. She forgot about the war, about the sheep, about everything but this man who had stolen her heart with his gentleness.

Chapter 7

"You have to go, Emmeline. I can't have you here in harm's way."

"Please." She clung to his arm. After their amazing night together, she finally felt she understood her husband, and she was finally his wife in every sense. And she had no desire to leave him now, especially not to stand up to Blake Randall alone. When he'd had to leave her to take his turn on watch in the early hours of the morning, it had felt as if her heart would burst with fear for his safety. "I want to stay with you."

His arm came around her, and he brushed a kiss across her temple. "I know you do, but I need you to go. Sean's not happy about having to take you, but you'll be doing me a favor keeping him out of it. Pierre and I will watch the sheep, and I don't think Blake will kill us in cold blood. I'll try to talk sense into him."

Sean stomped around, saddling the horses. Unused to being ridden, the team snorted and sidestepped, throwing their heads up and swishing their tails.

"You make for Parker's place. Stay with your sister there. I'll come for you when I can. And keep Sean with you. Tell Matt to leg rope him like a wandering hog if he tries to get back here."

The boy jerked the girth tight and shot Joe a filthy look but said nothing. After the flaming row they'd had at first light, there was nothing left to be said. At least nothing that would change Joe's mind.

Emmeline let Joe boost her into the saddle. The animal shifted beneath her, and she grabbed the reins and a fistful of mane. "I always wanted to learn to ride, but I never thought it would be like this."

"You can do it, Emma-girl." Joe patted her hand and winked at her. "You be careful."

"You too, Joe."

He tugged on her hand, pulling her down for one last kiss. Sean snorted and kicked his horse into a gallop. Her own horse took off, dragging her away from Joe, thundering over the ground. She clung to the saddle, at first terrified, but when she didn't fall off and her body caught the rhythm of the horse's movement, she relaxed a fraction. The wind whipped against her cheeks and blew her hair back. Sean didn't slow the pace and didn't look back to see if she followed until they had gone several miles. He eased back on the reins, and as his horse slowed, so did hers, to a bumpy trot then to a walk. The animals blew, sides heaving.

Her chest rose and fell from the exertion and exhilaration. She'd done it, ridden a running horse across the prairie. "That was amazing."

Sean shrugged, but his look was one of begrudging admiration. "Thought you'd holler for me to stop a long time ago. You've got some grit."

The terrain rose steadily away from the river bottom, and the horses climbed at a walk. She checked the angle of the early morning sun. "How long will it take us to get to

Matt and Gwendolyn's place?"

" 'Bout an hour."

"But it took so much longer by wagon."

"That's because you went by road to the homestead. We're going cross-country, and we moved the flock closer to Parker's boundary to graze along the river."

In spite of the trouble they were leaving Joe and Pierre in, Emmeline couldn't help but thrill to the notion of seeing one of her sisters so soon. She had so much she needed to talk over with Gwendolyn, and she ached to be sure her younger sister fared well.

By the time the hour was up and they approached the Parker spread, Emmeline's legs trembled, and her backside ached.

The back door of the ranch house swung open, and Emmeline recognized the familiar form of her little sister.

"What happened? Are you all right?" The words tumbled out of Gwendolyn's mouth as she closed the distance between them.

Emmeline all but fell out of the saddle into her sister's arms. Her knees wobbled, and she clutched Gwendolyn's shoulders. "Is Matthew here?"

"He's at the barn."

Sean took the trailing reins of Emmeline's horse and headed toward the big wooden structure.

"How many men does Matthew have working here?"

"Why? Why are you here? What's going on?" Gwendolyn helped her to the porch and into the kitchen. Without waiting for an answer, she pushed Emmeline into a chair and filled a glass with water. The young girl in the wheelchair came into the room.

"You remember Betsy, Matt's sister? Betsy, this is Emmeline. Here, drink this, then tell us what's going on."

Part of Emmeline's mind registered the fact that her little sister seemed to have grown up a lot over the past three months. And she was wearing a wedding ring. So at least that had been settled. She shouldn't be surprised that Gwendolyn had changed. She had changed and grown a lot herself.

Boots sounded on the porch, and Matt strode inside followed by Sean. Emmeline spilled out the story of Blake Randall and the trouble Joe faced. Sean helped her, filling in some bits she wasn't aware of. When she mentioned that her husband was a sheepherder, Gwendolyn gasped.

Matt listened, asked a couple of questions, and when she'd finished, turned and plucked a gun belt from a row of pegs by the back door. His face set in hard lines. "Sean, get to the bunkhouse and round up whoever's there. Tell them to send a rider to Garvey's and Kittrick's and get as many men as they can muster here right smart. We'll all ride together to Joe's camp."

Emmeline swallowed. Though she'd prayed for someone to help Joe, she hadn't dared think that her cattlemen brothers-in-law would come to his aid. "Joe doesn't want any bloodshed. I'm sure he doesn't expect you to ride in there. He just wanted a safe place to keep Sean and me. He's not a coward." She stared hard at Matt, willing him to believe her.

"I've known Joe Barrett for a while now, and he's a lot of things, but a coward isn't one of them." Matt's assertion was balm to her soul.

Gwendolyn squeezed Emmeline's hand. "Joe's part of our family now, and family sticks together. Of course Matt will ride out to help him."

"I'm going with you." Emmeline rose, stifling a groan at her already sore muscles.

When Matt opened his mouth to protest, Gwendolyn straightened. "If you were in trouble, Matthew Parker, heaven and earth couldn't keep me from your side."

Matt removed his hat, shoved his fingers through his hair, and studied her. "If I had known how contrary and stubborn you are, I might not have married you, woman." A warm light in his eyes belied his hard words, and Gwendolyn went to his side, putting her arms around his waist and resting her head against his chest.

Emmeline blinked. Things had changed drastically since her last visit. Matt and Gwendolyn obviously cared a great deal for each other. Their closeness made the ache to be with her husband even greater. Was Joe still all right?

Matt sighed. "A range war is no place for women, and Joe'd have my hide for a parlor rug if I brought you with us."

"I'll explain to him that you couldn't keep me here."

He grimaced. "You and your sister are sure cut from the same cloth."

By afternoon, the ranch yard teemed with horses, armed men, and noise. Jane and Evelyn had come with their husbands, and the four sisters embraced, wiping tears of joy and talking all at once. Love surrounded Emmeline, but her heart was out on the range with her husband, and though she wanted to stay, she knew she must go.

"I'll be back, and I'll bring Joe." Though her muscles had stiffened up, she forced herself to mount the horse Matt had brought for her. Sean was also on a new horse, and he took up a position on her right.

"Sean, Joe was clear that he wanted you to stay here,

but"—she held up her hand to stay his speech—"I won't make you stay behind. But, please, you have to promise me you'll take orders and not be foolish. Joe doesn't want any bloodshed, and if you let your temper get the best of you, someone's going to get killed."

Sean clamped his jaw, stared at his hands on the reins for a moment, then looked up, a clear, mature light shining in his green eyes. "I'll mind myself. I won't seek out trouble, and I'll look after you. I don't want anyone killed, but I sure am glad we're doing something instead of just taking it on the chin like we have been."

"Joe has a very good reason for handling things this way. After this is all over, maybe you can see things from his point of view. He cares about you, and it hurts him when you argue."

Matt conferred with Harrison and Gareth, issued orders to the men, and swung aboard his gelding.

Emmeline found herself in the center of a hoof-pounding, heart-pounding posse. Sean stayed at her side, and they thundered over the prairie. With each hoofbeat, she prayed they would be in time to help Joe.

∽

Joe kept the dogs circling the tightly bunched flock. Shep went one direction, Robbie Burns the other, and when they crossed paths, they ignored each other, focused only on their job of keeping the sheep together. The sheep, knowing something was different, stood still, heads up, tense. Pierre, on the far side of the mob, kept his back to the animals, staring up the slope in the direction of Randall's property line. A low outcropping of rock jutted up from the prairie a few paces from where the Frenchman stood, handy cover if things got out of hand.

The hands of Joe's plain silver watch seemed to crawl. He stood near the wagon. His rifle leaned just inside the door.

Please, Lord, don't make me have to use it. I don't want to go back to that place. I don't want to kill Blake Randall. Orla is my friend, and I don't want to shoot his son.

Robbie was the first one to sense Blake's arrival. His black-and-white head came up, and he gave a low *woof.*

Joe's stomach clenched. Riders crested the hill and fanned out, dark against the afternoon sky. Blake Randall sat his horse in the center of the line. Ten, twelve, fifteen, eighteen riders.

Against two shepherds.

"I figured you were too stubborn to leave. That was a mistake, Barrett." Blake's shout made the already tense flock even more volatile. Several ewes bleated.

"Blake, I'm asking you again to leave us alone. This is the kind of thing that starts a range war, and nobody wins. Men die, animals are killed, and the thing just goes on and on."

"You're the only sheepman left on this range, and after I run you out, that will be the end of it. You're all alone down there. I hope you had sense enough to send your woman away."

"Emmeline's not here, but I'm asking you to remember your father's wishes. He gave me his word I'd have no trouble from him or his riders."

"He's dead, died this morning, and these riders aren't his. They're mine. And I'm clearing this range of those sheep. If you get in our way, I'll cut you down."

Joe's heart thundered in his ears, and he had barely an instant to breathe a prayer when Randall's men started down the slope. He picked up his rifle, his throat squeezed tight. A sick, faraway feeling invaded his stomach. *Please, God, I don't want to kill him.*

He took aim at the black horse.

The thundering in his ears grew louder, and the ground shook. Bleating and baaing, the sheep scattered ahead of the riders. His finger tightened on the trigger. If he could bring the horse down, perhaps Blake would come to his senses. Just before he squeezed off the shot, Randall's riders pulled up, horses rearing and tossing their heads.

But the pounding of hooves didn't stop. Behind the wagon, streaming around it like water breaking around a rock, horses and riders flowed. Joe caught a glimpse of golden hair, and his heart stopped.

Gareth Kittrick, Harrison Garvey, and Matt Parker positioned themselves between the sheep and Randall's riders. Sean swung from the saddle and strode across the campsite to take up his position beside Joe. And Emmeline sat on her restless horse as if she'd been born in the saddle, her eyes finding Joe's.

"Blake, aren't you a bit far from home?" Gareth's voice carried to Joe.

"This ain't none of your concern, Kittrick. Nor yours, Garvey. And Parker, I'd think you'd be siding with me against this lousy sheepherder since he's grazing ground you need to fatten up your cattle. Us cattlemen need to stick together. Now that my pa's dead, I'm in charge of things, and I say we run the sheepherders out!"

Matt rode his horse forward a few steps. Cowboys flanked either side of him, rifles across their saddles, leather creaking, eyes intent. The riders Emmeline had brought outnumbered

Blake's at least two to one.

"Blake," Matt's voice carried back to them. "Your father would be ashamed of you, harassing his friend like this. You need to understand something about family. Family sticks together. That's what we're doing here. Maybe you didn't know it, but we all married sisters. That makes me and Harrison and Matt and Joe brothers-in-law. We'd take it pretty hard if we found out you were causing Joe any trouble. Not to mention how unhappy it would make our wives. I might not be able to hold these men back if that happened." He shrugged.

Harrison spoke up. "This is the kind of thing that gets out of hand in a hurry. Men wind up doing some mighty foolish things, and folks get killed. I don't claim any love for sheep, but this is open range, and Joe Barrett is family. We'd appreciate it if you all cleared off and left him alone."

Emmeline slid from her saddle, let the reins trail, and came toward Joe. She removed the rifle from his hands and gave it to Sean. Without a word, she slipped her hand into his and squeezed.

Blake Randall's glare could've started a fire, but he was smart enough to know when he was beaten. He motioned his men to retreat. "You've won this day, but I'll be back."

Matt legged his horse until he was alongside Blake and could grab the reins near the bridle. "You misunderstand us. This is the end of the feud. If we hear that so much as one of these lambs has come under distress as a result of you or your riders, we'll come hunting you down."

"I can't believe a cattleman would defend a sheepman like this."

"Cows or sheep don't come into it. It's a family thing.

Now git, before I forget what a good man your father was and tan your hide."

As the riders disappeared over the hill, Joe's wire-taut muscles relaxed. Emmeline sagged against his side, and he cradled her against him.

"How'd you do it?"

"Do what?"

"Get cattlemen to defend us?"

"They aren't cattlemen, they're family. Weren't you listening?" Her beautiful blue eyes mesmerized him.

"I think marrying you might've been the smartest thing I ever did."

"Might have?" She jabbed him in the ribs. "I had my doubts for a while, but you turned out to be a pretty good catch yourself. Like a knight on a white charger, you rode in and stole my heart."

In spite of the onlookers, he couldn't resist kissing her sweet lips.

Epilogue

The kitchen wouldn't hold everyone, so they set up tables in the yard. The brand-new pine boards of Joe and Emmeline's house gave off a resin scent that almost overwhelmed the smell of supper. Joe clasped her right hand, and she held her left to Matt. Surrounding the table, the sisters and their families all bowed their heads for the blessing.

Gareth prayed, "Father, we thank You for Your bounty and Your blessings, and that especially includes bringing Evelyn, Jane, Emmeline, and Gwendolyn to us. We ask that You would make us good husbands, bless us with children who will grow up to follow You, and that You would go before us. Thank You for this food and the hands that prepared it. Amen."

Joe squeezed Emmeline's hand and raised it to his lips for a quick kiss. "Amen."

Emmeline let her eyes rest on each face. How much they had all changed over this summer. Jamie had grown a couple of inches, and he rarely left Gareth's side, talking like his stepfather and even aping his walk. Evelyn's countenance had softened, as if something inside her had finally relaxed and she could enjoy life again. Gareth teased her every chance he got, and Evelyn returned in kind. Gareth's daughter, Maddie, looked nothing like the little hoyden who had protested the wedding. Garbed in a dress and pinafore now, she looked sweet and happy, though when they'd been building the house, she'd worn overalls and worked like a carpenter.

Jane, though pale and thin due to recent illness, blossomed like a rose every time Harrison looked at her. The news that she would be a mother in the late winter had all the sisters in raptures. Harrison's father beamed as if he had thought the whole idea up himself. And Harrison clearly doted on Jane. Their own new house had just been completed.

Gwendolyn passed Emmeline a dish across the table. Matt leaned over to whisper into Gwendolyn's ear. She blinked, blushed, and swatted his shoulder with a laugh. Her happiness and his were almost tangible. Betsy, next to Gwendolyn, giggled at something Sean said. Those two had been inseparable since the moment Sean laid eyes on the girl. He didn't seem to care a plugged nickel if she was in a wheelchair or not. Harrison's father had made some inquiries back east about treatment for the girl's ailment, and plans were in the works for a trip for the Parkers to somewhere in Arkansas that boasted hot springs said to be good for weakened muscles. Emmeline had a feeling when it came time to go, Sean might tag along. They were young, but with Betsy's prognosis being what it was, time was precious.

Joe nudged her elbow. "You going to eat, or just daydream? You thinking about the house?" He dropped his voice to a whisper. "Or are you thinking about getting rid of all these people so we can finally be alone?"

Her face heated, and she put her hands to her cheeks. He

laughed as he always did when she blushed. "I was thinking, if you must know, about how dreams can come true in strange ways. Not a one of us got what we were expecting. Who knew that a bunch of ranchers could really be gallant knights in disguise?"

Joe's eyes softened. "So you're not still pining to be a cowgirl?"

"I wouldn't trade my shepherd-knight for all the cows in Wyoming. And my sisters are going to hold fast to their Sagebrush Knights, too."

"That's good, because we'd never let you get away."

Even though Erica Vetsch has set aside her career teaching history to high school students in order to homeschool her own children, her love of history hasn't faded. Erica's favorite books are historical novels and history books, and one of her greatest thrills is stumbling across some obscure historical factoid that makes her imagination leap. She's continually amazed at how God has allowed her to use her passion for history, romance, and daydreaming to craft historical romances that entertain readers and glorify Him. Whenever she's not following flights of fancy in her fictional world, Erica is the company bookkeeper for her family's lumber business, a mother of two, wife to a man who is her total opposite and yet her soul mate, and an avid museum patron.